"Please, Doctor, don't look or talk down to me or your patients here," Emma said. "The locals may call me a baby catcher, but at least it doesn't imply I do all the work."

"Stop mincing words!" Griff said angrily. "I don't need your lectures or your help, but you are sure as hell going to need mine to survive here."

Holding her ground, she glared up at him.

"But I am not," he went on, "the enemy, the devil incarnate, Ms. Weston. Yes, I believe I can do a better, safer job here in this developing health center than you can out in some distant cabin—"

"They aren't cabins anymore, not most of them. If you'd make a few house calls, you'd—"

"—and better than at your so-called Baby Farm Birthing Center."

"Which you haven't seen," she pointed out.

"Invite me, then," he said, raising his dark eyebrows. "Emma," he continued, his voice almost a whisper, "give a novice around here a break. Trust me at least a little."

"Karen Harper delivers unforgettable romantic suspense."

—*Romantic Times*

Watch for the newest blockbuster from
KAREN HARPER

DOWN TO THE BONE

Available August 2000
Only from MIRA Books

KAREN HARPER

THE
BABY
FARM

ISBN 1-55166-520-4

THE BABY FARM

Copyright © 1999 by Karen Harper.

All rights reserved. Except for use in any review, the reproduction or
utilization of this work in whole or in part in any form by any electronic,
mechanical or other means, now known or hereafter invented, including
xerography, photocopying and recording, or in any information storage or
retrieval system, is forbidden without the written permission of the publisher,
MIRA Books, 225 Duncan Mill Road, Don Mills, Ontario, Canada M3B 3K9.

All characters in this book have no existence outside the imagination of the
author and have no relation whatsoever to anyone bearing the same name
or names. They are not even distantly inspired by any individual known or
unknown to the author, and all incidents are pure invention.

MIRA and the Star Colophon are trademarks used under license and registered
in Australia, New Zealand, Philippines, United States Patent and Trademark
Office and in other countries.

Visit us at www.mirabooks.com

Printed in U.S.A.

Special thanks to the people who believed in this
book and in me:
Meg Ruley, Amy Moore-Benson,
Dianne Moggy and Martha Keenan.

As always to Don, for our jaunts
to and through Appalachia.

And to my medical sources and friends:
Julianne Moledor, M.D.
Nancy Armstrong, R.N.
Laurie Miller, R.N.

1

Shelter, Kentucky
April 20, 1995

A car horn blared, then began a pulsing throb that drowned out even the tattoo of rain on the tin roof. Emma Weston jumped up from the breakfast table so fast she banged her knee.

Groaning, she limped onto the side porch, and squinted through the gray slant of rain at an old black pickup scabbed with rust. Many locals drove similar trucks. The throb of the horn accented the beat of loud country music pouring from the truck cab. She couldn't see who was driving, but someone rolled down the passenger's-side window.

It was Wade Poteet, freckled and as gangly as a cornstalk. Newly in his teens, he was the eldest child in a family of seven from way up Mudbrook Holler. What was he doing here? she wondered. No Poteet should be needing a midwife.

Even when the music was turned down, she couldn't hear what he was yelling, so she shrugged and raised both hands, palms up. Dripping wet even before he got out, his feet caked with red mud, Wade barreled up onto the porch and shook himself like a dog.

"Everything to rights at home?" Emma asked, her stomach already churning with concern.

"It's Miz Amrine at the old Settle place. Says she needs you real bad."

"Oh no. Is she having pains or bleeding?"

Though already flushed from exertion, the boy reddened to the roots of his hair. Most Appalachian males didn't want any part of women's work, and bringing babies into the world was surely that.

"It's just I been fixin' up that old tractor she got settin' in the shed to sell," he went on in a rush. "Gonna buy nice things for the baby, she said, and pay your fee with it. But she come a' runnin' out all het up and shouts to fetch you quick."

"You're a good neighbor, Wade. I'll go right up to see her," Emma said and tore into the house.

Amrine Settle was not due for at least several weeks, and she'd showed no warning signs. Worse, she lived alone in a ramshackle place where they'd turned off her electricity and phone for not making payments, and she wouldn't let Emma pay the bills. The stove, refrigerator and downstairs lights worked off an old generator. At least Amrine still had running water, though many a mountain midwife had washed a newborn in a rain barrel.

Even before she heard the truck drive away, Emma had dropped her fetoscope, to monitor fetal heartbeat, and hanging infant scales into plastic sacks and placed them in her big duffel bag. Grabbing her kit, she stuffed in scissors straight from the sterilizer. Seizing a new bottle of Betadine, she closed it into a resealable bag. She darted to the fridge for her special labor-aide, a mix of honey, water, salt, lemon juice, crushed calcium tablets and curing herbs.

She snapped her kit closed and zipped the duffel bag. From the old deer-antler rack by the door, she yanked off the neon-green, hooded slicker and pulled it over her T-shirt and jeans. Grabbing the beeper, she rushed out the door.

"Damn," she whispered and turned back to lock it, something she often forgot to do in these changing times when tourists and thieves were too often one and the same. She stuck the key under a crock of pansies.

Sprinting for the big shed where she kept the Jeep, she remembered she hadn't left a note for Ola Grady, who would be walking in. The girl was scheduled for a prenatal checkup, but her clients understood emergencies, and they all knew where the key was. *Amrine needs you real bad,* she heard the boy's words again. She and Amrine had always needed each other. They'd been good friends as long as she could remember.

Emma glanced at her watch. Only seven minutes had passed since Wade had come. At least she had the thick plastic top already zipped on the Jeep.

She looked in the rearview mirror to back out and glimpsed how worried she looked, older than her twenty-seven years. Her tires spit gravel. She roared past the old farmhouse she'd been slowly renovating and the sign she'd painted herself, now slick with rain and swinging in the wind: Shelter Birthing and Women's Health Center, Emma Weston, C.N.M. But locals called it the Baby Farm.

"Dr. Cusak'll see you now, Ola."

Griff Cusak hunched his broad shoulders and grimaced. He could hear the piercing voice of his licensed practical nurse, Wanda Keck, clear back here in his office. He needed an R.N. and a softer-voiced receptionist, but Wanda was it for now. Since he'd been sentenced to three years in Shelter, he'd had to do without a lot of things he'd taken for granted in Lexington. He could only hope that his Lady Bountiful, the health center's sponsor, Delia Lowe, soon found someone who suited them both.

"You sure you're eighteen, Ola, like you put down here?" he heard Wanda shrill. "I swear I thought you was born the year my brother Lester, so you'd be—why, barely fifteen."

Fifteen? Another underage, unwed, pregnant girl, Griff thought. This might be the hills of southeastern Kentucky, but hadn't anyone ever heard of birth control?

"I'm goin' in with her," an older woman whined. "I'm her ma, and she wants me there."

"I *know* you're her ma, Ginger. But she's obviously not a kid anymore, having one a her own. 'Sides, Dr. Cusak has his own way a doing things so—"

Griff hurtled out of his office and poked his head into the otherwise empty waiting room. The two Grady women resembled each other with their kinky red hair and long faces—though Ola was bulbously pregnant.

"That's fine, Wanda," Griff said, holding the door open and forcing a smile as he took the clipboard from her. "If Ola agrees, Mrs. Grady is welcome, too. Ola?..." he prompted, trying to get the girl to make eye contact with him.

He thought she would refuse to follow him, but her mother shot her a sharp look. "Sure, okay. But I been seeing Emma Weston, the midwife," Ola blurted, getting up slowly. Her mouth turned sulky, her ice-blue eyes more cold and defiant.

"So your mother told Wanda on the phone." He tried

to keep his voice calm as he ushered them down the hall toward the examining room. "It shows good judgment you've decided to seek more complete care now. And since you're well into your last trimester, I want you to get what I would hope is an extensive file from Ms. Weston for me, so I can more effectively bring your little one into the world."

"Emma says, even at my age, it's important I take charge of—"

"Emma Weston says a lot of fancy things, don't she?" Ginger muttered and grabbed her girl's arm. "See, doc, her pa and me din't even know 'til this morning she been goin' down the valley to see the baby catcher. She'll be fine just livin' with kin in Cincinnati the last month and deliverin' in the hospital there."

"In Cincinnati?" Griff said, running a hand over his close-cropped hair.

Ginger nodded. "But I said one visit to a doctor here in Shelter 'fore she went'd be the right thing to do. Miss Delia said so, too, said just one a my quilted table runners would pay the bill. But I got money to pay, 'cause the Gradys ain't beholden to no one."

"I'm sure Delia meant to say that *regular* prenatal appointments with a *doctor* are absolutely essential," he said, indicating that Ola should sit on the end of the raised examining table and Ginger on the extra chair. He put a hand on Ola's elbow to help her up. Both women sat slumped, glaring at him now instead of at each other.

Griff was getting used to stepping into the middle of messes in Shelter, including the fact that too many women had been going to the new midwife as if this were still the nineteenth century instead of nearly the twenty-first. He didn't give a damn if Emma Weston had a nurse's degree or a certified nurse midwife specialty. He ranked home birth, especially among these ignorant, isolated mountain people, right up there with blowing rabbit tobacco smoke in ears for earaches or carrying a buckeye in the pocket to fight rheumatism.

He glanced at the clipboard with the lengthy, blank prenatal exam chart attached and said, "To begin with, let's just talk about your family history, Ola, then I'll do an examin—"

"Family history?" Ginger interrupted, but Griff held up his hand to quiet her.

"I done all that with Emma," Ola said, crossing her arms over her breasts and staring at the nutrition chart on the wall. "So you just weigh me and check for fetal heart tones, and I'll give a urine specimen, then..."

Griff's head jerked up. He'd either underestimated this girl or the midwife was turning her patients into walking prenatal-exam experts.

"See what I mean?" Ginger Grady said, smacking her hands on her knees. "The baby catcher what delivered me and mine din't fill my head with stuff like that. And her pa and me wondered why she done changed from the nice, obedient, God-fearin'—"

"Pa-fearing—" Ola muttered.

"Now you just see here, girl," Ginger shouted.

"All right!" Griff thundered. "I'll just start with taking Ola's blood pressure before mine goes off the charts."

Emma sped through the little valley town of Shelter. Rain beat down in waves as her windshield wipers whined and whipped the wet gray from her vision. Familiar signs whizzed by: Fallen Rock Ahead and Are You Prepared to Meet Your Maker?

"Not today, 'cause I've got to help Amrine," she said to herself, but she quit talking when she saw that her breath instantly steamed up the front window.

The road began to climb, so she shifted gears. Runoff from some strip mining higher up was swirling red and white on the pavement, and she knew that acidic stuff could get slick.

She made the right turn up Mudbrook, a curvy, one-lane dirt road with a few pull-offs on the right in case you met another car. On her left was a narrow bank that dipped to Mudbrook Crick with its churning, coffee-colored water still full of snowmelt.

She gripped the steering wheel so hard her knuckles went white. *She needs you real bad.* As much as their lives had grown apart, even the years Emma was away at school, she and Amrine had stayed in touch. She pressed the accelerator even harder.

The road wrapped around Big Blue Mountain with rock walls on the right and the vast, open river valley on the left below. Rain was running down the cliff face still etched with spring ice.

She shuddered. She had planned to talk Amrine into coming to stay at the birthing center when her delivery date approached, but now her friend might have to deliver at home. Emma couldn't let anything go wrong, not for Amrine, the baby or even herself. Some people around here were just waiting for her to have a bad birth outcome so they could ruin her. Memory of her own family tragedy flashed at her, and she shuddered again.

She thought she heard thunder crack. Or were they blasting out a road across the mountain again? In this weather?

Suddenly the Jeep fishtailed on the slick mud. It was like being on ice. She tried to turn toward the rockface and a pull-off spot, but the rear spun out. She'd never lost control like this, never—

Her scream echoed in her ears. The Jeep turned half-way around, facing downhill, scraping its side. And came to a stop halfway into a pull-off.

She sat shaking, her pulse thudding harder than the rain. Hiding her face in her hands, she leaned on the steering wheel.

She had to get to Amrine.

Emma tried to start the Jeep moving but the wheels spun, digging her in deeper in the mud and slick runoff. The vehicle was tilted so that maybe only two wheels touched. She killed the engine and craned around to try to peer out, but the rain blurred her vision. Pulling up her hood, she rolled down the window. Blessedly, the rain was letting up a bit. She saw no one, heard nothing but running water and the light thrumming of raindrops on the hood of the Jeep.

She got out and looked at the deep skid marks she'd made on the mud-slick road. And then saw both back tires were flat.

Dear God, someone had *shot* at her. She saw one bullet hole; she knew what they looked like. Pa and her brother, Jake, had often used old tires for target practice. She didn't take time to look for a hole in the second tire before scrambling to the front of the Jeep. With only one spare and two flats, she was doubly stuck here.

Emma grabbed her gear and ran, fearful of being alone where someone had a gun, but more scared of leaving Amrine alone longer than necessary. Besides, if someone really had it in for her and was hurrying to catch up, she'd be a sitting duck if she stayed with the Jeep. She had several enemies in town. Worse, she had two in her own family, Pa still under lock and key, but Jake on the loose from prison.

She hustled hard uphill, frequently looking back. At least there were few places a pursuer could hide in the bare spring woods. And she was climbing so high the thick cloud mist that snagged on the peaks would hide her from anyone below.

Her feet kept skidding. Slick red clay mud, limestone with occasional sinkholes, and loose shale ran through these parts. She was high enough now that ice-glazed rocky outcrops made it tough going.

She was sweating. And out of breath. Not enough exercise, even though she urged her clients to take daily walks. In her six months back in Shelter, she'd been working too hard, worrying too much, remembering and fighting too many things.

Not only was she struggling to establish her baby clinic to help local women, she was desperate to prove she could succeed at delivering babies. So much bad had happened in her past. In fact, there was a saying in these parts that nothing good ever came out of Cutshin Holler, the home where she grew up. And when she let herself remember things sometimes, she could see why folks said that, she really could.

Emma's father and Jake used to get likkered up and raise hell. And on one particularly bad night, they had killed their neighbor, Cory Eubanks. Emma had just turned thirteen. After Pa and Jake went to prison, Mama had tried to keep the tiny farm going. But then Emma's younger sister, Sissy, got pregnant at fifteen and went into premature labor in an ice storm with only seventeen-year-old Emma to help her. The baby, a tiny mite of a girl, had died in Emma's hands. Later that same year, a freak farm accident killed Mama. Emma had tried to save her too—but could not.

Even after the wealthy Delia Lowe took Emma and Sissy in and mothered—and smothered—them with gifts and love, Emma sometimes blamed herself for the ruin of her family. At his trial, Jake had shouted that it was Emma's fault that Pa had killed that man. After all, she'd stood up to her own father with a gun when he went for Mama that night, and he and Jake had roared off into the night, fit to kill for sure. As for Emma's sister, it had taken Sissy years of struggle in a shaky marriage to get pregnant again, years Emma was away at school and not there to help her. For all this, Emma was left standing, somehow, even today, holding the bag of blame, not just in other folks' eyes but—when she didn't buck herself up real good—in her own, too.

She checked her watch. It had been nearly an hour since Wade had seen Amrine. She prayed her friend remembered to keep calm, to focus her energy. She had urged Amrine to take control not only of her body in childbirth but of her life after her boyfriend, Len, had abused and deserted her. She had counseled Amrine, Ola and her seven other current clients on more than mechanics of birth, which was all a doctor would do, including the mightier-than-thou new one in town, Griff Cusak.

Suddenly, Emma stopped and sniffed. In the mingled forest smells of loam, rich decay and dampness, she picked up the scent of cucumber.

She froze and looked around, wide-eyed. That was the telltale sign a cottonmouth was nearby.

She saw it then, in wet, brown leaves, dapple-skinned. It coiled, then almost lazily opened its pure white mouth to display its fangs and—

She darted back, dropping her duffel bag, slipping to sit down hard. The snake struck at the bag. Emma scooted farther back while it settled and swayed away. Praying there was not a nest of them, she edged forward to retrieve her bag, dragging it close before she hefted it to her shoulder again.

One of her grandma's old superstitions chattered at her: *A snake across your path means you have a new enemy.* Emma didn't believe in such sayings and signs, yet she guessed Griff Cusak could be that new foe. Sure, Hal Eubanks hated and harassed her because Pa and Jake had killed his brother, Cory. And Delia detested her these days for being defiant. But Griff and she had tangled, and he was the only outsider—a new person—who was fast becoming an enemy.

Watching every step, looking ahead instead of back and down, she crested the top of the knob where she knew she could see Amrine's place.

Thank God, smoke drifted from the chimney. Things looked normal, with the rocking chair and bench on the porch where Emma and Amrine had talked just two days ago, watching wrens nest in the hanging gourds Amrine had strung from tree branches. The tall, blasted corpses of last year's tomato vines still stood, tied to stakes. Pale corn shocks, shredded by winter wind, shifted and rattled along the rotted, split-rail fence.

"Amrine, I'm here!" Emma cried. "How-do?"

No face at the window, no answer, but Amrine was probably intent on her pains. Emma realized too late she'd left her cell phone in the Jeep. Amrine hadn't had a car that ran—or gas money—for weeks. There was only that tractor Wade was fixing, and there was no way Emma was touching that to get help. If anything went wrong and they needed that doctor in town, or even the hospital clear in Highboro, she would have to hike out.

Mud and ice patches or not, she ran now. Her feet sounded hollow up the board path to the house, then echoed deeper on the front porch. Trained as a midwife to rely on observation, she began to reconstruct what Amrine had been doing when her pains must have started.

It looked as if she had been sitting here listening to her radio, which was still on the windowsill, putting out muted static now. She had obviously been unstringing and shucking dried pea pods off a thread. A bowl half-full of peas was by her chair, and she'd spilled it in her surprise or haste.

Emma shoved the door inward; she knew it would be open. Folks up this high in the hills and hollers still hadn't taken to locking up. She sniffed stew-pot smells—and the pungent aroma of cigarette smoke, when Amrine didn't smoke.

"Amrine, I'm here!" she called again.

The single log in the low fire shuddered to silence in the front room. No voice, no movement. Emma dropped her things and tore into the downstairs bedroom that had once been the parlor—Amrine didn't use the up-stairs—and found the bed made, though it looked as if Amrine had lain down in it to rest, then moved heavily off. She smelled cigarette stench again.

She looked in the bathroom. Amrine's toothbrush and paste and cosmetics were gone. Maybe snatched in haste, a lipstick had dropped on the floor and rolled against the old claw foot of the tub. Emma picked it up and put it on the sink. Careful of sagging stair treads, she went upstairs and looked in every empty room. Strange, but as barren as they were, with a few, big wooden pieces of furniture left, the rooms didn't feel empty. Bad memories lurked here, too. She shuddered and ran back downstairs.

Emma stood, frustrated and fearful, in the center of the kitchen. The stove wasn't on, but a pot of soup, warm to the touch, put out its faint aroma. Amrine's mad-money jar, mostly small change, sat on the old linoleum counter next to the unwashed meat knife she'd been using to cut up stew meat.

"Am-ri-ine!"

Emma spun around to stare straight into the clear blue eyes of a framed picture of Jesus. Help me, she thought. Help me find Amrine.

"It must've gotten so bad," she said aloud, "she gave up on me, maybe started out for help. But who was here smoking?"

And then she saw the trail of dark splotches on the kitchen floor. She gasped and bent down. It was tacky and dried in some places like...

"Blood," she said, sniffing it. The acrid, coppery scent pierced through the stew and smoke smells. "Yes, blood."

Could Amrine have been spotting that much, with the drops so close together? But wouldn't her underwear or clothes have caught it, if that was the source of the blood?

Emma picked up the knife on the counter. Some dried blood, but not like the other. She hunched down again on the faded red-and-gray-checkered linoleum floor to look closer. The drops did not diminish in size and the trail went right into the bedroom where they suddenly stopped. That was good, wasn't it?

She retraced the drops to the counter where they started, then glanced at the cracked ceramic tabletop.

On it sat a crisp fifty-dollar bill and a note in Amrine's loopy handwriting, which looked a little shaky.

Dear Emma—
    Guess my pangs was false— Len come by and said he loved me and all so I'm going with him to his new place. Sorry about the quick notice— I'll write after— The money for all you done—
                                            Amrine

Len! Yes, that made sense. Len smoked. Then Amrine could be in danger.

Emma studied the note, which bore one blurred, bloody print of a big thumb on the back of the page. False pangs? All of this rang false. All of it.

2

Emma sniffed the note and fifty-dollar bill. Only the note smelled faintly of cigarette smoke. Keeping both flat, she shoved them in the big pocket of her slicker. Her hands were clammy; the crisp new bill stuck to her skin. She wondered if Len Roscoe had robbed a bank or something worse to get it. If Amrine had left with him willingly, Emma was real disappointed in her. If she'd left unwillingly, she was scared to death for her.

"That bastard!" Emma muttered between gritted teeth as she hurried out the door. Len had knocked Amrine around before she got pregnant *and* after, and she still went with him because *'he loved her and all'*? No way. Not after the talks Emma and Amrine had had about standing on one's own feet and fighting back.

"Or didn't you believe me that you don't have to play it like life deals it, Amrine?" Emma whispered, leaning against a porch post. "You know I'm living proof of that!" She hit the post so hard it shuddered the old roof.

Then, just to be sure her friend was not lying close by, unconscious from blood loss, Emma dropped her bag and strode to the privy, a two-seater with a view Amrine's grandparents had once been proud of. The damp breeze ripped through her hair. She was sweating but felt chilled to the bone. She slowed when she heard an owl hoot in broad daylight. Everything seemed wrong.

Before she rounded the corner of the slightly tilted outhouse, Emma looked both ways, then down into the valley through the scrim of delicate dogwoods and redbuds. She peered around the corner to see that the edge of the hill was narrower than she recalled. She looked back at the outhouse. Both doors to the compartments stood open.

A bad memory jumped at her: her brother, Jake, sneaking up to scare her and Amrine years ago, grabbing at their underpants, which were down around their skinny ankles, while they chattered away through the thin divider. The hell-raiser had hooted louder than the owl.

She shook her head and shuddered, trying to stomp down her fear of Jake. At his trial—it had been reported in the Lexington paper as well as the *Highboro Herald*—he'd said he'd get her, no matter how long it took. She'd tried to put that threat out of her mind the thirteen years he was in prison, first in juvenile detention, then the real thing for stabbing another prisoner. But she couldn't ignore the fear any longer, now that he'd walked away from a work team at a minimum-security prison where he'd been transferred for good behavior after ten more years.

She shook her head. Jake—good behavior? If so, he had staged it to get out to get to her. That's what haunted her now. Her only hope was that the local sheriff was obsessed with recapturing him, and Jake knew not to come back here. Didn't he?

As she looked into the first narrow compartment of the latrine—nothing—the wind creaked and slammed the other door closed. She shuffled over to open it. In the cold months of Amrine's pregnancy, living alone, she had used a slop jar inside the house. Cold running water was restricted to the kitchen and downstairs bathroom sinks.

This old outhouse still smelled faintly like a chicken coop. Holding her breath, Emma curled her fingers around the worn wooden handle and yanked the second door wide. Nothing but cobwebs and a scattering of mice nests.

Scolding herself for her bad case of nerves, she moved quickly away. She was letting everything get to her, overreacting. She had to forget the past. Just as when a birth went wrong, she had to keep calm, read the signs. She still had one more place to look for Amrine or signs of her.

Stopping to retrieve her duffel bag, Emma picked up her pace as she headed toward the slant-roof shed where Wade had been repairing the tractor. Emma supposed if he'd fixed it, she might have climbed up and driven it down the road to her Jeep, for Mama had taught her to handle a tractor. But she knew as sure as hellfire, she'd never drive a tractor again after the tragedy.

She nearly slipped in the mud between the shed and house, then noted something else. Tire tracks, big ones, maybe from a truck with the cab and bed set high, almost like tractor tires. Had Wade driven the tractor to his house and run into someone with a car heading down her way? No, lots of Appalachian folks had big tires on their trucks.

Farther on, the tracks blurred, digging into the ground. Lumps and globs of mud had been thrown as if the engine had been revved to speed away on this narrow road that linked the Settles' place to Mudbrook.

Emma pictured Amrine coming out here slowly,

hands to her belly or back, to send Wade for help. Len must have come for her after Wade lit out, so she was definitely having pains, perhaps bleeding before Len came. If so, maybe her panic to get help had made her leave with him.

Emma heaved such a sigh her shoulders slumped before her muscles tightened again. Though she dreaded it, she'd have to check with Dr. Cusak in town, make sure Amrine and Len didn't stop on their way out—or maybe, if she was hemorrhaging, she was still at the health center or had been transported to Highboro Hope Hospital.

Checking to see if the tractor was still there, she took one step into the shed. She glared up at the machine, looming over her. Despite the dimness and dust, fitful light through the rotting walls threw streaks that made the old hulk seem to shake as if its engine were coming to life. Scars of rust the same color as the drying blood inside the house nearly hid the once-shiny crimson color.

Suddenly Emma heard the shrieks of terror and agony again, the engine of the monster droning, her own screams for help—

She jumped at a shout, a real one. From outside.

"Amrine?" she cried as she ran back into the light.

Mike Bonner, a real estate agent and antique dealer from Highboro, who was also renovating a house and barn for a country home nearby, slammed the door of his new black truck as he got out. Bonners' Appalachian Dreams was scripted on the side with the larger letters *B, A,* and *D* blazoned in gold. Some Shelter folks thought it should read not *B.A.D.* but *S.O.B.* since Mike and his wife, Trish, were city folk—New York City, no less—who bought, renovated, decorated, then sold old homesteads to outsiders for big bucks.

Mike might be a wealthy outsider bringing in outsiders, but he'd gotten Emma's farmhouse for her from the Dixons at a fair price before it went on the market, so she owed him for that. And the Bonners were saving a lot of old farms and pumping money into the ailing area. In their early forties, the Bonners had owned some sort of consulting firm and obviously knew how to run a business. Trish had given Emma decorating advice and found her some beautiful old wicker she'd insisted on restoring for her—and in the process had become Emma's best new friend. She didn't know Mike as well, but she knew Trish adored him, and that was good enough for her.

"Emma, you okay?" he asked. "I saw your truck down below."

"Someone shot my tires out. But Amrine sent for me so I came straight up—literally."

"You're not kidding—about the tires or the trek up here. Now I see why Trish says you're Wonder Woman," he said with a stiff grin and just enough tease in his voice to make her glad to see him.

Mike Bonner was classically handsome, had a voice with no twang and stuck out around here like a freshly-painted house. He always seemed to stand at attention, putting anyone else's slouch to shame. Emma thought he should be advertising Cadillacs or cabin cruisers. Toothpaste-ad white teeth, green eyes and a dimple all added to the impact of his looks. He was so picture-perfect she felt uncomfortable around him, except that the love of his life, the pixielike Trish, was plain with a dash of cute. And the man couldn't help how he looked.

He came around his truck in the mud. "What's wrong with Amrine?" he asked. "A little early for her baby, isn't it?"

"That's what I'm worried about. You—you didn't come up here looking for me when you saw the Jeep, did you?"

"Partly, but I've got some groceries Trish sent for Amrine," he explained, gesturing toward the narrow back seat of the truck. Emma felt touched, even though she knew the Bonners made a practice—and a show—of kindnesses. Some said it was their version of public relations in the hills. Food baskets if someone was ailing or had a place to sell, Christmas poinsettias for Shelter First Baptist, an array of Easter lilies in the sanctuary just last week, free ice cream on Decoration Day, always candy for the kids. The Bonners had only lived in Kentucky for four years, but they had made a big impression one way or the other.

"The groceries are really nice of you," Emma said, "but I think Amrine's gone. Where, I don't know, but I'm going to find out. Can I ride back into town with you to get help for my Jeep and check on her? Only one spare and two blown tires or—"

"Or you would have changed them yourself. Sure. Climb in. Emma, are you sure you're all right? You look so pale—like you've seen a ghost."

She almost laughed but wanted to cry. "I was just surprised she lit out. I'll be all right," she said. "Thanks for your concern."

She hoped he wasn't being nice because he wanted her to sell the Old Weston homestead way up Cutshin Holler—something he'd mentioned more than once.

Emma took a last, futile look at the tire tracks Mike had sliced through. His were similar in size, but the pattern—she could no longer tell. Her inherent tendency to be suspicious threw another thought at her. As she opened the passenger door and lifted her gear onto the clean plastic floor mat, she tried to sound nonchalant.

"Don't tell me," she said, hoisting herself onto the tall step to the truck cab. "You've been trying to get Amrine to sell."

He settled in the driver's seat and snapped his safety belt on. "You mean, she was fixin' to sell?" he asked, his voice teasing again. Both he and Trish occasionally tried "to talk mountain," as Trish put it, not in a mocking way but with a fierce fascination. But now it annoyed Emma to recall that Mike often answered a question, especially one he didn't like, with another question.

When she turned to stare at him, he added, "Not exactly, though I have felt her out."

She noted his already wind-burned face flushed, maybe from wishing he hadn't put it that way. But Emma's mind and fears were racing. Perhaps Len had found out that Appalachian Dreams wanted the place and insisted Amrine sell. Len was always after a quick buck any way he could get it. And when she refused, maybe he'd roughed her up, then taken her to Tennessee or wherever he'd gone when she'd got up enough gumption to get a restraining order against him. Then, when she started bleeding, hopefully he'd gotten scared enough to stop at the doctor's in town. He sure wouldn't bring Amrine to Emma, the friend who'd urged her to stand up to him.

"I said, Emma—" Mike's voice interrupted her thoughts "—you'd better get a little sugar in your blood. You look pale." He was extending a Tootsie Roll wrapped in twisted paper. He always had them around to give kids—beware the stranger offering candy, Trish had kidded Emma once. Though her stomach was twisted just as tight as the wrapper, she took it.

"Mike, drop me at Delia's instead of the gas station, will you?"

"You mean," he said, his voice still teasing as they bounced downhill, "to that highfalutin new Shelter Health Center with Delia Lowe's fancy, Lexington-imported doctor? Sure, but I thought Trish said you two weren't getting along."

"Delia and me, or Dr. J. Griffin Cusak and me?" she asked so sharply Mike's head snapped around to stare at her again. She recalled that Trish had said Mike and Griff were friends. And she'd just answered a question with another question.

Emma could feel her heartbeat soar as Mike dropped her off in town. Shelter was a little southeast Kentucky boom-and-bust coal town huddled in a bend of the South Fork River, but it had seemed like a big city to a girl growing up in backwoods, high-ridge Cutshin Holler. Over time, Shelter had become both her refuge and her prison.

In the sixties, Shelter had awakened from its delusions of coal-fever grandeur to face down-and-out reality, even though President LBJ's Great Society programs widened the town's main road to a highway. Today it consisted of a scattering of houses along a main street—the highway—lined with a mix of empty buildings and surviving stores with brick facades. The saloon, movie house and bank had closed. The open establishments included Quincy's Pure Oil Station; the Tastee-Freez; the elementary school, and the Top Line

Hardware Store, which now also offered a banking ATM and groceries, as well as tombstones.

Holding up the middle of the block was Lowe's Five-and-Dime, where nothing cost that little anymore. The other end of town had Arletta Versey's place, where the fading sign still read: A Home-Cooked Restaurant. Next came the church, then the Lowe mansion surrounded by its own large lawn guarded by tall cottonwood trees and a knee-high spiked iron fence.

The town matriarch, Delia Lowe, widow of the local coal-mining baron, had built a pillared place outside town and had turned her husband's old gray stone mansion into a health center. She had recruited the area's only doctor from Lexington by paying off his medical-school bills and offering him who knew what else. Chit-chat had it that Griff Cusak had agreed to his mountain exile for three years. Emma was all for medical help so locals wouldn't have to go clear to Highboro, but Delia was forcing things and Cusak was pushing his ways on everyone. Worse, she knew she'd need him if a birth went bad. They'd already had words off and on—too many to suit her.

As Mike beeped his horn and pulled away, Emma scraped mud off her shoes on the edge of the sidewalk in front of the health center. Geraniums already filled the window boxes and sculpted beds around the small fishpond where she used to wade. The top dormer windows under the low brow of copper roof seemed to frown. From under her blowing bangs, she looked up at the big bays across the second floor where she and Sissy once shared a suite of rooms, which Delia had converted into an apartment for Griff Cusak.

Emma shook her head as she gazed at the house, once full of such warmth and love—and need. But why did

Delia think love was the same as adoration of and obedience to her? Delia had actually expected her—tried to convince, then coerce, then force her—to stay with general nursing, then commit to working here: *It can be our dream together, Emma, side by side, like mother and daughter. Becoming a midwife will be like taking a step back into the past, and, God knows, you of all people need to look ahead, not back. After all I've done for you and Sissy...*

She owed Delia a lot, Emma admitted as she started up the walk, but not the abandonment of doing what was right for women and babies around here, and certainly not servitude to a dictatorial medical outsider who thought he should manage women's births, babies and lives.

She twisted the brass knob and shoved the heavy walnut door inward. From the black-and-white marble-tiled hallway, she turned into the parlor that was now the waiting room. On carved rockers sat two elderly patients, both of whom lived within walking distance to town. She nodded and said her how-do's.

"Oh, Emma, what're you doing here?" Wanda Keck's voice squeaked as she whirled around from her computer screen that was blank as far as Emma could tell. "I s'pose you're all riled the doctor's got your patient seeing him now..." She shot a guilty glance toward the closed door to the next room.

Relief flooded Emma, then fury. Amrine was here, but in what shape? Surely Cusak wouldn't deliver a preemie here, or if so, he'd need help. She rushed to the door and opened it with such force it slammed into the wall. A hallway loomed, but she could hear Cusak's deep voice—he drawled high-class bluegrass without a hint of flat mountain twang. Despite Wanda's shouting and scrambling after her, Emma hefted her gear and strode straight toward the examining room.

Griff ignored Wanda's muted squeals. He was getting better at shutting out that voice, he thought smugly. He had finally calmed down Ola and Ginger Grady and had gotten something accomplished here, though he wanted to conduct the internal exam with Wanda in attendance and not the hovering Ginger.

He rose from the chair where he'd been laboriously filling in data he'd pried out of the girl—information a good nurse could have gotten—so he wouldn't have to call the midwife. Suddenly the door to the room swung open, banging his shoulder and pinning Ginger in the corner.

Emma Weston stood there like an avenging angel, breathless, muddy, windblown, dirty-faced and mad as hell.

"Amr—" she got out before she gaped at Ola. "What are you doing here?"

Ginger squawked from behind the door and pushed it open, bumping Emma farther into the room. Griff's narrowed gaze locked with Emma's wide stare as Ginger shouted, "Emma Weston, how come you din't tell me and her daddy our Ola been comin' to you?"

Ola shrieked, "I din't want to come here, Emma, but they said I had to, so—"

Wanda lunged into the small room, wringing her hands, though she looked as if she'd like to wring Emma's neck. "She just ran right by me, doctor. I tried to stop her, but—"

"I'll stop her," Griff shouted over the mingled din of women's voices. He seized Emma's upper arm, turned her around and, though she tried to shake him off and bump her big bag into him, propelled her ahead of him out and down the hall toward his office. He had never touched her before, except to shake her hand several months ago. It surprised him that such a petite woman could be so much stronger than her shapely, soft appearance had led him to believe. And he'd always thought of her as being taller. She must be only five-three, he realized, because he stood more than half a foot over her.

She protested, but he kept going. She wasn't the only one irate. Though he knew better than to touch her further, his palms tingled to shake some sense into her. Before she could land a kick at close range, he steered her into the doorway of his open office. For one moment, her duffel bag stuck between them, wedging them there, face-to-face.

Like many of the locals with their Scots-Irish heritage, she had auburn hair, but hers was neither stringy nor long. Emma's was a clipped, no-nonsense style, but when she flipped her head, her full bangs bounced and the short sleekness cupped her chin and swayed to emphasize her full mouth. Unlike many of this mountaineer stock with their pale blue eyes, hers were a velvet brown, set off by cheekbones starkly angled. A few in these parts claimed Cherokee blood. He could see it in Emma today when she was on the warpath.

She flung herself into the office. Breathing hard, he followed, closing the door behind them calmly, quietly, though he wanted to slam it off its frame.

"What the hell do you think you're doing?" he demanded as she dropped her bag like a barrier between them and spun to face him.

"It was an emergency," she said, fighting to keep control. Every time she was near this man rage churned in her wild as a spring stream. "I was looking for one of my clients—and here I found another." Not budging now, she kept her chin up, arms akimbo.

"Clients? Patients, you mean," he said, crossing his arms over his chest. He wore chinos, a denim shirt and a tie, no less, under his pressed, crease-sleeved white coat with *Dr. Cusak* on the pocket as if he were in some high-tech research facility.

"You have all the answers, don't you, doctor? But the word *patient* suggests a pregnant woman is ill, and she's not. What she's going through is natural and should be kept that way. Whereas a *client* hires you to help *her* do something."

"Who," he said as if he hadn't registered her comment, "are you talking about besides Ola?"

"Amrine Settle sent for me—early labor pains. When I got there, she was gone. She left me payment and a note that said she went with the baby's father."

"Well, hallelujah. A happy ending to at least one single mother's plight around here, one patient taken care of."

She crossed her arms over her breasts and said, "When I was rushing to her, someone shot both my back tires out, and I've been in a panic since then that she's in trouble and I can't help her."

His dark brows lifted. "Shot your tires out? I'm glad you're safe, but neither of us can cure these people's love for their damn guns. I'd say some hunter just missed, but—both tires?"

She nodded. "And in the rain. I almost spun off the road up on Mudbrook, not that you would know the area since you're a town doctor."

"Look, Ms. Midwife, if I went making calls everywhere and sitting around yakking like they expect, I wouldn't have time to do my job. Besides, if someone shot at you, maybe you don't have all the answers for winning people over around here," he goaded. "Not to mention you evidently didn't know Amrine so well then."

"I did know that she was abused by this guy before, and I found a trail of blood at her place."

"Blood? Are you sure it's hers?"

She detested this man, but she hadn't thought of that. Could Amrine have stabbed Len in self-defense? "I don't know," she said, her voice breaking, "but that's why I thought—hoped—they might have stopped here."

He shoved away from the door and came closer. "You actually," he said, his voice increasingly sarcastic, "hoped a pregnant woman—one who has complications that now make her a patient, I might add—would stop to get a trained doctor's help? Golly, Nurse Midwife, here in a place into which Delia is pouring money to provide the best in equipment and future personnel you can't even hope to—"

"That's your solution, isn't it?" she interrupted, balling up her fists. "Money, equipment, technology, personnel, your Lexington M.D. degree..."

"I know you're not a *lay* midwife, Emma. I know you've got an RN and a specialty beyond, but you're a nurse, not a minidoctor, so—"

"So never mind educating the mother-to-be, counseling her, building her up, right? Just drug her, control her."

Cusak smacked both palms on the desk but came no closer. "Build her up?" he thundered. "I take it, you don't mean with folic acid and vitamins. You know, there are psychiatrists and social workers in Highboro for that.''

"Typical!'' she shouted and began to pace two steps back and forth in the small corner between his desk and bookshelves. The impression of wood grain, rich leather and thick carpet seeped in to make her even angrier. "As if,'' she said, flinging gestures at him, "these mountain women can afford to just drive into the hospital thirty miles away any old time—maybe after their horseback riding or tennis lessons at the country club. That's the clientele you hobnobbed with during your internship and residency, isn't it? But here you are, sentenced to pay off medical school bills in hillbilly junction!''

His eyes narrowed and his knuckles turned white where he steadied himself on the edge of his desk as though to prevent himself from lunging at her. She could almost hear him grind his teeth. She took the advantage of his hesitation but lowered her voice.

"Please, doctor, don't look or talk down to me or your patients here. The locals may call me a baby catcher, but at least the term doesn't imply I do all the work—that I control a woman's labor and manage her pain and *deliver* that baby, as you like to put it.''

"Stop mincing words!'' he shouted, stepping over the bastion of her duffel bag. "I don't need your lectures or your help, but you are sure as hell going to need mine to survive here.'' Holding her ground, she glared at him. "But I am not,'' he went on, "the enemy, the devil incarnate, Ms. Weston. Yes, I believe I can do a better, safer job in this developing health center than you can out in some distant cabin—''

"They aren't cabins anymore, not most of them. If you'd make a few house calls, you'd—''

"—and better than at your so-called Baby Farm Birthing Center."

"Which you haven't seen. I guess that would be the ultimate house call, wouldn't it?"

"Invite me then," he said, his dark eyebrows lifting. He did not touch her, but she felt as if he did. "Emma," he said, his voice almost a whisper, "give a novice around here a break, trust me at least a little."

Her lower lip dropped at his sudden shift in tone and use of her first name. She stared at him from the distance of three feet where he'd stopped, hands out, palms out, almost as if he was beseeching her—or was going to embrace her. He had fine hands, broad palms, long fingers lightly dusted with ebony hair. So clean, especially compared to hers right now. She had to keep herself from thrusting her hands, childlike, behind her back. Seldom did she think much about her appearance, but she must look like something the cat dragged in.

What really shook her was the realization that, perhaps, after all, Dr. J. Griffin Cusak did have a bit of the comforter and healer's instincts. And in the sharp cross light from the window, she could see on his face what were either worry or age lines. One little crease perched over his broad nose and others crowded the corners of his light blue eyes, fringed with lashes as dark as his close-cropped hair. She'd heard he was divorced, thirty-eight and had gone to med school late, that he had left an earlier career to pursue his desire to be a doctor.

The left corner of his straight, firm lips moved once, as if in a grimace. She became aware he was looking at her mouth. Her knees went weak and her stomach cartwheeled. He was waiting for some answer, and she couldn't recall what he had just said.

"Obviously, doctor, I didn't mean to barge in today." She cleared her throat. "I apologize for that." She felt both warm and chilled; she had to get out of here. She edged past him to retrieve her bag. "I'll see Ola and her parents later, but right now I've got to find Amrine."

She made for the door. In three strides he held it closed where she had opened it a few inches.

"As for your accusations," he said, his voice deep and low, "about the way doctors oversee births, this is the modern age, even here, and the best of it must come. It's a blessing today's women can have their pain controlled."

Without turning her body toward him, she turned her head. Their faces were inches apart.

"In this modern age, Dr. Cusak, especially here, women's pain cannot be controlled. It's been a long, hard process for mountain women to find the heart and strength to even imagine controlling their own pain—their lives. And controlling their bodies to birth their children can show the way. Please let me out."

He did. Not daring to look at him again, she went into the hall and toward the back, past the door to the kitchen where she used to spend time helping Delia bake cookies, especially on the cook's day off. Once, Emma had said she wanted to send some of the chocolate-chip ones to Pa and Jake, but Delia had said absolutely not. *"Trailer trash like that doesn't deserve to be your family, and you aren't to so much as think about them anymore. Real families are not who births who, but who takes care of who,"* Delia had declared.

Emma could still see her shaking the wooden mixing spoon so hard that dough speckled both their faces. She had thought for a moment that Delia would hit her, but

her looks and words always battered so deep she didn't
need a weapon.

"*And don't you forget it, Emma, even if you refused
my kind offer to change both your and Sissy's last
names to mine. I can't begin to tell you the hell I've
gone through to be a Lowe and you dare to just refuse...*"

Now all was silent in the back hall where the old
kitchen door sported a dead-bolt lock and was marked
in black letters that read, LAB. PRIVATE.

Before Emma could stop herself, she slammed the
door on her way out.

3

"**Em**, I've been looking all over for you!"

Even without the familiar voice, Emma would have known who was shouting. No one else called her Em. She turned in the wide doorway of the gas station garage to see Hank Welling bearing down on her.

"What's up, Hank?" she asked, extending her hand before he could grab and hug her. Hank had been her childhood sweetheart and had never quite accepted that those days were over—for her, at least.

"Saw your Jeep up on Mudbrook—and the tires. I've been stopping at houses all the way down to see if you'd hiked there for help. I changed the one tire from the spare you had, so I'll just drive you up to change this one for you, too." He said all this almost in one breath as he pointed at the tire the garage owner, Quincy, rolled toward her.

"Thanks, Hank," she said, bending to roll the tire out of the garage herself, "but you've already done enough. Quincy said he'd run me up." She knew she looked silly; her bag of precious equipment she'd been toting everywhere kept bumping the tire.

"I gotta drive back up to see Asa Poteet on business, anyway. Come on then," he insisted, taking the tire from her and gesturing Quincy back to work. "I know you can change your own tire—change your own life,

Em—but I'm going that way. Don't be ridiculous, come on, okay?''

Reluctantly, she followed him to his government-issue car. He'd mounted its body on bigger tires so it looked like one of those demolition-derby vehicles, but a low-slung Chevy would never handle the back roads otherwise. Hank supervised the distribution of medical benefits in Lowe County for both silicosis, a disease caused by the inhalation of sand dust, and pneumoconiosis, or black lung disease. Ever ambitious, unlike most mountain men, Hank also moonlighted for an insurance agency that oversaw mine injuries, like the ruptured disks Emma's brother-in-law, J.G., had sustained.

"So how've you been, Em, other than someone taking a potshot or two at you?" he asked as he put her tire in the trunk of his car. He quickly lit and dragged on a cigarette. Because he'd seen what bad lungs did to a man, she was amazed he'd never given up smoking. Now here he was, lighting up near the gas pump.

"Can't believe," he told her, tossing the long butt down and grinding it out with his heel, "some idiot didn't recognize it was your Jeep."

"I'm afraid some idiot did, but who?"

"Oh, heck, under any circumstances, I never see enough of you, my girl. Come on."

His tone was light, but his expression was, as usual, achingly intense. He dressed in what Emma and Sissy jokingly called "Appalachian preppie," with button-down pastel shirts and round, wire-rimmed glasses that seemed at odds with his macho car and fierce passion for whatever he set his heart on.

As they got in, Emma bit back her retort that she was not a girl anymore and certainly not his. She hoped his hunger for success wasn't based on winning her back, but his dad had died from the black lung, so that was probably—hopefully—what really drove him now. She'd tried to stay friends, but at arm's length. Trouble was, he was always knocking himself out to help her and had sent several clients her way. He visited so many homes and knew what was going on around here, and she'd hate to have him for an enemy.

"Em," he said the moment he slid in the other side of the car, "you're not thinking it might be Jake, are you?"

"No," she said, crossing her arms over her chest, but her insides cartwheeled just at the mention of her brother's name. "Because," she went on, trying to steady her voice, "when I jumped out—even though I headed up that hill fast—he could have picked me off like the jackrabbits he used to shoot for fun."

"Unless—" Hank clamped his lips shut.

"Unless what?"

"Unless he means to make you suffer—worry—first. You know, play with you the way he did some of us when we were kids, tormenting and bullying—"

"It wasn't Jake," she insisted. "He's been missing for nearly three months, and he hasn't come back. He knows better with Reg Merrell still sheriff here. Besides, thirteen years is a long time. Even Jake could have changed, so let's just forget it."

"Right, okay," he said, holding up both hands, though he kept his thumbs hooked around the top of the steering wheel.

"I saw when I got in," she went on in a blatant attempt to calm herself and change the subject, "you've got all your audiovisual gear." She twisted around to glance in the back seat at his slide projector and plastic trays. "You set to give another health talk?" At least, she thought, Hank spent time visiting people, educating them, convincing them to take responsibility for their health and safety, unlike Griff Cusak, who acted as if the health center were his castle, to which the serfs must come to beg for help.

"Wouldn't exactly call it AV stuff anymore, Em," Hank said, smiling at her before he pulled out on the highway and had to watch where he was going. "It's all computer-generated and run by my new laptop. And I'm on-line to spread the word now, too. Just put my own Web site up. Maybe you'll want one soon."

"Around here? I may use on-line research and E-mail, Hank, but no webs of any kind, at least for a while."

He grinned and tapped her knee before pulling his hand back next to the other on top of the steering wheel. "Which reminds me," he said. "Sissy told me your hard drive crashed and lost the filing system you're setting up, so you know who to call for help."

Her sister and brother-in-law, Sissy and J. G. Presnell, whose house they were passing now, were Hank's close friends. It made things doubly awkward because J.G. still hoped she and Hank would get together. Sometimes, to Sissy and Emma's dismay, J.G. tried to play matchmaker and had them all to the house at once, as if they were double-dating like the old days. But nothing was the old days anymore, Emma thought, not even here in these hills.

"Thanks for the offer," she said, "but the system's still under warranty, so I think I'd better use it. As soon as I—we—get this tire changed, I'm going to stop at the Roscoe place." She craned her neck to look down the Roscoes' twisting lane as Hank drove higher around Big Blue. "I've got to find out where Len lives now.

You wouldn't happen to have his address, if they won't give it to me, would you?'' she added, angling slightly toward him. ''Or, do you know where he's gone?''

She scolded herself for breaking her own rule not to ask him for help, but Amrine might need her. ''The Roscoes claimed they didn't know where Len was,'' she reminded him when he hesitated, ''to stop Sheriff Merrell from serving their son with that restraining order a few months ago. At least they didn't shoot him off their property.''

''Don't know where Len's gone. Good riddance to bad rubbish. But for you, I'll try to find out.'' He shot her such a big smile that it softened his sharp features and lifted his receding hairline. ''Secretive, trigger-happy and maybe dangerous, to boot, that's the Roscoes. How about I just stop there after I change the tire and let you know what I learn later, okay?''

''Thanks, Hank. It's good to have someone I trust to help me out on this.''

His description of the Roscoes hit Emma hard. It was what folks always used to say about Pa and Jake, as well as ''Nothing good ever came out of Cutshin Holler.''

''You forgot to say you'd had abdominal surgery,'' Griff told Ola, who was still sitting with her mother in the waiting room when he gave Wanda his previous patient's chart to file. He'd seen the navel-to-pubic scar on Ola's belly during his exam but hadn't wanted to upset her more at the time.

''What if she did?'' Ginger Grady demanded before Ola could answer. ''She had her 'pendix out. What's that got to do with this baby?''

''Absolutely nothing, Mrs. Grady,'' Griff assured her.

"It has to do with giving a complete medical history. Listen, if you're wanting a ride home," he added to stem another outburst, "I'd be happy to drop you off before I go to lunch."

"Pa's coming," Ola muttered, hunching her thin shoulders as if she could hide her bulk. "He's late, that's all."

Just then, Griff heard a commotion in the hall and a woman's raised voice. Emma back again? Dragging in that lost patient? The mere thought of facing her again—or of working closely with her—made his pulse pound.

When he opened the door, he pulled Delia Lowe, holding on to the outer knob, off balance and into the waiting room. Her other hand grasped some old coot's arm. The man was mud-spattered and cussing up a storm. And no one did that around Delia Lowe, let alone try to buck her.

"Delia," Griff said, steadying her. "What's the matter here?"

"Sam Grady broke his wrist and insists it will heal on its own," she said and, loosing her hold on the man, rolled her eyes at Griff. "It's just made him slightly more contrary and cantankerous than usual."

As ever, despite the ruckus, Delia looked totally together, her champagne-hued hair held back in a smooth French twist to accentuate her attractive face and her makeup in soft pastels, which, with her slight plumpness, banished lines and made her look much younger than her sixty years. Today her denim jacket and long skirt sported huge embroidered sunflowers that matched her bright yellow silk neck scarf.

"Just here to get my womenfolk," the grizzle-haired Sam said in a gravelly voice. He held his right arm tight to his wiry body. When Griff bent to examine it, he muttered, "Pay it no mind. It'll fix itself soon 'nough."

"Mr. Grady," Griff said, "it may heal itself, but so crooked you'll never hold a hoe or gun straight again. You are right-handed, aren't you?"

As Sam shrugged, Griff became aware that Ola and Ginger stood beside him, but neither offered one peep of compassion or concern. Once again, he fought to control his frustration with these backwoods, backward people.

"Don't think I can't pay," Sam muttered, his face clenched in a frown. "I ain't gonna be beholden to you no more, Miss Delia."

"I wouldn't think of it," Delia said, rolling her green eyes again at Griff. "And I know you don't believe in preventive medicine, Sam," she went on in the soothing tone Griff was so familiar with. "But that wrist needs tending—please."

"Don't need a big to-do," Sam mumbled in his monotone. He rolled up his mud-speckled, plaid flannel sleeve. The wrist was swollen and discolored already. From its askew angle, Griff could tell the break was bad, though the bones had not pierced the skin. Sam would probably hardly flinch to have it set, but Griff figured he'd better use Demerol to knock him out for the procedure, that is if the man *let* him use sedation.

"So, what happened, Mr. Grady?" he pursued, gesturing him across the waiting room toward the hallway.

"Slipped on the gol-darned hillside fixin' to go after a thievin' coon."

Griff was glad Delia had dropped back to talk to Wanda and the Grady women. These old geezers hated women fussing more than a doctor interfering. What was man's work and woman's work was clearly delineated in these hills. Gardening was about all men would stoop to around the house, and hunting was strictly off-limits to females. Griff got Sam up on the examining table and, as he turned to the sink to scrub, it hit him.

"You live up near where Mudbrook turns off the highway, don't you, Mr. Grady?"

"More'n fifty years. Ma's folks 'fore that."

"The place where those quilts hang on the line for sale. You were going after a coon with a gun, I take it."

"Reckon not with a welcome-to-the-spring garden sign."

Griff bit back a grin. "So, what kind of rifle?"

"What's 'at got to do with this busted-up arm, doc? Anybody with a lick of sense knows a shotgun's 'nough to get a coon."

Frowning, Griff vigorously soaped his hands and wrists, then saw he was out of latex gloves. Damn, he needed a nurse here.

"I'm going to x-ray that wrist and have Wanda bring in some plaster-cast materials, Mr. Grady. Just sit tight a minute." He closed the door behind him, partly so the man wouldn't leave.

He called Wanda on the phone intercom from the other examining room, ordering gauze, padding and an arm stockinette for Sam's cast. Reaching for two latex gloves, he considered Grady's possible motive for taking a shot at Emma's Jeep. He'd just learned this morning she'd been treating Ola secretly, hadn't he? Too late, Griff realized he'd touched the phone and both doorknobs. While he rewashed, Delia poked her head in the open door.

"Old Grady's one of the worst of the mountain

bears,'' she whispered with a wink, then stepped in. "Once others hear you helped him, it will help us.''

Her strength and optimism had convinced Griff to come here, but he knew how fast her sunniness could turn to storm. Still he said, "What would help me— help us—Delia, is if you get a good nurse in here as soon as possible. Wanda's fine with the front desk, and she's learning the Medicare forms, but we need a nurse *now*.''

"I told you, I'm looking for just the right person.'' She clasped her manicured hands as if in prayer. "Not just anyone will do. Most people don't want to drive in or live here.''

"Tell me about it.''

A frown creased her high brow. "The point is, I'm looking for desire and dedication—just like with you. But you're down in the dumps again, aren't you?'' she demanded, her voice no longer soft-pedaled. "And with a full office this morning, for once, I take it. Griffin, I thought we had an understanding that it would take a while to build the health center up. All things worthwhile do, believe me.''

"We *do* have an understanding, Delia. Now, would you mind opening the other door for me, so I don't contaminate these?'' He held up his hands as if he'd just scrubbed for a major operation.

"Don't change the subject on me, my man,'' she scolded, blocking his exit with her arms folded. "If you're getting depressed again about the real reason you're here, then—''

"Which is, you mean, not to medically save mankind in defunct coal country?''

"Which is,'' she countered, wagging a crimson talon at him, "not just to pay off your medical-school debts as everyone believes. And because, if you go back to Lexington, no one will take you in because they know what happened back there.'' She made a sweeping gesture as if to encompass the entire universe. ''Not to mention the fact that I've given you more than a chance—a shelter—here.'' She stepped forward to stare straight into his eyes. ''You've said you're grateful, Griffin, but you could at least show a little more patience in this partnership we're forging.''

He almost challenged that description of their relationship, but instead said in a measured tone, ''All I did was remind you I need that nurse, Delia.''

''And all I did,'' she whispered over her shoulder as she opened the door, then preceded him into the hall to turn the other doorknob for him, ''was remind you that I know what no one else here does about you, Dr. Griffin Cusak.''

Emma was unsettled to see Hank's car in Sissy and J.G.'s yard when she arrived for dinner that evening, but maybe, she thought hopefully, he'd found out Len Roscoe's whereabouts.

She went in through the screen door, following the rich cooking smells and the sound of Sissy singing a plaintive, old mountain song, ''Brown Eyes.'' Her twenty-five-year-old sister's consolation through hard times had been her beautiful voice, which she shared with other needy souls whenever possible. Shut-ins, old folks, sick children—Sissy's haunting voice had blessed many. Emma loved it when she did the old gospel hymns of inspiration, but mountain songs like this one unsettled her.

Tonight Sarah Weston Presnell was picking out her own accompaniment on her guitar, which rested on her bulging stomach. She was nearly eight months' pregnant with her precious, second child. Hank was sitting nearby on the couch. J.G. was settled in his favorite straight-backed chair.

If Sissy's husband, J.G., had been born farther south, he would have been nicknamed Bubba. But John George Presnell wasn't just a good-time boy, he was deep—and moody as winter wind. Whereas Sissy had always been a looker with her pale blond hair and pert features that enhanced her perky personality, J.G. seemed as bland as his light brown hair and brown eyes. But he was no fool and was firecracker jealous.

Hank scooted over and patted a place for Emma on the quilt-covered couch, but she remained standing. Despite Sissy's smile and J.G.'s welcoming nod, Emma's insides still twisted tighter.

Sissy's time was getting so close and she'd—they'd—lost the first baby nearly ten years ago. J.G. had been in Germany in the army then, but there'd never been any question he'd come home and marry Sissy. Though a bit of a hell-raiser, J.G. had finally settled down to be a good husband, at least until his accident in the mines two years ago.

The pain of his injury—and maybe their financial struggle when he wasn't working—had made him drink more and had trimmed the fuse on his temper. The longer he was laid up, the more possessive of Sissy he became, especially when she took a short-lived factory job in Highboro. He even began to belittle her singing. Emma prayed the baby would lift the bitterness from his heart—and the burden of losing the first child from her own.

"Today I feel so sad and weary," Sissy sang, *"I*

*want a love that cannot be. All I need to make me
happy, let those brown eyes smile at me…''*

Her voice was husky—sexy, men always said. She
didn't even have that faraway look she often got when
she sang. She was looking at J.G., right here, right now.
Despite his chronic back pain, it was a wonder he sat
still, especially since Sissy's low-cut blouse positioned
her breasts right on the top curves of the guitar. Though
Hank was a good friend, Emma was amazed J.G. didn't
send Sissy to get something else on, but he was evidently too entranced himself. That was a good sign for
their marriage, wasn't it?

Everyone applauded the song, and Sissy blushed as
she unhooked her guitar and took an awkward bow. She
looked so healthy and happy that Emma tried to stem
her fears that something would go wrong with the birth
this time.

"Oh, golly, 'scuse me, y'all, no curtain calls right
now. Gotta check on our supper," Sissy cried, gesturing
for Emma to follow her out to the kitchen.

"J.G. looked like an appreciative audience for once,"
Emma observed once they were in the kitchen.

"Mmm. Hank just told him his payments—I mean
benefits—will go up a bit. I guess he knew it ahead of
time, 'cause he's had more money lately. Bought me
this new blouse in Highboro for a gift, so thought I'd
model it for him."

"Aha."

"Aha what, big sis?" Sissy asked. "Don't you go
analyzing everything again or I'm gonna scream instead
of sing. Here, toss these greens for me, will you?"

Emma seasoned the dandelion greens with sugar, salt
and pepper, then tossed them with the hot vinegar and
water to wilt them down. "You've got enough for an

army here. Been putting on a pound or two myself eating with you and J.G. a couple times a week," Emma admitted, arranging sliced, hard-boiled eggs on top of the greens.

"Delia might come by, too," Sissy admitted, hustling to ladle bean soup and ham hock from the pot to a tureen. She took corn bread out of the oven and replaced it with a huge rhubarb cobbler. "Says she's got some local gig for me, *and* it pays."

"She pays, you mean. Listen, Sissy," Emma said as they both hefted dishes to carry into the dining room. "If she offers to cover a high-risk specialist for you in Highboro, you just let her know I'm going to pay for that. We don't need to be accepting anything else from her."

"Emma, it makes her so happy to do things for folks. I know you two never patched things up, but if she's got someplace for me to sing, big as a house or not, I'm gonna take the job. With the baby coming, every little bit helps. 'Sides," she continued, "J.G. says we're not taking any more big gifts from you and, if we need a specialist, we'll pay him ourselves."

"Hank told me you did a real fishtail up on Mudbrook, Emma," J.G. observed later at the table as she spread butter on her corn bread. "You know when it's raining," he said, "that road's not passable, not even jackassable."

Everybody laughed, though they'd all heard J.G.'s one-liners a hundred times. Emma noticed he hauled them out whenever Sissy got too excited about her singing, and she'd just been chattering about that paying job again.

"You know, Sis," J.G. said, "you already sing kind

of breathy, and with carrying that baby, maybe you just ought to cool it for a while, holding that guitar against your belly, breathing for two and all that. You know, go back to singin' after," he added with a side glance at her bulk.

"You mean *long* after," Sissy dared.

J.G. frowned and glanced at Emma. "Tell her she shouldn't be tiring herself out, midwife. I'm gonna personally see nothing goes wrong this time."

Emma felt as if she'd been slapped. "So am I, J.G., but singing is not going to hurt her if she doesn't tire herself. As for nothing going wrong this time, we'll get her a specialist."

"He didn't mean nothing 'gainst you, Emma," Sissy said, reaching out to grab her sister's wrist across the corner of the table.

"No, not a thing," J.G. put in, looking down into his empty soup bowl. "It's just that it's taken us a while to get another one in the oven, right, hon?" He smiled at Sissy and she nodded back, but Emma could have cut the tension with the butter knife she still gripped.

"Oh, golly," Sissy said, getting up during dessert, "I hear another car pulling in. Maybe it's Delia."

While Sissy headed for the door, Emma finished her last bite of cobbler. Delia's presence would kill her appetite, anyway. She heard the woman's voice outside as she half listened to J.G. and Hank's quick, quiet exchange.

"Sissy's getting all het up over this stupid paying job is 'bout as welcome right now as tick season, Hank," J.G. muttered, narrowing his eyes at him as if Emma weren't even there. That had been one thing she'd found hard to take when she'd come back from years away. The menfolk would sometimes carry on deep discussions and make big decisions as if a woman wasn't even in the room or in their lives.

"I hear you, man, but she's got raw talent," Hank insisted. "It can't hurt for her to sing gospel songs or hit those rest homes in Highboro. It meant a lot to my ma when she lost Pa, and Sissy sang her all those heaven-bound songs."

"I just want her—and others," J.G. said, glancing at Emma as she got up, "to remember, though I ain't got much education, I got some sense, that's all."

Emma took a few empty plates on her way out to the kitchen, ignoring the long look Hank cast her way. At least he had whispered earlier that he hadn't learned Len's address or phone number from the man's Roscoe kin and doubted she would. She needed to think of some other way to track him. Maybe he'd gotten a Tennessee license plate. She'd probably need someone official to make inquiries, but she doubted Sheriff Merrell would help.

Delia's voice rang out in the house. Emma was tempted to go out the back door, but that would be the second time today. Besides, she wanted to thank Sissy for dinner. As night fell, she paused, drying a few dishes, staring at her serious, sad reflection in the window. For one moment, she saw Griff Cusak's face as he'd looked today, rugged but gentle, too.

"Oh, that's sweet of you," Sissy was saying. "Look, hon, a quilted teddy bear from the sewing co-op Miss Delia sponsors."

"I don't want to jinx anything," Delia said, "but I think you're close enough to have a baby shower now. I thought maybe Emma would throw you one, but it would be better up at my big house, and who knows she wouldn't have some wild emergency right in the middle of things.''

Emma's neck and shoulder muscles tightened. Delia had to know she was here, so this was all more deliberate guerrilla warfare. Though Delia was the beloved guardian of Shelter, Emma considered marching out there and throwing a plate at her. Delia had done that once to her when she'd tried to explain her dream of getting an education to return to help local women.

"I want to help them my way and not the way you've got all laid out in concrete and cash, Delia," she could almost hear herself shout.

"No, you listen to me, my girl. If, after all I've done for you and Sissy, you don't have the decency to show respect and gratitude for the love I've showered on you, as your foster mother—''

"You've made yourself my guardian, but I don't have a foster mother. I had a mother, and she's dead—''

"You're dead to me from now on, Emma Weston of Cutshin Holler!" Delia had screamed. Then she'd launched a dinner plate that hit Emma's shoulder and shattered against the wall.

That night Emma had left Shelter to begin her struggle of working low-paying jobs to put herself through nursing school before she could even begin to specialize to become a nurse midwife. It had been a long, hard, lonely haul, and now...

The plate she was drying almost slipped from her hands, but she grabbed it.

"The real reason I came, Sissy," Delia was saying in the other room, "was to invite you to sing at the Decoration Day social here in town—if you're not lying in then.''

Lying in, Emma thought. Delia might have a new,

modern house and health center, but sometimes she seemed to be living in the past. But then, too much, so did she. Emma hated it when she and Delia had something in common.

Sissy's squeal of delight made Emma jump. She went back out into the dining room to clear more dishes. Delia had evidently just given Sissy a big check for the Decoration Day gig.

"Oh, Delia," Emma said, trying to sound nonchalant, "you've missed the main course, but some of Sissy's fabulous rhubarb cobbler is left."

"I hear someone shot out your tires today," Delia said, the smile sliding from her face. "Dare we fear the prodigal son has come home and someone should kill a fatted calf?"

Sissy gasped. Hank shuffled his feet, and J.G. grunted.

"After three months?" Emma challenged, but her voice shook. "No, my theory is—" she drew the words out as every face turned her way "—someone's been telling folks I need to be scared off or stopped so women are forced to have their babies at the health center, whether they want a home birth or not. But Sissy's going to have her baby under a specialist's care in Highboro."

"I told you I don't need to," Sissy piped up. "Emma and I've been doing all the prelim exams and exercises," she told everyone, her voice rising. "There's no complications, so Emma and the good Lord are gonna get me through this just fine, I'd bet everything on that."

"If you ask me," Delia said, glaring at Emma, "that's exactly what you're doing."

4

Griff Cusak sometimes escaped the health center—and Delia—by driving the hills at the end of the day. Trouble was, it never helped him to escape himself. Worse, the day after his run-in with the midwife, he found himself going by the Shelter Birthing and Women's Health Center for the third time. And pulling in.

His stomach knotted as if he were a patient facing some dread disease—and the only specialist in the world who could cure it. Stupid thought, he scolded himself. He was the healer in these parts and was willing to fight for that right.

He wasn't certain whether to walk to the front or side door of the L-shaped, two-story, white house, but Emma evidently saw him and came out onto the long side porch. Too late to back out now.

He jammed his hands into his leather-jacket pockets as he walked slowly toward her. She gave him a flutter of a wave. He'd never seen her in a skirt before, a long, denim one with a cobalt-blue blouse open to show a slash of ivory throat. He wondered if she was going out or had people coming in.

"I was just driving by," he called, "and wondered if you'd found Amrine yet."

"No, and I've made a lot of calls today to locate the father of her child. I'd hoped she'd call, but she hasn't."

"It's only been one day. And *I* should have called

before I came," he said, propping one loafered foot on her bottom step and staring up at her.

"That's all right." She hugged herself as if for warmth. "Unless I get a call, I'm done for the day. You mentioned a tour of the center—you want to come in?"

So she wasn't going out. He saw she wore white terry-cloth slippers. The breeze blew her skirt to the curve of her hip and lifted her hair to expose the nape of a slender neck. He knew it was an illusion, but she almost looked fragile for one moment, as if she needed a protector.

"Fine. You have a lot of plants in there," he observed, indicating the small glassed-in porch beyond this open one.

"My herbal hothouse," she explained. "That's comfrey and chamomile hanging to dry for the labor-aide I just might market to get some money for this place, except it has to be mixed fresh."

"Anything else in the labor-aide, or that a secret?" he asked as he held open the screen door and stepped in so close behind her he could smell the delicate scent of her hair—like fresh woods in the rain. His nostrils flared as if he could breathe her in.

He saw she had an old pottery crock of spring wildflowers on the table, so that must be the scent. He shook his head to clear it and studied the large kitchen with two smaller adjoining rooms. She had just finished eating alone; her dishes were still on the table cluttered with mail and a *Midwifery Today* magazine.

"I'd share my recipe with anyone who really cares," she said, jolting him back to what he'd asked. She ticked off ingredients on her fingers. "Honey, water, salt, lemon juice, baking soda, crushed calcium tablets and whatever herbs I think will most benefit that particular client.''

He thought she really sounded like one of the traditional granny women they still talked about around here, but he said only, "If it works, it works, even if it's a placebo." No way he was going to screw this up by insisting she keep lots of liquids away from a laboring woman or questioning her calling her patients clients again.

She showed him her windowed office area in the breakfast nook, with its computer and file cabinet, and the windowless pantry that served as her equipment room, with its sterilizer for scissors, speculums and other instruments, which were kept neatly on shelves. The whole place seemed open, warm and light, but too homey to suit him.

The front rooms of the tall-ceilinged, old place made up the patient-care area, including the parlor, which was her waiting room. Plants and wildflowers again, he noted, books and magazines—all dust catchers or pollen-laden. On the wall were proudly displayed heart-framed photos of the nine babies she'd delivered in Shelter, though five had been home births. The room was papered and the furniture upholstered in mix-and-match flower or check prints of pale blues and bright yellows.

"Is all this fabric fireproof?" he blurted before he caught himself.

"I was waiting for Dr. J. Griffin Cusak to get here," she said with a tight smile. "The point is, comfortable, natural decor tells people what you think of the birthing process. If a woman's going to a hospital, she tends to expect indignities and numbs herself for them, and that's almost symbolized by the cold surfaces of stainless steel, stark walls, utilitarian everything. But birth is a miracle and a mystery, Griff," she whispered, gripping the back of a rocking chair and tilting it slightly toward him. "Sometimes in its presence I tremble because the power of it is so strong."

Transfixed, he stared at her; she looked flushed, transported. If he'd thought of her a moment ago as delicate or fragile, he was crazy. Why this holistic, earth-mother stuff she was spouting didn't sound quite as off-base as it should have, he wasn't sure.

She evidently approved of the fact that he didn't argue. She smiled again and touched his elbow to move him toward the other downstairs rooms. "I wouldn't ordinarily show you the bathroom," she admitted, "but this big, claw-footed tub serves clients who might want a water birth."

He couldn't help it; his lower lip dropped and his eyebrows lifted. Two ladder-back chairs faced the tub as if for a conversation, and unlit beige and cream-colored candles of all sizes lined a high shelf. It looked more like a place for a seduction, but then he'd been without a woman for too long. That's what was wrong with him.

"I've read," he told her, clearing his throat, "that rural midwives sometimes end up as health-care givers to the whole community, but I'm here now."

As she turned away to show him the birthing room next door, he heard her whisper, "You sure enough are," but he didn't take the bait to argue. They stood so close in the narrow door of the next large room, evidently once the dining room, that he could feel the warmth from her and wondered if she could sense his heat.

"This space does double duty," she explained, indicating a standard examining table. "In this area of the room, I do Paps, pelvics and prenatals. And that's the birthing bed."

He gaped at the double bed between two windows where the early-evening sunlight streamed in. Set up on a small dais, it was a gentle pool of pale blue and green pillow shams printed with water lilies and a matching spread. He couldn't have been more surprised if she'd showed him her own bed, inviting and intimate.

"It's slightly elevated to protect me from what we call midwives' back—too much bending and arching," she said. "Of course, it gets stripped down and sterilized. Out come the blood pressure cuff, fetoscope and infant scales, but I want a woman who comes here for a birth to be completely comfortable with it from all the time we've talked and planned together."

"That is something, I admit, a doctor doesn't have and is probably the poorer for—in-depth talking and planning, I mean."

"I believe," she said, turning to face him, "that is the nicest thing you've ever said to me."

Their eyes met. Her lower lip trembled before she moved away.

"I live upstairs," she said as if to fill the awkward silence where they could hear themselves breathe and the gentle whoosh of the old furnace coming on. "But I've put most of my money and time in down here."

"It's a very—unique place. Now, about our patient, Ola."

She looked surprised. "Yours now, evidently," she said as she led him back to the kitchen and poured two cups of coffee.

He sat down across from her, not wanting to break this tentative truce but knowing he had to. "She's underage, Emma. I realize people around here make their own rules, but you should have informed her parents. They were rightly upset." He paused. "Don't look at me that way, because I didn't come to accuse you. It's just I think it's highly probable that Sam Grady blew out your tires. He's obviously a crack shot, and I doubt if he broke his wrist chasing coons in the rain on some hillside by his house."

She nodded, frowning, lightly hitting one fist on top of the other next to her coffee. "I wanted to dig the bullets out of the tires," she explained, "but a friend did it for me—and said he threw them away. It didn't matter, anyway, because I'd need some ballistics expert to link them to a particular gun. Reg Merrell, the long-time county sheriff in Highboro, would probably say it was a prank—or just a bad shot. He knows me for bugging him about things before."

"The restraining order for Amrine?"

She hesitated. For one moment she looked angry—or was it anguished? "Right, Amrine," she said quickly. "So all my—and your—suspicions and proof, and this cup of coffee, will get us nothing. Almost any man around here can hit a bobbing deer's tail at two hundred yards with their single-shot rifles and can navigate these hills in the rain.

"I did think, though," she added, staring down at her hands as she sat across from him, "I might go up on that ridge above Sam's place and look for footprints or bullet casings."

He sat up straighter. "You want another good pair of eyes, I'll go, too. And I thought maybe you'd show me the Settle place—the blood you mentioned."

"All right," she said, standing. "Just give me a min-

ute to change. But you'll never make it in those loaf-
ers.''

"I keep my running shoes in the car.''

"Dig them out, because the Jeep will handle where
we're going and your big car might not.''

"I usually drive the health center van—but that's my
dad's old Chrysler, and I just drive it to blow out the
dust sometimes..." He blinked back tears, rising
quickly to glance out at the car before she could see his
face.

She was halfway down the hallway before she turned
back. "Griff, if I'd have told Sam and Ginger about Ola
seeing me, I'd have lost her. She said she'd run off to
Louisville to get a job, and I didn't want that.''

"Louisville?" he said, surprised. "Her mother says
she's going to live with relatives in Cincinnati and deliver there.''

"What? Maybe we'd better stop to see them, too,
together.''

"It's blood all right, too much of it," Griff said as
he hunkered down to scrape with his thumbnail on Amrine's linoleum floor. Though it was still light outside,
it was dim inside. Somehow the old generator had quit
so the few ceiling lights weren't even working. Emma
didn't dare open the refrigerator door because everything must have spoiled. She'd have to come back soon
to clean it out.

"Unfortunately," she said, bending over his shoulder, "I knew that." She suddenly remembered the note
with the single bloody thumbprint she had never retrieved from the pocket of her slicker. She'd better take
that to Sheriff Merrell, even though she'd probably have
to eat crow to ask for his help.

"We'd have plenty of blood here for DNA testing, if there had been a murder."

"Don't even think that!" Emma protested as she stood and sagged against the kitchen counter. "She left a believable note for me—at least for someone who doesn't really know her."

He straightened. "But you don't believe it."

"She wouldn't go with Len, not after what'd he'd done before, not after she sent Wade to me for help. I'm terrified Len hit her—maybe even cut or shot—"

"Whoa!" he said, holding his hands up. "You just told me not to get carried away. I think she was spotting vaginally. Come here and look at the pattern of these blood spots."

Despite the poor light, she saw instantly what he implied. "They are heavy where she first stood here at the counter cutting up the stew meat," she said as they shuffled along the path of drops between them, "but then they head away in an orderly fashion, as if she's walking, not rushing, not staggering."

"Right. No splatter marks or pattern. So it wasn't an extremity wound where she splashed or flung blood, nor an artery, because it didn't gush. But—"

"It was still heavy enough she needed help," Emma finished for him. "It came right through her clothes, unless she was in her nightgown with no undergarments on."

"You knew her. Did she go around like that?"

"She might have, but I doubt she'd go out to the shed, half-dressed, to get Wade, unless the pain really panicked her. I can ask him. I want to know if he brought her that stew meat, too."

Heads still down, shoulder to shoulder, they followed the drops into Amrine's bedroom.

"She could have lain down to get the flow to stop," Emma theorized. "Or put on panties or a pad, but somehow she stopped the bleeding." She sighed. "A good sign, I guess."

It was then she saw a notepad wedged partly under the pillow on the bed. "Look," she said, grabbing it. "This is probably where she wrote the note to me. It's the same paper. If she was lying down here for a few minutes, someone must have brought it to her."

She tilted the notepad sideways to the sinking sunlight but saw no impression of writing on the top piece of paper. Deepening shadows reminded her they'd have to keep going if they were to search the hillside before dark.

"What's that?" she asked Griff as she turned from the window to see him staring at a small piece of paper he'd picked up off the floor. "Not another note?"

"Just a Tootsie Roll wrapper," he said with a shrug.

"I think Mike Bonner might have been talking to her about selling her place," she said, looking once more around the silent, darkening kitchen as they went out. Remembering Mike and Griff were friends, she added, "But I'm sure he's not tied to this. He's given candy to scores of people around here, including me."

"An old generator for electricity, no toilet, no phone," Griff said, still looking around as he followed her out into the yard. "It's like a time warp. I can't believe it."

Emma turned to glare at him as she climbed in the driver's seat of the Jeep.

"I used to live the next holler up," she said, her voice sharper than she intended as she turned the ignition key. "This place once looked like Buckingham Palace to me. Let's just get going or it's going to be too darn dark."

"I can't believe it," Griff said again. She really didn't like this man and certainly didn't trust him—Delia's confederate—so the magnetism he exerted infuriated her.

"What now?" she asked as they stood on the fold of hill that lifted from Mudbrook Road and sank again toward the Grady homestead. "The smoke coming out of their chimney? Lots of people still heat with a stove or fireplace."

"No, I mean a little family graveyard practically out their back door."

"No one's been buried there for years," Emma explained. "Public-health regulations have caught up to Shelter, too, doctor."

Fortunately for him, he didn't respond to that. It hadn't made her feel better that they'd located the exact spot someone had lain behind a dead tree trunk to take careful, if quick, aim at her Jeep. They'd found two spent .22-caliber casings. It was one of the shells of choice around here, so that didn't narrow it down at all.

Below them, they surveyed the Grady house with its chicken coop, ramshackle barn, smokehouse and work shed strung out down the narrow, twisting valley that followed the crooked stream called Knob Crick, tumbling down from Big Blue. From here, Ginger's plastic-covered quilts hanging on the front line to advertise themselves looked the size of postage stamps.

"Let's get back down to the Jeep before we can't see a thing," Griff said. He took her elbow firmly, but she didn't budge.

"I just want to look down the path Sam would probably have taken up here when he took his shots. It must have been a spur-of-the-moment thing, because how would he know I'd be driving to Amrine's unless he was involved with her disappearance, and I doubt that. The Gradys have never been too neighborly. Other than taking to my dad and brother, they kept to themselves.''

''Your brother doesn't live around here, does he?''

''He's been gone quite a while. I—I actually don't know where he is now.''

''I just thought of something else,'' he said as if to change that topic for her. At least his question about Jake meant Delia hadn't told him all about her family. ''Sam said he was going after coons,'' he went on, ''but don't they usually come out at night?''

''Yes, but if they can sneak food during broad daylight, they'll do it. I hate it when you shine a light on them when they're in the garbage or garden and their eyes glow. I wasn't scared of much as a kid, but I hated that. It was like they were really desperately hungry ghosts or demons from the depths of the forest.''

She suddenly realized how silly she must sound, but he only nodded. ''Before I started school,'' he said, ''I used to be afraid of the dark outside my bedroom window. Then one night, my dad carried me outside so that I could see it really wasn't dark as it looked from inside. I could see and walk around, especially in the reflected stars or city lights. I was never scared of the dark, inside or out, again.''

''Your father,'' she whispered, barely getting the words out, ''must have been a good, wise man.''

He looked away as if he couldn't find more words. Strange, she thought, to be sharing inner thoughts and fears with this man. Less surefooted than she, he picked his way slowly over fallen limbs, wary of the poison ivy she'd warned him about earlier. She could only hope that a good rash of P.I. made whomever had shot at her miserable.

"You know this area well," Griff observed.

"My daddy used to be Sam's hunting buddy years ago, that's all. Amrine and I used to ramble all around these parts."

"You said your brother moved away, but do your folks still live around here?"

"Both gone," she said so quickly and calmly she prayed he'd realize that topic was closed. If he thought they were both dead, so much the better.

The path down to Knob Crick Holler was still there. If she wasn't pretty sure Sam might just take another shot at her, it would be the closest way to call on them tonight. She'd rather wait until tomorrow, but it would be best to confront him and Ginger with Griff's help. And she wasn't planning that she and the good doctor would be together any more after tonight.

She glanced down at the cluster of gravestones, that stood like broken teeth, pioneer graves, some of people who probably knew Daniel Boone. Her gaze drifted to the back of the work shed, which wasn't visible from the house. Sam had never gone to the mines but had done odd jobs on-site or hauled them back here to fuss over. It was not miners' benefits or social security that fed the Gradys lately.

"I don't believe it!" she cried, echoing Griff's earlier words.

He put both hands on her shoulders as he came to stand behind her and peer around at the same angle through the blowing trees. "He's hiding a moonshiner's still back there with that stuff behind the shed or what?" he asked.

"Nobody moonshines anymore unless it's for their own family," she said, shaking her head at how much he had to learn. "Patches of pot are the choice of a quick cash crop, but I haven't heard Sam's done that."

"So what are you looking at? Those appliances on the back stoop? I've seen lots of those sitting out on porches and in side-yard dumps."

"But close to the house, not hidden back away," she insisted. "Those look in working order, maybe even new. There's a huge chest freezer. Surely Ginger's not suddenly making that much on quilts. I wonder if Sam's been storing them for someone who's stealing them or is fencing them himself."

He tightened his grip on her shoulders. "Let's go ask—indirectly."

"And let him know we've been back here snooping? Still," she muttered as she led the way to the Jeep, "Ola has those narrow hipbones. We've got to make them promise to keep her home where she can come to one or the other of us to have that baby."

"She ain't here, so we won't be needing neither of you'ns for her," Sam bellowed. He stood in the front door with firelight dancing behind him. Emma could see a new coon pelt stretched on a frame leaning by the front door, so maybe he really *had* been after thieving coons. At least there wasn't a rifle in sight, but maybe his broken right wrist would slow him down with one. He held a cigarette in his left hand. Ginger peered forlornly out the front window, plainly silhouetted.

"Where's Ola gone then?" Emma dared, standing her ground next to Griff just off the porch. The faint stench of flesh from the pelt wafted to them, and she wrinkled her nose. If the Gradys told her that Ola had left with the father of her baby, she was going to scream. Ola's child had been fathered by her third cousin at a week-long family reunion in Hazard County last summer, but no one—even Ola—would so much as speak his name.

"Gone to Lexington to live with my kin," Sam said. "Leastwise 'til the baby come. Maybe get her a job and stay there."

"Lexington?" Griff whispered beside her. "First Cincinnati, then Louisville, now Lexington?"

Emma felt sick to her soul. Not only because Sam and Ginger were lying, but because Ola had lied, too. And because Emma had seen a wife and daughter lie to cover up the terrible things their husband and pa had done before.

5

As she heard her husband's key in the lock, Jidge Collister blinked back tears and stared out the condo window. The span of light and glowing supports of the Golden Gate Bridge hovered over the darker Presidio area and inky bay. As usual, Ben closed the door too loudly as he came in.

"Is he finally asleep?" he asked curtly.

"In bed, still fussing off and on." She stared at him in the black mirror of their sixth-floor patio glass door instead of turning to face him. She hugged her arms tightly to her full-figured body. "I don't know if your walk or drive or wherever you went after you stormed out this time settled you down, Ben, but it's stirred me up."

She spun to face him so fast her hostess gown belled out. He had said tonight it would have been better if Mitch had never been born, and she'd never forgive him for that.

"I've had it," she announced.

"With me or our little bundle of joy?" he countered, throwing his car keys on the marble-topped table. They skidded off onto the Aubusson, but he didn't retrieve them.

"I'm at the end of my rope with the whole situation!" she cried. "Those people lied to us. The perfect

Caucasian child, they said. But Mitchell is—he needs help."

"If you're ready to admit that, at least there's one fewer liar in the world."

"Why can't you be supportive in this? Or else get mad enough to go after them?"

"Go after whom, Jidge?" he shouted, holding his ground in the foyer.

Down the hall, their two-year-old started wailing. Jidge made no move to rush to him. For one moment she almost hated the child the way she hated the agency people. The way she hated Ben for not loving Mitchell anymore, for not loving her enough not to blame her for the baby being...damaged goods. The whole thing had been her fault, but she'd been desperate, though not as deadly desperate as she was now.

When Ben's face softened and he opened his arms to her, she almost flew into them, but it was too late. Jamming her knuckles to her lips to stifle a sob, she ran down the hall to Mitchell's room.

"Hi, my sweetie, Mommy's sweetie, my handsome boy, yes," she crooned until he settled down to murmurs and then silence.

When she looked for Ben, he was gone again, his car keys, too. Jidge felt dead inside, but then her fury at the unfairness of it came raging back.

She walked to the chinoiserie lacquer commode and opened the top drawer. Beneath their cashmere scarves and leather gloves lay the small quilt that Mitchell had been bundled in at the airport and, under that, the pistol she kept in the house for protection.

At least the moon was almost full, because Emma knew better than to try to use her flashlight out here.

To reassure herself, though, she felt in her jacket pocket to be certain it hadn't fallen out in her climb back up to the spot where she and Griff had stood earlier, over-looking the Grady place. Sam was one of the few hunt-ers in the area who had never kept coon hounds that would howl at an intruder, but still she wouldn't risk walking past the house to get back in the holler, even at two in the morning.

She hadn't been able to sleep after Griff left. She kept waking up, thinking she heard sounds outside, even in the house. She had to admit that Sam and Jake weren't the only ones who might want to scare or hurt her. Hal Eubanks and his kin had never forgiven her family for Pa and Jake killing his brother, Cory. It wasn't exactly the Hatfields and McCoys, since she and Sissy were careful never to respond, but she'd had proof Hal still hated her. Just like at Sissy's, years ago, Emma had had rotten eggs and later a bucket of chicken blood—the Eubankses had always raised and sold chickens and eggs—thrown on the house just after she moved in. Lately, though, there'd been no other blatant Eu-bankses' calling cards, and she'd tried to put them out of her mind.

Obsessed with examining those brand-new-looking appliances out behind Sam's work shed, she'd dressed and returned here. If she had something to hold over Sam's head, he might tell her where Ola had really gone. But even if she found out he was hiding, fencing or stealing every Maytag, Whirlpool, GE and Frigidaire in the state, she'd be crazy to report him to the law. It might make the sheriff excuse her for giving him grief in the past, but in blood feuds, no one went to officials or outsiders, settling their own scores, instead.

In the blowing, shifting darkness, Emma moved

slowly, touching tree trunks for support on the way down the path she had showed Griff hours ago. She wished he were here, then scolded herself for such weakness. She'd have to do this and plenty else on her own. She'd had to be the strong one for years and would steer clear of a man who weakened her in any way.

Emma stopped moving and breathing when she heard a strange hum. A hive of wasps or bees on the underhang of the shed? No electric wires or phone lines came clear out here. Her eyes were quite accustomed to the dark but the overhang threw shadows the moonlight couldn't penetrate. No one could see this spot from the house. She could risk the flashlight.

She jumped when the overhang creaked in the wind. Her flashlight beam jerked and skimmed the old tombstones about twenty feet away. Shadows lunged, and she gasped as a terrible memory flashed at her: Pa and Sam boasting they'd used those headstones for target practice when they were dog drunk. She turned and stepped on something she thought was a snake and jumped again.

"Damn it, Emma," she muttered to herself as her narrow beam illuminated an electric cable that coiled out from the shed and into each of the appliances. The hum was louder than just this freezer running, and the washer and dryer weren't operating. The sound must be coming from an electric generator in the shed.

She realized now that she'd been wrong about Sam being in on a theft ring. It was no crime to hide some fancy new items out in the back forty, but why not keep them closer to the house? And why such a huge, expensive chest freezer for the three of them? This thing was the size of a coffin.

Emma put both hands on its cold metal handle. She

hadn't let herself think it, but maybe she'd really come to take a look into this thing. Perhaps its proximity to the graves had made her dare to think some pretty dreadful things.

We'd have plenty of blood here for DNA testing, if there had been a murder, Griff had said earlier. He'd been talking about Amrine, but Ola, too, had left when Emma didn't think she would. And Emma knew that Sam, like Len Roscoe—like her own father and brother—were capable of violence. The Weston menfolk had always reeked of suppressed wrath, and it had too often exploded, especially when they were drinking. Sam had hidden it better but she could sense it seething beneath the surface. And if he had been mad enough at a midwife to pump two bullets into her tires, hoping maybe she'd spin off the slick road into a swollen stream, how mad would he be at his own daughter for going behind his back?

Trembling, Emma pulled the handle and, with a grunt, hefted the lid of the chest freezer straight up. A cold, white cloud lifted into her face. She blinked it away and trained her light down on a packaged, dismembered, skinned body.

She gasped and dropped her flashlight inside the cold depths. Shuddering, she had to feel for it against the frozen flesh. She couldn't just run, not now, not leaving her flashlight here to be found. Worse, there was more than one body here, something smaller.

She retrieved the flashlight, steeled herself for what she would see, steadied it and snapped it on.

"Venison?" she whispered.

It must be a deer carcass, stored in huge haunches not yet cut into roasts and steaks. What an idiot she was!

But there were also clear-plastic-wrapped smaller bodies, some with hair. Unskinned dead coons—three of them—and a few squirrels nestled in the kind of clear covers Ginger used to protect her quilts. Even through the thick plastic, one of the coons stared straight up at her, but he'd been dead long enough that his eyes didn't glow.

"Ugh," she muttered and shook her head to clear it. She let the lid fall back harder than she meant to. She leaned shaking against the freezer.

What was wrong with her? Ginger would surely protect Ola from Sam, wouldn't she? But Emma had once overheard her parents arguing about Sam fooling with Ginger's younger sister who had stayed with them for a while. What if some mysterious, even mythical, third cousin was not the father of Ola's child?

Emma almost dry-heaved. Those dead animals waiting to be skinned were bad enough, but what other secrets were hidden here in Knob Crick Holler? Surely, if Ola or Ginger—even Sam—had said something amiss to tip off Griff about the paternity of the child, he would have mentioned it to her.

Squinting into the darkness, Emma hurried toward the path up the ridge. Now she had two missing clients to find.

The next day Emma went looking for Wade Poteet at the hardware store where he worked. He wasn't in but, as she was heading for her Jeep, she saw Griff sitting at the front window table at Arletta's having lunch. She was going to call him to be sure he had no suspicions about the paternity of Ola's child.

Incest. There, she'd put a name to what she was thinking, at least, though she wasn't certain she'd have the guts to bring it up with Griff and tell him her proof was strictly a funny feeling. Still, when she saw he was eating alone, without Delia anywhere in sight, she knocked on the window and waved.

Looking surprised and pleased, he held up a finger and threw his napkin then a crisp five-dollar bill down before he scraped his chair back. She saw someone at the next table gesture him over and he stopped.

Emma walked slowly down the sidewalk toward the church to wait for him. And ran right into Hal Eubanks, coming the other way, his arms loaded with two paper sacks full of something. Big and burly, Hal was in his forties but looked sixty with his grizzled beard and hunched, lumbering walk. He had a dirty John Deere ball cap pulled low over his eyes and wore jeans and a black flannel shirt that looked as if they'd been through the wars. He'd never been quite right since his stint in Vietnam.

The Eubankses, luckily for her and Sissy, were almost recluses who lived up a short lane just off the highway. A lot of kin lived in their ramshackle, old place—a sort of bizarre television Walton family. Hal was the patriarch, married to Modeen. Besides their mama, the clan included one of their daughters, Tammy, and at least one of her kids, besides Hal's widowed sister-in-law, Letha, and her oldest boy Estes's family. Other Eubankses drifted in and out.

"Oh, Hal, haven't seen you for ages." Emma tried to sound friendly. "Hope everyone's doing well. How's Modeen and your mama?"

His scowl told her nothing had changed. He cursed low and hawked spittle at her feet, just missing her shoes. "That son-of-a-bitchin' brother of yourn's still on my list—all of you."

When she stood her ground, he shouldered past her and walked on. Late-night sneakiness was more their M.O., but she wondered if Hal or Estes could have shot out her tires. How would they have known she'd be on Mudbrook right then in a driving rain? Whoever shot at her could not have followed her up there but was lying in wait.

Considering how shook-up she felt now, at noon on Main Street, she'd hate to run into Hal off somewhere or at night. At least, she could tell, when she turned to see Griff hurrying toward her, he hadn't seen or heard her exchange with Hal.

"I thought it might just be a dream that we were speaking civilly to each other yesterday," he said, smiling. He pulled a denim jacket over his shirt and tie as he stretched his strides to catch up. "I just wanted to be sure you aren't going to take another stab at the Gradys alone."

She almost told him what she'd done last night, then didn't. Before she could decide how to question him about Ola and Sam, he asked, "Are you feeling all right? You look exhausted."

"Is that your doctor's diagnosis? Midwives are often beat, but I don't have another client's baby due until next week. Except for worrying about Amrine and Ola, I'm fine. But...losing two for two that way—" she shook her head "—is not good odds."

As if by mutual consent, they strolled toward the Lowe mansion. "You don't have any other single mothers under your care, do you?" he asked.

She sensed he was not joking or criticizing. "All married, pretty happily, I'd say, including Clary Doyal—you know, the mailman's wife—who's having her fourth. Also a cousin of mine by marriage and my sister, although she almost hemorrhaged to death when she lost her first baby, so I'm making sure she delivers at the hospital in Highboro. I'm not the mad midwife on a mission that you think I am.''

They turned down the narrow, grassy alley on the fringe of Delia's property. White and purple columbine nodded at them. "Then I think we still have a truce," he said.

"You'd better realize your boss of all bosses is furious with me for not toeing her line. After Delia let me and my sister live with her after my mother died, I committed the unpardonable sin of thinking for myself—wanting to fulfill my own dreams—and not agreeing to be your nurse.''

He stopped and spun to face her. "You're kidding. She asked you to be my nurse? When?"

"Years ago, before there was a you. Demanded it, in fact. Said I owed it to her and Shelter. Listen, Griff, I just came to ask if the Gradys so much as hinted who the father of Ola's baby might be when they were in your office.''

"They refused to give a name," he said with a shrug. "Some distant cousin. Ginger said it, and Ola nodded. I didn't know if that was common around here, and they were touchy enough, so I kept my opinion on marrying cousins—second or not—to myself for now.''

"*Second* cousin? Here we go again," she cried, smacking her hands on her thighs. "They aren't the sharpest bunch around, but they ought to at least get their stories straight. Ola told me more than once it was a third cousin. I just don't trust Sam for more reasons than maybe shooting out my tires.''

They stood close together now, whispering intently. "Lying about where she's gone and the father's identity,'' Griff said as if thinking aloud. ''I tell you, Ola is scared to death of Sam, and Ginger is, too. But that doesn't mean he fathered her child.''

It both relieved and annoyed her that he'd read her mind. ''But you'd considered it?'' she pursued.

''No, but I see you have, and you know them better. If I'd thought that, I'd have managed to ask him a few questions while I was setting his wrist yesterday—or else...''

He shook his head and muttered, ''Now they've sent the girl away, and we can't prove anything until she shows up.''

''Or until I find her. I have a sick feeling I'll get Ola's address out of the Gradys about as fast as I'll get Amrine's out of the Roscoes.''

''One other thing I've been thinking,'' Griff admitted, narrowing his eyes as if to assess her reaction. ''I don't suppose midwives see too many C-section scars.''

She frowned at him, uncertain what he was implying. ''Certainly not as many as doctors see,'' she said. ''Do you know how many C-sections in this country could be avoided and are just done for—''

''Spare me the lecture,'' he said, holding up his hands. ''That appendix scar of Ola's was strange. Appendectomy scars aren't usually that long, unless there's a crisis and the surgeon does an exploratory abdominal, then finds out it's the appendix. It could actually have been a C-section scar.''

''That's crazy. She's only fifteen now. And her uterus is tight and strong.''

''But if she's never gone through a normal labor and delivery, at her age it could be. I'm just saying maybe, considering the Gradys' truth ratio. But I'm glad we can discuss our differences and work together on things,'' he went on in a rush. "I'd also like to see you and Delia get along. As you said, she's done so much for you, not to mention for the town, for me. Why can't we all be on the same team?"

"Rah, rah, Delia. You're definitely her man," Emma said, looking past his shoulder to the house across the lawn. As if their speaking her name had summoned her, Delia appeared, holding open the drapes in a second-story window—supposedly Griff's private quarters.

If Delia owned Griff, Emma told herself, as she did so many others, she wanted nothing else to do with him. But she knew she was the liar now, because, despite everything, she was attracted to the man. Surely she could control that, fight it, then just walk away. And at the same time show Delia she could not control her.

"Thanks for the consultation, doctor," she told him. Leaning forward, she kissed his cheek, then hurried back toward the street, leaving him gawking after her.

Following Emma's gaze, Griff spun around just in time to see Delia drop the curtain. Fuming not as much at her as at Emma, he stepped over the knee-high side-yard iron fence and made straight for the house.

He went in the side entrance and took the old servants' stairs to the second floor. Delia had an office and bathroom at the back; the rest of the space was his private territory—if anything was sacred working for that woman.

Her office door stood ajar. Wearing a quilted skirt and vest over a pale blue blouse, she sat straight-backed in her upholstered desk chair, opening mail as if nothing had happened. He went in and leaned on her desk with both palms flat.

"Nothing else to stare at out windows?" he asked.

"I'm just wondering," she replied, not looking at him, "if you've decided to recruit an office nurse for yourself. If so, you're wasting your time with Emma Weston."

"Her calling is elsewhere."

Delia snorted. "So is her sense of duty and loyalty, so let the buyer beware." She squinted up at him. "I took in Emma and Sissy Weston when they had no one. I clothed them, fed them, schooled them, loved them. Emma wanted to be a nurse, so I said I'd pay for college. But after her first year, I found out she'd been wanting to be a midwife all along. When I suggested she plan to become the nurse for this dream of mine, she refused. She became more and more belligerent about playing baby catcher—and here in Shelter when I've set up this center and there are other places in these mountains that would welcome her with open arms.

"Griffin," she went on as she kept slitting envelopes open with her silver penknife, "I treated her like the beloved daughter I never had and she betrayed me."

"Look, Delia, I don't want to get caught in the middle, but are you angry with each other just because she wanted to be a midwife instead of a nurse here?"

"Just?" She jumped up, gesturing with the penknife as if she was unaware she held it. "She'd be neither nurse nor midwife if I hadn't taken her in. She'd be nothing but trailer trash, breeding babies she didn't want, not delivering them. Peddling ginseng, or quilts like Ginger Grady to make ends meet, or planting patches of pot and risking arrest from federal agents, even if Sheriff Merrell knows enough to ignore it."

"Wait a minute," he insisted, holding up both hands. "You actually believe there is no way a bright, determined woman like Emma could have saved herself on her own?''

Her shoulders slumped dramatically as she turned away to lean on the window frame and look out at the bright day. ''God knows I'm not criticizing her beginnings. I started out dirt-poor. If it hadn't been for my looks and being in the right place at the right time, there but for the grace of God go I.

''But,'' she plunged on, turning back to face him and pointing with the penknife, ''whose side are you on? Emma's out to convince women they don't need you or this health center you've promised to help me build, and here Shelter's got one of the highest birth rates in the nation and highest fatality rate for kids. You think people really want a sixth or seventh child to rear with the poverty level what it is?''

''I know, I know. It's why I think she's wrong to push her services, but maybe I can convince her that—''

''Malarkey! You know the mountain people don't want a doctor unless there's a crisis, and she's loose telling everyone that pregnancy is no crisis. Don't tell me she's bewitched you?''

''The kiss you mean?'' Griff laughed. ''No, she hasn't bewitched me. As a matter of fact, I'm aware she's using me.''

She sank onto her chair, then tilted her head so far back she looked down her nose at him. ''I just pray you're not happy to cooperate.''

''Hardly. But maybe if there's a certain level of trust, she'll realize she needs me, needs the center, so that—''

''I hear testosterone, not brain cells talking. Griffin, she comes from a long line of volatile, aggressive, dangerous people. If you want chapter and verse on the Westons of Cutshin Holler, I'll tell you.''

"You have my undivided attention."

Delia heaved a huge sigh. "Later. It's a long story. Now look what you've done," she said, flinging her arms out helplessly. "You've gotten me all so upset I almost forgot my good news. Any more of this and you'll have to put me on Prozac."

He waited, breathing hard. He hated that she held so much over his head, beyond what people around here knew.

"You mean a nurse, I hope," he prompted.

"Only for three days a week right now, driving in from Highboro, but she's highly recommended and experienced. If we treat her just right, perhaps we can convince her to move here. Her name is Pamela Stark and she loves people, especially children. She'll help us to attract more pediatric patients—maternity, too. And she's single, quite attractive, though very tall."

He got the message that he was to welcome her with open arms. "Pamela Stark, good," he said. "I can't wait to get her here."

The truth was, he couldn't wait to get his hands on Emma. She was not going to use him, not in her feud with Delia or her battle with the health center, nor as a man. But then, he admitted, the latter, at least, might not be so bad.

"Well, lookie here," Sheriff Reg Merrell practically sang out as Emma entered the Lowe County Sheriff's Office in Highboro that afternoon. He stood across the small office by the coffee machine, an area separated from the receptionist's and dispatcher's desks by a waist-high wooden railing and gate. Sleek, mounted deer heads—a doe and a twelve-point buck—gazed calmly down at the scene. As usual, it looked as if nothing was happening here.

"How-do, sheriff," she called to him. "May I talk to you for a minute?"

"Don't have much choice, being a public servant and all." He ambled over and swung the gate open for her. He was old enough to be her father and had been in office for decades, though hair dyed black and daily jogging kept him looking younger than he was. After a divorce that had surprised everyone, he'd recently remarried a much younger woman. Emma had heard he'd taken up tennis, no less, when his passion had always been hunting. If she didn't know better, she'd think he'd had a face-lift, but that was impossible.

"You heard from that hellfire brother of yours?" he asked as he escorted her into his small, private office surrounded by walls of opaque glass, with no ceiling.

"No. And I didn't come to talk about Jake or the past."

"But you'd let me be the first to know if he come callin'?" he said, indicating she should take the wooden chair while he perched on his desk. She hated him hovering, but at least he was going to hear her out.

Emma's stomach knotted even tighter. "I can take care of myself, sheriff, but I'm here because there are some who can't."

"Namely?" he said, swinging his booted foot. The boots were new with unscarred heels, and a gold Rolex shone from his wrist. It seemed Reg Merrell had decided to go upscale in his old age and new marriage.

"I know you never served that restraining order directly on Len Roscoe," she said, "but he's broken it to come and take Amrine Settle away, maybe by force."

"Maybe, huh? You don't know?"

"She left a note saying she was leaving with him and a new fifty-dollar bill that Len must have given her." Even as she said that, it occurred to her that Mike Bonner always carried new-looking bills, as if Trish had ironed them. Could Mike have given money to Amrine to buy food, or as a bribe to sell the farm? She shifted in her chair while the sheriff's blue eyes pierced her.

"Hell," he said with a sharp laugh. "The fifty don't sound like Len, but maybe all's well that ends well."

"I don't think she would have left with him unless under duress. There was blood on the floor—possibly spotting from an early-labor complication. And there is this bloody thumbprint on the note itself," she said, producing it for him.

When he rose, opened a desk drawer and pulled on a latex glove before taking the piece of paper from her, she realized she might have made another mistake. Not only could that print perhaps be traced, but there might also be latent ones on the paper, and she'd been carrying it around in her slicker pocket in the rain. Would Reg Merrell treat Amrine's disappearance like a crime, an abduction?

"What do you make of it?" she asked when he took his time reading and examining the note.

"Not necessarily her blood or thumbprint," he muttered, looking up at her at last. "Things're often not what they seem, and you're a rank amateur in this. I'm taking the note though, and I'll look into it. You just stop at the front desk and tell them to take your prints so's the lab technician can eliminate those."

"All right," she said, "but I was wondering if you would also try to trace Len through his Tennessee license plate, if he got a new one, or his old Kentucky one. I've already called hospitals between here and

Nashville where he supposedly went to find work, and I'm getting desperate enough to start calling Nashville factories to ask if they've hired him.''

"Desperate—that's Miss Emma Weston, all right," he said and stood, only to slump his gangly frame in the chair beside hers. He put the note in a plastic bag and peeled off the glove. When he gripped the wooden chair arms, she saw he wore an expensive-looking onyx-and-diamond pinkie ring.

"So I should do this just on your say-so, huh?'' he demanded. "On woman's or midwife's intuition, that it?''

Her hopes fell, but she went for her other ploy, sitting up straighter and twisting to face him. "The point is, since Len was back in Lowe County, his kin probably told him you tried to serve a restraining order, so he's out there somewhere thinking he's really put one over on you. I may be desperate to be sure Amrine's all right, but he's defiant—against you.''

"You know what I'm thinking, Emma?'' The sheriff leaned forward, not looking at her, elbows on his spread knees, staring at the scraped and scratched wooden floor between his boot tips.

"What?''

"That you got a lot a nerve coming in here with no direct proof a nothing, just like you had no proof talking to that reporter from the paper when your mama died. I once cared deeply for her—deeply, Emma.''

"I know you dated her years ago, before you left Shelter.''

"Sweethearting her, that's what we used to call it,'' he said. His voice softened, and he sighed. "But then she got pregnant with you and married that son of a bitch. Bet you won't challenge me for calling him that, will you, girl?''

Emma just shook her head. She shouldn't have come. Nothing good ever came from trying to deal with Reg Merrell. Too much water under the dam, Mama used to say, when Pa and Jake shot up the Eubankses and Reg Merrell took such joy in tracking and arresting them.

She stood and turned toward the door.

"Another reason," he said, "I can't take your always fighting me, hating me, is 'cause you look like her—spitting image. So it really riled me when you accused me of not rushing out there to help her when she got hurt."

Emma turned back to him. "I don't hate you, not anymore, and I'm sorry I told the reporter you were slow in getting there. I was crazy with fear and grief—and anger—that day. Maybe ever since." When she blinked, tears matted her lashes but didn't fall.

"Yeah, me, too," he said and wiped under his nose with his sleeve. "Go on then. I got no cause to do it, but I'll check around 'bout that Roscoe bastard's license plate and a few other things—on one condition."

She nodded.

"That you quit trying to play detective or sheriff or whatever you been doing."

"Just playing best friend to Amrine."

He snorted and gestured she should get out. Biting her lower lip, she started away.

"And keep an eye peeled for Jake," his rough voice pursued her, "'cause someone can't just vanish like that!"

6

"Did you find out where Amrine went?" Mike Bonner called from his truck, then swung off the road into Emma's driveway.

She waved, put down her hoe and leaned her elbows in the passenger's-side window. "No luck so far," she told him.

"People in town are saying she ran off with Len Roscoe," Mike said, extending a Tootsie Roll to her.

She took it and asked, "But you *did* say she didn't want to sell."

"I didn't say that, but no, she didn't. No more than I can get you to part with Cutshin when it's just sitting empty and is—as they say around here—a heartache to you. If you hadn't bought out Sissy's share, I bet she'd sell. But since we're friends, I'm promising you right now, I won't mention this again. You don't want the place touched, so be it."

"If there ever is a time, I'll come to you first. You know, I found one of these," she said, twisting open the piece of candy, "in Amrine's bedroom."

He frowned at her. "Which means what? I was there, more than once, but not in the bedroom. All I did was tell her that view behind the outhouse could bring a fortune for her to start a new life if she'd just let me knock it down—the outhouse—and show the place."

"I wasn't implying anything. I know you distribute

candy all over. But since you do hear what's happening most places, let me know if you ever hear a hint of where she or Len have gone, will you?"

"Of course," he said. "And if you want me to make inquiries, I will. Please, Emma, let Trish and me help any way we can."

"You've already been so kind, helping with my furnishings. I really appreciate Trish's decorating help and all."

"Then remember I'm your friend, too, not just Trish," he added as he waved and drove off.

Emma hadn't hoed one more row for the green-onion starts and lettuce seed when another car pulled in.

Griff. In the health clinic van. He stopped and got out.

"That's a big garden for such a small hoe," he said as she leaned on it while he came closer. "You ought to just rent a tiller or a tractor."

"We country people don't take much farming advice from city folk," she told him. Yet she flinched inwardly at his mere mention of a tractor. Surely he didn't know about her mother's death.

"Right. I guess that would be like you giving me advice about surgery or something like that."

She narrowed her eyes at him. The tension between them was always there, waiting to snap.

"I'm not going to plant much of this garden, anyway," she admitted, glancing at the big rectangle for a truck garden, "because I'll get too busy and it will go to seed and weed."

"I see you've got your beeper on, so you're probably waiting for a call."

She nodded, relieved to be able to talk midwifing again. "Clary Doyal, just up the road. It should be soon, but she's grossly overweight, and I can't be sure about her due date or the baby's presentation by palpating her.''

''Then she should have had an ultrasound. Does she have high blood pressure?''

''No, and this will be her fourth child, so she's pretty predictable—and a real hater of hospitals, by the way, since her first baby died there. Absolutely won't go.''

''Ah, a midwife's dream patient—client.''

She couldn't keep back a smile.

''I hope you don't bill Clary or me for this time,'' she teased.

''No, but I'm thinking,'' he said, coming closer, though his white running shoes sank in the reddish loam, ''of billing you for that kiss yesterday. Of course, I guess I could charge our avid audience, too. That was the whole point of it, right—upsetting or defying Delia?''

She went back to hoeing with a vengeance. ''I couldn't care less what your mistress—master, I mean—thinks.''

''Right. And I couldn't care less that you kissed me just to spite someone else—but I do.''

His hand closed around hers on the hoe, staying it. Her heart was thudding. Why did she always look and feel so grubby next to him? She pulled away and dug into the earth with the blade again, deeper, harder.

''One thing I never took you for,'' he said, ''is a coward.''

She stopped and turned to face him, one hand on her hip.

''This is crazy,'' she said. ''Why don't I just get you the rake, and we can fence with each other.''

He grinned. ''Let's not. Let's tell the truth and, as I

said when you came storming into the clinic, trust each other a little bit. And enjoy our differences, all of them,'' he added as his gaze skimmed her body with such intensity that she felt he'd caressed her.

As she stared mesmerized into the blue sky of his eyes, she lost her train of thought. He was so close she could see herself reflected in each liquid black pupil. Desperate to stop even the thought of his kiss or caress, she ached for both. She felt leaden-footed and light-headed.

They tilted together slowly. Their breath intermingled, their lips hovered, slightly open. She could smell the scent of his soap or aftershave, tart pine.

The kiss, soft then sweeping, escalated with his hands hard on her back and hers on his firmly muscled shoulder blades. Time slowed as she felt every inch of his skin she touched. Her chin skimmed the rasp of his stubbled jaw. His lips were both hard and soft. The tips of their noses touched, bumped. She clung to him at this new assault on her senses that so overwhelmed her sanity.

Her breasts tingled, pressed flat to his chest. Their hips and thighs pressed warmly together, skin and muscle through denim, as if to prop them up.

Sometime later, someone roared past the house and laid on the horn. Reluctantly, almost tipsy, they stood apart. Flushed, glowing, she tried to build up her defenses again when all she really wanted to do was invite him in, feed him, hold him, please him. Damn, this man was dangerous. She had to—somehow—fight this, fight back.

''You said I had an ulterior motive for the kiss yesterday,'' she said. Her voice sounded almost as husky as Sissy's at her most sexy. When he let her go, she locked her knees to stand. "So were you thinking turn-about's fair play?"

His dazed expression crumpled to a frown. "What's that supposed to mean? That Delia sent me to seduce you to my evil, technical, medical ways or what?"

Though it was her fault, she regretted she had broken their bond and shared mood. "The thing is," she said lamely, "our philosophies hardly mesh, so—"

He hooted a hard laugh. "This isn't philosophical, Emma, it's physical, at least right now. Aren't you the one who likes to preach that women should get more in touch with their own bodies? I'd like to help with that."

"Back to your normal, mocking self," she accused, traipsing out of the garden. "This has, at least, been very enlightening."

He followed her and seized her arm to spin her back to face him. He looked furious. "I don't know what the hell you're talking about. You like to kiss and run, is that it? Enlighten me."

"Tell Delia she should give you a bonus, or was handling me in the job description from the first? Not only are you to control these independent mountain people, but me, too."

"You know, I'd like that," he said, crossing his arms, maybe to keep from grabbing her. "But Delia wants me to steer clear of you, and I'm finally starting to see why."

At least when she slammed the door, she put another barrier between them.

When someone banged at Emma's side door as she got out of the shower later, she groaned. If that was Griff Cusak back again—

"Oh," she said as she peeked out her bedroom window and recognized the shiny, new truck that matched Mike's except this one was fire-engine red. She pulled the sash up higher and shouted through the screen, "Trish, I'll be right down!"

"Yo!" her friend called jauntily, walking backward into the driveway to look up. She cupped her hands over her eyes to see in the sun. "I've got something to show you. Midwife Weston, come on down, if you're not busy with any mothers-to-be right now."

"No, good timing. I've got a few minutes before I have to head out to see Clary Doyal."

She pulled on clothes and hurried downstairs. When they were first becoming friends, Trish had bemoaned going through an early menopause, so she'd never be a client. But both she and Mike had been supportive of Emma and her profession. Trish seemed fascinated by it.

"Oh, you brought the wicker!" Emma cried as she opened the door and saw an armchair, low table and three-tiered plant stand arranged on her side porch, just where she intended to put them. Trish grinned like a kid, which she resembled with her close-cropped red hair and elfin, freckled face. How she'd hooked a man as handsome as Mike Bonner, Trish had joked more than once, she'd never know. But Emma knew. She was charming and fun and as good-hearted as the best of mountain folk.

"The other chair's not done," Trish explained, bouncing on her heels. She wore faded, patched jeans and a huge T-shirt that said Bonners' Country Peddler, which was what they called the part of their business that dealt with antiques reborn from junk. "And," she went on, her hazel eyes sparkling, "we haven't even started that wooden swing. So, hey, I'm parched. Got any more of that great herbal tea?''

They chatted over several cups of tea, while Trish quizzed her on how everything was going with building up her clientele. Emma updated her on the search for Amrine but didn't mention Ola. The conversation reminded Emma of how sad it was that Trish hadn't had a child of her own, but she seemed to have accepted it, and the Bonners had evidently been too career-oriented to adopt.

"If I were twenty years younger, I'd become that midwife partner you're going to need someday, kiddo,'' Trish told her as they walked out on the porch to admire the wicker again.

"It's never too late to change careers. I think you and Mike have proved that already. You're following your dream together. You know, I'm really going to be crushed if you finish Big Blue Farm and move on. Your home base in Highboro's beautiful, but—''

"No way, José, we're selling Big Blue, however many other places we fix up,'' Trish said. "I've put too much work in there, and the big barn out back is perfect for the refinishing workshop. You know, I love how untouched it still is here.'' She gazed out at Emma's garden and the sweep of hill to the woodlot beyond.

"So,'' she went on, evidently pulling herself out of some silent reverie, "what's the latest episode in the handsome new doctor soap opera? Let's call it something, like maybe *General Health Clinic* or *As the Girl Burns*.''

Emma shook her head at Trish's howls, then caught the contagion of her humor. At least she could laugh over it. Then the mood changed again as her friend refused to take even a down payment for the wicker when Emma knew the Bonners could have gotten ten times the price they'd first quoted her.

"Nope," Trish insisted. "It's our contribution to a good cause—the baby business." She gave Emma a quick, one-armed hug, which buoyed her mood even more. Emma walked her out to her truck and waited to say goodbye as Trish got in.

"Oh, I meant to show you," her friend said, leaning down to fish around in a big plastic garbage sack she had on the driver's-side floor.

"Look at this quilt I got from Ginger Grady—one to fit that little hearth crib Mike found last week in the Poteets' attic."

Perhaps, Emma thought, as she stroked and admired the intricate pattern, that's where the Gradys were getting their money for new appliances. Perhaps Trish was buying sacks of quilts.

"It's beautiful," Emma told her. "With quilting, at least, Ginger's the sharpest woman in town."

It was nearly eleven that night when Emma returned home from visiting Clary for a fourth time that day and saw she'd forgotten to leave a light on. Clary had not yet gone into labor, but she had started to dilate, and Emma was going to lie down for an hour, then go back with everything she'd need to wait out the delivery.

She'd felt uneasy all day and not only because of Griff. She was not one of the mountain folk who had the sixth sense, but she felt something was due to go wrong. At least Clary lived just four miles away and she'd already delivered at home twice with her aunt, a midwife from Tennessee. Her first birth experience in a hospital had been disastrous, and she'd vowed never to so much as look at one through binoculars again. At least Clary, unlike most women in the area, had her husband's full support as a birthing coach. They'd been great to Emma from the moment she came home, so doing a good job on this meant everything to her.

She turned the Jeep around and backed it up to the side porch so she'd be ready to head right back out. A neighbor lady was going to take the Doyals' kids, Vinie, age five, and little Jess, still a toddler. Everything was in place, so why was she so nervous?

"'*Cause she's gained too much wei-eight,*" Emma sang her own slow words to one of Sissy's mournful mountain tunes. "*And I just ca-an't tell, if that babe's gonna come out strai-aight.*"

She admired the ghostly wicker in the dark and thought about sitting out here until she settled down, but she decided she'd better use the entire hour to rest. It could be a long night and beyond. She unlocked the back door and went in. Wearily closing and locking it behind her, she headed for the stairs without turning on lights.

But she sensed something different, out of place. She stopped in the black hall, gazing into the silent waiting room. She gasped.

A silhouette of someone sitting in the rocking chair in front of the window loomed larger than it must be. Wan moonlight made the shape sexless, formless. The rocking chair creaked once.

"I heard you tell someone at church," Delia's voice sliced through the silence, "that you had an open-door policy here."

"I had the doors locked, Delia. And I'm busy with an impending birth. Or were you prepared to wait hours?"

"You know," she said pleasantly, rocking now,

"you put your extra key in the same spot I used to, under the flowerpot on the porch. Sometimes I still cannot believe I helped to rear you and you turned against me so."

"We both made mistakes," Emma said, walking slowly over to turn on a light. Both of them blinked like owls. "One of them was that we've kept this personal. We disagree about bringing health care to birthing women, that's all." Emma shut her mouth when she realized she sounded like Griff. Damn the man, he'd been working on her head as well as the rest of her.

"I didn't come here," Delia said as she rose from the rocker, "to convince or be convinced—simply to make you a final offer."

"Meaning you want to buy me out and exile me to some other place again?"

"Don't corrupt everything I say, child. Modern training or not, you believe in midwifery all mixed with the old granny-woman herbs and healing—"

"I've gone a bit beyond putting an ax under the bed to cut the pain, Delia."

"Pain, yes. But my point is that the Lowe Health Center and the large staff I'm assembling there is to be my dead husband's legacy to this town, so you must go elsewhere to help those who think they need or want you. I'll make it worth your while."

"That's always been your creed—money talks," Emma said. "And don't tell me the health center or anything in this town is Piercy Lowe's legacy. It's yours—your kingdom. And if Griff Cusak and Wanda Keck are your idea of a large staff—"

"See how much you know. I've got a trained nurse coming in, who was in the pediatric ward at Highboro Hope. I should think you'd like to have an 'open-door women's health center' someplace that needs one, with an assistant, perhaps, instead of going it alone in this drafty farmhouse, scurrying out on these dangerous roads in storms and late at night. I still say you're dead wrong in pursuing this here.''

It was the closest the woman had ever come to a threat.

"Even though I have an open-door policy here in my home and health center," Emma said evenly, "it's only for those who wish me and my clients well, and you don't. I have a long night ahead and would appreciate it if you'd leave."

"I should have thrown you out and just kept Sissy. I pray to God when you realize you cannot come up to my doctor's standards that you won't take some poor patient down with you, even though that might be the end of you around here once and for all."

Emma didn't trust herself to speak. She gritted her jaw so she wouldn't push Delia through the window. She yanked open the front door, then shoved the screen open for her.

"And stay away from Griffin Cusak," Delia said as she swept past. "He mentioned a few hours ago he never wanted to have to deal with you again, so no more back-alley kisses."

Emma longed to slam a door for the second time today, but she didn't want Delia to know how much she'd upset her. She closed it quietly, turned out the light, then watched as Delia walked down the road to where she'd evidently left her car—or her broomstick— somewhere in the black, blowing night.

Emma's alarm clock on the nightstand was silent, but she almost felt it ticked in beat with her heart. She found herself flopping over in bed to look at it every five minutes. It wasn't only Delia's visit that had upset her, but everything else lately.

As it had the other night, the house groaned and creaked in the wind. She might as well get up and go to Clary's, she told herself, and rolled out of bed. She washed up, added shoes and a sweatshirt to the clothes she still wore, turned out the upstairs lights and went downstairs.

She had kept both porch lights on after Delia left. They threw the shadows of the thrashing trees across the black lawn. The claws of one limb kept scratching as if something outside wanted in.

She felt for the light switch in the hall, then the one in the kitchen and clicked them on. One cup of coffee, then she'd get the Jeep and go—

With the coffee can in her hand, she glanced out at her wicker furniture on the lighted porch. When she dropped the coffee can, grounds cascaded over her feet. She stepped through the grit to press her face close to the glass in the door.

She screamed. The wicker had been rearranged. The chair was pushed away, and the table had been dragged close to the door, almost blocking it. On it was set a horrible tableau.

In a crude cradle made from tree limbs lay a small dead raccoon on its back—a baby. A cross was stuck in the headboard of the crib to make sure she knew the cradle was a coffin. With a white cap stuck on its head and a fetoscope tied to its paw, was a dead skunk, leaning over the corpse, propped up with sticks stuck through the wicker tabletop.

Emma crumbled into the corner behind the door, covered her face with her hands and heaved wracking but silent sobs. She got the message. But from whom?

7

Emma wasn't sure how long she stayed hunched in the corner. When her cell phone rang, she got up to dig it out of her purse on the kitchen table. She punched the talk button but held the device stiffly away for a moment. Was that horror on the porch going to be followed by other threats?

But it was Carter Doyal on the phone, saying they were ready for her.

"I'll be right there," she promised. "Tell Clary everything is—it's going to be fine. Tell her to keep calm."

She was tempted to just run out the front door—not to look at the grotesque display again—but she realized that must be her fetoscope out there. She scrabbled through her equipment and found it missing. Whoever had done that outside had also been inside. If Delia could find her key under the crock, who else had? Or had Delia done this?

She took her gear and went out the front to avoid disturbing the evidence on the porch. Shouldering her bag and holding a butcher knife, she locked the front door behind her, rechecked it, then darted around to the side porch.

The smell of dead skunk nearly knocked her down. She knew she should at least photograph the scene, but she had to get going. Holding her breath, she looked around, tiptoed up onto the porch and grabbed the fetoscope. The skunk rocked on its sticks as she pulled the instrument from where it was tied with twine to the dead animal's paw. She saw the corpse was partly impaled and a big bullet wound bloodied its striped back.

Shuddering, she pocketed the fetoscope, to keep it separate from her sterilized instruments. She'd boil it at Clary's, even though it might contain fingerprints. She slid the pansy crock away to see her key was still there. It glinted up at her, and she grabbed it. She made sure her side door was locked and ran for the Jeep.

Heading for Clary's, she could not shake memories of the stench or the sight. Its message, however, was not so clear-cut now. Did that bizarre display accuse her of losing Sissy's baby so long ago? Or, since the standing figure was in a nurse's cap, did it threaten future catastrophe for one of her clients, as Delia had prophesied? And who, she asked herself, was the messenger?

"It just don't feel right this time," Clary told Emma and gripped her hand a few minutes later. Emma had managed to get control of herself, but she wasn't sure Clary could do the same. "That's it, can't say no more."

"Now don't you go getting in a funky mood on me, Clary Doyal. Come on now, tell me what you're feeling."

They were both twenty-seven, Emma thought, yet this was Clary's fourth child. Though they led such different lives, Emma empathized with her, feeling or sensing something, but not being able to explain what exactly. The two of them were momentarily alone in the Doyals' second-floor bedroom because Clary had just kissed her kids goodbye. Carter was going to take them out to the neighbor's waiting truck.

"Well," Clary said slowly, "it kinda feels like it's a' settin' sideways in me."

Dear God Emma prayed. *Don't let* that *happen.* Clary was describing a transverse lie, which could lead to a breech presentation and dangerous birth. Not only would the mother suffer, the baby could get stuck in the birth canal and suffocate or strangle on its own umbilical cord. Though the odds were against that in light of Clary's three previous successful deliveries, Emma knew to listen to a woman's feelings and fears. She bit her lower lip to force from her mind the picture of that dead baby animal in its crude coffin.

Emma's earlier worries came home to roost: she had not been able to read the presentation by palpating Clary's abdomen, when she prided herself on being good at that. Usually she could feel where the baby's head and bottom were positioned, but Clary's weight and an excess of amniotic fluid had made that impossible.

"Tell you what," she said, gripping the woman's shoulder. "Since you're not in labor yet, let me try to feel the child again. Have you got any last-minute feelings about it being a boy or a girl?" she asked to distract her as she lifted Clary's cotton gown and felt her belly again.

"A boy, I think. Want to bet?"

"I'll bet you a new layette outfit against one of your berry pies," Emma said, hoping the chatter would relax the woman enough that she could feel that little body so dwarfed by this big one.

As Emma began, Clary moaned and shifted her bulk, then stopped moving, straining intently to listen as her kids fussed and wailed down the hall. Suddenly, five-year-old Vinie's cries made Emma jump and Clary tense under her touch.

"I wanta go to Disney World!" the little girl shrieked. "I wanta to go there, Daddy. Can't we go, 'stead of have another baby?"

"She seen those ads on TV," Clary said, taking sporadic breaths as if she'd run miles. "You know, the ones that got those pro athletes—sayin' that's where they're going now that they won and all. No way we could afford Disney."

Emma tried to palpate again as they heard the footsteps recede downstairs, the front door bang, and the kids' cries fade. Her frustration grew, but she didn't let Clary know.

"She started labor?" Carter asked as he came back in. He had brought her sterilized fetoscope back up to her in a plastic baggie, just as she'd asked. Emma wished she had another one to use but they were expensive and she needed it to monitor the baby's heart.

She explained everything to Carter, omitting the potential dangers of a breech, since she didn't want Clary getting more stressed than she already was. Little Vinie's screaming had made the woman's womb go tight as a drum. Emma was still fighting to calm herself, and she feared Clary might sense her nerves, too.

Emma silently bemoaned that this wasn't working. Maybe it was time to risk turning the baby, referred to as version, but she refused to try that without someone to monitor the fetal heartbeats. And the only one with expertise in close enough proximity for that was Griff Cusak.

No way, she told herself. For several reasons, that would never work. His letting her deliver a breech here?

His assisting her? Working with her at all? Not when Delia had said Griff never wanted to have to deal with her again.

"Clary," Emma said, pulling her client's gown back down and bending over to put both hands on her shoulders, getting right in her face. "I want you to stay real relaxed while you and Carter and I discuss something important. Partly because of your own feelings that this might be a breech birth—and because I think you might be right—we need to consider a transport."

"To the hospital?" Clary cried, bucking almost upright. "No, no! My first little son died there with a cord—a cord—"

"Prolapse," Carter put in, sitting on her other side to seize her hand. "But with Emma there, that sure won't happen again."

"I thought you two was on my side!" Clary shrieked. "Cart, you promised. I trusted you, Emma. I can still fire you, and Cart and me can do it ourselves."

"It's because you trust me that I'm giving you this advice," Emma said, her face still close to Clary's, her voice strong but low. "Now, I'm hoping you will remain very calm, and I'll call—"

She began to pant. "No. You do anything you—have to here. But I'm not leaving—not unless it's feetfirst, so—"

"You stop that crazy talk, woman," Carter said. "All right, we're stayin' here. That right, Emma?" he demanded, his shock of corn-blond hair sticking up from raking his hand through it.

Fearing this would escalate to a nightmare where no one could work together or trust each other—or relax enough to birth a child, Emma nodded. Clary smiled grimly in a victory Emma could only pray would not kill her and the child. And that could surely happen if she tried this alone.

"This is Dr. Cusak."

His voice sounded raspy. He was in bed. He'd been asleep.

"Griff, Emma Weston. I'm sorry it's so late, but I have an emergency, and I'm asking you for your help."

"You?" He sounded as if he'd jerked awake. "Someone shoot at you again?"

"Help for a client, Clary Doyal."

"Oh, yeah, obese but not hypertensive. You're there now?"

"Yes. I recommended transport to Hope, but she will not go and her husband backs her up."

"The situation?"

"I'm afraid of a breech, because I think the baby's **lying** transverse, but I can't tell.

"Great, Emma. Just great," he said, his tone sarcastic. "Will she come in here to me?"

"She says she's leaving only feetfirst if she's not delivered here. I'm going to try version, but—"

"But you need me to bring out my electronic fetal monitor."

"No, my fetoscope would work, if you could help me. Griff, she has a large gynecoid pelvis, and the baby isn't large, I'm sure of that, at least. She's my client, so if you'd agree to consult and assist…"

There was a second of silence where she could hear his breathing.

"As damn dangerous as this is, all right. I know the house. I'll be there in fifteen minutes."

Her knees shook, even as she leaned into the corner

of the Doyals' kitchen. Griff was coming. He was coming to help.

"Version is a tricky maneuver," Griff told Emma in a hushed tone as they stood in the doorway of the bedroom while Carter went to bring a pile of pillows. "I've never done it because modern medical science works around such a problem."

"I've done it before," she whispered. "I've even known mothers who managed to massage their babies into vertex positions. One woman visualized it, and it happened."

He rolled his eyes but didn't say what he was thinking. He had thrown on jeans and a cutoff sweatshirt, so he hardly looked like the immaculately turned-out Dr. J. Griffin Cusak right now. Dark circles shadowed his eyes like bruises. Stubble darkened his cheeks to make him look mean and hungry. But his voice was calm, and he had spoken softly to both Clary and Carter when he'd come in and put down his medical bag, which Emma had been amazed to see. Why did he have that bag if his policy was not to make house calls? She steeled herself to be strong for when he'd inevitably try to take over.

The three of them positioned Clary on her back in the middle of a blanket on the piecework rug, with three plump pillows under her to elevate her hips.

"I already had her drink a little wine to relax her," Emma informed Griff.

The unbelieving shake of his head was barely perceptible. She ignored it and knelt next to Clary.

"Now remember what you learned about staying relaxed, Clary," Emma instructed. "If you're stressed, your body will release hormones that will inhibit cer-

vical dilation. If you just work with your body and don't
fight it, you'll secrete your own pain relief."

"Endorphins," Clary murmured, and Griff looked
surprised enough to drop the fetoscope he was frowning
over as if she'd asked him to bleed the patient or do a
witch-doctor dance. Should she tell him later where
she'd found that fetoscope tonight? Then it hit her: how
many people would even know what that instrument
was? Or had someone mistaken it for the more common
stethoscope?

Again, she shut out her own problems and tried to
feel the baby's position, this time while Griff listened
to its heart rate, staring at his watch and reading off like
a machine to her, "One hundred twenty—that's great,
go ahead."

"One hundred and twenty," Carter echoed.

It bothered Emma that Carter repeated every number
Griff reported, but she didn't stop him. She'd had him
scrub and put on latex gloves like she and Griff wore.
Carter had a brilliant mind for numbers—memorizing
them, not using them. The *Highboro Herald* had recently done a feature story on the Shelter mailman who
never forgot an address. Despite this selective photographic memory, he could easily forget what he'd had
for breakfast or where he'd put his car keys.

Emma's technique was to massage the baby into
place, keeping its head flexed and rotating it in the direction it was facing. She tried, then tried again.

"I think it's resisting," she said, trying to keep positive despite her disappointment. She let the fetus drift
back, then tried to shift it again. Damn, but there was
plenty of room in there. Why didn't it turn?

"Down to 110, 100, 90," Griff said as Carter echoed
each number.

"I hear you," Emma told him, not wanting to give up but realizing she should. She felt crushed her efforts hadn't worked, but relieved she and Griff had at last agreed on something.

The two of them huddled briefly in the hall when Griff was heading for the bathroom and Emma was returning.

"If anything goes really wrong," he told her, standing at close range, "I'll back you up they refused transport."

"You just tried to talk them into it, didn't you?" she whispered. "You didn't believe me she wouldn't go."

"I think we'd better argue later."

"Just remember, she's my client, Griff, my responsibility."

"That's right, because if she were mine, I'd knock her out with anesthesia and transport for a fast, safe C-section. I'm just hoping her bulk means we're wrong about a transverse lie."

"I'm pretty sure I felt the head, not the bottom, on top."

"Well, 'pretty sure's' medically sound enough for me," he said.

She glared at him and went back in to Clary.

Their hope for a normal, vertex presentation soared again when Clary's complete dilation and labor went faster than it would with a breech. The baby suddenly seemed to lunge for the birth canal. Emma noted Griff nodding silently when she urged Clary to stay upright and coached her not to push, even though she wanted to. She also saw that the grunts and howls Clary made at times startled Griff. She knew he'd like to manage that, too, but Emma always felt a woman, at least in normal labor, should do whatever felt right to her.

"You're a big help," Emma encouraged the nervous father. "Now you just sit right behind Clary and keep her upright in this pushing stage. Later, you can help support her legs."

Again Griff looked uneasy, even annoyed, but she'd deal with him later. This approach was far better than strapping a woman into cold metal stirrups.

She had him check the baby's heart rate again. Its location told them they were definitely going to get a breech, but which kind? Some were worse than others.

"Come on now, Clary," Emma urged. "You just pant—blow—that's it, blow out your belly on in-breaths. Carter, you go ahead and do it with her, like this." The three of them panted together for a while as Griff watched, frowning.

When Clary's pains intensified, Emma tried to ignore Griff except to give him calm orders. At least her doubts about him being able to work the fetoscope had been wrong. Though he was probably thinking they were back in the Dark Ages, without electronic fetal monitoring, he handled the instrument skillfully. But she knew, if he were in charge, by now he'd have Carter standing way back and Clary shaved and cut open for an episiotomy or C-section. Instead, she was giving Clary ice chips and sips of labor-aide under his steady stare. She was wondering if he was waiting to take over, when they saw what the breech presentation would be.

"Oh, oh, it's coming now, Emma," Clary shrieked as if neither man was in the room. When Carter held her legs for her, she asked, "Can't I get on my knees like last time?"

Griff looked startled again, and Emma realized he'd

probably have a fit if a woman wanted to deliver in any position but prone in the birthing straps and stirrups.

"No kneeling if this is a breech," Emma said. "You just push now. You're doing great and—"

Emma gasped, then bit her lip as one of the baby's feet popped out, dangling from the knee down, even kicking.

"Footling breech," Griff said, then moved his mouth to form the silent words of either *damn* or *damn rare.* He bent over Clary to press the fetoscope to her bulging flesh again.

Emma's and Griff's eyes met swiftly as if to say, *This has to be fast now. Get it out. It can't get stuck. Not much time.*

Under Griff's steady gaze and occasional calm calling out of the baby's heart rate, Emma went to work.

"We're going to do a breech extraction, Clary," she explained, "so you just hang in there. Push for us, but just when you feel a contraction. When you do, push hard."

She knew not to pull on the visible leg or try to free the other until the baby was born to the navel. First Emma, then Griff, kept manual pressure on Clary's belly in the direction of the baby's descent to hurry it and keep the head flexed. Their fear was that the head, coming this direction instead of crowning first, would snag.

One leg flopped out to join the other, and Emma supported them so they wouldn't tear Clary.

"All right, you're doing great, just great," Emma assured her. "We've got half a baby here, right to his little belly button." Ordinarily, Emma would not have revealed the baby's sex and let the parents have the thrill of discovering it themselves. But nothing was ordinary about this birth, and these parents needed encouragement.

"You were right about a boy, Clary," she continued. "You won your bet. Now I'm going to pull down a loop of cord here to create some slack for the rest of him."

She nodded her relief to Griff as they both reached for the umbilical cord to feel the pulse—strong. A good sign. Their fingers touched; Emma felt doubly jolted by the thrill of this birth with Griff here. Energy coursed between them, a passion she was sure they both felt.

She wrapped the baby's lower torso in a towel to keep it warm and grasped the hipbones carefully, curling the butt on her hands and her fingers over the slippery pelvis and thighs. Holding her breath, she gently rotated the body to get the shoulders vertical.

She blinked back tears as she worked, because they had only about five minutes to free an airway to the baby's mouth. She knew Griff was listening now for the telltale gurgle that could be a deadly sign—that the baby was trying to breathe while still inside the birth canal.

The first shoulder popped out, and she and Griff gave a little cheer.

"Home stretch now, babe," Carter told the exhausted Clary as the first hint of dawn streaked between the curtains by the bed. "Got us another boy and gonna name him Weston Griffin Doyal, that's what we're gonna do!"

But there was no celebrating yet. Though the other shoulder birthed as easily, both arms were still inside. Emma brought them down by slipping her index and middle fingers up the baby's back, going over the shoulders and down past the elbow to the forearms. She caught the arms and swept them down across the baby's chest to free them.

As if Griff knew every muscle of hers was screaming, he rubbed Emma's lower back, then returned to putting pressure on Clary's abdomen while Emma rolled the slick little body in her hands so he was facedown.

"Clary, I'm going to reach a finger up inside to make an airway," she said. But she could not manage it. The cord would still have to provide the oxygen supply. With one hand on Clary's belly and one on the cord to check the pulse, Griff's face was stamped with concern.

Emma had done two breeches before, but only in training, assisting her mentor. Still, she told herself, she had a good touch, the sense of feel. She silently talked to herself as if she were a separate person in this crisis, trying to be aware of her client and her surroundings— even Carter and Griff—but concentrating fiercely on what she must do.

Let his weight help clear the perineum, pull down and out. Don't jerk or twist. Gently, pull gently.

And then the descent of the warm, wet body simply stopped. The head had snagged. Griff realized it, too, shifting from one foot to the other, not speaking.

Emma tried again, flexing the head, which was born only to the back hairline, indicating the baby's chin rested on his chest. The face was now resting in the hollow of Clary's tailbone but still inside her body.

"Rate of ninety, going lower," Griff whispered, feeling the cord, since the fetoscope was useless now.

"Ninety...ninety," Carter whispered, making Emma want to scream at both of them to shut up.

The stuck upper forehead must be pressing on the cord, yet the airway was not clear for the baby to breathe. She knew ninety was an infrequent heartbeat, a sign of worsening distress.

"About eighty and dropping," Griff said.

"No!" Clary screamed and, for once, Emma wished she didn't educate her clients so completely. Suddenly fighting her husband's restraints, Clary tried to shift her bulk. The baby shuddered in Emma's hands. "Emma!" Clary howled.

"Hold her still, Carter," Emma ordered, raising her voice for the first time. "I've got to get his head out."

She lifted the body to try to ease the chin and forehead. Griff let go of the cord to put both palms on the pubic bone to help press the little head down and out.

Emma was trembling. Sweat stung her eyes, blinding her. She ached all over, her muscles burning, her heart thudding. She leaned against Griff's solid shoulder for support as she twisted the tiny body, lifted, pulled.

"Come on, baby," Griff whispered, his voice rough. "Come on."

Somewhere through her panic, Emma wondered if he was talking to the infant or her. Again she saw that terrible tableau on her back porch—and recalled Sissy's lost baby. Things couldn't get worse, but they did.

The sucking sound of the child trying to breathe sounded like a scream in her soul. The cord was collapsed; he was trying to make it on his own where there was no air. The little body was going blue in her hands.

"Push, Clary," her voice sounded strong and sure. "Push now!"

Suddenly the nape of the tiny neck pivoted and freed itself, and Weston Griffin Doyal was born into her hands.

Emma suctioned and stimulated the baby, and he thrilled them all by wailing and turning from blue to white to a healthy pink. She cleaned little Weston and laid him, naked but covered, on Clary's belly while Carter cooed over him. After the placenta came, Emma and Griff stepped into the hall to give the Doyals a moment of privacy.

"I was so scared," she whispered, hugging herself.

"And I was so impressed." He rested his hands—which were shaking, too—on her shoulders. "Clary's perineum didn't tear, no episiotomy," he recited. "And no anesthesia. I've never seen such rotation and handling skills."

"That's the second-sweetest thing you ever said to me," she murmured. Still smelling of Betadine, she wrapped her hands around the inside of his forearms and they propped each other up without touching otherwise. She was shocked to see his watch said 9:00 a.m.

"I'm sorry," she said slowly, "that I slammed the door on you yesterday. I've been really uptight about Amrine and Ola—and Delia—but that's no excuse, and it's my problem." She decided then she would not tell him about the dead animals on her porch, though she wanted to. She'd clean it up herself, bury the evidence of someone's hatred and just go on. "Or else," she added, "I'm not very good at relationships—our kind, I mean."

He leaned forward and his lips moved in her damp hair. "What is our kind?"

"Remains to be seen," she admitted and yawned. "The only thing I'm sure of now is that I'm exhausted and sweaty and hurting, and Delia's going to have your head. She came calling last night, offered to buy me out and said to stay away from you."

"I wouldn't have missed this exhilarating, seat-of-the-pants experience for anything."

Her heart fell; he'd said she was skilled, but he still thought she was crazy to be in the situation in the first place. The chasm between them loomed again.

She was so tired she just shook her head. When she moved, his stubble was like sandpaper on her forehead but she did not step away. This quiet intimacy of shared success—of helping to start a new life—was a big bonus on top of that beautiful baby. Whoever had meant to curse her, it had not worked.

"Anyway," she said, stifling another yawn, "for your missed sleep and consorting with a baby catcher, I owe you now."

"You do," he murmured. "Big-time."

Though she was utterly exhausted, she steeled herself as she pulled the Jeep into the driveway to bury the dead animals that were on her side porch. Again, approaching the porch, she stopped and stared.

The animal corpses were gone. The furniture was back in place as if she'd hallucinated the scene.

But her nostrils still flared with the faint whiff of death. And when she got close to the table, she found remnants of bark where someone had stuffed sticks into the table to hold up the skunk-nurse hovering over the dead baby in its cradle.

She saw two tiny flecks of dried blood on the white wicker tabletop. She thought of Amrine's blood at her own house. If the sheriff wasn't going to help, she'd get back to investigating her friend's disappearance on her own, no matter what got thrown in her way.

8

Griff regretted that he'd told Emma their relationship was just physical, because his passion for her had plunged far deeper. He was obsessed with finding out more about her, and not from Delia.

So the next day after he saw his last patient, as exhausted as he was from being up all night for the breech birth, he went looking for answers about Emma Weston in the place that had bred her. Driving the health center van, he finally found the twisting lane that led to Cutshin Holler, about a mile higher around Big Blue than the Settles' place. No signs marked hollows here—hollers, the locals called them—any more than they did knobs or cricks that they knew like the backs of their hands.

His isolation in the midst of these people hit him hard. These hills were a place where you were only a stranger for five minutes, but a newcomer for fifty years. Sadly, the patients he knew best were outsiders, such as injured hikers and tourists or other relative newcomers like Mike and Trish Bonner. Mike was highly susceptible to skin rashes, and when Griff had first treated him, they'd struck up a camaraderie.

Griff knew the Bonners were close to Emma, so he could question them about her. Eventually, he'd hear Delia out—Emma, too, if she'd discuss her past. It was a tricky thing, though, because he sure as hell didn't intend to talk about his own past.

A few yards down the lane, he saw a sign that read Posted Keep Out. This kind of warning was fairly common in the area, but he laughed aloud. When he approached Emma as a man or a doctor, she ought to wear that sign around her neck.

Deciding not to risk driving the van farther, he got out, locked the doors and walked. He paused in a scattering of pink dogwoods above the narrow clearing that had once sheltered a house. Remnants of charred wood and a scorched, tumbled stone chimney were all that remained of the small place. Evidently that fire had been one of who knows how many mountain tragedies that had hardened Emma's backbone and her heart.

He moved along the ridge to view the entire narrow hollow. A shallow rill, no doubt Cutshin Crick, ran jaggedly through here like a string of crystal. He could make out land once cleared for a big garden and two small fields beyond, though both slanted sharply uphill to contour a wooded knob. When he saw the rusted, single-width trailer hunkered down on cinder blocks, he frowned. Delia had called Emma trailer trash.

Watching where he stepped, he started down on uneven turf thick with spring growth. A few minutes later, he reached the trailer. It had boards crudely nailed across all the windows except one. The place no doubt held nothing of value, but the urge to look inside overpowered him.

The screen door had a fist-size hole, and the wooden door stood open. He shaded his eyes to peer in, but the sun reflected silver off the screen. It was his imagination, of course, with the charred house skeleton across the way, but he thought he smelled smoke inside.

He wondered if Emma had looked for Amrine here.
Len Roscoe could have used the trailer for a hideout.
Could that be why Emma hadn't passed them on Mudbrook Road, or had she missed them when she hiked
up through the woods?

"Hello," he called, rapping his knuckles on the
screen door, then "how-do," however strange the
mountain greeting felt on his lips.

Nothing but whistling wind and birdcalls. He opened
the screen door, which screeched in protest, and stepped
in.

Someone had been here recently; he *did* smell cigarette smoke. It could be a vagrant, hiker, hunter or a
local who knew the place stood vacant. Still, the skin
on the nape of his neck crawled as he examined an
open, empty can of SpaghettiOs and a cup with a coffee
ring. The tiny rooms were stripped of appliances and
furniture, but he found a crude pallet of moss and leaves
inside the single, small bedroom.

Emma might be angry he was poking around, he
thought, but he should tell her someone had been living
here. Or, if she visited as seldom as he thought, maybe
she just didn't care.

He went back into the glare of sun and sucked in
fresh, crisp air. Like Emma, the hollow had strength and
natural beauty, but for a woman like that to have come
from this....

He stood staring for several minutes, seeing nothing
but her face, both bold and bashful. It hit him then: she
had been somehow abused here—by her father, maybe,
considering how she'd reacted to Sam Grady. He prayed
it hadn't been something as sick as what they feared
about Sam and Ola. Or had she been hurt by someone
who came courting, a loser like Len Roscoe? Griff had

heard she'd dated Hank Welling. Maybe he should talk to him, but then she'd really have his head.

As he started to hike out, he remembered one other thing he wanted to see here. Wanda Keck had mentioned that, after Delia stopped supporting her, Emma had put herself through college. Besides working any odd job she could get, she'd sold what the locals called 'sang. She had secret places up here, Wanda said, where she picked the best ginseng in the county. It was precious both as a root and leaf herb, used in a variety of ways, everything from organic food to medicine to an aphrodisiac.

"Aphrodisiac, that's why she's been getting to me," he muttered. His mouth lifted in a rueful grin as he climbed, his gaze skimming the new growth of spring vegetation for the distinctive, hand-shaped leaves he'd looked up in Delia's old library.

But he saw no signs of 'sang. It was probably too early for it, he reasoned, or else she kept her stash hidden so people wouldn't poach it. The stuff, Wanda said, was worth its weight in gold, yet it would be just like Emma to value it because it was also supposedly good for female disorders. Actually, he thought, that was his problem lately—a life disordered by females, two of them who couldn't get along and had him trapped in the middle. And despite his occasional rebellions, he had no choice but to do what Delia wanted.

Then he spotted a patch of what must be ginseng with its delicate shoots starting to sprout. He went closer and hunkered down beside it. No, this looked newly planted, not natural. The ground was still freshly turned.

"Oh, hell!"

Emma—or someone—was growing illegal marijuana here.

* * *

Emma gripped the printed, pink-and-blue flowered vellum invitation so hard it bent in her hand. The ornate calligraphy swam before her eyes. She didn't even catch Carter Doyal's final words he shouted about the new baby as he got back in his postal delivery truck and pulled away.

You are cordially invited to a baby shower
In honor of Sissy Presnell
On Saturday, April 29, 2:00–4:00 p.m.
Hostess Delia Lowe, Hill House

It didn't mention an RSVP, because who would turn down the equivalent of a royal summons? At least, Emma thought, she had been invited, of course, on the same afternoon *she* had decided to give her sister a baby shower. Had she told anyone else ahead of time except Trish? Could it just be coincidence? Anyhow, that plan was now ruined because no way could Sissy's friends afford a gift for more than one party.

Completely, cleverly, in the usual bloom of bounty and gush of goodwill, Delia had outmaneuvered her again. This was the way Delia operated, with emotional jerks and jabs. Surely she could not be behind the dead animals on her porch. No, that crude calling card had to be from Sam, who'd had those frozen coon carcasses in his freezer, or even Hal Eubanks. There was also Sheriff Merrell, a born hunter, but it seemed his new wife was making a new man of him, in some ways at least.

For the tenth time that day, Emma made a circuit of the house, checking doors and downstairs windows. Each time she came home now, she looked in closets and under beds, exactly what she needed to do in Amrine's house, to see if she could turn up anything to find her.

On the way to Amrine's Emma stopped at the Poteets to talk to Wade. It was an overcast day, perfect for a visit, though Emma wasn't in the mood.

"Morning, Mabel," she called through the screen door to his mother. Wade's father, Asa, still worked the mines, though he drove fifty miles a day one way for that privilege. The Poteets had seven youngsters, all younger than Wade, more girls than boys, though Emma had lost count the five years she'd lived away. After school, Wade helped earn extra money when he could, doing odd jobs, sweeping out the five-and-dime, fixing flat tires and doing oil changes at Quincy's Pure Oil in town. Wade's dream was to run a gas station just that grand.

"How-do, Emma," Mrs. Poteet called back as she came to the door. "Set a spell?"

"I'd surely like to," she said. Though she felt frustrated and frenzied, she knew mountain manners. They settled in rocking chairs on the porch. After the first round of small talk, Emma said, "I was wondering if I could speak to Wade. I tried to look him up in town, but they said he's been sick."

"Wheezin' something dreadful, that boy. You can't catch the black lung from hangin' 'round those old guys at the station, can you, Emma? You know, kinda like what they say 'bout secondhand smoke? I was goin' to ask your old beau, Hank, 'cause he does all them fancy picture shows warning about the lung, but it plumb slipped my mind."

"No, Mabel, black lung's not catching. I'll bet Wade's just got a bad spring cold."

Emma was touched that Mabel had asked her opinion about Wade's health, if not because her reputation was growing around here, then because her grandmother had been skilled with curing herbs.

A thin, freckled girl, maybe age five, brought out two glasses of cold springwater and a plate of oatmeal cookies. Though Emma smiled and waved, three other girls peered out through the screen door at them, hanging back, munching on their own treats.

"So, my boy's not in no kind of trouble?" Mabel asked, still rocking.

"No, he's been really helpful fetching me for Amrine that day she left."

Mabel nodded despite the sudden screeches from the kids in the house. One thing that amazed Emma was that Mabel operated at a slow speed when this many kids underfoot might have done her in.

"Pearl Mae," Mabel called in to the oldest girl, "you go see if your big brother's decent. Tell him Miss Weston here wants to talk to him.

"You think his wheezin' could be asthma?" Mabel asked, turning back to Emma. "I been a' dosin' him with comfrey root, but handlin' it makes me all itchy."

"You've got to handle comfrey with gloves, Mabel. But if it's not a cold, considering all the early blooms we've had this year, it's more likely he's just got a kind of sinus or hay fever from all the pollen. Was he better that day it rained so hard, when he came to get me for Amrine?"

"I rightly believe he was."

"The rain would have cleared the air of pollen that day," Emma explained, "so that's probably it. I'd say goldenseal—you know, Indian yellow root—made into a good tonic might help him to get better, and that's in the woods right now…"

Her voice drifted off as she recalled Griff's warning about a midwife playing general-health adviser. *But I'm here now,* he had said. Emma cleared her throat. "You know, Mabel, it might be a good idea—before you dose him anymore—to have him pop in to see the doctor in town. Asa's got medical coverage, doesn't he?"

"Sure. Ain't had no use for a doctor, but for the babies comin', and if I had it to do again, which I ain't, I'd come see you."

"I'm grateful, but things are changing, Mabel—for general health care, I mean. You think about Wade seeing Dr. Cusak, won't you?" she encouraged as the boy came to the door and walked out onto the porch, announcing himself by an explosion of sneezes. His hello sounded as if it came from deep inside a barrel. The girlish shrieking from the house got louder. Mabel sighed, gave Wade her chair and ambled inside.

Emma asked Wade a few questions, assuring him she was just curious. Yes, he said, he'd brought Miz Settle that stew meat and she started cutting it up right then, promised him some of it when he got done with the tractor, too. She was dressed in a loose housecoat when she sent him for the midwife. And she looked pretty much like she was hurting, so he ran cross-corner to the road and caught a ride.

"And Miss Settle told you she was going to sell that tractor to get some money, right, Wade?"

He nodded, wiping under his runny nose with his sleeve. "Gonna pay you, get things for the baby," he said, still nodding. "'Course, then, she din't pay me, not even with the money that man gave her."

Emma stopped rocking. "What man? Len Roscoe?"

"No, not Len—that new city guy bought her big, old china pitcher and bowl that morning—roses painted real fancy on it."

Emma knew the exact set, which, like most things in the house, had once been Amrine's grandparents' property. "Do you mean that antique dealer, Mike Bonner?" she prompted.

"That's him, give her a fortune for them old things. Two new fifties, I seen it and told Ma she should sell more old stuff we got, like that little cradle in the attic that same guy bought."

Emma nodded, her mind racing. Why hadn't Mike mentioned he'd bought things from Amrine? Emma pictured the crisp fifty-dollar bill Amrine had left for her.

"How much did she say she'd give you for fixing that tractor, Wade?"

"Twenty, ma'am. But I'm not sure I got it goin' again, and Ma said not to go up there 'il Miz Settle comes back."

"Well, she left me one of those fifties, and I know she meant for you to have your pay from it," she told him as she fished in her purse for a twenty. His face lit as she held out the bill to him.

He folded and pocketed it, muttering, "Much obliged."

"Wade, did you see anyone else on the road that day? I'm wondering if you could have passed or seen Len Roscoe driving by?"

Strangely enough, he looked upset, but she decided he was only focusing on telling her what he knew. "Sure I did," he said excitedly when she thought he wasn't going to answer. "Always did soup up his trucks with lightning bolts and racin' stripes on the side, real neat, Len did."

"You saw him when you were in the truck, coming to find me?"

"Before—when I was hikin' out over the hill to hitch a ride. Saw him passin' down below, just flyin'."

"Was he heading up or down Mudbrook then?"

"Up, pretty fast on that slick road, real daredevil-like," Wade said admiringly. "Wish I could've flagged him down, but with the rain and all, don't think he saw me."

"Did you notice if he had Tennessee or Kentucky license plates on his truck?"

"Nope," he said, frowning in concentration. "Too much mud. But there's somethin' else I saw."

She leaned forward in her rocker. "What's that, Wade?"

"You know mountain soldiers like his own kin done fought for the Union in the old days. But there he was, that big reb flag a' hangin' in his back truck window right by his gun rack with his rifle."

Emma pulled the Jeep around the back of Amrine's house by the kitchen door, figuring she'd have to haul out spoiled food from her friend's refrigerator. But she checked to see if the seldom-used front door key was hidden under the drain spout rock. She found the key and pocketed it. This place needed to be protected now. For several reasons, the old open-door policy was fast fading in the hills.

Then, as she had taken to doing at home, she walked quickly around the outside perimeter of the entire house, to be sure that nothing strange was on the porch or peering in windows. She wished the day wasn't so gray.

At least her flashlight would help with the generator down. She wanted to get this part of losing Amrine over with, to close up the place and preserve it for her friend's return.

She emptied spoiled food into two sacks—the smell reminded her of that dead skunk again—and washed the inside of the refrigerator with water and baking soda. Then she systematically searched drawers, cupboards, the old desk, then odder places: a half-eaten box of cereal and a sugar canister. She pulled up worn drawer lining in the linen closet that smelled of mothballs and peeked under the mattress and corners of rag rugs. She wasn't certain what she was looking for—anything to suggest where Len was living, she guessed.

She turned on Amrine's transistor to have some sounds, some company. She turned the dial, settling for oldies music, though the station's idea of old was the 1970s.

Emma was surprised to see a lot of Amrine's regular-size clothes still were hanging in her closet. If she was planning to live with Len after the baby came, was she going to buy a whole new wardrobe? More proof she had not planned this, that she had been coerced or worse. Emma went through the pockets of everything and shone her little flashlight beam on the closet floor. No dead animals around this house but a lot of dust bunnies.

Carrying the radio, she went up the sunken stairs to drag out two boxes of old shoes from the closet floor. Though she'd been poor all her life, Amrine had loved shoes and, from the looks of these, she mustn't have thrown out a single pair since her feet stopped growing at size eight. Emma could remember some of these pairs and the places they'd been together when Amrine had worn them. She heaved a huge sigh as she slid the box back in the closet.

Then she froze. And frowned. A sound downstairs? A door opening with a bang? She hadn't locked it. The key was back in her pocket.

She clicked off the radio and strained to listen. This bedroom overlooked the back of the house, so she'd have to run clear across the hall to see if a car had pulled up in front.

She heard a man's voice, kind of whispery but rough and mean.

"Get upstairs and do exactly as I say or else. You're my prisoner and don't forget it. And don't make me use the gun."

Emma's heart began to slam against her ribs. Had Len brought Amrine back? And had a gun?

She tried to remember Jake's voice when he'd whispered some threat. Could he be back, living in this empty house? Maybe he'd heard Amrine had gone. He had always liked the Gradys, and they were just a hike over the ridge the other way from Cutshin.

She scooted into the closet, shoving the box of shoes and radio ahead of her. She pulled the closet door nearly shut, careful not to close herself in. If it was Len and he intended to hurt Amrine, maybe she could jump out and surprise him to get the gun. But if it was Jake...

"No bed in here but we don't need one, do we?" The man's voice came closer. In this room. They'd come into this room. She knew that voice, but couldn't place it.

"I said I'll do anything you say, but please don't hurt me."

No, not Amrine's voice, thank God. Too quick. But who were these people, and what was going on?

Slowly, carefully, Emma shifted to her knees to try to get a glimpse through the keyhole. Her line of sight through the crack of the open door wasn't wide enough.

"Just don't make me hurt you then. Get undressed— nice and slow so I can watch your every move. I'm going to have to do a complete strip search."

This was insanity, a bad movie. They must be play-acting.

"I thought you might force me to do this," the woman said, her voice both shaky and husky.

"Get going then, or I'll turn you right over my knee for starters."

"Please, I said I'll do whatever you say, if you just don't hurt me, sheriff."

Sheriff? Sheriff Merrell?

Emma jerked so hard her head bumped against the closet wall, but the intruders were evidently too en-grossed to hear. The urge to sneeze hit her, and she jammed her finger under her nose. She should make herself known, but this was more than embarrassing now. She needed this bastard's help, had asked him to look into finding Amrine, and he was here cheating on his new wife.

The action in the room kept heating up. Emma could glimpse a lot of naked white skin as he pressed the woman against the far wall. She saw the blur of his brown uniform, so he wasn't getting undressed. Emma couldn't see the woman's face, but she was blond, fairly young and very willing, despite her corny protests.

The talk got dirtier, the action wilder. Emma began to sweat and shake from rage as the sounds of a spank-ing filled the room and then, on the floor, the pair grap-pled and groaned over her fake protests and cries for help.

Emma sat in the corner of the closet with her eyes shut tight and her hands over her ears. For all she knew, that could be Reg Merrell's new wife; Cindy Sue Merrell was young and blond.

"Mmm," the woman said when the thumping and moaning stopped. "I love it when you wear your uniform and take me off to some awful, deserted place like this. You think that woman who lived here really was kidnapped by that Len guy?" she murmured over Reg Merrell's labored breathing. "And maybe that Jake Weston is on the lam around here, looking for some woman to abduct. Is he really as dangerous and crude as you said?"

"Cindy, I swear, all that's gonna have to wait for another day. I'm gonna do a quick look-see downstairs where Amrine lived so I can say I did. Now get those clothes on your beautiful backside then come on down. You insist on this kind of stuff, you got to show some patience when I have to work."

"I know that," she whined. "But you're gone so much, don't get riled if I want to go with you sometimes."

Emma heaved a silent sigh of relief. At least they were going downstairs. But what if he saw her Jeep and came back looking for her? She heard him clomp down the stairs, his steps much slower than when he came up. She peeked out to see Cindy, half-dressed, stop to yawn and stretch. Reg began banging cupboard doors downstairs. Why didn't this woman hurry up so they could leave?

Then, Emma watched in silent dread as Cindy, still tucking her blouse in her slacks, reached for the knob to the closet door.

So much flashed through Emma's mind. She had to

try to get Cindy not to scream. Tell her she'd keep their secret if Cindy didn't blab to her husband. But Emma knew women, and this one was a screamer and—

"Cindy, get the hell down here!" the sheriff bellowed so loud that he sounded as if he was in the room again. "I can hear a call comin' in on my squad-car squawker even from here. If somebody's spotted that jackass Weston, I'm gonna be there first!"

"Oh, yeah!" Cindy said and spun away to clatter down the staircase.

Emma slumped in the corner of the closet until she heard them pull away, with the siren going, no less. At least one good thing had come out of this mess today, maybe two. First, the sheriff was obsessed with rearresting Jake, and that was fine with her. And second, though she hoped not to have to stoop so low, she knew something about him and his new wife he wouldn't want anyone else to know at any price.

9

"I hear we have a midwife problem here in Shelter," Pamela Stark said as Griff took her on a tour of the health center facilities with Delia bringing up the rear.

"I see our founder and chairwoman of the board has briefed you thoroughly," Griff commented as he showed Pam the layout of the storage room just off the hall behind the two examining rooms.

As Delia had said, Pam Stark was tall; he had to look slightly up at her, especially in those high heels. Hair so red it had to be bottled accented her strikingly chiseled physique, which he assumed, she got from hours of working out. She seemed poised and confident, and, thank God, she had a well-modulated voice that made Wanda at her best sound like a screaming banshee.

"Griffin's policy with such substandard medical competition," Delia said when he did not pick up on Pam's midwife comment, "tends toward not only tolerance but cooperation."

Pam arched her auburn eyebrows. "How hostile is the midwife?"

"Emma Weston only wants the best for her clients," Griff said, staring Delia down even though he knew better.

"And her best can be dangerous for the women and babies around here," Delia retorted.

Griff set his jaw. Delia had not been pleased he'd

helped deliver Clary Doyal's son and then praised
Emma's manipulation skills to free the child just in
time. "Oh, yes," she had said, narrowing her eyes at
him. "I can see her manipulation skills are excellent
and getting better all the time."

Pam kept looking from one to the other, then declared, "So, we'll just work harder to show Shelter's
pregnant women and mothers they need modern medical care, not a link to the past, whatever function the
old granny-women and baby catchers once served."

Pam smiled at Delia, then Griff. Her teeth were so
perfect they looked capped, but he had to admit her
smile was stunning. The perky package, Griff thought,
almost overshadowed her slightly astigmatic stare and
the long, plain face which could have made her look
dour and depressed.

"I like your positive attitude," he told her.

Delia exhaled, as if she had been waiting for him to
approve. "I'm sure," she said, patting both their arms,
"you two will be a fine team, and I'll leave you to get
more acquainted. I'm throwing a baby shower for the
midwife's younger sister, and I've got loads to do."

"So," Pamela said as Delia went out," she's friends
with the midwife's family?"

"From way back," Griff explained. "But then everything's from way back around here. Let me show
you the lab, hopefully to be overseen by a tech soon."

"Just a sec," she said, surprising him by kicking off
her heels, then retrieving them when they skidded down
the polished hall. "I'm grateful we won't stand on cer-
emony around here—and I'm glad I'm not stepping into
some sort of minefield. I know we can keep that midwife thing under control," she added with a grin, pre-

tending she was being careful where she stepped. "Lead the way, doctor!"

Still shaken from the scene she'd witnessed at Amrine's, Emma knocked twice on the Bonners' back door before she heard someone coming. Mike opened it, obviously surprised to see her.

"Hey, sorry, if you've been knocking a while," he said, massaging the back of his neck with one hand. "When I get on-line, I wouldn't hear the Battle of Armageddon start. Did Trish know you were coming over? She's out somewhere."

"I just wondered if the last piece of wicker or the swing was refinished yet." Actually, she wondered much more than that and was glad to get Mike alone for a minute.

"No, sorry. Heard you liked the other stuff, though."

"Loved it," she said, repressing a shudder as she recalled the tableau on her table. "If it weren't going to be on the porch, the wicker would look great with one of those old-fashioned, white ewer-and-bowl sets, you know the kind I mean?"

"Sure," he said, thrusting his hands under his armpits. His white-and-black tennis sweater had Brown University scripted small on the ribbed neckline. "I've seen those antique pitcher-and-bowl toilet sets, and I think we've even bought a few around here."

She couldn't believe he didn't mention Amrine's, but maybe that set was already promised to someone else. Or maybe, since Emma had questioned him about trying to get Amrine to sell her land, he thought she'd resent his buying anything from her friend.

"How much do you think I'd have to pay for a set?" she pursued.

"Ah, depends on what shape it's in, the era and detail of workmanship. If it's something special like a Spode or Copeland and not just out of the old Sears Wishbook, a couple of hundred per piece, I'd guess."

The phone rang. "I'll let you get that and be going," she told him.

"No, wait. Sorry I didn't ask you in. If that's Trish, you can talk to her and set a time to get together—find out about the wicker and all that." He spoke over his shoulder as he stepped back into the kitchen. Through the screen, she saw him pick up the cordless phone on the cherry table. The huge room was done in barn oak and rare old chestnut and country antiques. This place was so beautiful she couldn't believe they had a mansion in Highboro, too. In the next room, which he and Trish shared as an office, Emma could see his computer screen glowing blank blue, so he'd apparently taken time to clear it before answering the door.

"Mike Bonner," he said into the receiver, then covered the mouthpiece with his hand to look at her. "Not Trish," he whispered. "I'll have her call you later."

She nodded and started away as he began to talk. Before his voice faded, she heard, "Left coast again? They do understand cross-country shipping ups the bottom line considerably?"

She looked out toward the big, renovated barn where they stored and refinished antiques. Mike had not lied, but she somehow felt he had.

That evening, as he worked on his dad's old car in the carriage house that served as the health center's garage, Griff heard a man and woman arguing out front. The man's voice was loud but slurred, the woman's low and pleading. Wiping oil from his hands on a rag, he jogged toward the house.

"I told you, Sissy," he heard the man shout before he could see them, "this pain's nothin'—nothin'."

"Not the way you've been carrying on. You're fibbing to me, J. G. Presnell, and you're not gonna be laid up again, not with this baby coming!"

"Thinkin' 'bout the baby, 'stead of me, huh?"

"I'm gonna ignore that. I know it's that pain talking now."

Griff knew the Presnells were Emma's family but had never spoken to either of them more than in passing. Though pregnant and shorter than her husband, Sissy was propping up J.G.

"Oh, Dr. Cusak, there you are!" she exclaimed, relief flooding her pink face.

"I've been performing surgery on my old car," he told them, holding up the oily rag and a wrench from his back pocket. "I didn't hear if you rang the bell. What can I do for you?" he asked as he took the man's weight from her so he practically dangled between them.

"J.G., tell the doctor or I will."

"Two bad discs, been on disability," J.G. muttered. Griff dropped his rag and wrench and fished in his pocket for the front door key to let them in. J.G. grunted with each step. The question was, Griff thought, was he drunk, oversedated, or was his injury so bad it was pressing on the spinal cord? If the latter, he'd need surgery and soon.

"Let's get you off your feet," Griff urged. "Did your pain pills run out?"

"They didn't run out," Sissy said. "My brave man flushed them down the toilet, thinking he was gonna just heal himself, like in the Good Book—'Heal me and I shall be healed, save me and I shall be saved.'"

"Sissy, shut up," J.G. muttered.

Flipping on lights, Griff got J.G. settled in the first exam room in a straight-backed chair. Sometimes a bad back was better on the vertical. It was after hours, but Griff knew he'd probably have to phone the doctor who had done the original diagnosis. No way was he going to risk getting caught prescribing powerful drugs for someone else's patient.

J.G. sat, propping himself up with his hands on the seat of the chair. He had a surprised look on his face, maybe because he'd ended up here. Evidently, like her older sister, Sissy could be very persuasive.

"Do you remember the name of the medicine?" Griff asked.

"Naw. All medicine's a bunch a long words," J.G. said through gritted teeth, his face contorted in a wave of panic. The scent of liquor hit Griff hard. He tried to block the memory, but his father's agonized face flashed through his brain, and here he stood with oil on his hands like black blood...

He jolted back to reality and scrubbed quickly. "Did you really flush those pills and then take a drink to help kill the pain, J.G.?"

"Tol' Sissy I din't take no drink."

"It's obvious you did, but I want you to tell me if you really did flush the pills or took them," Griff pursued, drying his hands and bending down to get in the man's face. "How about the truth, J.G.?"

"You're good, doc, you know 'at? Miss Delia says you're good, and I thin' so, too. 'Course, I know Emma doesn't want you 'round—"

"J.G., *you* just shut up now," Sissy interrupted. "You haven't talked this much in weeks!"

"—and I got plans," J.G. went on to Griff, ignoring his wife, "for Emma gettin' back with Hank. Yeah, doc, I swear to you I flushed the pills and that's why I needed the drink, so maybe I better get me more pills if you got some 'round here—"

He snorted and hiccuped, then put his head back against the wall in midsentence.

"I think," Griff said, straightening, "the fact he's been conscious and somewhat coherent this long indicates booze but *not* mixed with the pills. I'm going to take his blood pressure and check his heart, so why don't you sit over there, Sissy."

She did, shifting her hips to slide back on the chair with her big belly cradled in her lap. She looked almost ready to deliver, but she could be just a small woman carrying a big baby.

"I'm gonna have his head, Dr. Cusak, for throwing out expensive pills. Why would he if he's in pain?"

"I've noticed the men around here like to pretend pain doesn't exist," Griff said as he worked to get J.G.'s vitals. If they were strong, he'd let him sleep it off. If they were erratic or plunging, he'd pump J.G.'s stomach to be sure he hadn't mixed liquor with pills. Good, he thought, holding the stethoscope to J.G.'s chest—steady and strong. Like many of these mountain men, he must have the constitution of a bull, and yet it was the physical and psychological stamina of the women that continued to amaze Griff.

"What you said about pain," Sissy broke his concentration as he rechecked J.G.'s pulse. "Lord's truth, it's a burden our men aren't too good at sharing. What's worse is he can't work regular no more. Can't hunt or

cut firewood. But the very worst is taking benefits and
getting watched by his friend Hank Welling 'bout disability fraud. J.G.'s no fraud! Oh, I could write a song
or two about it all, I reckon.''

"I hear you're a fine singer," Griff said, leaning
against the examining table while J.G.'s rhythmic
snores accompanied their voices. "Do you ever use
your own past, you know, family things, for inspiration?''

"When I can stomach remembering.''

"I—do understand," he said as their eyes met and
held.

Sissy and Emma did not look alike, he observed, yet
the kinship was there, bone deep, in the set of the determined jaw, the flashes of buried sorrow and the anger
in the eyes. And if he knew Sissy's past, then he knew,
at least in part, Emma's too.

"Losing Mama," Sissy said, "and the way she died,
was the worst, but that wasn't the first.''

Her words seemed to lilt with rhythm and rhyme as
if she were singing. He assumed their mother had died
of some terrible disease like cancer. He'd ask Emma;
they could share the loss, though there was no way he'd
be sharing more than that.

"Emma said," he prompted when Sissy said no
more, "that both your parents were dead.''

She shook her blond head. "You misunderstood her.
Mama's dead, but not Pa or our older brother, Jake—
just dead to us. We both kinda think of it that way.''

She hesitated, fooling with the strap on her purse.
"When I was a kid I used to pretend I was Loretta
Lynn—you know, the country singer. I'd just go around
singing that coal miner's daughter from Butcher Holler
song. But she's real proud of her past and Emma and

me aren't a bit proud to be from Cutshin and to be a murderer's daughters.''

Griff gripped J.G.'s shoulder, making the sleeping man wince. Griff had been trying to avoid Delia lately, but he silently cursed the fact he hadn't demanded she tell him everything of Emma's past.

"I'm sorry I don't have more to report yet, Mrs. Collister," Reed Gorham said, shifting his position on her couch. "Frankly, you're really rushing me."

"But I'm paying you overtime rates, and it's essential you fill me in as far as you've gone."

Jidge heard Mitchell fussing down the hall, but he'd have to just carry on until this was over. If Ben had not moved out, she'd have called the sitter and gone to Gorham's office on the sly. But now she didn't have to sneak around. And just in case Ben decided to try reconciliation later, she had to push things along.

Reed Gorham heaved a silent sigh that lifted then slumped his narrow shoulders. He looked more like an accountant than a private detective, she thought, with his bland but meticulous appearance and his nervous hands.

"Then here goes," he acquiesced in his quiet, clipped voice while shuffling his notes again. "First, Mrs. Collister, using your suggestion that the woman who delivered your son to you at the airport had some sort of Southern or hillbilly dialect, I theorized that baby quilt could have come from a five-state area. Then I spent most of my time trying to match the initials *G.G.* on the quilt to copies of Interstate Compacts filed in those states around the time of your son's birth. Which helped me narrow down the search to three states, assuming your son's parents gave the child up legally.''

"If not," she said, thinking aloud, "the adoption facilitators would be getting into kidnapping over state lines. Your guess is they'd try to cover their rears by staying within the law or appearing to be legal."

He frowned at her, as if annoyed she'd usurped his next revelation. "Exactly," he said and gulped as if he had just come up for air. "Details—it's all in the details. Frankly, without on-line info these days—"

"Refresh my mind on the term Interstate Compact."

"It's the legal document that a birth mother must sign to allow her child to be adopted in other states. The originals are privileged information, but an initialed, dated facsimile is public record. The original gets filed in or near the county seat of birth. The facsimiles I viewed on-line."

"And...?"

"And found G.G.s in three states. That's the catch. No G.G. signed a compact in the time frame of your son's birth, though there were other first-name initials with a *G.* last name."

"So you have narrowed down the search to three states, and no doubt, specific counties within the three states?"

"Oh, yes. Ah—" he flipped open his small black leather notebook and skimmed a fingertip down the page "—Jackson County in Ohio, Cumberland County in Tennessee, or Lowe County in Kentucky, all in the Appalachians, and all with *G.* last names of—ah, the donors."

"And you've prepared a written report on this for me?"

"I will later. Right now it's just my notes, so—"

"I want those notes," she declared as her excitement increased. Mitchell's crying down the hall helped her decide as she stood. "Mr. Gorham, I'm going to pay you in full and terminate your services. I'm pleased with your information and think you've done timely and resourceful work."

"That's it?" His voice rose to a squeak. "I assumed you wanted to meet the parents or expose the adoption facilitator, or—"

"I hired you to do a job and you did it," Jidge said, "so I'm going to get my checkbook."

"But you aren't certain which of three counties. It could be none of them. Look, I can clear my schedule of cases here and fly east to narrow it down more. You're—you're certainly not taking things into your own hands?"

"Don't be ridiculous. I've changed my mind, decided to let it go, that's all," she lied, opening the drawer of the antique Oriental commode.

She caressed the cold metal skin of her pistol, which was lying there, then took out the checkbook and pen, clicking the ballpoint nervously. When she found who was to blame for Mitchell's tragedy—and who had made that tragedy her business—she'd pull the trigger of her gun, just as easily as that.

"Pa used to drink a lot and knock Mama around, Emma, too, when she tried to stand up for Mama," Sissy told Griff. "Our older brother, Jake, he was Pa's boy all the way, wild as he was.

"The night everything really blew up, Pa was drunk as a dog, Jake, too, and Pa come after Mama for rough loving—rape, if the truth was known." Sissy shook her head. "But that night Emma took the third rifle and loaded it and told Pa she'd shoot him if he touched

Mama again that way. Leveled that barrel right at him, when she didn't like guns, nearly never touched one.''

Gooseflesh chilled Griff's skin, and he hugged himself. Sissy stared not at him now, but into space, into the past. He was aching to ask who their father had killed, but he kept quiet.

''I was watching from the door of the small downstairs bedroom Emma and me shared in the house. This was way before it burned. Thought Pa'd turn and shoot her—Emma, I mean—just the way he'd threatened to put a bullet in Mama more than once. But Emma stared him down with her finger on the trigger, and Pa just roared out of there with Jake right behind.''

She cleared her throat before she went on. ''Later that night Sheriff Merrell came looking for Pa, 'cause him and Jake had shot up the Eubanks family down by town and killed Cory Eubanks, who owed him a couple dollars or something. Gonna get enough money to put Emma on a bus to hell, Jake said at his trial.''

Fury flooded Griff, but he fought to control it. ''Jake was sentenced, too?''

Sissy looked startled he'd spoken. Her eyes focused on him. ''For assault, but not to maximum security, not a life sentence like Pa. Anyhow, Jake just up and walked away from his work detail a few months ago, so who knows where he is. I been praying he don't come back here.''

Griff's nostrils flared. He hoped that open trailer and makeshift pallet out at Cutshin weren't a clue as to where he had last been.

''There's more,'' Sissy said, ''but I can't bear telling it, Dr. Cusak—''

''Griff. Please call me Griff.''

''All right, Dr. Griff. I just can't bear talking 'bout it

right now—how Mama died later and the house burned, not with this baby in me taking in everything good or bad that happens to its own mama right now.''

Griff wondered if Emma had been preaching fetal sentience, the theory that talking, reading, singing to an unborn baby was healthy. "Tell you what," he said, "why don't you just sing a lullaby to J.G. while we load him in your truck and get him home so he can sleep like a baby."

Sissy smiled wanly, almost wistfully. "You got a nice way 'bout you. Nothing personal on my part I didn't come to you with this pregnancy. Miss Delia wanted me to, but Emma's set on me having a specialist in Highboro, and we're going to see him tomorrow, me'n Emma. Emma says the baby's head's engaged already, so that means I'm prob'ly just a couple weeks away from delivery!"

"I'm glad to hear that. Here, you just open doors, and I'll handle your man."

Griff realized, though, the more he learned about Emma, the less certain he was he'd ever be able to handle her.

"Oh, come on, Trish," Emma said, hands on her hips. "I know Mike saw Amrine that morning she left. I know he at least bought the ewer-and-bowl set from her, but didn't tell me even when I gave him the opening."

They stood at the end of the lane to Big Blue Farm where they'd nearly run into each other as Emma was leaving and Trish was coming in. They'd gotten out of their idling vehicles to talk. Though Emma was uptight, she'd decided to ask Trish to explain what was going on. Emma actually didn't think there was much Mike did without his wife knowing it.

"Calm down, girl." Trish threw an arm around her. "Emma," she drawled when Emma stood stiffly and didn't answer, "I know you're shook, but you're starting to sound like the Spanish Inquisition and Mike and I are on the rack."

"I just can't let Amrine's disappearance go," she said, pulling gently away. They stood looking now not at each other but out over the blue-green mountain peaks snagging clumps of storm clouds.

"I think you'd better work on it," Trish advised, "before all this affects your work. It's already playing havoc with your personal relationships—believe me."

"I know, I know," she admitted with a sigh. "It's just I'm going crazy worrying about her, and nothing fits."

"Now here's what does fit," Trish said as Emma turned to study her friend's face. "Amrine mentioned to Mike weeks before she had a couple of things to sell, and he just happened to stop by that morning. He probably has the china toilet set promised for big bucks somewhere and he didn't want to hurt your feelings."

Emma nodded. She had overheard him promise to send something to the West Coast on a special order.

"Actually," Trish went on, her voice getting even sharper, "he probably didn't want to make it sound as if he could just give it to you, like we want to with the wicker and the swing."

Guilt swamped Emma. These people had been nothing but kind and generous to her. And what was she going to accuse them of, anyway? They weren't guilty of anything except maybe siphoning antiques out of the area, but they paid well for them and no one forced folks to sell.

"You're right about Amrine's disappearance affecting my work and relationships," Emma said, thinking of Griff and Delia, too. "I don't mean to take it out on others or you but I hate all these dead ends. Worse, Sheriff Merrell called me on my cell phone a little while ago to say he can't trace Len Roscoe through his license plates."

She shook her head. That liar had dared to phone her from the scene of an accident to tell her he'd done a thorough search of Amrine's house. How she'd like to have told Merrell she knew what he was really doing there. He'd made a real point of saying he was calling from the scene of an accident, as if that was some kind of veiled threat.

"He told me to mind my own business," she admitted. "But it *is* my business. I've got two very pregnant clients missing when they shouldn't be."

"Two?"

Emma explained about Ola, leaving out her suspicions that Sam Grady might have fathered his own grandchild and shot at her. Trish was supportive again, boosting her hopes that nothing was wrong in either case and that both women would eventually return with their new babies.

"How 'bout you come to dinner this Sunday evening, and we'll have us a big to-do," Trish said, her eyes sparkling, her lilting attempt at local lingo making Emma smile again.

"Sure, since Sissy's shower is the day before."

"I know. I'll be there, and wait 'til you see what I found for your baby sister's baby!"

Emma pictured the little cradle from the Poteets with

a quilt from Ginger Grady, though that would be absolutely too much for a baby-shower gift, however generous the Bonners were. But she would like to see someone outdo Delia.

"So," Trish said in her exaggerated twang, "you can just quit a' frettin' and, by dad, I'm gonna fix you a right fine meal where you won't have to do one lick of work. I think I'll just fetch in that fancy new doctor hisself for it, too, kinda play mountain matchmaker."

Emma gave a mock groan, but they parted with smiles. Emma was nearly back out on the highway before she realized how cleverly Trish had mimicked mountain speech.

Delia popped her head in Griff's office near dinnertime. "How's Pam going to work out?" she asked.

"She's very efficient, very upbeat, so, very well, I'd say."

"All right!" she said, beaming. "Onward and upward. Griffin, would you like to come eat at Hill House this evening, instead of Arletta's? Down-home cooking or not, I'll bet you have her menu memorized."

"Thanks, Delia," he said, tilting back in his chair, "but I think I might just use that great kitchenette you had built here. Then maybe top things off with a Tastee-Freez from way the other end of town—big time, you know."

"And I thought you were a city boy at heart. Which reminds me," she said, stepping in and closing the door, though no one else was still around, "I meant to warn you about something."

He stood, because he knew by now he might as well be on his feet when her tone of voice shifted like that. Her expression hovered somewhere between anger and anguish. His stomach knotted the way it had when he stood to hear the jury's verdict that had decided his entire future.

"Someone at the Highboro hospital," she said, speaking low, as if the room were bugged, "I can't say who—you know I went there to check on leads for our lab tech—said that your name was familiar, but he just knew it couldn't be you who was on trial in Lexington—something about stealing drugs, he said."

"Great, just great," he muttered, his voice dripping sarcasm. "A warped version of a much worse scenario, but I don't want any version. Still, if rumors start, I'm going to face them head-on with the truth."

"No!" Her voice cracked as she lunged at him, gripping his wrist in both hands. "Griffin, no, are you demented? It would ruin everything. That's the real reason I don't want you getting close to Emma, because she'll find out, pry something out of you, use it against you. That will be the ruination of our plans here. I just think," she added, losing her grip on him and stepping back, "you should stay away from her, that's all."

"Look," he said, stepping past her to open his office door, "I don't want my past to come walking in here to find me any more than you do, but we can hardly lie about it or cover it up. It's not exactly like I'm on the lam with new ID papers and a reconstructed face." He frowned as he recalled Jake Weston again. "Nor," he added, gesturing her out the door, "is it going to keep me from seeing or speaking to people around here— Emma, whomever. As you told Pam, I *do* believe in cooperation instead of competition or trying to control someone."

She narrowed her eyes. "I see. Believe me, I do see."

He met her stare before she broke it, walking past

him out the door. In the dim hall she turned back partway as if she were addressing the far wall.

"You really don't get it, do you?" Delia cried. "That
we have to do things my way here to survive and pros-
per? That Shelter is your last chance and that the ice
under you is very, very thin? But, if you want to deal
with Emma Weston that way, you'll need my help—
cooperation, as you call it."

"Fine. I'll take cooperation anytime."

She whispered something he couldn't quite hear, but
he would have put money on the words *ungrateful bastard*. She walked slowly toward the front stairs—she
never took the old servants' staircase—as if expecting
him to run after her or call out for her to stop. But he
was getting tired of toeing her lines, which she'd drawn
all around him in the sand—or on the thin ice, as she'd
put it. When she disappeared down the stairs, he went
back into his office and grabbed the phone. He dialed
Emma's number, but when her answering machine
came on, he hung up.

10

Nearly thirty chatting, smiling women gathered at Hill House for Sissy's baby shower on Saturday afternoon. Emma had only been in the new house twice, but she was struck again by what it said about Delia's transformation from caterpillar to butterfly. On her flight out of soul-grinding poverty, Delia had reached the heights in many things, but she sure enough still showed she had red Appalachian soil on her high-heeled Italian-leather shoes.

The rooms of Hill House were spacious with lofty, distant views of Delia's domain, but too much floor space loomed between guests who lolled back on the soft, sunken, leather couches or perched on raspberry-print upholstered chairs. Once Delia noticed the women were shouting to be heard, she suggested they pull the chairs closer to the couches to make a circle.

Reproductions of French paintings, maybe some the real thing, graced the walls, intermixed with Delia's own paint-by-numbers art and an occasional huge, gilt-framed portrait of her or her deceased husband on a cruise ship or standing in front of the Eiffel Tower. Stark modern lamps and a sculpted marble-and-glass coffee table so large they could skate on were mingled with a few heavy Victorian chestnut pieces Delia had brought from the mansion in town.

The guest bathroom had gilded faucets and maroon,

flocked wallpaper with swooping cherubs guarding bright-print hooked rugs and a crocheted chartreuse and pink toilet-paper cover. The huge kitchen had painted Italian tiles, country French wallpaper and colonial cabinets. Besides jumbling many decors, Delia McGhee Lowe had taken all kinds of lessons—music, elocution, art, accounting—when she married Big Blue Mine owner Piercy Lowe, a childless widower thirty years her senior. But there were no lessons available for escaping her beginnings in Bitter Crick Holler, a far piece up a mountain road.

"I am much obliged to all of you," Sissy was saying as she started unwrapping her gifts, "'specially to Delia for putting all this together."

"It was the least I could do," Delia announced from her seat next to Sissy while two maids she'd hired from the caterer in Highboro zipped in and out with glass trays of punch and tiny sandwiches. A huge, decorated cake and silver urns of coffee and tea were displayed on the dining room table. "And I certainly consider Emma my cohostess," Delia said, surprising them all, "though with her busy schedule, there is no way she could have carried this off herself, so I was happy to help."

Everyone applauded, including Emma, who was sitting on Sissy's other side next to Trish. Emma was touched that she'd been included in Delia's extensive efforts. She'd like to think she'd been wrong about Delia trying to scuttle her plans for a shower just to show her who was in control again.

Sissy displayed Trish's ribbon-and-balloon-decorated gift first. If it wasn't the old Poteet crib graced by a Ginger Grady quilt, Emma speculated silently, they were someone else's heirlooms. Emma almost asked

Trish, but she didn't want to remind her friend she'd been suspicious of Mike for buying Amrine's things before.

"Oh, look," Sissy cried and showed everyone what she had unwrapped. "A little set of dish and cup with baby rabbits and this tiny spoon and fork!" Delia had instructed Wanda Keck to jot down who gave what, though Emma herself would have happily done it.

"I heard Sissy say," Trish leaned over to whisper to Emma, "you finally got her to the specialist in town. I hope you'll rest easier about her now."

"I'll rest easier about her when that baby's here. Did she tell you the ultrasound indicates a girl?"

"She did. Her first one was a girl, right?"

"Yes, but this baby won't replace that one. Once lost, lost forev—"

"Emma, I'm sorry," Trish said, reaching out to touch her arm. "I didn't mean to bring that up. It's just, I'm really pulling for all of you in this."

"I know you are," Emma said, blowing her nose as everyone cooed over a music box that played "Rock-a-bye, Baby." "Thanks for sticking with me when I get a little weak."

"Weepy, maybe, but never weak," Trish said. "Not you. Listen, though, I was just thinking, since she's going to deliver in Highboro, Sissy—her husband and you, too, if you want—could come stay with us in our place there when her due date gets close. That way she can't get caught by a storm. You know we're about four blocks from the hospital."

Emma waited until the oohs and aahs swelled, then died again. She hadn't told Trish all the details of losing that first baby, and was surprised she must have known about the ice storm that had isolated her with Sissy while Mama was trapped in town.

"I'll talk to Sissy about that," Emma said, reaching out to squeeze Trish's hand in return. "And thanks again—for being a friend."

Trish's freckled face lit. "My mother always used to say 'A friend in need is a friend indeed.' Which reminds me, I threatened Mike that if he bugs you about selling that homestead of yours again I'm going to grill him instead of shish kebabs tomorrow evening."

"I've asked Griff to pop over in the van later to help Sissy get these things to her house," Delia told Emma in the aftermath of hugs and farewells at the shower. "With that back of his out of kilter, J.G. can just stay put."

"Since you'll have Griff and the van, you won't need me," Emma said. She bit back a comment about Griff's job description growing every time Delia snapped her fingers.

"I thought you were all for cooperation. No, never mind—let's not get started that way," Delia said, holding up both hands. "May I talk to you for a moment out on the deck?"

Emma sensed Delia was in fact asking and not ordering because she looked nervous, even contrite. Then why not have a chat? Emma thought as she nodded and followed Delia out into the crisp April breeze.

"I'd like your advice on something," Delia began as she spun to face her. They stood along the board railing amid potted pansies, rather than sitting in the cushioned redwood chairs. However much Emma was used to Shelter scenery, this sweeping view of the valley and distant mountains stunned her. The only other house close by was the Eubankses' old place with the patches of small hillside fields they still farmed.

Emma locked her arms across her waist and stood her ground. "Ask away—if I can help."

"You know you could always help me by just being civil and kind. No, don't get in a tizzy now. You and Sissy are the only daughters I've ever had. Yes, I realize," Delia went on hastily, "adopted daughters in a way and for only a brief few years, but I do have a heart, you know."

"Of course I know that," Emma said. "I do cherish many of our times together. It's just that you seem to have some idea that if I disagree with you—or want to go my own way—I'm being hard and hateful. That isn't so."

"You know," the older woman said, almost as if she hadn't been listening, but simply holding on to what she would say next, "you're the only child in town I've let call me Delia, not Miss Delia like they all do, like there is some pedestal, some barrier or wall to separate me from them, some—"

"Some lofty palace or two," Emma put in with a sweep of her hand to encompass Hill House and the old mansion on the edge of Shelter below.

Emma stared at her, waiting for an explosion.

"True," Delia said, looking almost sheepish. "And I suppose the progressive, even aggressive, vision I have for Shelter will always mean walls of some sort. Emma, I don't want to push things too fast, but I want to build a small library in town, renovate the old bank building, maybe put a day care in there, too. You told me once that you wanted to provide some sort of day care for mothers who use your facilities, so let's not butt heads on this, all right?"

When Emma just nodded, she plunged on, "On the library shelves I'd want a large children's collection, self-help books, pride-of-heritage volumes, and a lot of health advice. And I'd specifically like you to help me choose the women's health and child-care books, if you would—though, of course, I'll use input from Griffin, too."

Of all the things Delia could have said, Emma had never expected this. "I—of course," she stammered. "I'd be glad to help—honored. It's a fine idea."

"Unlike the health center, you mean."

"*You* don't really think *I* don't want the health center, do you? It's simply that you've tried to force me and everyone else to be a part of it in your way, then made things so adversarial when I stood up for what I believed."

"Perhaps you're right," Delia said with a sigh. She hit a balled fist lightly on the wooden railing. "We can all learn from each other, can't we?"

Though thrilled by Delia's shift in attitude, Emma wondered why. Was it because Sissy was having a baby and Delia wanted to appropriate it as her own adopted grandchild, even her heir, and she knew she had to win Emma over? Because Griff had convinced her to be kinder? Because she regretted what had passed between them? Or because she had finally met her match in mountain stubbornness?

"Well? Do you mean it?" Delia asked. "You'll help?"

"Of course, I mean it. As long as you're no longer trying to buy me out or force me out of Shelter."

Delia gently grasped her wrist. "I won't lie to you. *I* think you may find this town too small for both of our missions, if you will. But I would like us to trust each

other, confide—to get along the way we did after your
mother died and then the fire—"

"Yes, fine," Emma interrupted before everything
came crashing back. She just wanted to be rid of the
past, to know Amrine and Ola were all right and to get
Sissy's baby safely here. Was that too much to ask?
"All right, Delia," she added hastily. "On this, we're
partners."

"Hi, Hank, this is Emma," she told him over the
phone late that afternoon.

"I'd know your voice anywhere."

"I just got back from Sissy's shower and found your
kind invitation on my answering machine, but I really
don't think it's a good idea."

"Come on, Em, just dinner," Hank urged her. "In
Highboro, not New York or Paris. La Pasta's a great
Italian restaurant. It's a chain, and I've been to the ones
in Lexington and Nashville. Good wine, good company.
If J.G. was feeling better, the four of us could go, but
I think you and I can handle a longtime friendship un-
chaperoned, okay?"

Emma squared her shoulders as if she was facing him
down. "I heard the restaurant's good, but I don't think
so."

"Got other plans?"

She didn't have any such thing until dinner tomorrow
night at Trish and Mike's, but she wasn't going to spend
time with Hank. She had too much else to worry
about—everything from dead animals on her porch to
missing women and their babies.

"I've a lot to get caught up with here. Thanks for
being so thoughtful, but I'm sticking to my guns about
us being over. It's best, believe me."

"I won't take no for an—"

She hung up quickly before he could wheedle or coerce her into dinner.

Hoping Emma was alone in the house—he saw no vehicles but her Jeep—Griff honked as he pulled into her driveway. The chrome and luster finish on his dad's old cinnamon-colored Chrysler Newport Custom gleamed, and he'd worked leather softener into the Tahitian bronze vinyl roof. Sometimes just driving it took him back to those easy, happy days before everything went wrong.

He saw the downstairs curtains move, then the porch door open. Emma stepped outside amidst wicker furniture and waved, then came out to greet him.

"That car always makes me feel we've turned the clock back," she said, giving the vehicle a real once-over this time, even stroking its long hood. Her hot-pink blouse was pulled tightly into belted, hip-hugging jeans, and her hair ruffled in the slight breeze. Again he felt a lurch of desire for her. Too bad he had several heavy things to lay on her, but he was determined to get her alone where she had to face them—and him—and not slam any more doors.

"What year is this big thing?" she asked.

"It's '73 with a nifty V–8 engine, and I've come to take you for a spin, chick."

She laughed. "I told you, my Jeep will get us farther around here."

"Actually, I'd like to take you to dinner, too. The best Shelter has to offer."

"Arletta's?"

"The Tastee-Freez. A chili dog and any kind of cone or sundae you want—soft drink, too."

"Wow."

"Yeah, wow. Let's go get seen together and let them all talk. Even Delia. I don't care."

Their eyes met; she smiled and nodded before she started toward the house. Her willingness, even eagerness, thrilled him. "I'll have to take my beeper and phone, though," she called over her shoulder. "I'm keeping close tabs on two clients, a real nervous first-timer near Highboro and my cousin's wife, Lottie Weston, who's due in a couple of weeks and is on the verge of hypertension."

"So you're watching for pre-eclampsia?" he called, but she evidently didn't hear him as she hurried into the house. Besides, he thought, wiping fingerprints off the hood with a rag he kept under the front seat, the baby business had nothing to do with the things he had to ask her tonight.

On the way into town, Emma told him about Delia's change of heart at Sissy's shower. He was pleased, but didn't tell her that he wouldn't trust her. Anyhow, she knew Delia by now. He wanted to fill her in about J.G. and Sissy's impromptu visit and tell her he knew about her father and brother, but he wanted to keep this light at first. It would help if she'd learn to trust him.

"So what's your real car like?" she asked, glancing around at the imitation-leather interior.

"This *is* my only car, other than Delia's van," he admitted.

"It's true, then, that you came here only to pay off medical-school debts? Not a lick of humanitarianism for us hillbillies. See, we can call ourselves that but outsiders can't."

"And I'm still an outsider. I wondered when you'd

get around to wondering about me as I do about you. Yeah, medical school on top of some old business debts—I got into something once that went sour. Not to mention alimony payments when I decided at my advanced age to go to med school and my wife wouldn't wait for her version of the good life. That's over now, though—she's remarried, I mean.''

He hesitated for a moment. He'd almost told her the real reason he'd sold everything except this car and one suitcase of clothes—but he changed his mind.

"I can afford this restaurant, though," he said, forcing a smile.

"We could go dutch."

"No way. Around here, we're going Scots-Irish, which means we eat cheap, then drink beer at your place after.''

Too late, Emma realized she was caught. Hank Welling drove by, not once but twice, turning his head their way while she and Griff ate at one of the three wooden picnic tables in front of the Tastee-Freez. It reminded her of her high-school years when any kid who could get a car or truck on a Saturday night cruised repeatedly down Main Street, turning into the Tastee-Freez, then back out again in a ridiculous circle. Damn that maladjusted, eternal adolescent Hank, Emma cursed silently. Still, she felt so happy she didn't care who saw them—Hank, Delia, even the sheriff who she saw go slowly by.

"Why are we going this way?" she asked when they were back in the car and Griff turned north instead of south onto the highway. Her exuberant mood quickly deflated to unease.

"I've got a confession to make," he said. "And whether or not you make any to me doesn't matter."

"What?"

"Emma, I drove up to Cutshin earlier this week."

She twisted to face him. "Why?" she said, feeling panicked.

"I just wanted to see it. But before you try to get the sheriff to arrest me for trespassing—"

"That'll be the day. I'm way past trusting him to do anything for me."

He looked strangely pleased at that. "I just don't want you to quit trusting me, over this or anything. I thought we worked well together the night Clary's baby came," he explained, "and I'm available for further consultations."

Her panic at the mention of Cutshin waned. He was being supportive and even flirty, wasn't he? "Then I'll consider our elegant meal tonight your admission price to Cutshin. But why," she added, craning her neck to scan the road behind them, "are we turning up Mudbrook now?"

"Would you believe a nice night for a drive?"

She could have almost relaxed, but she couldn't rid herself of the feeling they were being watched or followed. Because of Hank, no doubt, or seeing the sheriff earlier. Or because this was just about where she was the day someone shot at her. Feeling more unsettled, she began wondering if she could really trust Griff as he'd asked. She sat facing stiffly forward, but each turn they took, she checked the rearview mirror.

Griff kept his eyes ahead, talking calmly as if he sensed her unease. "Do you know someone's been living up at Cutshin in the trailer?"

She gasped, then shook her head, as if to reassure

herself. "Folks know the place is deserted," she admitted. "It could be any hiker or hunter..."

"I agree, but your first thought was maybe your brother's back, right? Sissy told me about all that."

"So she said. But he'd be crazy to come back where the law would look. When I asked Sheriff Merrell to help me trace Amrine, he mentioned Jake more than once, so I'm sure he's checked there. The man never forgets an insult to his idea of law and order in *his* hills."

"If he checked Cutshin, he may have found something there besides Jake."

"Like what? Why are we here?" Emma was starting to get worried. "What if it was Jake and he's still around? You aren't taking this car all the way into the holler, are you?"

"Not clear in, but I'm not worried we'll find Jake. It looked like whoever was there left. And if he comes back and sees I've touched his things, he'll move."

"I'd still rather not stop here. Sorry, but this just isn't the place I'd choose for a nice Saturday-night outing."

Griff drove the car up the bumpy lane a short way to hide it from sight of the road before he killed the engine. He turned to face her, his hand sliding along the back of the seat to grip her shoulder.

"You stay pretty much away from here, don't you?" he asked.

"I check on it now and then and visit a lot in the fall when 'sang root is ready to harvest."

When he just nodded, she realized he'd been doing more research on her than she had imagined. That disturbed her but cranked her interest in him up a notch. She almost thought—hoped—he might embrace her, but instead he said, "Emma, I'm not accusing you of anything, but I saw patches of pot planted on the ridge overlooking the hollow, and I think you'd better get it out of there before somebody else sees it. Especially if the sheriff might check here for J—''

She was out of the car and striding up the lane before he caught up with her. "It's not yours, is it?" he demanded, pulling her around to face him. She tugged away and kept walking.

"Legally, if it's on my land," she threw back over her shoulder, already out of breath. "But hell no, it's not mine!"

"Listen," he said, grasping just her elbow this time. "I'd help you pull it out and burn it, but—"

"I'm going to bury it. I'd never burn anything here, not since the house went. There's a curse on this place, I swear there is, but I'm not selling out, no way, not on Cutshin and not on my so-called Baby Farm."

He took her to the edge of the ridge to point out the patch of pot. "What I was trying to say is," he explained, "I don't want to be found anywhere near illegal drugs—you understand. But I had to make sure you aren't caught with it, either."

"I'm not only concerned about repercussions on my license," Emma explained hastily. "If you're caught growing it on your property, the law can confiscate it— not only the pot, the property. Now, wouldn't Reg Merrell like to have that to hold over my head?"

"I didn't know," Griff said. "I should have told you sooner. But Sissy just told me about Jake the other day."

"It's not your fault, that pot patch, and—other things. I only hope to God it's not Jake's doing."

Emma was grateful that Griff was waiting on a vantage point overlooking both the road and the hollow, so he could let her know if he saw someone coming. It gave her time to calm down and realize she owed him for this warning. He had checked the trailer again, too, but yelled up to her that no one was there, though the spaghetti can and coffee cup he'd seen were gone.

Her skin had prickled when she heard that. She kept glancing into the darkening forest. That feeling of being watched weighed heavy on her again, but she was trying to tell herself it was just nerves. If Jake had not come after her by now, he wasn't coming back at all. Sure, a certain amount of torment might suit Jake. But he'd never been patient, unless prison had taught him that. That was her theory, at least, so she should stop worrying.

After she was done pulling up the plants, she washed her face and hands in the crick, then darted in to check the trailer. It was exactly as Griff had described: nothing proved Jake's presence.

"So much for that *cannabis dangerous*," she told Griff as they walked away from the trailer. She was feeling better already. His bringing her up here to get rid of the evidence of someone's deceit and contempt made her feel even closer to him. He had believed the plants were not hers, believed in her.

He stopped and sat under a tree, then patted the ground beside him. "So where did you bury the pot after you tore it up?"

She sank beside him, her back to the same tree, her legs bent to match his. "I stuffed it all down a big groundhog hole I found. That's going to be one high-flying groundhog."

They shared a little laugh before silence stretched between them again. "So why did the cabin burn?" he asked finally as they gazed down into the hollow. He took her hand and held it against his jeans-clad thigh. That scrambled her thoughts, and she had to concentrate on what she wanted to tell him.

"While Sissy and I were at school, someone set it from inside, torching beds and some curtains." She leaned her shoulder against his. "The sheriff never established who. I guess it could have been the Eubankses. Some said Hank Welling, since I'd just broken up with him, but I didn't believe that. Sissy said once maybe even Delia did it to make us come live with her because the two of us were hanging on here after Mama died. And please don't ask me about that—not tonight."

"Sure. I understand," he said, putting his arm around her so she settled against his chest instead of his arm. The man radiated strength and heat. And the way he'd said he understood—for some reason she believed him.

"Actually," she added, "whoever burned the place probably did it to hide the fact they'd ripped off most of the rare chestnut beams that made up our ceiling and doorways and evidently took the best old furniture, too. Unknown timber rustlers, Sheriff Merrell finally put in his report."

"So timber rustling's been going on a while in Appalachia?"

"It's been rampant for a decade or so. They cut down hardwood trees or rip wood out of old barns or houses to sell on the black market for upscale homes. But the rustlers don't usually burn buildings afterwards, since it calls attention to the theft. On some deserted farms or high woodlots, folks don't realize the wood is gone for months."

"I'm sorry, Emma, about everything bad that happened here, but surely there were good times, too. You could still make some good times here.''

She cuddled closer to him. The slant of his chin and bulk of his shoulder cupped her head perfectly as he turned toward her. Their thighs pressed together. She felt good, even here at Cutshin, safe in an unspoken bond, because for the first time she was certain that he, too, had a past he kept fenced off, maybe one he had to overcome. She didn't want to think about the past anymore, because it was right now that she wanted him.

A storm seemed to have started in her, shaking her to the core. She reached for Griff and clung to him. Their mouths met, then their chests as they sprawled under the tree in the thick tangle of grass. They rolled a little down the hill, bouncing, laughing. He lay partway on top of her, gazing down at her on their soft bed of leaves as dusk deepened.

She gazed up at him against the fading, spinning sky and clouds, memorizing his cheekbones and the little squint lines at the edge of his eyes that disappeared into thick sable lashes. With her index finger she traced the slight shadow of his beard line, feeling the rasp of his skin. His firm, moist lips opened, and he said, ''Damn, we're almost lying in poison ivy.''

That jolted her. ''I told you this place was a curse.''

''Let's go back to the car,'' he suggested. ''I don't want you to end up like Mike Bonner with this stuff all over your skin, though, of course, I wouldn't mind treating you for it—up close and personal.''

He stood and pulled her to her feet. ''You mean, play doctor?'' she asked as they walked down off the ridge toward the car, arms around each other's waists. This banter almost made her forget the feeling of being watched.

"With you, I'd play doctor anytime, anyplace." He laughed.

She felt herself blush, something she never did. She was warm all over despite the freshening breeze.

"I've got to admit," he said, sounding as nervous as she felt, "there are intriguing advantages to driving this big, old car."

"Easy to impress a date on a Saturday night—after the Tastee-Freez?"

"Wide single seats for good old-fashioned necking."

He unlocked the car and let her in while he went around to the driver's side. She felt not sixteen again, but dangerously adult, infatuated with possibilities. He slid closer. She clicked down the locks. Unlike in modern cars, no console with gearshifts separated them.

She welcomed his strength and need, letting her own desire sweep through her. He cradled her against him, his hand roving her back and waist. She bucked slightly to come closer as kisses and caresses made her senses spin.

She slid onto her back, her legs stretched along the seat by the steering wheel, while he sprawled partly beside her, partly over her. This man had been around; he was good at this. His mouth was everywhere along her jawline, down her throat, into the opening of her blouse and the damp valley between her breasts.

She ached toward him, her hands in his thick, short hair as he unbuttoned her blouse. He tugged it from her jeans and moved one hard hand to cup her rib cage, then her bra. His thumb skimmed the lacy top of it, dipping lower. When she moaned, he covered her mouth with his again and let his fingers work their wildness.

"Not enough room, even here," he whispered against

her ear. "I keep seeing that big, elevated bed back at your place…"

"The birthing bed? I don't know, this old car sure goes fast," she whispered with a throaty laugh. "But that just might be a possibility—someday when you really believe in the power of midwives."

"One of them, anyway," he breathed. "I already do!"

Her hands felt his solid back muscles that plunged to his narrow waist, and she kissed him until she was so dizzy that—

Bam! Bam! Suddenly the car shook and bounced.

Emma shrieked. The first thing that came to her mind was Jake.

"What the—" Griff sat and pulled her upright.

She yanked her blouse closed. It was dark outside but through the front windshield they'd steamed up, a big, blurry face peered in at them.

"Sheriff here! Now get the Sam hill outta there!"

Griff rolled down his window and stuck out his head and shoulders.

"Oh, doc, it's you," Reg Merrell said as he walked around to the driver's side. Emma saw him holster his pistol. "Didn't recognize the car and didn't have time to call the plate in. I been checking these parts now and again for an escaped felon and—that you in there, Emma?"

She was flushed and furious, but she fought for control. "That's right. Jake's not here, though, someone has been."

"Don't think I ain't looked around," the sheriff continued. "Took a coupla things to get them fingerprinted, too. By the way, got your note back from the lab and your prints are the only ones on it. I told you not to play sheriff.''

She held her breath, waiting for an accusation about the patch of marijuana, but there was only an awkward silence. She was tempted to tell him she had witnessed how he himself liked to play sheriff. She'd only use that information if she had no other option.

''Well,'' he added, ''guess it's still rightfully your land.''

''It is, sheriff,'' she said angrily. ''Though since I'm seldom here I can't control everything that goes on.''

''Looks like you was doing okay—what I could see through that steamed-up winder,'' he said, annoying her by muffling a snicker.

''Is that it, sheriff?'' Griff asked, his voice tight. ''If so, we'll be on our way.''

''Sure, go ahead. Does my heart good to know the teens 'round here don't have no monopoly on sweet-heartin'.''

Emma opened her mouth again to tell him he'd proved that himself at Amrine's, but again she kept quiet. She wanted to scream at him, about everything, but she had to keep control.

''He's always hated us,'' she said, leaning to her side of the car after Griff cranked up his window and drove away. ''He's the first one who said nothing good ever came out of Cutshin.''

''The man's an idiot,'' Griff muttered. ''*You* came out of Cutshin.''

11

Emma drove slowly, with her headlights on, but once she started up Mudbrook, she didn't worry about meeting another car. No one would be out at this hour. By dawn she had worked herself into a tizzy about that pot being planted on her land. What if there was more of it Griff hadn't spotted? With Sheriff Merrell lurking around looking for Jake, he might stumble upon it and confiscate the land. She wasn't worried about Jake being there. He'd always had a certain natural cunning, so surely his own home was the last place he'd go to hide out. That can and cup must have been left by some drifter or hunter.

She found the Cutshin farm lane almost by feel and didn't drive in very far. If she didn't hate guns so much, she would have liked to have had one with her this morning. If she needed protection, she'd have to make do with the butcher knife she'd brought with her to chop down any more marijuana plants she found.

As she hiked in, she took heart in the fact that the day was brightening. Starting on the far side of the ridge from where she'd pulled up the pot last night, she walked the familiar twists and turns. Thank God, there seemed to be no more marijuana, but her secret 'sang patches looked pretty good considering they were so young. She retraced her steps to the site of the single patch of pot she'd found, then decided to clean it up a bit more. Putting her backpack down, she hacked at a few of the stems that were left. All she needed was to have them resprout later. She stamped down the mess she'd made, then picked the thick red soil from her soles with the big knife point.

And then she saw it. A bare place that looked like a small grave.

She stared silently at the rectangular plot. It, too, had been stamped upon and not by her. The feet that had done this were a man's—the prints were large and there was a distinct design, probably from running shoes. She wondered if Griff had seen the bare place when he was here the other day and stamped it down for some reason.

But what really upset her was a memory of Jake. When he was young, he used to bury animals he shot for fun in a tiny graveyard just down this ridge; he even put up crude crosses sometimes.

As she stood, frozen in thought, the day went darker. The lurking fog reached out to envelop her. It leaned into her, holding her here, pressing her down. She scanned the silent trees. The hair prickled on the back of her neck and along her arms and wrists under her jacket. Her stomach clenched.

She wanted to run, but that had never been her way. Instead, looking all around, listening intently, she knelt and, in a frenzy, began to dig with her knife blade.

The soil came up in red clods. Below, it was packed looser. She cut the base of her little finger when the blade hit something, but she ignored it and kept digging, more carefully. She snagged something again, dropped the knife and began to dig with her hands.

Mama had wanted to bury Sissy's baby here with the nice view, but family graveyards weren't allowed any-more, and the little mite had been buried in the church graveyard in town. With Amrine and her baby missing, and Ola gone, she wondered again how and where their babies were.

Her hand touched something. She shrieked, though the fog seemed to muffle the sound. Something small buried...

She gasped.

Side by side lay a tiny raccoon and a skunk. The skunk still had its little nurse's cap tied to its head with twine. She saw no cradle coffin, no cross. But the fact that they had been buried here—

She scraped the earth back in place with first the knife, then her feet, and stomped it down. In five minutes, she was in her Jeep, driving much too fast downhill through the hovering fog.

"Now get out of here, all of you," Trish ordered. "At least until I've got these shish kebabs ready for the grill." She made shooing motions as if her guests were the herd of cows that bordered the farthest fence of Bonner land. "Then, Michael dearest," she called after them, "you and Griff can grill while Emma and I get the table set. Go on and show Emma what we're doing to that swing of hers in the barn."

Emma, Griff and Mike trooped outside with their wineglasses. "Have you seen all the things they're working their magic on out here?" Emma asked Griff as Mike slid open one side of the big double door of the old barn they had rebuilt and repainted. Evening sunlight slanted into the crowded space, highlighting floating dust motes and the jumble of furniture inside: chairs, tables, bureaus, mantelpieces and headboards in various stages of rot or restoration. They wandered through the crooked aisles of chaos.

"Did I tell you, Emma," Mike was asking, "we're going to hire and train some locals to strip and refinish these for us? We can't keep up with it ourselves."

"That's great. Maybe some local craft jobs will keep our young people from leaving the area."

Griff watched as the sun silhouetted Emma's shapely legs through her long, azure skirt. The full hem shifted around her sandaled feet. To his amazement, she'd done her toenails pink. He thought she looked softer and more vulnerable even with the touch of mascara and eye shadow that brought out her huge, brown eyes. Unfortunately, she had shadows under them, too. Gold hoop earrings glinted against her sleek hair. The effect was light-years away from jeans and running shoes. Last night, he'd taken her home, and they'd just talked after Sheriff Merrell's brazen interruption. But tonight, who knew?

"Over here," Mike was saying, "is the old porch swing, but I think it's just mountain ash. It might not be worth restaining, but we'll spray it white to match your wicker."

"Which I still intend to pay you for," Emma insisted.

"No way." Mike downed the rest of his wine and set the goblet on a water-damaged chest of drawers. He frowned at the two of them, though Griff knew it was from some thought of his own. "Wish we could take it out in trade," Mike went on, "because Trish would still like a child. But adopting a kid through legitimate channels takes so long we'd be hobbling around with canes by then."

Griff glanced at the back section of the barn which, at one time, must have been horse or cattle stalls. New wood closed it in, though it matched this old stuff pretty well. Mike had said it was a receiving room for junk and had quickly shoved the door closed when Griff had accidently leaned against it when he'd been here picking furniture for his bedroom above the clinic. Today, before he could ask if Mike had cleaned the area out, Trish rang the big dinner bell, and they headed toward the house.

"Gentlemen, start your kebabs," Trish said, flapping a checkered tablecloth like a racing flag. Griff thought she was a hoot, though, in his experience, people who were always on sometimes hid dark things.

"You won't believe this, Emma," Trish said, "but your beeper went off a moment before I rang the bell."

"Uh-oh. I should have carried it with me. Excuse me a minute, everybody, but I've got to check on this."

Griff watched Trish hand Emma the beeper and hover close while she checked it. "It's Ruth Wicklow's number in Highboro," Emma said. "That's a farther drive than my other patients, my cousin Rooster and his wife Lottie."

"Rooster?" Mike mouthed to Trish as Emma called her client on the Bonners' cell phone from the porch. Griff watched her; she looked as disappointed as he felt that she might be leaving. He only half listened to Mike quietly quizzing Trish about why someone would be named Rooster.

"Because a lot of them have wacko nicknames," she explained in a low voice. "Emma said he's red-haired and always had a cowlick sticking straight up, so that's enough around here." She rolled her eyes. "You know, diagonally parked in a parallel universe. Those Westons are the ones about to have their sixth baby after five girls."

"Now I told you," Emma said into the phone, "there's no such thing as calling me too soon. I'll be right there. What? Think of it as practice labor, not false labor. Sure, the body does it for a couple of real good reasons, and we'll talk about that. Right, in about a half hour.''

Griff couldn't think of one good reason for false labor, especially when it just got everyone stirred up—doctor and patient—too early, but he should have known Emma would have a midwife answer that calmed her clients.

Trish said, ''Emma, you should have made it forty-five minutes so you could eat and then run, but I'm packing you some of these appetizers. And if it's a false alarm, you get her settled down and come back. We'll hold dessert.''

''I'm sorry to run, to miss this,'' Emma said, and Griff's stomach clenched when she looked directly at him. ''But don't you dare wait for me, because you never know.''

When Griff finally pried her loose from Trish's questions about Ruth Wicklow, he walked her to her Jeep.

''In her next life, Trish wants to be a midwife,'' Emma told him, as if to apologize for her friend, ''though she's seen the disadvantages.'' He opened her car door, then closed it, leaning in to put his elbows on the bottom of the open window.

''I know being on call is tough,'' Griff commiserated. ''I was like a zombie in residency. I could sleep standing up. But if you don't make it back tonight, there will be other nights when the only emergency will be how we feel about each other.''

She looked speechless for once, though he had the distinct feeling she was upset about something and wanted to tell him. This woman was really starting to get to him. She only nodded, avoided his eyes, then looked directly up at him.

"About tonight—besides us, I mean. The funny thing is that sometimes I get almost psychic about when a baby's due. I feel that now, though this sounds like false labor."

"You're on edge because of Amrine and Ola and because things got so wild when Clary delivered."

"No, that's not it. Ruth's a nervous Nellie and her pains are totally incoordinate, *and* she's early, but I just feel it's time for a baby and that she—someone—really needs me."

He took her hand off the steering wheel and leaned farther in to kiss her palm. "Good luck to my favorite midwife."

He sensed she was going to tell him something else, but she didn't. He watched as she pulled away, then went back to help Trish and Mike make supper for three.

"I'm glad she's found something in her life besides her career," Trish told Griff as Mike handed him another glass of wine. "C.N.M.s can burn themselves out in ten years, and she's working on it, agonizing over lost clients to the detriment of herself and others."

"Red alert, red alert, Dr. Cusak," Mike said, pretending to speak into the end of an upturned kebab as if it were a microphone. "Trish says the rate of divorce among midwives is high, and I can see why."

"Mi-ike," Trish protested, swatting at him. "You don't have to repeat everything I tell you. But," she added, taking Griff's arm and smiling while she wagged a finger at him, "you're just what the doctor ordered for her."

* * *

"I want Emma! I want Emma here. Len, you promised. Emma wouldn't do it like this!"

Amrine could still hear her own screams, echoing in her head. The contractions had come so hard, so close. Her water had broken, then pain broke her in two. The pain will be worse, Emma had said, if you don't relax, but how could she? Len had brought her to this place called the Southern Pregnancy Service. A nurse named Mary Lou had hooked her up to a fetal monitor, and they had restrained her and put a needle in her arm.

"No!" she had screamed. "No restraints. No drugs!"

Even now, she hurt, groggy, still on Demerol, though it had dulled the pain. Dulled it everywhere but in her heart.

Suddenly she remembered the worst of her ordeal. She had signed her name on some sort of paper they had thrust at her. *Amrine Settle,* she had scrawled. Signed her initials *A.S.* on something, too, because Len said she had to, some sort of paper to allow the baby to be treated in a hospital if there were any complications... Complications...

She fought to clear her mind. Her eyes flew open to face a new nightmare. She'd had her baby! That muted crying—it was a baby, *her* baby, not her own voice pleading anymore. Dear God, help me find my baby, she prayed as her eyes darted around the tiny, dim room with the pockmarked ceiling she remembered hovering over the nurse's head.

"No!" Amrine whispered, but the realization hit her hard. Once she'd gone into labor, Len had talked adoption. Too expensive to have a kid, he'd said, and she sure as hell wasn't going back to Shelter to that shack to raise it alone. His plans had come as a complete shock to her. She'd never considered it, not giving away

her flesh and blood, though Mike Bonner had jokingly
called his buying her antiques as adopting them and had
paid her good for them, too. But that money was long
gone now.

"Len!" she cried, or at least thought she did. But no
one came. Voices and a baby's cries drifted from somewhere else.

With great effort she raised her head to look down at
the fetal monitor. But it had turned into some sort of
Velcro strap wrapped around her middle as if to keep
her here. Her arms and legs were free, at least.

She jerked her arm to stop the Demerol drip. Did that
nurse think she was too stupid to read the word *Demerol*
on the hanging plastic pack? She and Emma had talked
about lots of things, and *not* using drugs like Demerol
was one of them. Then she saw she'd already somehow
yanked the needle from her vein. Maybe that's why the
pain had waked her up.

She could hear Len talking to someone, and she
strained to make out what he was saying. She needed
to get closer. Weak and shaky, she sat up and fumbled
to rip away the Velcro tie. She slid to the edge of the
cold, metal delivery table. Under the hospital gown, she
wore only panties and packing, but she didn't stop to
search for her clothes. This was nothing like what
Emma had promised her. Mary Lou had not acted like
a midwife, not like a supporter and helper.

She careened across the small space to lean against
the wall. Creeping along it to the door, she managed to
turn the knob. She was not locked in.

"So how's good old Shelter?" she heard Len say.
"Yeah, like you said, signed, sealed and delivered."

He must be on the phone to someone in Shelter. Calling his parents to tell them about the baby? But, delivered? That sounded as if he was talking to Emma.

"No," his voice went on, even louder now. "I ain't takin' no damn trip to Disney World. Screw you, lady. You want me goin' to the law—I mean to cops *not* bein' paid off—or to those noon news bastards around here? Five thousand cash, and Mary Lou here wants her thousand in small bills this time. Huh? Yeah, you got it." He slammed the phone down.

Trying to make sense of the tumble of words, Amrine peeked through the crack in the door. She saw a series of small rooms, with Len and the nurse standing in the second one. And in the adjoining room that separated Amrine from them, lay a baby in a low, clear plastic bassinet fussing and kicking against a small pastel quilt, its red face screwed up, ready to cry again.

Suddenly, nothing, no one else mattered. Amrine lunged for her baby.

"You know," Mary Lou was saying, "despite the messy means, I feel the ends are justified. Your daughter will go to a well-to-do family who really wants her, so—"

"Yeah, well, the bitch says," Len interrupted, "she's gonna have the carrier here in a coupla hours. Can you give Amrine somethin' to keep her out longer? And check her, 'cause I don't want to take no chances she'll start bleedin' again like she did when I hauled her out of Shelter. Who knows but missin' this kid, she might not be willin' to let me plant another one in her."

Trembling with mingled rage and tenderness, Amrine picked up the baby and cradled her against her breasts. The mite felt as if she weighed a ton. She'd face them down, Amrine resolved, she'd die before she'd give up her baby to some carrier.

But the thing was, she was pretty sure who "the bitch" was. Len hated Emma, and he'd called her that more than once before, even to her face. And who else but Emma knew that she would be alone and in pain after she sent the Poteet boy for her? Len had said Emma had located him and told him to take good care of Amrine and the baby, so who else but Emma knew where they were now? *Delivered... like you said.* Those were Len's words on the phone to Shelter just now. She had trusted Emma, but there was no one to trust now.

Amrine pressed against the side wall of the small room, rocking the child, ready to claw her way out when they came for her. But something as hard as Len's rifle barrel pressed into the small of her back and she spun to see a second door. A closet or a way out?

She turned the knob and found herself in a dim hall. Barefoot in her flapping gown, her newborn in her arms, she staggered toward the bloodred exit sign.

"Give me one good reason I should be in such pain if I haven't really started labor," Ruth Wicklow whined, gripping her husband Jess's hand so hard Emma saw him wince. "If that was just practice labor, I'll never handle the real thing, never."

Emma was both surprised and dismayed that Ruth was carrying on so because her contractions had been widely spaced, more like cramps, and had soon stopped. Besides, Ruth worked as the receptionist at Highboro Hope Hospital, where she must have learned to keep calm through a crisis, not to mention that she'd been around doctors and nurses enough to know coping skills. Her husband owned and operated the only health food store in Highboro, so he was into natural health care and extremely supportive. But, obviously, Emma's early concerns that it was Jess who wanted natural childbirth, and not Ruth, might be coming home to roost.

"First, Ruth," Emma said, moving her chair closer to where the Wicklows perched on the edge of their bed, "the easier type of premature-labor pains, which sound like what you had—"

"How can you judge that?" Ruth snapped, dabbing at tears with her free hand. "You didn't get here till they quit."

"—were most likely just the baby's head engaging or some cervical softening," Emma went on in her best soothing voice, deciding to ignore the accusation. "That's absolutely good. And if you'd had the harder type, with contractions coming closer to ten minutes apart rather than twenty before they petered out, that would indicate your uterine muscles are flexing and strengthening for the birth later."

"Do you think my muscles aren't flexed and strong enough?"

"I think a hot bath and sleep will put you back on track by tomorrow morning." Emma could feel her self-control slipping. She was juggling too much lately to keep calm through all this. "Why don't you do that? You're not dilated and your water never broke, so relaxing is going to really help here."

"Mmm," Ruth murmured, sniffing. "Easy for you to say, not having gone through this yourself."

There it was, Emma thought, the criticism she dreaded most because it was true. The chink in her armor—that and the sometimes crippling fear she tried to keep at bay that she could lose another baby someday the way she had Sissy's.

"But think how many births I've seen," Emma cajoled, fighting to keep her voice calm. "And if I find myself a good man, I assure you, I'd love to experience this beautiful miracle for myself from the other side."

"I didn't mean it like that," Ruth said as her husband helped her stand. Emma rose to give her a quick, reassuring hug. "Not saying you're over the hill or something."

Emma packed her things while she listened to Jess's and Ruth's muted voices in the adjoining bathroom, then water gushing into the tub. Still, Emma couldn't shake the feeling that Ruth had really needed her, that the birth was imminent—and she'd been wrong.

Jess came out to walk her downstairs. "Sorry you had to stay so long, psyching her up," he apologized, shaking his head. "But I've got to tell you, her friend Pam Stark, who used to work at Hope, has been after Ruth to switch over to Dr. Cusak since she's working with him now. Ruth said he's the one who suggested it, though Mrs. Lowe weighed in on it, too."

Emma almost stumbled and grabbed the banister before Jess could steady her. Was it possible Griff could be trying to steal another client? And here she'd told Mabel Poteet to take Wade to see him. Maybe she'd been a bit too starry-eyed lately, taken in by Griff's support and personal allure, as well as Delia's supposed change of heart. She'd actually believed she'd swayed Griff, at least partly, to her beliefs. Like an idiot, she thought she had lured him, too, seduced him, even a little, when he and Delia could have been amusing themselves by pirating her clients in a more underhanded way.

For the first time, she wondered if, since Griff knew more about her than she had ever guessed before, he could be using some of her past against her. Maybe he'd warned her about the pot to make her trust him. Maybe, also, he was on a campaign of terror to scare her away with nurse-skunks and dead raccoons. Griff had found that pot and could have stomped those running-shoe patterns into the soil. How well did she really know him, anyway?

She shook her head to clear it. No, dead animals was not Griff's style any more than it was Delia's. She was letting her fears run away with her.

She cleared her throat, but her voice still broke. "It hurts me to say this, Jess, but Ruth, and you, must do what you think is best."

"I think," he said as he held the downstairs door open for her, "as uncomplicated—and undrugged—as possible, that's best."

Emma turned to face him on the lighted porch. "Do me two favors, please. One, talk to Ruth about what *she* really wants, and I'll come out sometime tomorrow to do the same. *She* has to believe in what *she's* chosen."

"Sure. Right. What else?"

"Get her to eat a lot of high-calcium food. Yogurt—you know that with your background."

"Got it. In other words, without saying so, keep her tolerance threshold for pain high, right?"

"Right," she called to him as she waved and walked away, out of the pool of light, to her Jeep. But she didn't feel right about anything on this night that had begun so well. She could see and feel those dead animal eyes still staring at her.

12

On the dark road home, a pair of eyes glowed gold, then demonic red. Startled, the doe froze in the headlights.

Emma's fears leaped to life. Those eyes... Although Emma knew it was safer to hit the doe than swerve, she turned the wheel and stomped on the brakes.

And careened into blackness.

How long the deep void lasted she wasn't sure. At first, she thought Jake was staring at her with those hellfire eyes, staring in her windows. Like when he was a kid, when he'd covered himself with the dissected, still-glowing bodies of lightning bugs so he glimmered in the dark when he'd jump out and scare her and Sissy while Pa just laughed. His eyes burned just like that when he stood up in court and screamed she'd killed Sissy's baby, as good as killed Pa and Cory Eubanks, killed him...

Emma's eyes jerked open. The Jeep was tilted in the ditch, with its lights out. Her head hurt. Seat belt or not, her forehead must have hit the steering wheel. For one moment when she opened her eyes, she actually saw stars, spinning, falling stars like eyes.

She shuddered and pulled herself back from the depths. Her door was wedged shut in the ditch. Dragging her midwife kit, she climbed out of the tipped Jeep from the passenger side. She hoped she had not hit the doe. The car didn't seem dented, and she saw nothing on the road where the animal had been.

She knew she'd need help to get the Jeep out. Thank God, she realized, she was near the Bonners' place. She could see the house and barn across the field from here through low-lying fog. She squinted to make out a single glowing light, though it seemed to be coming from the barn and not the house. Trish had said to come back but it must be too late now. Emma was grateful she was remembering things, because she didn't want a concussion.

She hefted her precious kit over her shoulder and began to trudge up the lane. Breathing hard, she decided halfway in to cut across the rolling field of wheat stubble. At least she was still capable of making decisions, she assured herself. The stubble seemed to snatch at her feet, but it was shorter this way.

After a while, she got confused, tried to recall where she was and why. Oh, that's right, someone had shot at the Jeep to blow her tires out, and she had to hike in to help Amrine. She set a faster pace.

As she got closer, she realized this was not the Settles' farm, but the Bonners'. Had Trish sent for her? She had to try to be brave, even if Jake and Sam, maybe J.G. and now Hank, too, hated her and were hiding somewhere out here.

She stopped for a moment and stared at the Bonners' big barn through patches of waist-high fog. Fog, just like this morning at Cutshin. But why had she been there? Maybe, she reasoned, she was here now to get the other piece of wicker or the swing.

She stopped behind a clump of maples about ten yards away. Standing in a single floodlight behind the barn were two men. Why behind it? Why not in it or at the house?

It was Mike—and J.G. Why was J.G here? What about his back?

"All right," Mike's voice carried to her, "here's your cut. Let's hope the next haul's closer. Here's the hush money for the others."

He was counting bills into J.G.'s open hand. J.G. said something she couldn't catch.

"And you'd better watch this sneaking out at night," Mike went on. "You've got your wife to take care of soon."

Emma suddenly realized she was not alone in this little copse. A shadowy figure ahead of her shifted from behind a tree trunk so his silhouette was in her line of vision. He didn't see her, as he was looking at the men, too. His glasses glinted in the reflected light. Hank! It was Hank.

Click, click, she heard. *Click, click.*

She tried to place the sound, then realized Hank was taking photos though there was no flash.

But in her confusion the *click, click* became the *bam, bam* of a gun. She saw clearly Hank had only a camera, but she threw herself down beside her duffel bag.

She huddled behind the tree as Hank turned toward her, then walked right past, carrying his camera, to be swallowed by the fog and night. She let herself fall into it, too, that deep, drifting darkness.

"Emma, come on, honey. Emma..." A man's warm voice curled around her, pulling her back from the cold void.

She sniffed a sharp smell. Ammonia capsule. She jerked alert. Her eyes flew open. She lay outside on the ground under a tree, covered with a blanket, staring up at Mike and Griff. Griff had called her honey.

"Where…"

"It's all right," he said. "Your Jeep's in the ditch, and Mike found you here this morning. I think you have a concussion so we're going to sit you up right here and check you out."

Despite the blanket, she was cold. The fog was gone, except in her head. Dew coated her skin and hair. "I'm all right," she insisted as Griff sat her up against the tree. "I remember I swerved to miss a deer. Those eyes…" She shook her head, but that hurt too much and she lifted her hands to her temples.

"What else do you remember?" Mike asked, kneeling down beside her, too. "Why didn't you walk to the house instead of the barn?"

"I don't know. Where's Trish?"

"She went to our Highboro house pretty early this morning," Mike explained, "and evidently didn't see your Jeep in the ditch. I'm the one who sent for Griff."

"I'm going to shine a light in your eyes to check your pupil reaction," Griff was saying, sounding all business. "Try to follow the light. I can't believe you hiked that whole field with a concussion."

The tiny beam of light pierced her eyes and brain. Emma tried to follow it, to follow her own train of thought. Her head started to pound again. She couldn't recall what had happened after she hit her head last night. Right now, one hand on her shoulder to steady her, Griff was holding a cold compress to the contusion. The compress felt good, but she wasn't going to fall into the trap of trusting him again. She had a big bone to pick with him over trying to pirate her client. She was both relieved and sad she remembered that.

"Your ocular reflexes are good," Griff told her, "but you're going to have to keep quiet and rest for a few days."

"I can't. I said I'd go back to talk to Ruth Wicklow today, and I need to check on Lottie. Her hypertension needs monitoring."

"And so do you," Griff said, his voice harsh. "I'll take you back to your place, but if Lottie or anybody else needs help today they're going to get Dr. Cusak instead of Midwife Weston."

"Oh, no, they're n—"

"I'm on call Mondays. You do know it's Monday, don't you?"

"Of course. I'm fine," she insisted as both men helped her up. She swayed into Griff. "Just tired and hungry, that's all."

"So, Griff," Mike said as he carried the blanket and her duffel bag toward the clinic van, "do memories ever come back *in toto* after minor trauma like this?"

"You never know," Griff replied as he got her situated in the passenger seat, even fastening her seat belt. "Anyway, only if there's a serious wreck or a crime committed is it of much importance."

The policeman put a long, plastic raincoat around her. Though the rain had stopped, it was cold and wet. Amrine had been staggering in exhaustion through the streets, trying to stay off the main drag, get away from Len, find someplace to hide.

For some reason, it popped into her head to tell these officers she couldn't remember who she was, but then they might try to take the baby from her. So she said only, "My husband don't want our new baby. I birthed her on my own. Please, is there someplace I can stay, just for now?''

The officer who had swept the raincoat around her looked so serious, but the other, older officer's stern face softened as he peered at the sleeping child she held so tight to her.

"Sure, ma'am, sure, a shelter for abused women. But we'd better get the both of you looked at in the hospital. Then maybe you have other family or a friend we can call for you."

His words clanged in her head: abused...shelter... friend. If Len had been talking to Emma, her friend was involved in some kind of baby-adoption scheme. Amrine just couldn't believe it, but she could not risk calling Emma or trusting her anymore.

Now with a little one to feed, when she could hardly feed herself, Amrine knew she'd never stand on her own feet, as Emma always put it. Always preaching, always pushing, but she'd loved Emma—still did. Only now she hated her, too.

The rain began again, and she started to sob. The baby began to wail.

The first officer opened the back door of the squad car and the older one helped her in, putting his hand on her head so she wouldn't bump it. The gesture felt like a blessing, like that time in Shelter she got baptized.

She felt safe until she heard the older officer say as they stood outside the car, "There's something really fishy here. We're gonna have to question her, haul somebody in."

The officers got in the front seat and turned up their heater full blast. Using their lights but not the siren, they pulled away into the black, wet night.

* * *

"Midwives need sleep when they can get it," Emma argued.

"Midwives with concussions need to stay awake to be watched," Griff countered. He was sitting in the wicker rocking chair on the porch, sipping coffee. "If your headache continues to lessen, you can sleep tonight. And I repeat, I did not put my new nurse up to trying to take Ruth Wicklow away from you. What Delia did, I don't know."

"You've got that right," Emma muttered. She'd been pacing, trying to remember something just out of her reach, something about last night. Now, admitting exhaustion, she was perched on the porch railing. She felt so nervous, so pent up.

"And the only reason," she went on, "I told Rooster he could bring his whole brood here this afternoon for Lottie's prenatal when you're still here is that I know my cousins are loyal enough they can't be talked out of trusting me."

"You must be feeling better," Griff groused. "You're back to being as suspicious as ever. Sad, though, if it takes family loyalty to get and keep clients."

"Better that than Delia's heavy-handed approach to dragging people in. Just remember that Lottie Weston is extremely shy, so don't get her shook up. I've known her for years, and that's what it takes here for trust."

"Obviously," he said, his voice cold. "I can tell where I'm not wanted, even if I am needed, whether my patient knows it or not."

Because the five little Weston girls, age ten and under, were impossible to keep quiet, Emma escorted Lottie up to her bedroom to take her blood pressure and run other tests while Rooster and Griff kept the kids from tearing things up below.

But Emma was worried. Lottie's puffy face showed fluid retention, and she'd complained her wedding band had become too tight. Many pregnant women had swollen ankles, but the swollen hands and face were signs of trouble. Griff had given Emma an eagle-eyed look that almost shouted, *She's borderline toxemic* even before this urine test Emma was studying confirmed the same.

"Lottie," she began, coming out of the bathroom to perch next to her on the bed, "I know it won't be easy with all the food you've got to fix for the troops, but you're going to have to change your ways until this baby comes."

"Like what?" Lottie asked. She seemed barely to be listening, cocking her head as if to follow the shouts of the kids outside where the men must have taken them. She nervously wedged her left thumbnail in the space between her two front teeth and scratched at the freckles on her nose, almost as if she were sucking her thumb.

"Like going on a low-salt diet," Emma told her. "Veggies, egg yolks only, fruits and cereals—and for protein, more meat than you usually get. No prepared foods, snacks and desserts like that junk food the kids like and you end up eating. I know how it is."

"Laws, I thought you was my friend."

"That's exactly why I'm telling you that your blood pressure is too high, teetering right at the danger level."

"But it ain't there. That's good, right?"

"That's good, but we can't let it go. If it climbs from this level of mild toxemia to pre-eclampsia, that's real trouble. Full-fledged eclampsia can mean serious complications for you and the baby—I mean bad.''

''E-clamp-sia. Like something clamping down on my belly? One of us could die?''

''We won't let that happen,'' Emma reassured her, ''because we're going to watch what you eat and get you on a diuretic, too. But you know what I'd really like to try if you give me the go-ahead?''

''Starvation?'' Lottie suggested with a rueful shake of her head. ''Laws, I'm just hungry all the time.'' She stood slowly and looked out the window. Her hair was not the russet of Rooster's but strawberry blond, and their little girls were all carrot-topped.

''I want to give Rooster a son,'' she was saying, speaking more slowly than usual. ''And this one's settin' different from the others, so's I have hopes. But if this one ain't, I'm going in to have my tubes tied, like you said. You think that nice doctor'd do that for me?''

''Dr. Cusak? It's a small incision. I suppose he would. But what would you think about a real rest leading up to the baby's birth, if I could arrange it? In Highboro, close to the hospital,'' she proposed, standing to walk over to her.

''What?'' Lottie squealed, jerking her head around. ''You not deliver me here, you mean?''

''I'd be there all the way. But I'd want you completely monitored when you give birth. Rooster could still be there, and the hospital will give a midwife permission to attend the birth when the mother requests it. If I can arrange it, I think Trish Bonner would let you stay in their house in Highboro for your last week or however many days you have yet.''

''I couldn't.'' Lottie shook her head. ''I know they're

rich and the house they got 'round here's big enough—''

"Listen to me. Trish has volunteered to help Sissy, and I know she would help you. You wouldn't even have to stay in the big house because they've built a nice little one by their pool. And one of the things recommended for mild toxemia is long periods of rest, lying on your left side and afternoon naps. Now are you going to manage rest and naps at home?''

"No way. But what about my girls?''

"Since Rooster's been doing that telemarketing out of your place, he'd be around home. I'll bet the neighbors would pitch in with the girls,'' she added, wishing Delia had already started that day-care center she'd mentioned. "I'd visit Highboro every day to check on you and bring Rooster with me the moment you go into labor—''

"Tell me true,'' Lottie said, seizing Emma's shoulders. "What can happen if I get worse?''

"You could have convulsions or go into a coma,'' Emma said, looking her straight in the eye. She knew no one else talked to Lottie as she did, since people thought the woman was slow. "Ten percent of eclampsia mothers die, and for sure there'd be fetal distress in the delivery.''

"I can't lose this baby, Emma. I think it's a boy. Just wish I knew.''

"We could get Dr. Cusak to take an ultrasound to check it out,'' Emma blurted before she could snatch the words back. But her own battles with Griff didn't matter if he could help Lottie in any way.

"Yeah, I'd like that. A picture of him, 'case somethin' bad happens, and a real nice stay at the Bonners' if she'll take me in. And you come to visit me a lot. Laws, who could ask for more…''

"I'll there for you, Lottie," Emma vowed, hugging her. But it scared her that she'd promised Amrine and Ola the same.

"I don't care how much you fuss," J.G. told Emma the next day when he picked Sissy up at her place. "I'm payin' you for those earlier checkups for Sis, and you're not chipping in on the specialist, neither."

Emma would have argued, but for the sharp tone of his voice and Sissy's shooting her a warning look as she climbed in the truck beside J.G. Emma bit her lip as her brother-in-law counted out new bills into her palm through the open truck window.

Something hovered in her memory then, something she wanted to recall, but it seemed just out of reach. She was probably flashing back to that fifty-dollar bill Amrine had left when she'd gone off with Len, she reasoned.

"I'm glad," Emma told him, "your back's better. It's good to see you driving."

"Yeah? Well, you'd help me out a lot more if you'd throw poor Hank a bone once in a while. He sees me trying to garden or driving, he says, 'Hey, maybe the disability payments can be tapered off, huh, buddy?'"

"Some buddy," Sissy put in. "Besides, Emma can date who she wants, and she told Hank no years ago. I think Griff Cusak is—well, more her type these days. Just like Miss Delia, Emma's bettered herself."

Before Emma could deny having any designs on Griff, J.G. said, "You know, Emma, I always thought you and Delia, being our betters with all the answers, had a lot in common, with your big ideas for changing things, changing people. So why can't you two get along?''

Emma knew she should keep quiet, but she said, ''I'd like to give the same advice to you. I thought you were really serious about keeping calm for this baby, so Sissy can keep calm, too.''

In answer, he stepped on the gas and roared out of the driveway. He might as well have been spitting that gravel and dust straight at her. Why, every time she tried to help someone, did something go so wrong?

The morning Emma drove Rooster and Lottie into Highboro, where they were going to leave Lottie at the Bonners', they stopped first at the Shelter Health Center, where Griff gave Lottie an ultrasound.

''It's new equipment,'' Griff told the prone Lottie with his hand on her shoulder while Rooster stood on her other side and Emma at her feet. Pam Stark darted everywhere in the room, efficiently busy.

''I'm using you as the inaugural test here, Mrs. Weston,'' Griff went on, ''so there won't be a charge for this today. Just relax. Nurse Pam is going to put some ultrasound gel on you, and I'm going to touch your belly with this magic wand called a transducer.''

''A magic wand, like the one that turned Cinderella into a princess,'' Lottie said, smiling at him shyly.

Again Emma admitted to herself he had a comforting way with patients. Too bad, she thought with real regret, she might never know if that bedside manner could work in more personal ways.

''Ooh, that stuff feels cold!'' Lottie said as Pam rubbed the gel on her. She lay bared from below her breasts to her pubic line, though amazingly, Emma thought, despite this being her sixth child and near due date, she was not as big as Emma would have expected. Skinny to start with, she was somehow holding the baby tight.

"Let's all look at the screen," Griff said as he began to move the transducer across her belly. "There, now!"

"Oh," Lottie said, craning her neck to squint at the screen. "Looks like one of them old black-and-white TV sets, with all that snow 'cause you can't get good pictures in the hills. Laws, there he is!"

Although grainy, the three-dimensional silhouette of a baby emerged from a black background. Goose bumps peppered Emma's arms. This thrill of new life—it was part of why she was a midwife. Now, if only the baby would be born healthy.

Rooster reached for Lottie's hand and squeezed it while they all stared at the screen. Pam annoyed Emma by leaning in front of her. She was tempted to push an elbow into her, but instead moved around the other side of the examining table.

"Lively as can be in there, Rooster," Emma said. "Look at that leg action!"

"But not," Griff said, shifting the transducer again, "in the position we want, to be able to tell the sex. Lottie, why don't you shift slightly onto your side. Nurse Pam will help you."

The minute he'd said that, Emma could tell he regretted it. "Emma, too," he added, avoiding her eyes.

"There!" Griff cried. "Did you see that? I think you have a boy there."

"Didn't see much but the little feller moving his leg again," Rooster said, leaning closer over Lottie. "Guess it takes your eye to see things clear, doc."

"Did you see it, Emma?" Griff asked excitedly.

"I'm not trained with ultrasound," she answered

evenly. "It went by too fast and now he's unreadable again."

Griff frowned and didn't meet her eyes. When they got no more definitive results, he asked Pam to sponge Lottie off and stepped into the hall with Emma while Rooster stayed behind. Griff put his shoulder against the wall and looked at Emma earnestly, almost eagerly.

"I know it was quick," he told her, his voice low, "but I saw male genitals, I'm sure."

"I believe you believe that," Emma said, crossing her arms over her chest. "But sometimes we see things that aren't really there. Lottie's record for girls is one hundred percent, the previous birth weights were light, and this baby is not big, either—though since *she* thinks it's a boy, I'd put stock in that."

"Over a trained doctor's reading of state-of-the-art equipment, of course. We'll see. If it's a boy, you owe me a Tastee-Freez, if it's a girl, I buy."

Before she could reply, he went down the hall toward his office, peeling off his gloves. Pam suddenly emerged from the lab, passed Emma without speaking, then, apparently on second thought, turned and blocked her path to the waiting room.

"It seems, Miss Weston," she said, staring down her long nose, "you continually need to use outside resources—this office, Hope Hospital. *I* hear your sister has a specialist in town. So if you can't beat them, why not join them?"

"If I didn't know better, I'd say you're parroting Delia Lowe's company line. Do you mean I should become a doctor's nurse like you?"

"I mean that subsistence care is not good in an area that has subsistence living. We all know that woman's own ignorance," she went on, pointing at the examining-room door, ''about nutrition and medical help probably brought on her dangerous precondition, not to mention her breeding like a rabbit, with five births in ten years! Obviously, midwife care is not the answer to that.''

''Without my presence and work in Shelter, nurse,'' Emma said, keeping her voice low so the Westons wouldn't overhear, ''it's highly likely Lottie and women like her might be dead right now, because they'd never come to a clinic or to Highboro Hope until it's too late. Her husband and a neighbor woman delivered her other healthy children—human children, nurse, not rabbits—at home. Please get out of my way.''

Breathing hard, Emma shouldered by her and went out into the waiting room. If she needed proof that Delia was still on the warpath, no matter what truce she'd declared, Pam Stark had said it all. As for Griff, she didn't want to keep fighting him, but every other man she'd ever cared for had, one way or another, betrayed her.

13

Jidge Collister was exhausted and frustrated, but at least she was here—if you could call the defunct Appalachian coal town of Jackson, Ohio, being anywhere.

She parked on the main drag, then slumped in her car, wondering if there were any B&Bs in town, because she couldn't fathom there being a decent hotel in a backwater like this. Not that she was planning to be in Jackson more than a couple of nights. After all, she had driven cross-country in three days because she couldn't possibly get her gun through security to take a plane.

Still feeling as if she were in motion, she closed her eyes, but all she could see was highway coming at her. She got out and stretched, then walked briskly into a doughnut shop for coffee. Caffeine, junk food, gas— and rage—had fueled her this far this fast.

Perched on a stool in the empty shop, she stared at the array of choices, then ordered two glazed doughnuts and black coffee. Hoping to get some information, she sat at the scarred Formica counter rather than in a small booth.

"Can you recommend anyone who makes quilts around here?" she asked the grossly overweight, blank-faced, young counter girl.

"Quilts?" she—her smudged plastic name tag read Rhonda—said, appearing to wake up. "They got great

Wedding Ring ones at Kmart, cheap, too, when they do the blue-light special.''

Jidge picked up a glazed doughnut, then glared down at her own wedding ring. She'd left Mitchell with her sister, saying she had to get away for a little while to decide whether to divorce Ben or not. She missed her boy already, but this had to be done, even if it took her to places like a doughnut shop on the edge of Appalachia, talking to Rhonda about Kmart.

"I mean handmade quilts," Jidge tried again.

"Not like for sale, 'less there's some at the church yard sale in September.''

"No one special makes them?''

"Lots of ladies do, I guess.''

"Sure, I see. Do you know anybody with the initials *G.G.?*''

"That's a funny question. Not right offhand. You one a those people trying to trace back family trees or something?''

"In a way that's exactly what I'm doing,'' Jidge said, more to herself than Rhonda.

She heaved a huge sigh and huddled over the worn maps she'd pulled from her purse. If Jackson didn't work out, Jidge assured herself, it was only a day's drive to either Cumberland County, Tennessee, or Lowe County, Kentucky. She supposed she'd just flip a coin to decide. The Shelter the Children adoption facilitator had used a discontinued 800-number that was impossible to trace without legal assistance, and she did not intend to leave a trail that led back to herself any more than she already had by hiring that private detective.

Chewing without tasting the doughnut, she wiped the crusty glaze from the sides of her mouth, and some of it fell on the map. She bent close to blow it off, then blinked and stared at the web of labeled lines and dots.

Outside of Highboro, the Lowe County seat in Kentucky, there was a tiny dot with the word *Shelter*. It was a crazy leap of logic, she knew, but could that be a link? As long as she was here, she'd ask and look around. But tomorrow, she thought, Lowe County, here I come.

"Don't it look like that *Gone With the Wind* house?" Lottie whispered as Emma pulled into Trish and Mike's long, curved driveway in Highboro. "Least, it looks like they're rich as Miss Delia," she went on, leaning forward to gawk at the white-pillared, porticoed house. Emma drove around to the patio as Trish had suggested.

In the back seat with Lottie's suitcase and Emma's midwife kit, Rooster leaned forward. "You deserve the peace and quiet, honey. Emma and me's only one phone call and a half hour away. But the hospital's four blocks. Glad you arranged all this, Emma," he said and patted her shoulder.

"Nothing but the best for us Westons," Emma said, trying to sound upbeat, though she was still worried about Lottie and was smoldering from tangling with Pam Stark that morning. Somehow everything kept unraveling.

Trish came out to greet them in turquoise tights and a long striped T-shirt. Mike bounded out behind her, dressed as nattily as ever. "We're so pleased you'll be staying with us," Trish told Lottie, giving the suddenly silent woman a hug. "I hope, Emma, she is only the first of many we can help this way, including Sissy, soon."

"You've been so great about this," Emma told her, while Lottie nodded. "We can't thank you enough."

"*My* thanks," Trish said, "is going to be seeing a healthy little baby real soon so—"

"Boy or a girl," Mike cut in. "Anyone taking odds?"

"Doc Cusak and Lottie both says a boy," Rooster said, snatching off his baseball cap and rotating it in his big hands as he talked. "I just wanted to say my piece, too, Miz Bonner, 'cause me and Lottie are beholden to both of you."

"Hey, now, none of that," Trish said. "We've got all this space for our own families that never quite get here for a visit, so we're glad to have the company. We've been spending more than half our time at our house near Shelter. Now, Emma said you might prefer to stay in the pool house there," she said, gesturing toward the smaller version of the big house. "But either there or with us is fine."

"I like that little one," Lottie told her and Trish nodded.

"Trish has sandwiches set up in the sunroom overlooking the pool," Mike said, "but I'll give Rooster a little tour first while you all get settled."

Trish took Emma and Lottie inside through open French doors. In the reflection of the windowpanes, Emma saw Mike expounding on something to a rapt Rooster as they walked around the pool. As always, Mike looked as if he was buying or selling something.

Her short hospital stay had done Amrine a world of good, but she knew the police were coming back to question her this morning. She'd told them nothing about Len because she only wanted quit of him, not to have to go to court. She didn't want that bastard—or Emma—to so much as have a hint where her baby was.

Though the women's shelter the nice social worker had described to her sounded real good, Amrine got out of bed close to midnight and pulled on the clothes they'd left for her. She could find a shelter somewhere else and change her story so the police wouldn't be all over her. You couldn't trust city cops, she thought, any more than you could trust Reg Merrell.

She pulled off the top sheet of her bed and used it for a backpack. She took both boxes of diapers they'd left, wishing she could also take the plastic bassinet Laurie slept in. When she borrowed some bills from her roommate Sally's purse in the cupboard where she'd seen her put it, she also memorized the name and address on her driver's license, because she sure meant to send the money back. She was pretty sure Sally was okay for money. She had a home and a husband who dressed real well.

Both babies and Sally slept soundly, even as Amrine carefully bundled up Laurie. She liked this place because they let you keep the baby in your room if the baby wasn't sick and you were nursing.

It was past midnight when she went down the back stairs and headed for the bus stop she'd seen from her hospital room window. But when the bus didn't come for a while, she got real worried. Nurses always popped in and out at night, and they would find her gone soon.

Finally a bus pulled up. "Only correct change after eight at night," the sleepy-looking driver mumbled. No one else was on the bus. Laurie started to fuss.

"Here, keep this five," Amrine said, holding it out to him. "It's the smallest I got."

He grunted and took it. Big spender, he probably

thought. And here she had nothing to her name now but this beautiful baby. If it wasn't for little Laurie, she'd probably use the sixty dollars she'd borrowed from Sally to get a gun and settle things with Len for good— and maybe Emma, too. But no, she knew she'd never have the nerve for that. She was just running.

Emma was dreaming that Pa and Jake were shooting at her as she struggled to get to Amrine. And a baby wailed and wailed, like a ghost. It wasn't Sissy's lost baby, for that little tyke hardly had the breath to blow in or out. Whose baby was it and why didn't Pa stop shooting at her so the ringing in her ears would stop?

She sat bolt upright in bed. At nine o'clock, she had been so exhausted she'd lain down in her clothes. She looked to check the time but the clock was blinking. The electricity must have gone off and on in this storm. When did that start? The storm and the phone—those had been the noises in her dream.

She grabbed the ringing phone. "Emma Weston here."

"Emma, Griff. I know I shouldn't use a phone in a lightning storm but Mike Bonner called to say Lottie's in labor."

"Why didn't he call me?"

"He said he didn't want you having to drive to High-boro alone, I guess thinking Rooster couldn't leave his kids at night. I don't know. He says tree limbs are down there, and it's been pouring buckets, evidently more than here. Are you all right? You sound groggy."

"I fell asleep."

"It's bad driving out there," he said, "but I can take the van and go with you to help you with Rooster if not Lottie."

She wanted to tell him no but she didn't. "I'll get Rooster and meet you in town. We'll have to drop his kids off at the neighbors'. Lottie's at the hospital? She was still holding her own the three days I saw her at the Bonners', including just this morning. And she wasn't dilating. Did Mike say anything about the frequency of her contractions?"

"He was nervous as heck and hardly thinks like a midwife. We'd better head for the hospital, though he didn't say where she was. His line had a lot of static, then just went dead."

"See you in town as soon as I can make it."

Just went dead Griff's words kept revolving in her brain as she tore out to the Jeep, getting soaked in the process. Her front headlight had been repaired after going in the ditch. Their glare on the slick, black pavement disoriented her. She told herself to concentrate on driving, to keep control. All she needed was another accident.

Just went dead, the thunder seemed to rumble, repeating Griff's words. Damn, but she felt a terrible foreboding, just as she had the night Ruth Wicklow had her false labor—the night she'd ended up in the ditch. Maybe she had more of the mountain sixth sense than she thought.

Griff insisted on driving the van and Emma let him, climbing in the back seat to let Rooster sit in front. Mike had been right about storm damage being worse in Highboro. Limbs and blowing debris littered the running streets. They heard distant sirens, but in a storm, lightning strikes often summoned the fire department. They followed an ambulance right up into the emergency entrance to the hospital.

While Griff went to park, Rooster and Emma ran in, assuming Lottie would have been admitted here and not formally checked in. The emergency squad bustled past them with a screaming, bleeding kid on a rolling gurney as Emma took Rooster up to the triage nurse.

"This is the husband and I'm the midwife of a woman who was admitted sometime this evening in labor, Mrs. Weston—Lottie," Emma told the gray-haired woman breathlessly.

The nurse scanned some sort of sign-in sheet, then turned to her computer screen. "Not admitted here and not in maternity," she informed them crisply.

Griff ran in, soaked. Emma saw him shake water off a newspaper he must have held over his head. "That can't be," she told the nurse, gesturing Griff over. "The man with whom she's been living called us."

The nurse raised one brow. "I'm sorry, whatever the arrangements. You'd best check with her boyfriend then."

"Not her boyfriend," Rooster exploded, banging his fist. "She has to be here!"

Griff and Emma tugged him away and huddled by the automatic sliding door. Outside, lightning slashed the sky and thunder shook the windows.

"With tree limbs down," Griff said, "it's possible they've been delayed—in the Bonners' car or the emergency squad they called. The squad…"

He ran back over to the triage desk to ask if a squad had been summoned to the Bonners' residence. Emma and Rooster followed. "What's their exact address?" the nurse asked. "Several squads are out that haven't returned."

Emma wasn't sure, but Rooster knew. The nurse consulted her computer screen again. "Yes, a squad was called at 8:37, but it has gone on to another call—a car accident across town.''

"Can you call that squad for us?" Griff asked.

"I'm sorry, but they're currently at a bad, busy scene and we can't..."

"Come on," Emma said, tugging both men's arms. "They only live four blocks from here. The squad probably delivered the baby, then got the other call so left her there. A woman who's had five children at home's not going to head for the hospital if she can help it."

They sprinted for the van through puddles that magnified the parking-lot lights from above. At least the electricity and phones, were working here, Emma acknowledged with relief. Rooster guided Griff to the Bonners', though they had to back out and go another way when a good-size tree limb blocked one street.

They careened up the driveway toward the big house just as the rain slackened and the thunder muted. Griff laid on the horn until Rooster stopped him.

"Lottie'll be sleeping," Rooster said. "She's always tuckered out after a birth."

The downstairs back room of the main house blazed with lights, though the pool house where Lottie was staying was dark. Leaves littered the pool, and the once-proud clumps of peonies were beaten flat into mud puddles.

"They musta took her inside the big house and helped her there." Rooster was muttering. "Well, now they got a doctor and a midwife both to check on her."

As calm as he sounded he began to pound on the doors. Lights upstairs snapped on to flood the patio.

"Rooster, wait, they're coming," Griff told him and put a steadying arm around him. Emma stood mute, staring at their reflections in the French doors.

They saw Trish pull away the curtain over the doors, turn back and call "Mike, it's them!" The door latch clicked. Rooster lunged as it opened.

"Is Lottie here?" he demanded.

"Yes," Trish said. "Upstairs—though we've got to get her to the hospital. We thought at first she was all right."

"What?" Emma demanded. "Was it false pains earlier, or did the emergency squad tell her it would be a while, then had to leave?"

The look on Trish's face chilled her. Trish shook her head. Emma saw her eyes were red.

"What happened?"

"She—she went into labor real fast and hard. Then the storm came—and the baby."

"Yeah, she has 'em quick. Was it a boy?" Rooster asked, looking wildly around.

Trish shook her head. Emma had never seen her so— serious, shaken.

"Girl," Trish whispered. "But then—"

Mike clamped Trish to him with one arm. "We did all we could, and we've called the squad for the second time tonight. With all that's going on, it might take a while to get here. We brought Lottie into the house, after she—passed out. God help us all, I'm so sorry. Before help got here, the baby died. The squad took it to the morgue, and after they left, Lottie slipped into a coma. I called the squad again, like I said. Listen, I hear it now."

If there was a siren, it got drowned out by Rooster's cry and Emma's scream.

They'd sat, stunned, first in the waiting room, then by Lottie's bedside in the ICU at Hope.

"Stabilized but comatose," Dr. Jack McGill, the attending physician, had told them, "so we'll have to give it some time. Right now, it's a deep-level coma, so don't be fooled by the fact she might respond to verbal or other stimulation. She might even utter a few words or show some automatic responses like coughing, yawning or blinking. And she is breathing unaided, so it could be much worse."

Immersed in shock and despair, Emma had thought nothing could be much worse. Just across from Lottie's door, Emma sat slumped against the wall, letting Griff hold her hand. They could see Rooster, his shoulders hunched, leaning against Lottie's high bed amidst IV drips, tubes and monitors, whispering low to his unconscious wife.

"She might have been on the verge of pre-eclampsia," Emma told Griff, "but she wasn't full-fledged, and I'd just seen her."

"You know it can come on suddenly, even a coma."

She hugged herself hard. "Not that suddenly, I swear it."

"If Rooster wasn't your cousin you might have to swear it—in a malpractice suit," he said, shaking his head.

She pulled away from his comforting touch. "Malpractice? You saw her lately. What would you testify?"

He looked terribly uneasy, and her stomach churned. Was there any way Delia and Griff could use a catastrophe like this against her?

"I couldn't even read the damn ultrasound right," he said, hitting the wall with his fist. "Besides, if anybody's liable, though they were just playing Good Samaritans, it's Trish and Mike, too."

"Too? Then you and Delia *are* planning to use this against me."

"What?" he said, jerking his head around. "I'm going to ignore the fact you said that because we're all exhausted and distraught."

"And you're not going to start tossing blame at Trish and Mike, either. I've been through the horror of being a layperson trapped with a sick mother and a baby in distress, desperate for help. That storm reminded me of another one once—an ice storm. I was trapped with Sissy when she first delivered, years ago."

He didn't look surprised. Had Delia or Sissy told him that, too?

"What happened?" he asked.

"We were both in our teens, and a freak ice storm trapped our mother in town, until—it was too late."

"So that's where you get this fierce calling. Honey—"

"Don't call me that!" she cried, hitting his hands away when he reached for her. "I can't trust you, so just leave me alone. I'll handle this."

"Oh, right," he said, his voice rising, before he evidently realized where he was and lowered it again. "Emma Weston, midwife, can handle anything alone. I swear to God, you don't have a clue how to cooperate with or trust a trained doctor, let alone a man who cares for you!"

He jumped up and strode down the hall, bumping into Mike, who must have been hovering around the corner, afraid to interrupt.

"I brought an extra car, in case anyone has to go back and others want to stay," Mike said in one breath. "Trish will be right in. Anything we can do to help, anything at all…"

Griff hustled him back around the corner. Emma sank into a chair with her face in her hands. Only then did her accusations of Griff—and his hurtful words—crash into her. How had things between them gone so wrong? But far worse was the loss of another baby she'd vowed to deliver safely into the arms of her client. It wasn't the same as with Amrine and Ola, but there had to be some link. Didn't there?

Emma sniffed hard, swiped tears off her face and stood. She marched into Lottie's room and told Rooster she would be back later after she checked on when the baby's body would be released.

"Tell them soon," Rooster said, letting go of Lottie's hand to grip hers. "No autopsy, neither. No one's gonna cut my baby up, and we'll get a good funeral for her in Shelter."

"But when there's a sudden death, sometimes the medical examiner insists on—"

"No autopsy!"

"Sure. I'll take care of that." Though she could not bear the thought of it, either, she ached to know the exact cause of death. She could only hope that, despite her protests, the ME would insist.

Rooster nodded numbly, squeezing her hands, mumbling his thanks. She gritted her teeth as she went out. She deserved no thanks, but condemnation for misreading the signs. And yet, she was still convinced she had been right.

She went down the hall and ran into Trish. "Emma, if there's anything at all we can do…" she echoed Mike.

"Where's Griff?"

"He said he had to call Delia, then he'd be back up."

"I see. I'd like to borrow that extra car."

"Oh, sure thing, fine," Trish said, digging in her shoulder purse for the keys. "A red Pontiac in the front row nearest the building by the bus bench. But where are you going? Can I go with you?"

Emma turned back. "I'm going to see about getting the baby's body released for burial and avoid an autopsy as Rooster wishes."

"Oh, I understand. Good. I'm so sorry, devastated. Be careful."

"No autopsy?"

14

Dawn broke on a broken world. Leaves, tree limbs and sodden garbage had blown about and stuck to the pavement, fences and buildings, including the flat-roofed, cinder-block Lowe County Morgue hidden on a back street in the city's small business district.

"Member of the deceased's family, you say?" the gaunt assistant to the ME asked as he sat at a wooden desk and studied a piece of paper. He was sharp-faced and balding, a reality he tried to hide by combing what hair he had straight up and over his shiny pate.

Emma wrinkled her nose: she smelled formaldehyde or worse in the small, closed area. The front office was tiny, and a dim hall reached toward the depths of the structure.

"That's right," she said. "Family member and a nurse, so I'm not squeamish. I want to see the baby and discuss getting her body released."

"I see. Last name Weston, like the deceased?"

"Yes, Emma Weston."

"But not a parent or guardian?"

"The mother is comatose, and the father won't leave her side. I'm here on his behalf."

"Oh, sorry," he said, blinking up at her. "Didn't know. Just got in." He looked down quickly to shift the paper around to face her. "Sign here, and I'll add the in and out times."

He moved ponderously as if to keep from having to get out of his chair. Didn't this smell get to people who worked here, Emma wondered, or were they immune to death?

"Be right back," he told her, standing slowly. "Got to make sure things are ready for a viewing. It may take a while—unless, since you're a nurse, you don't mind stepping in the lab. It'd be faster."

"All right," she said and came around the desk to follow him.

He held up a hand like a traffic cop. "I've got to get the deceased out first..." His voice faded as he went down the hall.

She sank into the chair he'd vacated, then jumped up to pace. She could not believe in the few hours between seeing Lottie yesterday morning and Mike's phone call to Griff, Lottie had gone into labor and degraded to an eclamptic state that could have caused her coma and the baby's death.

In midwife training, they always referred to losing an infant as a "bad birth outcome." In the face of this tragedy, that wording had never seemed more cowardly or ridiculous. Griff would probably deride that, as he did much of what she believed in and stood for. She tried to convince herself that, next to this catastrophe, her loss of him was nothing. And yet she ached for him already.

"All right, Ms. Weston," the man called from down the hall. "This way, please."

"The father has requested that there be no autopsy," she told him, her voice shaky as she walked toward him. "Do you need to speak to him on that?"

"Doesn't look like the ME's planned one. The stats sheet lists no foul play. You know of none, do you?"

She shook her head, but vowed silently that she *was* going to find out if there had been. There were no motives and no culprits, but something strange was going on with the babies and mothers who were in her charge.

"But then why was the baby brought here instead of pronounced at the hospital?" she asked.

"The record says the squad pronounced, but there has to be a certificate of death, and paramedics can't go signing those—doctors, either, if there's a hint of anything slightly off."

She almost argued he'd just said there was nothing amiss, but when he opened the door, she kept her mouth shut and followed him in. The whitewashed work area was starkly lit with naked, overhead bulbs. Metal gurneys, marble tables, stained enamel sinks, drains in the concrete floor and a wall of large metal drawers made the little room feel even colder and tighter. Her feet began to drag. A large, white enamel door, which looked like it accessed the cooler, was across the way. A cluttered table in the corner held an X-ray machine and several hot plates. She almost bumped her head on a set of hanging scales. She was starting to tremble. Her frustration had segued to apprehension.

"Totally inadequate facilities," the man was muttering more to himself than her. "Damn state government's got to realize we need a new morgue, even if we are in the hills. Now, Ms. Weston, the body will be stiff from rigor mortis and not from the cooler it was in," he said as calmly as if they were discussing ice cubes.

The tiny form lay on the farthest marble-topped table, bundled tightly in a white sheet. When she instinctively reached for the baby, the attendant said, "I'll handle the deceased."

Though she wanted to scream at him for being so emotionally distant, she understood that he could not get too involved. For one moment, she wished she could be that way. But she could never manage that. She always got involved in other people's lives, maybe losing some of herself in the process.

When the baby lay bare—as he had said, the little limbs were rigid—Emma just gaped. Griff's ultrasound prediction it was a boy was indeed wrong. The child's rather copious hair was pale brown with no hint of red. She did not resemble the Weston brood, but then newborns sometimes did not look like kin after a tough or extended birth, which this baby's slightly elongated skull suggested. But Rooster had said Lottie's previous deliveries were quick.

The oddest thing was that this child was a big one, more than eight pounds and surely longer than the child Lottie had carried. Emma had palpated her belly just yesterday. And yet, this baby had to be Lottie's. Didn't she?

"That's it then." The man's voice came from very far away. "I'll see that the remains get signed out to a funeral home, you just tell me which one. Ms. Weston, you aren't going to faint, are you?"

"No," she said, jolting back to reality, "I sure am not."

She turned away without another glance at the body that every instinct told her was not Rooster and Lottie's child—though they'd probably shun her or lock her up if she claimed that. She headed straight for the door out of here and toward as many doors as she needed to knock on—or knock down—to get some answers.

* * *

The Shelter First Baptist Church was packed for the funeral of Emma's tiny second cousin, whom she was increasingly certain wasn't a Weston at all. Still, it was such a comfort to Rooster to have the community help shoulder the double grief of his dead child and his stricken wife that Emma kept her suspicions and fears to herself—for now.

Besides, going over everything again with Trish and Mike and interviewing the rescue squad hadn't given her one clue as to how two babies could have been switched—and what could have happened to Lottie's child. Meanwhile, she'd spent almost every other waking hour with Rooster at the hospital.

With several gospel songs, Sissy's beautiful voice lifted everyone's hope for a better future in this world of woe. If the fact she was heavily pregnant made folks wipe their eyes even more, maybe that, too, Sissy had said, was part of God's plan.

At times like this, Emma realized she was wrong to be angry with God for not letting her save Sissy's baby. After all, that loss had set her on this path to help other mothers and infants, though lately she seemed to be failing again. The Lord's answers for solving this mess were as foggy as the hills lately.

Sissy sang,

"Just as I am, though toss'd about
With many a conflict, many a doubt,
Fightings and fears within, without,
Lamb of God, I come, I come."

Emma stared at the tiny poplar casket, wide at the shoulders and narrow at the feet in the traditional Appalachian shape. Bouquets of wildflowers filled the church and, when Sissy's last plaintive notes faded, the steeple bell began to toll. Ordinarily it would be one peal for each year of the departed soul's life, but today, it just kept going.

In the small, attached Fellowship Hall, a covered-dish dinner awaited everyone after the burial out back. Life would go on for these mountain women in their black mourning clothes and their men whose sleeves were tied with black ribbons. And, Emma thought, for more fortunate parents like Clary and Carter Doyal. On the other side of the aisle, Clary had her head bowed as she cradled their new baby. Carter was staring above Pastor Porter's head as if searching for answers from on high, when Emma knew he was probably just memorizing the numbers of next Sunday's hymns displayed in their little rack. And that gave Emma an idea: since Carter had a photographic mind for numbers, he might be able to help her.

You don't have a clue how to cooperate with or trust a trained doctor, let alone a man who cares for you! she recalled Griff's last words to her. Most of the mourners sat behind Emma, including Griff, who had escorted Delia. Her continued largesse had provided a burial fund, though many others in the community had also contributed to it.

Finally the funeral oration was over and the congregation turned to the aisle to face the coffin, balanced now on four men's shoulders. They carried it out and led the procession around the back of the church and up the hill into Sunrise Cemetery.

It was an old burial ground but there were still empty plots, high up where tombstones caught the first morning sun. Emma's mother was buried here with her grandparents and Sissy's infant daughter. Following

J.G. and Sissy on the narrow gravel path among the stones, Emma stubbed her toe on the uneven turf, and a man's hand firmly grasped her arm.

Her insides cartwheeled; she turned, expecting Griff. It was Hank.

"If there's anything at all I can do for the family, especially for you, Em, just ask, okay?"

"That's very thoughtful," she said, but gently tugged her hand back when he tried to tuck it through his arm. She had to admit, though, he looked grief-stricken.

"Events in the church," he said quietly, out of the side of his mouth, "make me realize you and I are wasting a heck of a lot of time."

"Events like funerals?"

"And weddings, baby dedications. It's inevitable, Em. You will come to me and regret all that's been lost between us."

She turned to look at him again. He had intoned that pronouncement like some Old Testament prophet of doom.

"Hank, our past is long past—dead. Bury it."

"A baby dying, it's a warning to all of us, especially you, for trying to deceive me. I saw you that night with Cusak when you turned down my invitation to dinner. I've seen you—"

"If you've been spying on me, you just keep clear, or—"

"Or what?" he interrupted coldly.

She frowned into his burning stare until she had to look away. Intense, dedicated and zealously loyal, yes, but Hank was getting dangerous. He looked far too distraught. At least if *he* was the one spying on her, that meant it wasn't Jake. But Hank's watching her reminded her of his watching someone else, but when and who?

She left Hank standing on the path and went to stand between Sissy and Rooster at the open grave, though she wished now she'd stayed with the women in the church who were tending the young Weston girls. The grave gaped small but so deep, like a hole in her life. Even though she hadn't been in attendance, she had lost her first baby as a midwife, and the mother might go, too. But it was so much more personal than that. Helping others, saving Sissy at any cost to herself—that was what her life was all about. Had she been wrong to be so obsessed with midwifery? Was she missing out, as Hank said, on her own life?

After Pastor Porter's final benediction, Emma stooped like the others, to drop flowers on the coffin in the ground. As the clods of shoveled red soil thumped on the small box, she and Sissy took Rooster's arms to walk back to the church. Their way was lined with mourners touching their shoulders and murmuring condolences. Trish and Mike were there, tears in their eyes, still agonizing over everything. Emma knew they partly blamed themselves, just as she felt some responsibility. That made her feel even closer to them.

Sheriff Merrell, ever watchful, was standing at attention in full dress uniform, as if they'd just buried some local dignitary. Clary and Carter hugged Rooster. It seemed everyone was there except the Eubankses, and they hadn't darkened a church door for years.

Once back inside, Emma steered Carter into a corner of the cloakroom. Before she could figure how to ask the favor she wanted, he said, "I keep thinking, Emma, there but for the grace of God goes my and Clary's new baby."

"That's true," she said. "The breech could have gone wrong."

"But for the grace of God and skills of our midwife, I should have said," he added, and she realized he had given her the perfect opening.

"Carter, I need your help in something—and I know you're an honorable man."

"What do you mean, want?" he asked, suddenly refusing to meet her eyes. He frowned toward Sheriff Merrell, who was standing across the hall by the tables of food, not looking their way, though Carter shuffled farther back into the cloakroom. Emma pursued, still talking.

"I really need to find Ola Grady. I think she had a fight with her parents and ran off to have her baby somewhere, and I've got to know they're all right."

"Sure, I can understand that," he said. He looked at her again; he seemed relieved about something she couldn't grasp, something maybe she *hadn't* asked.

"I hope this won't go against your grain, but I just thought—with the way you remember addresses and all—"

"Only the numbers."

"—that you might have noticed, on your mail run, if the Gradys, maybe just Ginger, have heard from Ola by mail. I supposed she'd be more likely to phone, but it would mean so much to m—"

"Yeah, she wrote her ma a coupla times."

"Can you remember even the numbers in the return address?" Emma tried to keep the excitement out of her voice.

"Sure, 'cause it was almost all numbers. 114 East—or West, not sure—17th Street, Number four. And it was a Lexington zip code."

* * *

After the meal, Emma went out to her Jeep with Rooster's two oldest girls, Louise and Annie, in tow. Clary, carrying Weston Griffin Doyal, stood there waiting for Carter, and they all stopped to fuss over the baby. Emma worried for a moment that Louise and Annie would be upset to see a new baby when they'd just lost one, but evidently life went on for nine- and ten-year-olds too. One of the Doyals' children, Vinie, who had screamed about Disney World the night her little brother was born, smiled shyly, obviously proud of her baby brother. Why, Emma thought, couldn't life just be this simple and sweet?

She let the girls chat while she unlocked the Jeep, then saw a piece of paper fluttering under her windshield wiper.

"Don't tell me Sheriff Merrell gave you a ticket," Clary called to her over the girls' voices.

Emma knew it was not that, though she wouldn't put it past him. It was a note, folded in half. "My name's even spelled wrong on the outside," Emma said, trying to sound casual. "It looks like a calling card from the Eubankses. I've gotten one or two before, none repeatable."

Hesitantly, Emma flipped the note over.

"Wouldn't think that bunch could so much as read and write, seein' how they keep their kids to home instead of school all the time," Clary said. "Truant officers—sheriff, too—ought to get after them."

But Emma wasn't listening. On the note were written the words YOR BROTHERS BACK.

The next morning before dawn—the first Saturday in May—Emma rescheduled her appointments and, telling no one, drove three hours to Lexington, taking a detour and continually looking back to be sure she wasn't being followed. For one thing, she wanted out of town just to think and breathe freer. At least now she had a number of possibilities for why she'd been feeling as if she was being watched. It could have been Hank, maybe even Hal Eubanks. Worse, it could have been Jake. But why hadn't he made a move?

By noon, she had figured out that the Lexington address she sought had to be West 17th because the number on East 17th Street was a dry cleaners. The place was an old house subdivided into four tiny apartments, two up, two down. Number four was up.

Her heart thudding, Emma climbed the back, covered stairs and listened at the door for voices or a baby's cry. Locking her knees and gripping her purse under her arm, she knocked on the door once, then firmly again. If Ola wasn't there, she was prepared to wait, though she'd probably ask around to be sure she had the right place.

But suddenly the door opened and there she stood, bone-thin, in jeans and a cutoff sweatshirt, her hair still looking like a Brillo pad. Ola gasped and covered her mouth with both hands, her pale blue eyes wide.

"I know it's a surprise, Ola," Emma said quickly, "but I had to see that you and the baby were all right. I can understand why you left. Can I come in?"

Ola shook her head at first, then took a step back into a tiny hall that led to a living-dining area carpeted in a drab olive shag. Emma noted that Ola must have been asleep; her eyes were bleary and her hair was flattened in back.

"I'd love to see the baby," Emma said as she hurried in before Ola could change her mind.

The girl seemed to surface from a stupor. She

grabbed several teen magazines off the sunken sofa, the back of which was draped with one of Ginger's quilts. She gestured for Emma to sit.

"You gave me a start, that's all," Ola said. "And wha'd you mean you know why I left? It's for a job I got here, that's all, a good one at a factory—makes boxes."

"That's great, but I'm assuming you had to get out of your parents' house, away from your father. I'm assuming a lot, I know," Emma said, sitting forward on the soft sofa, "but if you had just told me what was going on, I could have found a way to protect you."

"Like what was going on?" the girl parroted in a weak voice, her stiff arms clamped to her sides.

"It was really brave of you to come to a midwife when your parents wanted to keep it strictly secret about the baby's father."

Ola gasped like a fish out of water. "You gotta leave. You can't come saying that, whatever you mean. Pa beat me for getting myself knocked up and by kin, that's all."

"You realize the baby's parentage can be tested. Now don't panic, I'm not saying I'm going to get you in trouble, because I'm not, but your father should be pun—"

"No, you can't!" she cried, starting to pace erratically like a caged animal, two steps out, then back while she snagged her fingers in her hair. "You can't take no blood from my baby."

Emma stood. "I didn't say I would. I'm just saying I need your help about the truth so—"

"You can't, 'cause my baby's gone."

"Gone? Gone where?"

"Got a good home, adopted—and don't ask me

where 'cause I don't know and don't want to. I signed and initialed papers and that's that.''

Emma just gaped. But, she reasoned, if the child was the result of incest, even rape, perhaps adoption was for the best. She wondered if the adoptive parents had been told the truth, in case there were medical complications later. If it was a private agency, it could be money from the adoption and not some factory job that paid for this refuge from her father. Despite having so much stacked against her, the girl had solved her problems.

"Adopted, I understand," Emma assured her. "Through what agency or doctor?"

"A private adoption. Don't go asking no more. Got a good home, he does.''

"You had a son?"

She nodded defiantly, then suddenly stopped her pacing and crumpled against the wall to slide down it into a fetal position. Emma knelt beside her, but Ola shook off her touch.

"Just leave me be," she muttered, turning her face to the wall. "I had a C-section and the scar still hurts bad sometimes. Too narrow in the pelvic to deliver without maybe hurting the baby. I know a midwife don't wanta hear that…"

As her voice trailed off to choking sobs, all Emma could think of was that Griff had theorized that Ola'd had a previous C-section. Surely this tragedy couldn't have happened before to this girl—breeding babies to sell. The mere idea sickened Emma as much as the possibility of incest.

"Can I take a look to be sure the incision is healing right?" she asked, touching Ola's shoulder. "Did they do it right across that earlier abdominal scar?"

"Quit asking questions! Get out, or I'll call long-distance to Sheriff Merrell and tell him you been after me.''

''If you call him, tell him to question and arrest your father.''

''Ma needs him,'' she cried, pressing her hands over her ears like a child. Emma feared it was the closest to an admission she might come.

''Is that why you're afraid to tell?'' she pursued. ''Your ma knew and didn't help you, did she? If you're worried about her making a living without him, she's got her quilts to sell.''

Ola was rocking now, sobbing silently, her arms wrapped around her knees.

Emma stood. ''I see why you decided to give the baby up for adoption, Ola, I really do—''

''You see nothing! Get out!''

Emma worried that someone might hear the girl's screams through the thin walls and come running. Tears in her own eyes, Emma started for the door then turned back.

''I'll leave now, but please call me if I can help you in any way, at home or here. I'm glad you've got a good job, but don't you let your pa take your money or scare you. I—I know what it means to have a cruel father. I'm just hoping he didn't buy those fancy appliances he's got hidden out back of his work shed on money from your baby.''

Ola turned to face her, teeth bared. Up from a crouch, she exploded at Emma, her hands like claws.

Emma jumped back, banging into the wall. Ola's nails slashed once, catching her on her lower jaw. Emma shoved her away and Ola bounced on, then off, the sofa to come at her again with a growl. Emma sidestepped and yanked open the door. She was partway down the stairs when Ola, still shrieking, slammed the door.

It was a restless night outside—just the way Emma felt as she paced through her lighted downstairs, trying to reason everything out. She'd pulled shut all the curtains, but she couldn't close out the dark. She heard the electrical and phone wires rattle and tree limbs scrape the roof and windows while the wind wailed. It wasn't raining, but she was starting to hate even windstorms.

She tried to concentrate, desperate to find links, reasons, answers. The pieces didn't even fit to make a puzzle. Ola's putting her son up for adoption made sense, but it did not align with Amrine's disappearance or Lottie's tragedy. No way either of them would agree to put their children up for adoption. If there were some sort of adoption agency working secretly in Lexington or the entire state, surely it was not just her clients that strange things were happening to. And she'd assumed Amrine had gone to Tennessee. So where was the place, the piece of evidence, or the person that tied all this together?

Finally after 1:00 a.m., already in her nightgown, and telling herself she had to get to bed, Emma began to click off downstairs lights, then started up the stairs. She was to the top of the landing about to turn on the hall light when she first heard the sound, new and different from the noise of the wind.

It was close, so close! But where?

Instinctively, she threw herself down on the stairs. It had come from the window on the landing just above her.

Again it sounded, a regular rap, rap, rap. Surely not just the wind or a branch.

She tried to make herself believe it could be a client or someone just wanting help, someone throwing gravel against the window to get her attention. But no, it was something knocking on the landing window at a height no one on the ground could reach.

She went cold as ice. No tree limb stretched toward that window. And even if there was one, it would never rap in such a regular fashion. She was exhausted, that was all, or else the concussion she'd sustained five days ago was making her delusional.

Keeping the lights off, she crept back down to see if she could sight anything from the first floor window nearest the knocking. She pressed herself to the wall and peered out. No one stood under the window. Could someone have climbed on the roof? In this wind?

The knocking came again. This time she imagined it was saying "Let-me-in." She fought to keep away the memories of that dreadful dead animal tableau with those horrid eyes. There must be a logical explanation for this.

"Let-me-in."

She went partway back up the stairs and knelt on the landing to peer out. Nothing but the shifting night with distant, dark trees' limbs thrashing in silhouette against the backdrop of her pale white shed. Her chin where Ola had scratched today felt sore when she leaned it on her hands.

She tried to calm herself. It was surely some branch caught in a drainpipe or in the eaves which the wind had bent down to rap on the glass. It could even be an echo from somewhere else in this old house in such a wind, she tried to tell herself.

Emma breathed slowly, in and out, using relaxation

techniques she'd shared with many a laboring woman. And then she screamed just as loud as one.

A horned, disembodied, demonic head with glowing eyes peered in the window at her.

She hit the landing hard and huddled there, gasping in terror. Her heart nearly burst from her chest. She wasn't sure how much time passed before she got herself together to look out the window again.

Nothing. Nothing there. No head—no strange sounds.

She put her face in her hands. If it hadn't recalled her accident with the deer, if it hadn't reminded her of childhood fears, she would have realized that it was a deer head and not a demon. But no way this was some practical joke.

"The head of a mounted stag," she muttered aloud, to steady her nerves. "Someone must have had it on a pole and tapped the antlers on the glass. And rigged its lighted eyes."

Under other circumstances, this might have been almost funny, but another animal corpse—or the cut off head of one—made the earlier warnings worse.

She heaved a shaky sigh. Many of the houses around here had deer-head trophies. Few folks knew she'd almost hit a deer the other night, but with her car in the ditch and people talking, word could have spread. Whoever was tormenting her was getting more desperate to warn her off or scare her out of Shelter.

As she crept upstairs to look out all the windows, Emma decided she would say nothing to anyone about this harassment. She would watch people closer to see who was waiting for a reaction. These threats and terrors would not stop her but instead spur her on.

15

Immediately after breakfast the next morning, Emma headed for the Gradys'. She was determined to shake loose something about how Ola's baby might have been adopted—and indirectly warn them away in case they were trying to get back at her for helping Ola. She figured Hal Eubanks had left the note saying Jake had returned—which could be a scare tactic in itself—but she still thought Sam might have shot out her tires and put the dead animals on the porch.

Emma's stomach knotted tighter as she walked past Ginger's double clothesline of plastic-covered quilts. For the first time, Emma realized that, not only did they provide promotion for her sales but also privacy for the house. People driving by on the road could not see the front porch or first floor at all.

"Ginger? Sam?" she called. "You home?"

The house stood silent, the windows like blank eyes. She knocked on the front door, then decided to look out in the back. Their dusty, mud-spattered truck was parked between the house and the back buildings, which were scattered down the holler.

"How-do! Ginger? Sam?"

The chickens squawked and fluttered when she checked the henhouse. She almost gagged at the sight of a hatchet stuck in a bloodstained, feather-flecked tree stump. She heard a muted radio playing a baseball game somewhere.

In the distance she saw Ginger, carrying an empty tray, come out of the smokehouse. Few folks used them these days, but she must have been taking out ham hocks, although no smoke rose from the crooked chimney. The woman looked startled and none too happy to see her, but Emma told herself that didn't mean she knew she'd seen Ola. Ginger just thought she was struck up with book learning.

"Is Sam around?" Emma called to her.

Ginger shrugged. "Somewheres. Why you askin'?"

"You know," Emma said, hoping she sounded nonchalant, "I've always hated guns since Pa shot Cory Eubanks, but I'm feeling the need for one and was hoping—Pa and Sam once being buddies and all—that Sam would lend me one of his. He's got quite a few still, doesn't he?"

"Like most hunters here 'bouts. What brung that on?"

"People harassing me at night, and next time they do, I'm going to use them for target practice," Emma vowed, trying to sound belligerent. "I'd mean to warn them with a couple of shots, but I suppose I might actually hit someone."

As Ginger gripped the plastic tray so hard her knuckles went white, Emma noticed it contained eating utensils. So Ginger had not just been carrying meat to smoke. The utensils looked used.

"Is Sam working in the smokehouse?" Emma asked.

"Huh? No. He's out yonder in his work shed. This is stuff from a long time ago when Sam used to put Ola in there for her sass. You set yourself down on the front porch 'round front. I'll fetch Sam, see if he got a shot-gun and shells for you.''

At least, Emma thought, it didn't seem like Ola had called them about her visit. Ginger marched her around to the front porch and sat her on the bench like a child who'd misbehaved. She opened the front door a crack, slid the tray in on the floor, then closed the door. "You must set there," she repeated and disappeared around the corner of the house.

Emma wished she had time to search the house. They might have the name or address of Ola's adoption agency. She got up, opened the door and reached in for the utensils. The fork still had sticky red stuff on it—and one soft SpaghettiO caught around a tine.

Her heart pounding, Emma opened the door and slipped into the house, stepping over the tray. She darted through the front room to the back kitchen windows. Ginger was hustling toward the workshed, giving the smokehouse a wide berth. What, or who, were they hiding out there? Could it possibly be Jake?

Emma knew she was risking a lot on a crazy hunch. She opened her purse and dug out her cell phone. If she was wrong, she'd never hear the end of it from the sheriff, but no way she was going to face her brother alone if he was really back. She'd never thought to look for him here, but she guessed she should have. Jake, like Pa, had always been friendly with Sam.

Her pulse pounded and her index finger shook as she punched an 8 in the 911 and had to start over. No, it would be safer to call the sheriff from her car. She didn't want to get trapped in the house. If they were hiding Jake out back, she could get Sam arrested for harboring an escaped criminal, if not for incest and stat-utory rape.

She had barely stepped out the front door when Sam came running around the house, carrying his broken arm awkwardly in its cast, with a panting Ginger bringing up the rear. No Jake, thank God, but she certainly had their attention. She had to get out of here.

"Wha's this about a gun, girl?" Sam said.

He was out of breath, too, and, from somewhere on his way around the house, he'd picked up a rifle. Just looking at his sly face made her sick. Still, with Ola's child gone, she'd never prove paternity. Right now, she just wanted to prove to herself Jake wasn't here—even if it took the sheriff to do it.

She started edging down the porch steps. "Someone's been on my property at night, and I want a better greeting for them next time. I know you've got quite a few guns."

"A fair passel," he said, walking warily up to the porch. He stood directly in her path with his good arm holding the rifle across a raised knee while he propped one foot on the bottom step. "What kind you think you kin handle?"

"A .22-caliber rifle," she said, hoping to put him on notice she suspected him of shooting at her Jeep, too.

He didn't blink an eye. "A .22's your pa's favorite."

"Jake's, too?"

The gun slipped off his knee before he grabbed it. "Well, now, guess so."

They stared each other down for a moment. Did he know she was calling his bluff? Her eyes kept darting around the corner of the house. She pushed past Sam and started away.

"What about a gun, girl?"

"I'll be back for it later," she called over her shoulder.

"I gotta tell you, Emma Weston," Sam shouted. "Never did cotton to smart-talkin' women—'cept, a course, Miss Delia. How 'bout you takin' a bullet or two right now though for always stickin' your nose in?" Before she could react, Sam shot the rifle straight up in the air.

She started running. He shot again as Emma shoved between two flapping quilts on the inner line, then tried to paw her way through the ones on the outer line. She'd have stood her ground if she wasn't so afraid that those shots were to summon Jake.

But when she popped through the second line of quilts to try to reach her Jeep, Jake, bearded and thinner, was standing between it and her. He looked unarmed.

"Well, well," he said, grinning, looking more like Pa than he used to. "I been wantin' to call on you and Sis, 'stead of just watchin' your busy little lives fly by. But here you are to see me. Ain't that nice."

He spread his arms as if to embrace her. When she tried to dart around him, he jumped sideways to block her way.

She ran back through the quilts toward the house, expecting Sam or even Ginger to try to stop her, but she saw neither.

She tore around the back of the house, hoping Sam had left the keys in his truck like Pa used to. If that's where the radio was playing, the keys had to be there. She yanked open the door, felt for them, skimmed her hand up over the dusty visor, and found nothing but a tumble of Tootsie Rolls.

"Hey, Emma," Jake bellowed not far behind her. "This any way to welcome back your long-lost blood kin? I need a nice, safe place to stay. I seen your Baby Farm up close and think it would be real nice. I'd love to see Sis real close up, too, but you're the one to blame for all Pa and me been through—''

She ran around the truck to put it between them, even though that put her deeper in the hollow, farther from the road. When Jake came around the truck, he'd picked up the hatchet from the henhouse.

Her mind raced faster than her feet. Could she outrun him past the little cemetery, toward the ridge, up into the woods? He'd always been quicker than her, on foot at least. She had to outsmart him.

He must have been in the smokehouse, a sturdy refuge. That's where the muted sound of the baseball game was coming from. She'd be trapped in there, but...

She jumped away from his lunging grasp, sprinted for the smokehouse and slammed the door. A kerosene lantern burned here so she could see to lock the door. Its hissing sound vied with the buzz from TV—not a radio—plugged into a cable that snaked under the door. She shot the bolt just as Jake must have hurled a shoulder against the door. The whole smokehouse seemed to shudder. The TV crowd began to cheer a home run.

"You want me to hack you out or smoke you out, Emma? Get out here so we can settle up! This's your last chance!"

She pressed against the back wall, remembering the times Pa had screamed at her. She didn't have to take this from them, just like Mama didn't, just like Ola or Amrine didn't. She'd told so many women that. Stand up for yourself—stand up to them when men or life are wrong or cruel and you feel trapped and cornered.

"Go to hell, Jake," she yelled back. "That's where you're going, anyway, if you don't stop acting just like Pa!"

"Why, I'll tell him you said that, when I break him out. But right now, I got somewheres to break in."

She stood trembling while Jake heaved the blade of the ax against the door near the locked latch once, twice. Again. The wooden door, heavy as it was, began to splinter. It reminded her of horror movies where some demented villain hacked screaming women down. No matter what, she was fighting back.

She got out her cell phone again and punched 911. If this didn't work, she'd call Griff. She was amazed the emergency line was busy. Trying to steady her hands, she punched it again. This time a woman's voice answered. Emma had to shout over the ax blows so the dispatcher could hear her. The woman tried to keep her on the line to confirm information, but Emma hung up and jammed the phone back in her purse. The ax blade bit clear through the door. She grabbed a big metal meat hook from the ceiling and held it horizontally behind one shoulder as if she was about to swing a baseball bat.

The wood splintered, then shredded. Jake yanked the remnants of it open and lunged through. She swung the hook at him. It snagged his arm, pulling his ax down. She put her entire body weight into hauling the surprised man past her, to his knees. She vaulted over him, leaping out into sun and air.

Behind her, Jake roared as she sprinted for the back of the holler. She thought about running into Sam's shop, but she didn't want to get trapped inside again.

She had nearly made it to the old cluster of tombstones when Jake yelled, "Got me a gun! 'Member how good I was with a gun, pickin' off rabbits and 'coons? Better than you, turnin' that one on Pa and me that night you got him mad enough to shoot Cory Eubanks. Shoot him just—like—this.''

She didn't glance back, but dived for a pair of old tombstones that leaned together. She hit the ground behind them just as a bullet pinged the top of one, sending shards into the air.

"Love it!" Jake yelled. His voice came closer. She was pinned down, doomed. "Target practice on the target I been thinkin' 'bout for years," he bellowed.

Talk, she thought. Make him talk. At least stall the inevitable.

"Jake, did you leave those dead animals on my porch?" she shouted at him, but kept her head down and her body curled fetuslike behind the stones. "That was pretty scary."

"Well, now, maybe I did…"

He shot the stone next to her and filled the air with fragments.

"…and maybe I din't."

"You've been living up at Cutshin on and off, right?" She had her face pressed to the ground. "Sheriff Merrell says you have. He's on his way here now. Hal Eubanks may be, too, because he left me a note you were back. He's as set on settling with you as you were on me."

"He'd be a dead duck—like you—if I didn't want to get you 'fore I tipped him off."

He shot again, but she heard the rifle ping. Was he out of ammunition? Maybe she should run. Then she heard him noisily reload.

"Were you staying here with Sam and tried to shoot out my tires, Jake?" she dared. With her heart pounding so loud, all she could think of was, thank God, he's after me and not Sissy. Sissy—the baby—would Emma live to see them safe now?

"You know, Emma, you always were a Goody Two-shoes. Playin' up to Mama, givin' me bad looks. Then you get rid of all of us and get that Miss Moneybags Delia to take you in. Stand up now, sister dear, 'cause I want to see your pretty, greedy little face again."

"Jake, you've scared me and won this match and got me down. Go on now before the sheriff gets here."

"You liar. You din't call him. Now I said," he roared and came to stand almost over her, "stand up! More'n once those was your very words—stand up for Mama, Jake, stand up to Pa..."

If she didn't stand, she knew, he was going to shoot her facedown or running. Maybe he wouldn't really shoot her and he just meant to scare her again—if that had been him at the farm those two nights. She scraped up a fistful of soil to heave it in his eyes. It was her only weapon. Her stomach clenched, her body shaking like she had a fever, she got to her knees to stand.

At first she thought she had made the low sound—a squeak of fear—but it got more piercing. When Jake recognized the scream of a siren, he leveled the gun at her, shouting, "You traitor. Traitor!"

Emma dived behind the last row of pockmarked tombstones as his gun went off. Then, as the siren screeched louder, Jake ran at her. She tried to cover her head, to curl up, but he only took a passing swipe at her with the gun, which came so close she felt the breath of the barrel. He jumped over her and raced down the hollow into the thicket of trees.

"Glad I was delivering something to Miss Delia's *and* you listened to me for once about calling if you saw Jake," Reg Merrell told her. He'd ordered a man-hunt and had called for hound dogs for tracking Jake as he'd done years ago. "Otherwise, I'd never have made it clear from Highboro in time."

"I know," she said. "I'm—grateful." It actually hurt her to say that, but the man had saved her life.

They were sitting in the front seat of one of the three squad cars that were parked with their bar lights still blinking. Emma glanced over at Ginger and Sam, who were being interviewed by another officer at a picnic table out their back door. Where they had been during Jake's attack on her, she didn't know.

"Think of any more for your statement?" Reg asked, squinting at his notes from where he sat behind the driver's seat. "You were trying to get a gun from Sam to—number one, indirectly let him and the Eubankses know you'd be armed in case they bothered you again, but you're not sure it was them. And, two, to see if he had a .22 like the casings you found up on the ridge after someone took potshots at you more'n two weeks ago, which you didn't report to me like you should have when you came whining for help about Amrine. That about right?"

She nodded grimly. He was still putting the worst spin on everything. Damned if she was going to tell him about questionable baby adoptions or incest until she had some proof.

"I don't suppose," she said, nodding toward Sam, "he's admitted to anything but hiding Jake, but that should be enough to get him temporarily locked up for housing a fugitive."

The sheriff hooted a laugh. "Hiding Jake? He didn't know a thing about Jake here. When Ginger spotted Jake just before you came, she was afraid for her life, 'cause Jake said he'd kill both of them if she didn't feed him. You said it was your idea to come here so they didn't set you up. Ginger's keeping a secret under duress from her man's all she's guilty of and Sam's not guilty of a thing.''

"You have to be kidding!" Emma exploded, jumping out of the car and leaning back in to stare at him. "Your report will be that Sam didn't know? And Ginger could have locked him in the smokehouse at any time, could have called you like I did—''

The sheriff slowly got out of the cruiser, and leaned both arms on the top of it to talk to her across the roof. "Not all womenfolk're pushy as you, Emma. You ain't related to that bastard brother of yours for nothing, so I'd advise you to just let it all drop and go back to midwifin' and try to do a better job'n it looks like you did with Amrine—and your cousin's wife and kid."

She glared at him, then just shook her head. She almost retorted that she thought his own wife was pretty pushy to want him to take her to deserted places to turn her on. And would the two lovebirds be using the smokehouse as a trysting place now that Jake had battered it in? But she knew he'd be after her worse if she let on what she knew about him and his wife.

"Can I go now, Sheriff?"

"Yeah, why don't you do that 'fore you get yourself in deeper."

Without another word, she walked to her Jeep, got in and drove away.

She called Sissy and told her to lie low, not to leave J.G.'s side.

"Mission impossible since he's gone for a couple of hours to see friends," Sissy told her. "But Jake really did come back…and tried… Emma, you come over here and spend the night.''

"Trish wanted me to stay with them at Big Blue Farm, but I'm not scared anymore. I'm sure Jake's the one who's been bothering me, probably with Sam and Ginger's help. Now he's lit out up toward Cutshin with men and hounds on his tail, so he's not coming back here.''

"Then I'm not worried, either. He'd have to hitch a ride back into town…''

"Just lock your doors and be careful. You hear me?''

"You sound like Mama sometimes, Emma. But I guess you felt you had to take over with me after she died, even when Delia took us in. I love you, and I'll be all right. The Lord's gonna take care of me and this baby I'm gonna birth, I told you that.''

Emma nearly jumped through the ceiling when the phone rang an hour later, interrupting her pacing and glancing out her locked windows.

"Emma, Sheriff Merrell here.''

"Did you find Jake?''

"Sure did, and only had to put two bullets in him. Treed him at Cutshin like a 'coon—or a skunk.''

She sucked in a breath at the way he'd put that.

"He's not—dead?''

"I was real tempted. Naw, just wounded. He's on his way to Highboro Hope, then my jail 'til he goes back to the big pokey. Didn't think I'd better let your doctor boyfriend patch him up or the doc just might try to help out by fixin' Jake up real permanent. The doc knows all about that.''

"What?''

"Nothing. You gonna thank me for saving your hide

a second time today? If Jake was still loose, I wouldn't put it past him to come after you at night anymore.''

"I said I was grateful. I'm the one who phoned for help to hand my own brother in, sheriff. I'm sure you'll see that the sad Weston story is recounted in all the papers again.''

She shouldn't have, but she hung up. Fighting tears, she punched in Sissy's number to update her on Jake. Though the grief pressed hard on her, she felt relieved, too. At least she was physically free from Jake again. She might not sleep well tonight, but at last she'd feel safe.

Emma had finally fallen into a dreamless slumber when she heard a sound. A tractor motor revving, then a woman's screams and pleas, eternal shrieks of the soul...

Emma sat straight up in bed and screamed, then threw herself onto the floor to kneel with her eyes screwed shut and her hands clamped over her ears. It was real, loud, the perfect, yet perverted, rendition of the day her mother died.

With horror she realized her nighttime tormentor was not Jake. It was someone clever, which surely ruled out Sam and the Eubankses. And tonight it was the worst form of torture.

Every muscle clenched tight, Emma gritted her teeth. Perspiration slicked her skin but she felt chilled and nauseated. Griff had been right: she couldn't bear this alone and she had to learn to trust him. She needed Griff. Needed him to hold her as hard as she'd held her mother when she died.

As she headed for the phone to call him, shots rang out. Instinctively, she hit the floor. Were those recorded or real? Who would go to this much trouble to scare her? Was it Hank, with all his audiovisual gear, who expected her to call him, to flee to his arms? Delia, who knew all the Westons' secrets and really wanted her out of town, even though she'd apparently offered a tenuous truce? Perhaps Mike and Trish?

She made the call. "Griff, it's Emma," she said as soon as he answered. "I know it's late, but someone's outside, making noises—trying to scare me. It's not J-Jake. They caught him. I thought I was safe. I need help and I'm sorry about what I said bef—"

"Hold tight. I'll be right there."

The whole nightmare scenario began again. As men's shouts rang out amidst the sound of shots outside, she heard Cory Eubanks's name shouted. Was all this supposed to sound like the night Pa shot him? And then the woman's screams and the tractor roaring began again, so loud that she didn't hear Griff's car until he honked the horn.

She had never been so glad to see that old Chrysler. He'd evidently scattered whomever was out there, because the first thing he said when he came to the door was, "I heard a roaring sound, but I didn't see anyone."

She threw herself into his arms.

16

"What a hell of a mess," Griff said as they stood in the dark house, peeking out between the curtains. She had told him about finding Ola, about going to Sam's and the nighttime harassment, and about her suspicions that someone was stealing babies.

"I heard about Jake," he said, "but I figured you'd be with Sissy, and I wasn't sure I'd be welcomed here again. You should have called me right away."

He put both arms around her, touched by her need for him. "I never realized midwives deserved hazardous-duty pay," he said, trying to keep her spirits up. Closing the curtains, he pulled her to sit in his lap at the bottom of the stairs. He wanted to comfort her, but she needed to tell him some things she must be hiding, though, God knows, he should be the one confessing here.

"I think it's time," he said slowly, calmly, "that you explain about losing your mother."

She nodded. "Of all that happened, it's the worst, the most unfair. I guess I blamed God for it, just like when I lost Sissy's baby, when it's not God's fault at all."

"I understand bitterness and anger. I watched my dad die of cancer—my dad and my hero." His voice caught. He almost blurted out the rest of it, but the truth might shake her hard-won confidence in him and he needed her trust.

She swallowed and gripped his left arm with both hands. He thought she had decided not to tell him, but finally she said, "After Pa and Jake went to prison, we needed food and money. My mother borrowed a tractor to plow the largest hillside field." She spoke matter-of-factly, as if reading from a newspaper headline, staring not at him but straight at the wall. "I saw her get crushed to death under it."

He sucked in a swift breath and held her tighter. "I'm sor—"

She shook her head so hard her hair whipped his cheeks and chin. "Don't stop me now if you want to know." She cleared her throat. "It's a common accident in the hills. You'll get one at the health center sooner or later, hopefully not fatal."

She started to cry, gasping for her next words, her shoulder heaving against his chest. "They tip real easy on a hill if you don't know what you're doing, and she didn't. I guess it was in all the Kentucky papers back then."

The papers, the press, those microphones stuck in his face. He saw and heard it all again, reporters shouting for a statement. Was he guilty, had he done it? Burying his face in her hair, he held her even closer.

"So I realize," Emma was saying, almost choking on her words now, "many people could know the details—if they wanted to fake a recording to torment me. I tried to get the tractor off her, but couldn't. I tried to drag her out while Sissy ran to the road for help, but it took them—the rescue squad and the sheriff—so long to come. Reg Merrell had dated Mama years before and she threw him over, and I blamed him at first, even in the papers, and he's never forgiven that."

When she hesitated, he asked, "You don't think Reg Merrell could be behind any of this?"

"He hasn't done anything but ignore me for years. And he's pretty busy with his new wife. I'm starting to think the brains behind it might be someone who wants me to leave midwifing, to leave the field open so more babies can be taken. Reg Merrell can't be tied to that, except..."

"Except what?" he prompted when her voice trailed off.

"Ola threatened to call him if I didn't leave her alone. And Carter Doyal kept glancing at him, real nervous, when I questioned him about something at Lottie's baby's funeral. But then—" she sucked in a big breath "—there's Hank. I threw him over the way Mama did Reg Merrell."

"History repeats itself?"

"No!" she insisted, sitting up straight to face him. "I've dedicated my life to history *not* repeating itself, with me or other mountain women around here."

"You and Delia seem the exceptions to that rule." He paused before continuing, "You don't think that Delia could be behind things like dead animals and recordings of—"

"It's not her style. But it *is* her style to hire others to do her dirty work f— I didn't mean you."

"It's all right. Besides, now I've got some better reasons to stay than Delia's paying off my debts."

"You know, sometimes I even think J.G. could be doing this, maybe with help from Hank."

"Things are that bad with you and J.G.? I think he'd better just concentrate on taking care of his wife."

She swiped at her tears with both hands, then, as he'd seen her do before, got hold of herself. Gently disengaging from his embrace, she sat beside him on the stairs. She turned and leaned toward him. "Griff, in your tenuous position, I'm not asking you to help me, but…"

It was exactly what he wanted to hear. "I'm with you, if you want me," he vowed.

The look in her eyes said she did, hopefully, in more ways than one.

After Emma fixed Griff breakfast, he hurried into town for two early appointments, ones he was proud of as he built up the health center, she could tell. Despite the glow she'd felt, sending him off with kisses after sleeping in his arms last night, she still could not stem her growing panic.

What haunted her now was Griff's saying that J.G. had better concentrate on taking care of his wife. As she thought about his comment, it brought back a memory: J.G. standing against a lighted barn with his hand out for money from Mike Bonner. And Mike telling him he'd better watch sneaking out at night, because he had his wife to take care of soon.

J.G. and Mike—maybe Trish, too—must be involved in something secretive and underhanded, so maybe they wanted to scare her off. But whatever was going on had to be something besides finding babies to be adopted. J.G. would soon have his own baby, and Trish had decided not to adopt.

Though Emma calmed down enough to see a new client, Susie Jordan, the third referral from Hank—for her first prenatal, she still felt deeply disturbed. She should be telling Susie, who was looking at her now with such trust, all bright-faced in the glow of her new pregnancy, *Your initial tests look fine, but I've got to warn you that you and your baby may be at risk. Some-one's out to get me, maybe so I don't discover who's taking my clients and their babies, and you and your little one could be next.*

As soon as the appointment was over, she called Sissy's house to make sure she had gone on her usual Monday-morning rounds, singing hymns at two nursing homes in Highboro. When J.G. answered, she hung up. Ten minutes later, she was knocking on his door.

However bad she felt, her brother-in-law looked worse.

"Been missing sleep lately?" she asked as he poured them both coffee and they sat across from each other at the dining room table. Morning sun streamed in the window, highlighting crumbs and stains on the plastic-lace tablecloth between them.

"My back gives me fits now and then," he muttered as he dumped two huge teaspoons of sugar into his cup. "I'd be better off just sleeping on a board. Now that Sissy's so big and sleeps all funny with pillows under her and all, I been using the back bedroom."

"Which also makes it easier to sneak out at night."

"Whoa!" he said, raising both hands. "You better not come in here trying to say I'm cheating on Sissy."

"Not unless you're doing it with Mike Bonner—for cash."

He slumped over the table, then came erect, grimacing when his back evidently pained him. "Mike tell you that?" he asked.

"I saw it with my own eyes the other night, when I had the concussion. I didn't remember it until this morning. J.G., I need some answers, and I'm not even sure what the questions are. What in God's name have you been doing?"

He took a big swig of coffee, then put down his cup to stare into its depths, swirling it with both big hands. "Life's tough, you know that. No one gets out alive."

"Can the jokes," she insisted, leaning forward toward him and tapping the table. "Have you been stealing antique furniture and selling it to the Bonners or what?"

He still didn't meet her eyes, but frowned at the wall behind her. "You don't know how bad it's been, not being able to give Sissy what she needs."

"Bull. She needs your support and love, and that's free."

He swirled his coffee so hard it slopped onto the tablecloth. He mopped it up with a swipe of the cuff of his shirt. "You, of all people, gotta understand pride. Bettering yourself—you done it."

"But not illegally. I don't know what you're doing, but I saw something else that night at Bonners—your old buddy-boy Hank taking pictures of you getting paid off.

He swore low, then slammed his cup on the table, splattering the rest of the coffee. He hurled the empty cup into the corner, where it cracked apart. After facing Jake yesterday, Emma didn't so much as flinch.

"I'll tell you," he said, pointing a meaty finger at her, "if you swear you won't tell Sissy."

"Not until after the baby, at least," she promised.

"Deal." He heaved a huge sigh that sank his shoulders. "It's timber."

"Timber? What about it?" she asked before she realized what he meant. Her voice rose. "Timber rustling? You?"

"I don't cut or haul the stuff—couldn't with this back no more—but I'm a spotter for locations. I tell cutters, they get it and pass it on to Mike, who has contacts and—''

''I can't believe you'd be part of the rape of Appalachia.''

''Oh, give me a break. That midwife or women's-lib talk? The rape of Appalachia? Do you always have to be so damn dramatic? Wood grows back, and some deserted lots are too shady with old trees...''

She put her head in her hands. His voice trailed off, so maybe he realized what a jackass he'd made of himself, how stupid he sounded trying to rationalize his participation in such a scheme, no matter how desperate he was for money.

''I'm gonna need the dough, Emma, 'specially if Hank Welling turns me in and my disability gets slashed. I guess I could even get sued. But I could keep him from doing that, if you'd only give him a little attention now and th—''

''That's it!'' she cried, smacking the table and jumping up. ''Maybe you can use me just like those trees to get what you want, right? Now I know why Mike acts so secretive sometimes. But we're talking about you right now. Don't you realize that it was probably timber rustlers who burned Sissy and me out at Cutshin? You could be in bed with the same bastards!''

She was partway out the door when he managed to catch up to her and swing her around to face him. ''You said you won't tell Sissy, but I want your word you're not gonna turn me in to Reg Merrell like you done Jake.''

''Jake was going to kill me.''

He shook her once, but pain flitted across his face again and he loosened his grip on her.

She straightened her shoulders and glared up at him.

"The code around here might be live and let live, but I don't know what I'm going to do. You've got to find something more honest than thieving trees or—"

"Or what?" he shouted. "Can you see me following Sissy everywhere like some lapdog or guitar-carrying sap while she sings for old folks or church socials? Or should I just stay to home and change diapers all day?" He banged his fist on the screen door so hard it popped from its frame. "I'm no killer, I'm not like Jake, but you tell all this, and I'll find some way to keep Sissy and that new baby from you. I swear I will."

She grasped for something defiant to say, but that was her worst fear now. Not that J.G. could stop her from seeing Sissy and the baby, but that some nameless evil, disease or death, would spring from the dark to harm them, to take them away like the others she had been close to.

Emma hated to do it, but she was going to tell Hank to keep clear of her—and her property—for good. Not wanting to face him alone somewhere, she went into town to waylay him at Arletta's where he met his mother for lunch every Monday—old Mrs. Welling's big weekly outing. The trick was to use this public place to keep Hank from throwing a fit, yet not upset his mother.

Emma called to Hank on the curb as he got out of his government-issued car. His face showed disbelief, then joy. His eyes actually looked teary as he adjusted his wire-rimmed glasses.

"Em, you've seen the light."

"No, but I've heard too many late-night tape recordings. Now, who do I know who's adept at all that?"

"What?" he cried, smacking his hands at his sides

in exasperation. "I don't know what you're talking about."

She had to give him credit: he looked totally baffled. "I'm talking about the sound shows I've been honored with, terrible shrieking, a tractor—"

"I swear to God, I don't know what you mean. I wouldn't do something like that."

"Any problem here?" a man's voice cut in. Griff had approached without her noticing.

"Hell, yes," Hank yelled, "there's a problem here. It's a paranoid woman who should be locked up just like her broth—"

"Shut up, Welling," Griff said as he stepped between Emma and Hank. Emma knew, the morning edition of the *Hillboro Herald* had already been printed, and so wouldn't have covered Sheriff Merrell's heroic deeds catching Jake, but it was obvious that Hank and probably the whole town already knew the latest.

"Tell him you came after me, Em," Hank said in a low voice when Griff looked even more belligerent.

"It's true," she conceded. "I needed to ask him about the nightly shows someone's been playing for my benefit. I can handle this."

The minute she said that, she realized she sounded as if she was cutting Griff off again. The three of them stood momentarily like players in a childhood game of statues, slung in awkward poses they had to hold.

"I'll keep my ears open about your problem," Hank said, "and try to help like I did with your finding Len Roscoe when you asked. And I'll be sure you get some other information you need, too."

"What inform—" she stopped midsentence as he shoved past her into the restaurant.

"I think," Griff said, "you've ruined his meal. After

confronting him, do you think he's responsible for the trouble you've been having at your place?"

"He seemed honestly shocked I asked. But I don't know any other way to go at this than full steam ahead. Something's got to spring loose somewhere."

This quaint little restaurant surely beats that doughnut shop in Ohio, Jidge Collister thought as she watched the local wildlife gather for lunch. She'd learned a lot in Jackson, not about a G.G. who made quilts or about babies or adoption scams, but about how not to arouse suspicion. Here, she was being a lot more careful. For the time being, under the assumed name Jillian Lister, she just watched and listened.

"I can't stay long today, Ma," the thirty-something, preppy-looking guy with wire-rimmed glasses told the dowdy, white-haired woman at the next table. "Something came up that needs seeing to."

Jidge noted he had entered the restaurant in a high huff. And that, except for his twang, he'd fit more naturally in a tony San Francisco restaurant than this down-home greasy spoon. She stabbed her fork into her chicken-and-gravy sandwich as she strained to eaves-drop.

"Oh dear," the old woman said, patting his arm with her liver-spotted hand. "You're always so busy lately. Not another trip out of town or more secret phone calls to those girls about their babies."

Jidge dropped her fork against the plate like a chime. No one so much as turned her way. Unfortunately, since the noise level was going up in here as more people came in, she might have trouble hearing what else the couple had to say.

"I'm just suggesting to several mothers-to-be I had

previously recommended Em to that they're better off at Delia's clinic, that's all," the preppy guy said. "Em's got to learn who's boss here, the power I can wield. And I've got some more research to do on-line about that doctor of Delia's, that's all."

Jidge scrambled in her purse for her tiny suede notebook to jot down the array of names before she forgot them. It was like an answer from heaven, a place to start digging. Now she'd just have to find someone to question about who these people were and what their links could be to Shelter babies. Meanwhile, so she didn't raise suspicion, she was going looking for antiques, then ask there about quilt shopping.

As they had almost every evening since the night of the storm, Emma and Griff drove to see Lottie, though this time they went together. After a brief visit in Lottie's room, Griff always went to the cafeteria with Rooster while Emma sat by Lottie's bed, talking to her in a low voice and picking up where her husband had left off. Rooster was staying at the Bonners' house in town while a neighbor and Clary Doyal helped with his kids. No way, though, Emma had already decided, would Sissy be staying at the Bonners' as Trish had offered. Not until she found out who was guilty of dealing in both live and dead babies.

"So, your girls are doing just fine, Lottie, and they miss you bad," she chattered on to the unconscious woman. "I want you to hear me now and come back to us. Those sweet daughters of yours and Rooster need you..." She bounced Lottie's hand gently and watched as the woman did one of her huge yawns that so excited them—even though they knew they only meant that her brain stem was still functioning. The hanging IV tubes flopped when she moved even slightly.

Emma shifted one tube to unkink it. Her gaze followed it up to the hanging bag. Unlike the others, this one wasn't marked. She stood to look at it closer. Just more fluids or glucose? Medicine? She knew what was in the other bags.

She shook her head at her total obsession with random suspicions lately. She was seeing crimes and double-dealings everywhere, and trusting no one but Griff. And, of course, there was poor Sissy, who had no idea what J.G. was up to and needed to be warned that something was threatening babies in Shelter—as soon as Emma figured out what that was. The fact that Sissy didn't know what J.G. was into, of course, proved that Trish didn't necessarily know what Mike was up to, either.

"You know, Lottie," she continued, bringing her mind back to her friend, "I'm thinking of bringing you a gospel tape Sissy made for the convalescent center. It's got your favorite 'Blest Be the Tie That Binds.'"

Her voice drifted off as she looked at that unmarked IV bag again. *The tie that binds,* she thought. She got up and went out to get the nurse.

"I'm a nurse myself," she began, leaning over the raised counter of the nurses' station, "and—"

"The midwife who attended Mrs. Weston's baby, I hear," the sleek-haired, young brunette said, squinting up at her through glasses that magnified her brown eyes.

Emma frowned, but of course, even Rooster could have told her that, and Emma herself had announced it in the E.R. the night Lottie was brought in. But she was certain this nurse—Gaynelle Pritchard, her ID badge read—had made the statement with censure in her voice.

"I'm wondering," Emma tried again, "if you could tell me what's in one of the IV drips in Mrs. Weston's arm."

"There are several," she said, not getting up. "Which one?"

"The unlabeled one," Emma told her, hands on hips.

That, at least, got her up to take a look.

"I—I'm not sure," she said as they leaned together beside Lottie's bed. Her glasses slid down on her nose, and she shoved them back up. "I'd have to ask Dr. McGill. The thing is, I'm not sure it was here when he did his rounds earlier."

"Would you page him about it, please?" Emma asked, more concerned. "Or just do a test on the fluid?"

"You're sounding quite an alarmist."

"I am quite an alarmist. Have you seen another bag that isn't marked? In this entire hospital?"

"No, but that doesn't mean—"

"Never mind then. I'll speak with your supervisor and have Dr. McGill paged myself."

"Hardly," she said huffily. "I was just fixing to take care of that."

By the time Rooster and Griff returned, there was no sign that anything was amiss. Emma kept her doubts to herself, even when Nurse Pritchard came in, removed the drip needle and squirted some of it into a beaker without a word. She replaced the needle into Lottie's arm. When she was gone, Emma slid it out herself and let it dangle, dripping on the floor. Nurse Pritchard might think she'd done that herself or, if not, Emma could handle one more problem.

When Emma and Griff walked out into the hall a few

minutes later, they saw the young nurse on the phone at the nurses' station, frantically nodding her head.

"Yes, doctor, yes I know," Emma could hear her say. "Yes, right away. I'll remove it but wait for you then. Oh—" she said as she turned and caught Emma and Griff listening, though Griff was now shooting questions at Emma.

Emma held up her hand and followed the nurse into Lottie's room. She frowned at Emma when she saw the needle was already out, but she didn't say a word. She unhooked the bag from its chrome holder and carried it and the tube into the hall as if it were a venomous snake.

"What is that liquid?" Emma demanded, trailing her as Griff came behind. "Tell me, because I'm going to find out anyway."

"It's pentobarbital."

"A barbiturate?" Griff demanded, his voice carrying in the hall. Other nurses and visitors looked up. "That's what doctors use to induce a medical coma. Who the hell prescribed that for a comatose woman?"

"We—we don't know," she replied grimly as Dr. McGill jumped off the elevator and came running, white coat flapping.

It was the prettiest sight Emma had seen in days.

17

When Amrine nursed little Laurie like this, she felt love flow into her as mother's milk flowed out of her. The room she shared with another woman was fixed up real nice. It reminded her of Emma's waiting room at the Baby Farm, with its pretty prints and pillows, things on the walls. And that made her miss Emma, though she still was scared Emma could have been the one Len phoned about placing the baby, about paying for the baby when Laurie was beyond any price.

Amrine knew she should look into bringing charges against Len and Emma, but she felt safe in this Atlanta shelter, and she didn't want to tangle with Len again. She'd made up a story about her man not wanting the baby, saying he'd kill her if she went home. But she guessed, other than changed names and places, it wasn't much of a story, after all. She'd just keep her mouth shut and try to get a job here. Until then, child support, food stamps, and Medicaid would get them through.

Just then, her roommate, Jenna, opened the door and stepped in.

"Oh, sorry," she said. Jenna always apologized and whispered and was shyer than Amrine had ever been. "Didn't know you was nursing."

"It's okay. It's your room, too. Come on in."

Jenna was a pale, plump blonde but her face and arms—more of her, too, which people couldn't see—

had purplish and gray bruises. Her right eye wasn't swollen shut anymore, but the puffy area around it was still black-and-blue.

Jenna stepped in and stood by the single window, looking out over a concrete playground. Shouts from a pickup basketball game floated up to them. It was a view Amrine knew by heart. This building in the shadow of a Catholic church had once housed nuns. The skyscrapers of Atlanta hung over the closer buildings, but Amrine like to imagine they were just hills and mountains.

"Sometimes I think it'd be easier to run away for good," Jenna whispered. They'd had a few talks, but it was the first time her roommate had said anything so personal.

"Then start over? You may be right."

Jenna slowly turned to face her with her arms wrapped around her middle like she was hugging herself. "No, I mean run away permanent. From the earth. Period. The end."

"Kill yourself?"

At the tone of Amrine's voice, the baby startled and her eyes widened, so she said, her voice quieter, "You better talk that out with the counselor."

"Anne's nice, but she's paid. It's not like she really cares."

"Maybe she was abused, too," Amrine said. "She understands."

"Understands herself, not me. Not how I can't fight back, but should have."

"I have—had—a friend always preaching that."

"Yeah, well, your friend was right. Even if we can't live each other's lives, she was right to say that. In a way, you did that. You didn't just go along with his ideas, Laurie's father's.''

"I guess that's right." Amrine smiled down into Laurie's adoring gaze, then up at Jenna again. "But how does fighting back square with wanting to do yourself in? Isn't that like the biggest abuse you could to yourself?''

"I don't know. I don't know anything anymore.''

For once Jenna's voice got louder, and Laurie looked her way. Jenna noticed and came closer, her stiff expression softening.

"I only know," Amrine said, "that my friend used to say not to quit, no matter what others said or did and no matter how bad and black things looked.''

"Did your friend have this?" Jenna asked, holding out both arms, wrist up, and shoving one long sleeve up her arm to bare its bruises, then the other. "And this?''

"Worse than that," Amrine said, realizing for the first time that she'd never seen a real bruise—a surface bruise—on Emma. "I used to get real mad at her for keeping after me, trying to mother me worse than she did her kid sister. I guess that kept me alive sometimes when— Listen," she interrupted herself, "if you don't tell Anne you're thinking suicide, I'm gonna. You got to get some help here so you can heal, outside and in. And don't you just go running off somewhere else, 'cause that's not gonna help.''

Jenna looked angry, then nodded and turned away, maybe so she wouldn't cry. She stared out the window again, and Amrine went on nursing Laurie. But for the first time, no matter what bad things Emma might be involved in, Amrine knew her friend's stubborn strength had birthed something good inside her.

* * *

"I'd put your new nurse, Pam Stark, right up there on the list of possibles," Emma insisted as Griff drove his big Chrysler out of the hospital lot and headed home. "She used to work in this very hospital."

"In pediatrics only," he pointed out, "so someone would have spotted her as not belonging in ICU. How about throwing me in the mix, too, since I knew right away what pentobarbital meant? Actually, I don't especially trust Miss Nasty Nurse back there on Lottie's floor, so are we going to look into everyone with enough money to bribe her? How about Trish and Mike? They live nearby. Or Delia. Of course, I've seen overworked hospital staff make some terrible mistakes on their own with no one behind it so—"

"You're not helping," she interrupted. "I realize I don't have answers yet."

She almost confided in him about Mike Bonner being in on the timber rustling, but then he'd really accuse her of seeing suspects everywhere. He'd probably insist on confronting Mike about it, and she didn't want to do that yet. Besides, timber rustling paled next to rustling Appalachian babies.

"You even told me," he went on, his voice quieter now, "that your false-labor patient, what's-her-name…"

"Ruth Wicklow."

"Right—that she still works at the hospital and was pretty hostile to you before she switched to having her baby there."

"Griff, I said you're not helping."

"I'm not trying to upset you. I'm just saying you need one hell of a lot more proof, some sort of link."

"I know. That's why we're going to have to wait for

Lottie to come out of that coma. I wish they could have given us a more definite answer on when. At least she's going to be all right. I don't know how I'm going to face her when I think her real child, probably a son, is out there, adopted by strangers somewhere.''

"And yet, there's no real proof anything's amiss,'' Griff reminded her. "Even if Ola gave her child up for adoption, even if Amrine's gone, even if—"

"I said stop it! Something's really wrong. There are reasons apart from me being a meddling midwife that someone could be trying to scare me away from Shelter!''

He reached for her hand, but even that didn't calm her. She knew she needed to talk to Trish alone about what happened, minute by minute, the night of Lottie's delivery. The Bonners' story had been believable and had jived with the emergency-squad guys' report. But she and Griff were not wrong about Lottie's baby being male and being smaller than the one they'd buried.

Emma's beeper went off and, not recognizing the number on the display, she called it right away. Susie Jordan, whose prenatal she had done earlier today, was on the line, sounding jumpy compared to how low-key she had been this morning.

"I'm sorry, Ms. Weston, but I've had second thoughts about using a midwife. I've decided to go with the health center in Shelter from now on, with the doctor there and all the equipment they have. No hard feelings, I hope—"

Emma frowned at Griff. "Hank Welling suggested me to you, didn't he?"

"Well—yes, but now my husband and I changed our minds."

"I thought you said your husband was out of town

until Friday and you wouldn't be able to tell him how well your prenatal went until he called tonight."

"Look, is this some kind of third degree? Please just send my records to the health center, will you?"

"Of course, I will. Susie, did Hank Welling or someone else talk you out of—"

The line went dead.

"Why the glares at me?" Griff asked as they passed the Shelter 3 Miles sign. "What was that about?"

"You just inherited my new client, Susie Jordan. Thanks, I think, to Hank, but I'm not even sure of that. If I've been looking for a pattern, my clients running like I have the plague is sure one."

"But you're blaming Pam Stark for one defection and Hank—"

"You know," she mused aloud as she turned toward him on the wide seat, "with all the community visits Hank's done over the years to black-lung victims and people who get insurance benefits, he's had access to a lot of homes and families. If he recommends doctors and midwives, he might just recommend an adoption agency, even push people into one, bribe them or something."

"Next time you corner Hank, take me along."

She nodded, wondering if she only had to worry about women who *had* been her patients but whose babies were *not* delivered by her. She hugged herself hard when she realized that included Sissy.

Emma used her cell phone to call the hospital again to check on Lottie, who was showing more motor reflexes but still not responding to verbal stimulation. The next road sign said simply, Shelter Kentucky, 2 Miles.

"I've got my weekly dinner at Hill House with Delia

tonight," he told her, "but I'm going to cancel so I can stay with you."

Her stomach clenched in excitement—or something that went far deeper. "I can't ask you to do that. Delia and I are almost getting along, so let's not get her stirred up."

"I don't want you out there alone," he said and reached for her hand again, not taking his eyes off the twists and turns. He squeezed her wrist, then got both hands back on the wheel.

"All right," he said when she didn't say more, "we'll compromise. I'll eat with Delia, then come out to stay the night. Look!" he suddenly cried, hitting the brakes. "That woman out of her car on that curve. She's going to get hit, standing there."

He slowed the Chrysler and coasted up behind her, getting as far off the road as he could. He hit his warning blinkers.

"California plates," Emma observed. "In Shelter? Wait, let me exit on this side of the car, or you'll get your door taken off."

"At the least," he agreed, watching another car whiz by. "If she's broken down, tell her we'll give her a lift to the gas station and Quincy can fix her vehicle. And watch you don't scrape your door on the rocks."

"Are you all right?" Emma called to the woman as they approached each other under the cliffside overhang.

"A flat, front right," the woman shouted back. "And on this turn where I could have careened off into that ravine on the other side. I'd certainly appreciate a ride back into Shelter."

Back into Shelter, Emma thought. Then she wasn't

just lost or driving through. "That's where we're going," she assured her.

"Thanks. Let me get my purse and bag."

Besides the California plate and the clipped, flat accent, there were plenty of things that screamed "foreign" about the woman. She was big-boned with bronze skin, probably Hispanic. Slightly plump, she wore a strikingly sophisticated pantsuit in olive green and lilac, accented with chunky, gold jewelry on her earlobes, wrist and wedding-ring finger. She had a huge, leather purse and a soft suede overnight bag she clung to as she hurried toward Emma on platform shoes.

"Do you and your husband collect antique cars?" the woman asked, eyeing the Chrysler. "I love antique anything."

"Have I got the place for you," Emma told her, "but this isn't my husband, just a friend. I'm Emma Weston and this," she said as they both got in, "is Dr. Griff Cusak."

The woman seemed to perk up at both names. "I'm really pleased to meet both of you," she told them with a broad smile. "This is so kind of you. Actually I'm looking for a place to rent a room in Shelter while I look around—antiques, quilts—just a rest off the beaten path. I'm Jillian Lister—please call me Jill—and I've been driving cross-country to give myself some downtime before facing up to a divorce. I'm from Santa Barbara."

"Sorry about the divorce, but glad you're here, Jill," Griff told her, extending an arm back over the seat to shake her hand. Her bracelet rattled musically. He put the car in gear and looked over his shoulder to be sure he could accelerate without someone bearing down on them from around the curve.

"Actually," she said, "I saw a man at the edge of the ravine with a rifle. I heard a pop, and my tire just went flat. I almost skidded out of control. It's crazy, but I think he must have been hunting and actually shot my tire out."

Griff hit the brakes. His eyes met Emma's in a stretch of silence until he said, "You two sit tight a minute and let me check."

"What did the man look like?" Emma asked Jill, her heart pounding as Griff got quickly out and closed the door behind him. They were on the other side of town from where her Jeep had been shot at, but that didn't mean anything since nothing was making sense lately, anyway.

"It was so quick, I couldn't say. Dark garments, maybe brown fatigues. You—you don't think someone would do that just because I've been asking questions in town, about where to find antiques, do you? I mean, I know I don't quite fit in, but there's not some anti-outsiders thing here, is there? You two have been so nice…"

"Jill, if you don't mind an old farmhouse, I've got an extra room for a night or two," Emma said before she remembered Griff might be staying, too. "I'm the local midwife, and my women's health center's downstairs in my house."

"That's so thoughtful. I'd insist on paying, of course, just like in a B&B."

"No way. I'd appreciate the company," Emma assured her.

"Yeah, looks like a bullet hole," Griff said, getting back in the car, not daring to meet Emma's eyes, "but I'll have them dig it out at the gas station. Jill, do you want to report it to the pol—"

"She doesn't know what the man with the rifle looked like," Emma cut in, "so what's the use? What could—or would—the sheriff do, anyway?"

"Suits me," Jill said, plopping back in her seat with her purse and bag tight beside her. "I don't want the police involved."

Griff nodded, then checked in the rearview mirror and took off around the next curve in the road.

"I'm so beat. I'll be asleep in no time in this quiet," Jill told Emma as they ate at the kitchen table. "Try living in a big city."

"Is Santa Barbara pretty wild?"

"Ah, at times," Jill admitted, finishing up her chicken salad with gusto. "You've got a great place here, and I'm fascinated by your work," she went on, bouncing up to clear her dishes as if she wasn't tired at all. But maybe, Emma thought, she was just wired from four cups of coffee.

"Being a midwife has been my dream, my life," Emma told her. "Lately, though, I'd almost rather own a dress shop for oversize—"

"Special-size," Jill corrected, wagging a finger.

"Right, special-size women," Emma nodded. "Right now working at your shop in Santa Barbara sounds good to me."

"Trouble with Griff, in other words," Jill said. "Sorry if I'm overstepping, but in a dress shop, believe it or not, I counsel a lot of women about life—stress, relationships, men. You probably do, too. Too bad," she added with a shake of her sleek head, "it's hard to counsel yourself sometimes."

"You mean your divorce?" Emma asked, joining her at the sink just in time to see a truck drive in. Trish.

"Uh-oh, looks like business for you," Jill said.

"Business for you. That's Trish Bonner, who owns that antique barn I was telling you about outside of town. She and her husband go back and forth between that place and their house in Highboro, but ask her if you can visit tomorrow. They've got furniture, old wood, even quilts like you mentioned. She showed me a darling one for a baby's crib not long ago, and she gave my sister one for a baby shower you would really love..."

To Emma's amazement, Jill beat her to the porch door.

When Jill finally made herself scarce by going upstairs to unpack, Emma decided she'd try probing Trish's Achilles' heel. "I don't mean to pry," she said, interested to see her friend's head jerk around in alarm at those few words, "but I've been picking up some vibes for a long time that you and Mike are considering adopting a baby."

"Oh, that," Trish said with a shrug. "It's an old, tired topic between us. It's just that we're so busy. I guess it's one reason I'm so fascinated by what you do. And—" her voice wavered "—why I wanted to help Lottie. You know, kiddo, I actually thought you were going to give me lecture number two about taking heirlooms from the area. But honestly, Emma, we're helping people out by buying things, and we would never take something they don't want to part with."

For one moment, Emma stared into her friend's clear hazel eyes, trying to read sincerity there, trying to assure herself Trish hadn't just swiftly, subtly shifted subjects. She almost brought up the illegal timber trade, but if Trish didn't know about it, she wasn't prepared to cause a rift between her and Mike, nor did she want to alienate another friend around here. Besides, if Trish was in on it, she'd probably lie, then warn Mike. The thing was, if she covered that up for him, what else might they be secretly dealing in?

Emma was glad she hadn't said more, because somehow, quietly, Jill had come back downstairs and was standing in the hall, apparently engrossed in baby pictures where she could surely have overheard them. It was Trish who pulled them from the awkward silence.

"What in heaven's name!" she cried as she stooped to look past Emma out the window toward the front lawn. "Do I see a child alone on the road?"

Emma hurried to look out. "I can't believe it—Vinie Doyal, Clary and Carter's daughter."

"She doesn't look to be more than five," Jill's voice called after Emma as she hurried to the front door. "You're an angel to keep rescuing waifs off the roads…"

Emma ran across the grass, calling, "Vinie, how did you get clear down here from your house?"

"I walked, a course," the little girl declared, and Emma saw that one hand held a bundle of clothes tied in a lump. "I don't like my brother you brought 'cause we can't go to Disney."

Emma couldn't believe the child was still parroting such nonsense. She took the bundle from her and led her up the lane toward the house. She could see Trish and Jill in animated conversation on the porch, and she hoped Jill was getting information out of Trish that Emma could pry out of her later.

Exhausted or scared, Vinie started to whimper. Emma knelt down and hugged her. "I'll bet your mama and pa are crying right now because they think they lost you," she told the trembling child. "We're going to have to call them. And as for Disney, where did you get the idea you could go there instead of get a brother? Brothers are better, believe me," she said, though her voice snagged over that lie.

"Why?" Vinie demanded, rubbing a dirty fist in an eye before Emma gently pulled her hand down and held it tight.

"Partly because they last a lot longer."

Vinie's face was dirty, and tears tracked down her cheeks and chin. For one moment, Emma almost envied her for being able to run away, to just cry it out. She bent to lift the girl in her arms.

"Come on now, Vinie. I'm going to wash you up and get you some ice cream, and we're going to call your pa to come get you. You love your pa, don't you?"

She felt the child nod against her. "Ladies," Emma said, "this is Vinie who was just taking a walk and—"

The child's shriek nearly broke Emma's eardrum. She kicked to be put down, then lunged toward a startled Trish, grabbing her denim skirt.

"You're the lady," Vinie cried. "The one said we could go to Disney!"

"What?" Trish said, half laughing, bending down. "I don't know what you're talking about, honey. Emma, what is this, some put-up Make a Wish Foundation request?"

"You talked to my pa down by the car," Vinie insisted, "but I saw you out the window. Then he came in and said it to my mama and I heard it. Can we still go? We can give Wes back."

Trish just shook her head and rolled her eyes. "Honest, hon, it wasn't me, and I don't know what you mean, unless I might have been talking to your daddy about buying some old furniture. Sorry. But if I find a Mickey Mouse or Sleeping Beauty doll, I'll see you get it.''

"I got no idea what she meant," Carter told Emma when he came to pick Vinie up as dusk descended.

"You talked to her, Pa," Vinie insisted. She was all cleaned up and full of ice cream and cookies. "I saw you."

"Now you just set there quiet, Vin, and I don't want to hear no more sass nor nothing 'bout giving your brother away!" Carter exploded.

Emma just gaped. A moment ago, he'd been hugging the girl, so glad to have her back. And he was usually so easygoing. For one moment, Emma wondered if there was something to the stubborn little girl's story. She remembered how Carter had seemed so afraid she was going to nail him on something else besides asking for Ola's address at the funeral, glancing toward Reg Merrell as if to be certain the sheriff didn't see them talking.

"She's just exhausted, confused and upset," Emma assured him. She sounded like she was describing herself.

"Sure, I know it," he muttered as he turned away. "Can't thank you enough—again. See you sometime."

"Soon," she said and meant it. Because as crazy as it sounded, anybody who even hinted at giving up a baby for anything needed looking into. And now Trish did, too, since the little girl had insisted she'd made that crazy offer. Lately, trusting a stranger like Jill, a confused kid like Vinie and her own gut instincts was starting to really make more sense than trusting the people she thought she knew well.

18

"**I**'ve been watching you," Pam Stark said, sidling
closer to Griff in the lab as he read a chest X ray on
the view box and she waited for a blood test to develop.
"And I got me a notion your back is killing you."

Griff flexed his shoulders slightly. She was right, but
his neck hurt, too. Though she made him uneasy at
times like right now, Delia's nurse had turned out to be
a good one.

"That's all right. I'll be fine," he muttered as she
began to massage his lower back in a slow circle. She
must be some kind of witch: he could feel heat radiating
from her hand, not to his back but to his groin.

"The doctor as martyr," she murmured, so close behind him her warm breath brushed the back of his ear.
She clamped her free hand around the front of his shoulders to steady him. It was more a wrestling stranglehold
than an embrace.

"Just relax a sec," she protested when he tried to
shift away. "Physicians seldom heal themselves."

Her kneading of his knotted muscles felt so good, but
damned if he was going to tell her that or let her keep
it up. She'd propped her hipbone against his, and a soft
breast pressed against his shoulder blade. He'd been
longing for Emma since he'd slept, holding her close,
three nights ago at her place, but no way was Pam going

to put out the fire. Gently, he disengaged himself, stood and moved away with the X ray in his hand.

"Thanks, but I'm fine," he repeated and purposefully put the countertop between them.

"Or, doctor as coward," she said, looking both defiant and hurt. "I was just trying to help."

"You do help," he told her, stooping to file the X ray in the lowest drawer. "I'm really pleased things have worked out for you to be here." He stood and faced her across the counter. "I've asked Delia to try to lure you to the health center for more than three days a week."

"Hmm," she said, surprising him by her lack of enthusiasm. "I suppose," she went on, grasping the edge of the Formica counter and tipping over it toward him, "I am lurable—but not by Delia."

If not the sensual back rub, the way she slowly licked her lips devastated any doubts he had misread her intentions.

"Let's clear the air, Pam. You're a very attractive woman, but it's more important to me to have a very professional nurse."

"I understand. I also understand that your *un*professional interests lie elsewhere. No, never mind denying it," she said, holding up her hands. "It's just that tension between us won't be productive here."

"Then let's not let tension get started. I said I'd love to have you here full-time, so the tension's not on my part. What are you doing your two days at Hope? Is it something you can leave?"

"Actually, Delia made me an offer I couldn't refuse to have a go at it here. She's paid me enough that I'm only working these three days and giving myself a sabbatical the rest of the week."

"I didn't realize that. I pictured you still working at Hope in pediatrics or—the way you've been recruiting for us—maternity, or even ICU. Someone at the hospital mentioned to me you'd worked intensive care a few years ago," he added in a rush.

He studied her face, hoping for some hint at whether or not she ever went back to the hospital. So far, Lottie's doctor had not discovered who had put the pentobarbital drip in her arm. They were still waiting for her to gain consciousness to throw some light on what had happened to her and her baby.

"Griff, since you brought up intensive care, I've got to say this." She opened the lab door to the hall and leaned against it with her head turned sharply to him. Her stance displayed her body in silhouette—her breasts thrust out and back arched to press her bottom against the door.

"Your work here's getting real compromised by your feelings for the midwife—so my work's compromised, too. I can read Dr. Griffin Cusak's rules of order all right. You give intensive care, even mouth-to-mouth, to a woman whose medical ideas are night and day from yours, while you hold your supporters and sympathizers at arm's length." She shrugged. "So be it then. No wonder, even with your brains and background, you ended up in hillbilly heaven."

She went out, leaving the door open. He was furious she would demean Shelter that way, now that she was part of it. But worse was his shock that he felt protective of this place and people *he* had once branded hillbillies.

As he headed back to his office, he wondered if Delia had hired Pam to seduce him, and if she'd report that he was not cooperating again. He had no doubt that

Delia would strike back if he kept crossing her. He'd just have to watch his sore back better.

Emma answered the phone in her office on the first ring.

"Emma, Griff. Don't hold dinner for me. An overheated radiator at the gas station exploded and scalded the Poteet kid—and Sheriff Merrell, no less."

"Wade? Is it bad? Have you called his mother?"

"Someone went to get her. I can't talk. I got the call from the garage a few minutes ago, and they're walking them in. I'll call you later, but—"

"Don't worry about making it here tonight if patients need you," she assured him. "Jill and I are getting along fine, and I'm going to send her to see Trish and Mike in the morning—just to see if she can find out anything. She's easy to talk to. Good luck with your first emergency—"

"First *medical* emergency. Talk to you later."

She heard him hang up, then another, quick click on the line. Was someone listening in? At the clinic? Surely not here.

She gently placed the receiver in its cradle and tiptoed up the stairs. Jill had said she was going to take a nap. Her bedroom door was closed, and there was no phone in her room. But the door to Emma's bedroom stood ajar when she thought she had closed it.

"See to the kid first, doc," Sheriff Merrell ordered as Quincy and two other men helped them into the health center waiting room. "He was closer and took it right in the face," he explained to the hovering Griff, Pam and Wanda. "'Course," he added when Griff was beginning to think there was at least something to like about the man, "it's his stupid fault for takin' the cap off the hot radiator."

"Nurse Pam and I can take care of you both right away," Griff assured him, but he took the boy by his shaking shoulders to usher him in ahead of the sheriff to a separate room.

Neither of them appeared to be in shock, though Griff wrapped Wade in a blanket and had them both sip saline solution through a straw. The left side of the boy's face, chin, neck and right arm had taken the worst of the hot water and steam. Second- and third-degree burns with blisters were already forming. At least he'd instinctively closed his eyes and saved them.

Griff's heart went out to the boy. He was amazingly brave, at least until the pain began to really set in. His face screwed so tight it hurt Griff to look at him, especially when Wade realized any facial movement was agony. As Griff carefully cleaned and dressed the worst of it, he kept a firm hand on Wade's shoulder to steady him.

"You're being very brave not to let your eyes water, Wade," Griff told him, avoiding so much as mentioning tears to a mountaineer, however young. "That salt water you're sipping is good for you but any kind of salt water on your face will hurt your skin."

"Okay," the boy whispered through puffy lips. Fighting back his own tears, Griff squeezed the boy's shoulders before he let Pam take over, and hurried to Reg Merrell in the next exam room.

"Just part of your cheek and jaw and this wrist?" Griff asked, quickly assessing what Pam had done.

"Just?" the man challenged, gripping the paper-covered edge of the examining table so hard it dented and crinkled. "Easy for you to say."

"I meant in contrast to the extent of the boy's burns," Griff explained. "He's got some third-degree but yours appear to be all second or first. An antibacterial dressing and analgesic ought to handle yours, and you won't scar like he will without special grafts or plastic surgery."

"Thank God. Got a young wife to keep happy, you know."

"Yeah, so someone said."

"Probably Delia. She's taken a real shine to Cindy."

When Griff added nothing more, the sheriff said, "The boy need the hospital?"

"I'm going to suggest it to his mother when she gets here, probably run him in myself."

Griff noted delicate scars along Reg Merrell's sideburns behind his ears. They looked like skillful face-lift incisions. It also looked as if he was coloring his hair dark though, no way, in his brief observation of mountain men, Griff thought, had he seen one who'd dye his hair. He bit his lower lip to keep from smiling as he carefully continued to salve the man's burns. A young wife's demands, yes, Griff thought, but the money to do all this, too.

"You sure got good newspaper coverage for rearresting Jake Weston," Griff said, partly to take the sheriff's mind off his pain and partly to probe his thoughts. "It's great that you could help Emma out the minute she called you."

"Damn, doc, you're s'posed to be making me feel better. Watch it. And Emma was just lucky I was seeing Delia when my beeper went off, or she'd a been dead meat by the time I got there."

Griff shuddered at the way he'd put that. Emma al-

ways did jump in with both feet, boldly, but dangerously, too.

"Mabel Poteet, the boy's mother, is here, doctor,"
Pam said, poking her head in the door.

"You go tend to her," the sheriff ordered, shoving
Griff away with one knee. "Your nurse got a lot
sweeter touch, ain't you, Pam?"

Griff's gaze snagged with Pam's as he edged past her.
"Glad *you* think so at least, Reg," she said.

As Griff hurried down the hall, he heard them talking
in low voices, but he didn't have time to think about
what they might be saying about him now.

"So they kept the boy for observation at the hospital?" Jill asked as she poured milk on her oatmeal the
next morning.

Emma nodded. "Griff said he stayed there most of
the night with him and his parents. I'm going to see
Wade and take him some car magazines as soon as I
can. The poor kid's dream is to own a gas station and
that's where he gets hurt."

"Well," Jill said slowly, her spoon suspended halfway to her mouth, "we all have dreams that turn and
devour us—nightmares."

Emma nodded, studying her new friend, sensing she
might say more, but she didn't. She must be haunted
by her looming divorce, Emma decided. She'd said she
had one small son, but that she'd easily get custody of
him. Beyond that, she hadn't wanted to talk about her
family.

"If Wade needs plastic surgery," Emma explained
when Jill said nothing else, "it's probably not covered
by his parents' insurance. But, poor or not, Shelter folk
will pull together to help."

"I'll pitch in. The world is cruel to kids, and they need someone to get them justice."

Again, Emma sensed Jill's passion for something she didn't say. In the awkward silence, she thought of Wade again and hoped Hank would go to bat for the Poteets on insurance and not just play judge and jury as he seemed to be doing with J.G.

"So tell me more," Jill said, startling her, "about the couple who own this antique barn where I'm headed this morning."

Emma had been slowly programming Jill to find out what she could about the Bonners' background, things Trish had never quite seemed to want to talk about. But maybe she'd tell a disinterested stranger something she wouldn't tell Emma. Not that she expected the Bonners to tell anyone they were exporting Appalachian babies as well as antiques and black-market timber.

"Although I consider Trish and Mike friends," she explained, choosing her words carefully as she spooned strawberry jam on her toast, "they're a bit mysterious."

She could tell that got Jill's attention. "For example," Emma went on, "they apparently left very lucrative careers running some sort of consulting firm in New York, but they never want to talk about exactly what they did."

"You don't think it was something illegal, underhanded, at least?"

"No way," she said, hoping she wasn't lying. "I'm just curious if it was related to what they're doing now. Oh, yeah, and being baby obsessed as I am," she went on, hoping this sounded like an afterthought, "I can tell Trish wants one, but when I mention adoption she clams up, and—"

Jill's arm jerked, and the china milk pitcher flew to the tiled floor and shattered.

"Oh, darn. I'm sorry," Jill said, pushing her chair back and jumping up. "I don't know what happened—no, let me clean it up. I didn't see it. It was right there, but I just didn't see it."

It was a pitcher Emma had bought in Lexington, a pretty, striped one but with no sentimental value. Despite Jill's protests, she got paper towels to help wipe up the mess.

"You know what they say about spilt milk," she told Jill, hoping to cheer her up.

"Yeah, but I don't mean to come on like a bull in a china shop when you've been so sweet to take me in."

Both on their knees, blotting up milk, they shared a smile before Jill shook her head again and said, "I'll look for one to replace it at your friends' antique barn today," she promised. "And don't bother to protest. You've been enough help already."

It was not until Emma's only patient of the morning left that Jill's words when she broke the pitcher came back to her: *It was right there, but I just didn't see it.*

Her own dilemma had to be partly a result of that. There must be something right before her eyes, something she'd slighted or ignored, that would give her the key she needed to link someone to Amrine's disappearance, Ola's baby's or babies' adoption, and Lottie's baby being switched with a dead child.

She paced back and forth in her waiting room. Trying to build her courage, she reminded herself that a midwife lived by her wits: observation, signs, interviews, even intuition. Lately, though, Emma felt she had the tenuous Appalachian sixth sense everyone in the hills believed in. Not that she could foretell the future, but she could sense when something was about to happen, to go wrong.

And she had never felt that more strongly.

But she wasn't going to wait for it to hit her, or to bury herself like some groundhog with a winter storm coming. She had to think back, go back, and look at everyone who was even slightly suspect again. And she couldn't leave checking out Trish and Mike to outsiders. She was going to have to look into them—and both their homes—on her own. First, she was going to stop being so wary of Reg Merrell. There was something really fishy about him having enough money lately to support a trophy wife and himself in such style.

Then something clicked.

She rushed to the kitchen and dug out the broken pitcher from her wastebasket. She'd wrapped the pieces in newspaper before she'd put them in the plastic garbage bag so that the sharp edges wouldn't cut through. She'd intentionally used the front page of yesterday's local section of the *Highboro Herald* with Sheriff Merrell's photo. REARREST OF ESCAPED LOCAL CRIMINAL, the headline read. The picture was of the sheriff smiling after capturing Jake. Emma had refused an interview and photo, but the story detailed how Jake had tried to kill her with a hatchet and rifle.

Milk marred the photo now, but she saw what had snagged in her mind. She'd ignored it before—a little detail—and that was what she could no longer afford to do, not in delivering babies or in discovering who was abducting and adopting them.

Yes, there it was, that onyx-and-diamond pinkie ring Reg Merrell flaunted. And the gold Rolex watch on the same hand holding his rifle. He'd also been wearing new, tooled boots that day she went to see him in his office. In a dirt-poor county that didn't even have enough of a tax base to build a modern morgue, Sheriff Reg Merrell had evidently been blessed with some sort of financial windfall. One way or the other, Emma vowed she was going to find out from whom and why.

It didn't take Emma long to find the sheriff's house in Highboro; it was listed right in the phone book. The large, new colonial-style house was in the development where Mike and Trish lived, and several large lawns displayed Mike's Appalachian Dreams real-estate sales signs.

The Merrell residence was not as big as the Bonners', but it sported pillars and a tennis court out back, which Emma glimpsed as she drove by a second time. She couldn't picture the sheriff in tennis whites with a racquet in his hand. Parking down the block, she pulled a baseball cap on and looked all around.

Emma's mind raced as fast as her heart thudded. Getting out of her car, she strolled up the block past the Merrells'. She knew enough about the sheriff's kin to doubt he'd inherited any money from them. And Sissy had said his new wife was a divorcée who had nothing but looks to offer. So maybe he was a recipient of the same kind of hush money Mike Bonner had handed over to J.G. for rustling timber. Or, maybe the Merrells were getting rich quick with profit from a black-market adoption scheme.

She was tempted to march up to the front door to talk to Cindy Sue Merrell, but about what, exactly? Besides, the woman would tell her husband, and it would all blow up in Emma's face. She wished she could at least look around the grounds.

When Cindy Merrell pulled into her driveway in a low-slung jade sports car, Emma tried not to gawk or panic. The woman shot Emma a passing look, but didn't slow down or stop. Still walking, Emma watched the garage door wide enough to accommodate three cars lift. Two parking spaces were empty, but an old pickup occupied one, looking totally out of place in this neighborhood, especially next to Cindy's car. It was probably Reg Merrell's hunting truck.

Emma quickly returned to her Jeep. She'd drive around to see if there was a way she could later cut into the Merrells' yard through a house on the street behind. The area was laid out very confusingly with curves and courts cutting into each other. She finally followed the outer boulevard into the right street and slowed so she could locate the house that was directly behind the Merrells'.

Since she'd come in from a direction she didn't know, she was surprised to realize where she was. She slowed then stopped. Though you couldn't quite see one house from the other with the deep lawns and leafed-out trees, it looked like the Merrells' place backed onto Mike and Trish's.

Emma shuddered as she got out of the Jeep and quietly closed the door. Even on a sunny spring day, the Bonners' house gave her the creeps. She much preferred their Big Blue Farm. The patio and pool area behind the house had been cleared of storm debris from the night Lottie lost her baby. As if the area was off-limits now, a bright blue plastic cover floated on the surface of the pool, and the patio umbrella at the round glass table was collapsed and tied.

Emma stood there a moment, undecided whether to

cut through to the sheriff's yard or to look around here first. Trish and Mike had told Jill they'd be at Big Blue so she could stop to buy antiques.

On a hunch, Emma headed for the pool house where Lottie had stayed those three days before she'd gone into labor. Emma knew the place well from visiting her with Rooster to monitor her progress. The place had a changing room, a big linen closet and a small bedroom, also a kitchenette, and a bath and shower room, so it could easily double as a guest house.

Emma walked to the back of the pool house to glance in the window, one she now knew looked out over the sheriff's backyard and tennis court. Why had Trish never mentioned the Merrells were neighbors, but then, why should she?

"I thought that was you," a woman said close behind her.

Emma jumped and whirled around. "Oh, Trish." She must have come out quietly from the house. "I heard you were at Big Blue."

"So you came here? What's going on?"

"It's just I'm still feeling guilty I couldn't predict Lottie's coma and her baby's death. Why are you here then?"

Trish started toward the pool and Emma followed. "I told you," her friend said, "you're going to drive yourself crazy. Don't you think you'd better learn to let some things go?"

Trish was Mike's wife, all right, asking questions instead of answering them. "I—just thought I should look around where she stayed again," Emma repeated as they walked around the pool toward the house.

"I've had the place cleaned, Emma. And don't you think I feel awful that catastrophe happened here?

We've all got to put it behind us. And I'm not at Big Blue because I have some family business to take care of. I'm driving to Lexington to fly to New York, just for one night. I told Mike your friend Jill was coming, though, and he's better with the antiques than I am.

"Actually," Trish continued, opening the French door to the back of the house and stepping in, "I was hoping you heard I was here and came to give me some good news about Lottie. Come on in."

Suddenly, Emma didn't want to be closed in with her. "You mind if we sit out here?" she asked.

"Fine. I've got to leave in a minute or two, anyway." Trish came back out with her car keys and purse and locked the door behind her.

"I'm afraid there's nothing new about Lottie yet," Emma admitted as they sat at the round, glass-topped table next to the pool.

"Comas can be lengthy, and who knows how she'll be when she comes out." Trish paused for a moment then continued. "I didn't want to say all this in front of Jill and poor little Vinie last night, but I was so sorry to hear your brother came back and went after you. Thank heavens Reg Merrell got there in time." She reached over to grasp her hand.

"Do you see Reg much, living here?" Emma asked.

"Too busy. You know us, back and forth, in and out, burning the business candle at both ends," she said, taking her hand back. The strange thing was, her voice was still perky but her face had gone stiff and still.

Trish's unease, as well as Vinie's wild accusations the night before, made Emma decide to take a risk. "Actually," she said, lowering her voice, though there was no one in sight, "I think Lottie will wake soon and have plenty to reveal."

"Meaning what?"

"I asked that a DNA sample of Lottie's poor little girl be taken before she was buried," she lied. It was something she had thought of, too late.

As though some unseen puppeteer had jerked her strings, Trish sat up straighter. DNA tests took weeks, but Emma was gambling she might not know that. She was starting to feel completely reckless, especially with Sissy's due date fast approaching. After all, Trish had said she could come stay here with them, too.

"DNA? But why?" Trish demanded, looking astounded.

"Because the ultrasound Griff gave Lottie showed the child was a boy. And I know from her prenatal exams that Lottie was carrying a much smaller infant than the one I saw in the morgue."

She intended to say more—that the DNA had proved the child was not a Weston—but she watched Trish carefully as that much sank in. The woman's lower lip quivered. She didn't look like the Trish she'd known— and trusted—at all.

"That c-can't be," she floundered. "It doesn't make sense. It's dreadful, impossible. Have you been to the sheriff with this DNA proof—which showed exactly what?" she asked, frowning intently.

Then, before Emma could answer, Trish stood abruptly. "I'll have to talk to Mike about this, perhaps our lawyer, too, the way you're looking at me." Trish's warmth had chilled to ice. "I told you I have to go, and I think you'd better, too. After I thought we were friends, you come out here poking around and now spring all this on me. I told you earlier your paranoia was going to ruin your relationships."

"There's much more at stake here than relationships.

Sit down and let's talk." Trish tried to move past her, but Emma grabbed her arm and jumped up, too.

"I told you, I have to go," Trish cried. "Now get off—"

Trish yanked free, then pushed Emma hard. Emma went off balance, almost to her knees with her back turned momentarily to Trish. As she got up, she heard a scraping sound.

Trish wielded the metal pole of the closed umbrella she'd pulled out of their tabletop. To shove her off the grounds? Or hit her?

Emma tried to grab it. Trish swore and swung it at her. Emma lifted her arm to protect herself, ducking the blow. Trish clipped her shoulder and sent her tumbling into the pool.

Emma hit the soft, bubble-quilted cover on her back, but when she tried to get up she began to sink with the huge piece of plastic collapsing around and over her. Worse, Trish poked near her with the pole, pushing the cover deeper into the water.

"Here, grab this, and I'll pull you out," Trish cried.

But when Emma reached for the pole, she yanked it away and shoved the cover down, careful not to directly stab Emma.

She tried to distribute her weight, spreading her arms and legs, but it was too late. Water poured in over the plastic, soaking her. She sucked in a big breath and struggled to claw her way up through the collapsing, clinging weight of plastic and water.

"Help, help," she heard Trish's distant cry. "Someone help! Sheriff! Cindy!"

Did Trish mean to save or drown her? Emma couldn't be sure. She was not shouting very loud, maybe just covering her attempt at murder. All the questions of the last few days spun through Emma's head. Where did that dead baby come from? Was it Trish and Mike taking the babies? Maybe with the sheriff's help?

Emma's first gulp of water threw her into a panic. The huge, heavy cover enfolded her, filling from both ends.

"Here, grab this!" Trish called again, her voice muted. If someone saw or heard, they would think she was trying to save a drowning woman. As Emma spit out water and gasped for air, in the thin crack of sky that was left, the metal point of the umbrella stabbed at the cover again and again.

Her head exploded with burning, stinging as she sucked in water. She managed to get off her back, to her knees, but still descended, deeper, deeper, her head underwater now.

Dizzy, leaden-limbed, swimming again in Cutshin Creek. Mama teaching her to hold her breath underwater.

Just like a puppy, move your hands and feet, Emmie! It's not too deep. Put your feet down, and you'll keep your head up.

Outrage and horror clumped into a small, hard ball inside her. Emma used her last shred of breath to push her feet down to hit bottom. She shoved away, holding her arms up over her head, reaching toward Mama.

And broke water in a crack between blue folds. A man and a woman—not the sheriff and Cindy—helped Trish haul her in with the damn umbrella pole. Though exhausted and spitting water, Emma paddled for the side away from Trish and clung weakly to the metal ladder, gasping, choking.

"Oh, I'm so glad you're here," Trish told the strangers. "I tried to get her to grab this, to hook the plastic with it, but I knew if I jumped in, too, we could both drown. Thank God you heard me,'' she addressed the people who must be other neighbors. "I think she hit her head, too, so she's probably disoriented about what happened."

The man hurried over to help Emma up the ladder to the concrete where she spit water and gasped for air.

"Should I call the emergency squad, young lady?" he asked, thumping Emma's back.

"No—I'll be—all right—now. I'll see a doctor— and—tell him everything."

She glared across the pool at Trish who looked shaken but defiant. But she knew better than to come over to comfort Emma. Trish had told a blatant lie that Emma had hit her head, but it was probably the most truthful thing the traitor had said in weeks.

19

Sopping wet, Emma fled. She drove back to Shelter, showered and changed clothes. She knew if she accused Trish of attempted murder, especially to Sheriff Merrell, the woman would skew what had happened, just as Sam and Ginger Grady had escaped responsibility for hiding Jake. As with her investigation into missing babies, Emma's suspicions were her only proof.

As she made herself coffee in the kitchen, she saw on the counter a pale green china pitcher the size of the broken one, and a note from Jill:

Trish away on business, but Mike was nice—wow, a Ralph Lauren male model hidden away in the hills. Bought several items I'm having sent west. I'm going exploring uptown—see you for dinner, my treat at that quaint restaurant, to thank you and Griff for rescuing a damsel in distress.

J.

Emma unplugged the half-made coffee, went back upstairs and collapsed, trembling, fully dressed, on her bed. She longed to curl up in it, though she couldn't bear to pull the covers over her. She wanted to shut out the images of going under, the drowning weight of this rushing, growing terror. Of her friends in Shelter—one who was missing and the other who might be to blame.

She sat straight up and clawed her fingers through her hair. Tonight, she'd get Griff caught up on everything, so she wouldn't be alone in this. She could confide in him, at least.

She felt weak and sick. But in ten minutes she was in the Jeep, heading back to the very beginning: Amrine Settle's place where Mike Bonner had visited to dole out two crisp, fifty-dollar bills that first morning. However carefully she'd searched the place and however haphazardly Reg Merrell had, there must be some clue or sign there she'd missed.

As she drove the twisting road up around Big Blue, Emma looked in her rearview mirror to be sure no one was following. She glanced nervously at the Gradys' place as she passed by. How sad Jake's being caught and confined was the only good thing that had happened to her for days. She decided then, though the place scared her, she was going to ask Griff to accompany her back there tomorrow to question Sam and Ginger again.

She had hoped the air up here at Amrine's would clear her head but it didn't. Despite the sunshine and lofty view, her feet felt like lead and her heart was heavy.

She parked the Jeep in front of the house, deciding that hiding it last time had caused her a lot of problems when the Merrells arrived for their little porn show. But when she got out, something looked really wrong here. Then she saw what it was—or wasn't.

She stared agape. The small stand of sturdy oaks and other hardwood trees that had guarded the northwest side of the house from winter winds was gone, butchered knee-high, leaving a naked patch of sky exposed.

"Oh, no!" Emma whispered, but the brisk breeze ripped her words away.

Surely after she'd confronted J.G., she reasoned, he wouldn't have been a part of this, unless he'd told himself it was his last hurrah. Or was it Mike and his cutters working without J.G.? Had they just ripped off this woodlot as they had from other deserted homesteads, or could Amrine have willingly sold them the timber to beef up her bank account for the baby—or for fleeing with Len?

After she searched here, Emma decided, she'd have to find some way to look through the Bonners' barn and house. Trish's clever attack was not going to stop her. She wanted to access Mike's computer, too, and wished she had Hank's know-how for that. Again, she recalled overhearing Mike ask on the phone, "They do understand that cross-country shipping ups the bottom line considerably?" Had he been talking about antiques, hardwood boards and beams, or human cargo?

She walked over and looked around the area where the trees had been cut: sawdust covered the ground like dirty snow. The site was a graveyard with the rough-buzzed trunks serving as their own tombstones. Twelve trees, she counted, not much, but the pride of the place.

"Damn their greedy souls," she muttered.

She dug the key from her pocket and entered the house. She went to work in a frenzy, even tearing things apart she'd been careful with before. She felt desperate, panicked. Something had to turn up, please Lord, she prayed even as she flipped over the picture of Jesus and the one of John Kennedy to look on the backs. Nothing.

But when she pulled the bed apart, something went sailing onto the floor. She went to retrieve the same scratch pad of paper she'd examined before. When she picked it up, and it ruffled open to the middle, she found a note scrawled in Amrine's loose, loopy handwriting. *Let M & T Bonars know about selling. They'll take real good care of all.*

"Selling?" Emma cried aloud. Did that mean a bowl and pitcher set or the trees or this place—or a baby? She sank onto the striped bed and studied each word, each phrase in the note. Amrine had spelled Bonners wrong, which maybe meant she'd never seen the word written out. *Had* Amrine considered infant adoption? There was no doubt about it—the people Emma thought she knew well she didn't know at all.

Emma nearly jumped out of her skin when she heard a door slam. Not the sheriff again. Or could Trish have followed her and—

Darting to the front, dusty window, she looked out. Hank stood looking in at her, shading his eyes. Then his feet echoed on the front porch, and he opened the door.

"I couldn't find you at home and just followed a hunch."

She almost accused him of following her, but she steadied herself. "Why are you looking for me?"

"I told you I'd get you some important information," he said cryptically and flashed the front page of a newspaper at her. Emma couldn't tell what it was, but it wasn't the one with the recent photo of Sheriff Merrell after he captured Jake.

"A follow-up story on Jake or the sheriff?"

"About Cusak. You'll be real interested." Hank bit back a grin as he stepped inside with the paper and a briefcase.

"It's dim in here. Let's sit outside," she said, then realized those were the same words she'd said to Trish earlier. They settled on the top step of the front porch. "Now what about Dr. Cusak?" she asked.

"About his lies. About what he's hiding. He's dangerous as hellfire, Em. You're not the only one who can run around getting the goods on people, you know. This'll convince you I didn't have a thing to do with trying to warn you off or scare you away. It's gotta be him, 'cause you're getting too close to the truth."

Hank flipped the newspaper open, and she froze.

Griff. With all the people she now didn't trust, she had fought so hard to keep faith in him through all of this. Suddenly, she was afraid to look, to hear. Her previous anger at Hank completely evaporated to leave only regret and fear.

"Got the initial stuff on-line," he boasted excitedly, adjusting his glasses. "Then had to go to the newspaper morgue to steal an actual paper. Heck, no photocopies for my Em on this. Knew I had to have the real proof."

She darted a look at the paper on Hank's knees, but, as if to taunt her, he'd now folded in half what appeared to be a big front-page section. He opened his briefcase to reveal more papers.

"I knew he hadn't told you, or you wouldn't have taken up with him so fast," he said smugly. "Want to hear my short version of his trial or would you prefer to read it yourself?"

Trial? The word chilled her, but Emma didn't answer at first. She knew there was something in Griff's background that haunted him, something more than debts and Delia that had brought him to Shelter. She was suddenly fearful he'd been accused of stealing babies from a hospital in Lexington, or he'd worked in a morgue where he had access to babies' bodies.

She had to get hold of herself. But, in this moment,

what scared her most was the realization she had fallen in love with Griff Cusak.

"Quit playing games and let me see the paper," Emma said.

"I'm fixing to, believe me."

With a flourish and a grimace that could be a grin, Hank flopped the Lexington paper open in her lap.

Once she read the headline, she was grateful she hadn't called Griff for help again. She dared not now or ever.

Emma felt she'd been struck by lightning.

She stared down at a year-old newspaper photo of "Dr. J. G. Cusak," sitting stoically between two dour-looking attorneys in a Lexington courtroom. The largest headline read, MURDER CHARGES STUN HOSPITAL COMMUNITY. The smaller one read, NEW DOCTOR ACCUSED OF ASSISTED SUICIDE OF FATHER.

"*His* father?" Emma whispered.

"Which doesn't mean he didn't do the same before and after," Hank said, shifting closer on the step to peer down at what she was reading. "Surely you've heard about those serial euthanasia kinds of quacks in hospitals. Coma, then death. Doctors like to call it managed death, you know. Keep reading."

She skimmed the text. The defendant's father, Stanley Cusak, had been diagnosed with lung cancer the same year "Griff" completed med school despite debts from a "previous business reversal," as his lead defense attorney termed it.

The defense vowed to prove that there was absolutely no connection between the drug-overdose death of the senior Cusak and the theft of drugs from the ICU at the hospital where the accused was in medical residency. If the cancer-ridden man had overdosed, it was on his own, not with drugs his son provided him. The drugs stolen from the hospital were, specifically, the powerful medications Demerol, quaaludes and pentobarbital. The cancer-stricken man had taken a huge number of quaaludes.

She sucked in a sharp breath and shook her head hard, ignoring Hank's "You better believe it!"

The pentobarbital aside, she knew Demerol was a drug often used to control pain in managed childbirth. Not only had Griff gone through this trial and terror—but he had worked in ICU where Demerol and pentobarbital were still missing and he still believed in controlling the way a woman gave birth...

"The point is," Hank was saying, "no one can trust him, and I'm fixing to show Miss Delia all this as soon as you sober up about him."

"Delia might already know this. She's no fool."

And if, Emma thought, Delia knew about all this, she could have used it for leverage to force Griff to keep an eye—and hands—on Shelter's troublesome midwife. Or else his stake in things was so high that he willingly set out to seduce a woman he disagreed with and didn't trust or like. If so, was he protecting more than just a bad past? If he was desperately in debt, what great lengths would he go to to make money he could hardly earn in that slow office in Shelter? Helping Delia run an illegal adoption scam would solve his financial woes.

She shook her head. She was getting crazy again. Everyone seemed guilty. Griff had helped her more than once, and Delia had done nothing but good for this area, even if it was in her own way.

"Of course, Miss Delia's not a fool," Hank's words pierced her own agonizing again, "so she *can't* know.

She needs a doctor for her precious health center, but not one with this hanging around his neck."

Emma turned to Hank. "Where are the later papers? Trials are so complicated. Was he found guilty?"

From his briefcase, Hank hauled out a thin pile of computer printouts of other newspaper articles. "Heck, it hardly matters," he told her as he tapped them neatly together on the step and handed them over. "He had expensive, hotshot, liberal lawyers out to prove something about people's right to die and all that. There's an article here about his legal team. Okay, he did get off. But he was still ruined—in Lexington, at least, and should be here, in Shelter."

He pointed to a headline that read, SUICIDE DOCTOR'S PARTNERS DEMAND RESIGNATION FROM SUBURBAN CLINIC; HOSPITAL RESCINDS RIGHTS TO USE FACILITIES.

"But you said he was found innocent," Emma insisted. "This does happen to be America and—"

"Oh, it's America, all right," Hank interrupted. "You might know they got him off on a technicality about the prosecutors' failing to disclose something, okay? Here, back in one of these last articles." He shuffled through the papers. "When he should have paid with years of his life in prison, all he had to pay for is lawyer fees and med school," he added disgustedly.

"And for his shattered reputation," Emma added.

"Oh great, defend him. He's taken a hypocrite's oath, not the Hippocratic one. And you're the one he's taken in the most."

Blinking back tears that had threatened all day, she flipped through the other photocopies Hank thrust at her: FATHER'S BODY TO BE DISINTERRED FOR BELATED AUTOPSY. A feature-page article entitled PATIENTS

TRUSTED CUSAK: A DR. JEKYLL OR MR. HYDE? An editorial headed THE GHOST OF DR. JACK KEVORKIAN HAUNTS LEXINGTON.

"Well?" Hank said, edging closer to her again, this time slipping an arm around her waist. "Don't tell me you're paying this no mind."

"What? No, it's terrible."

"Damn straight it is. Like I said, I'm going to Miss Delia. But what about you—him—us?"

His implication this would make a difference between her and Hank wasn't worth a comment. If anything, it had made the mess between them worse. She thumped the pile of papers back into his open briefcase and got up, shaking off his touch.

Emma felt a huge, suffocating weight again, as if she couldn't breathe, as if that pool cover and water were rolling tighter around her. She felt deep grief for Griff, but why hadn't he told her any of this, especially when she and Sissy had shared their most sensitive family problems with him? She should have known not to want and need the man so desperately.

"Em?" she heard Hank's voice as if from a distance as she went to lock Amrine's door, then walked slowly toward her Jeep. "You can't just run away from me anymore," he insisted, blocking her way to the driver's-side door. "We're not done talking yet."

She stopped three feet from the Jeep and crossed her arms over her chest. "Yes, we are. You've done what you set out to do. Get out of my way."

"What have I done?" he demanded, shifting to block her key from the lock. "Nothing but help you, and you're running straight to him. It wouldn't be safe, and I won't let you."

"No, I'm not running straight to him, but that's none of your business. Move!"

Emma tried to push past him, but he grabbed her arm. The whole scene with Trish flashed through her mind. She dug her keys into his wrist. He loosened his hold on her and jumped back, swearing under his breath.

"Hank," she said, holding up both hands, one still dangling her keys, "I don't want to hurt you any more than I'm sure I already have over the years. But I am not flinging myself into your arms or at your feet. Ever. Got that?"

"So this is the gratitude I get for trying to protect you—save you from Cusak and yourself. You're acting moony lately. My mother told me once not to get mixed up with the Westons, and she—"

"And she waits pitifully for you to take her out to Arletta's restaurant once a week, so she can see her boy," Emma interrupted, hands propped on her hips. All her frustrations and fury poured out. "He doesn't have time for her otherwise because he's so obsessed with his job and evidently with getting back a woman he dated in high school when he's never gotten beyond that stage emotionally."

"Oh, great, try to shift the subject from you and Cusak by attacking me," Hank said angrily. "I didn't steal drugs or kill my father! You know, I don't regret telling potential patients to stay away from your Baby Farm."

In a split second, Emma decided to see if she could bluff Hank. "Don't you think I know what you've been doing? And what else have you been telling my potential clients? That your noble insurance company won't cover their next delivery after so many kids, and they ought to think of giving their next baby away for cash?

Or maybe even for a family trip to Walt Disney World?''

He looked so stunned—this man she thought she had learned to read over the years—that she almost cleared him of suspicion, in an adoption scheme, anyway. It was that same look he'd had when she'd accused him of scaring her at night.

"Where are you getting such crap?" Hank shouted, grabbing her wrists again so hard she felt her hands go numb. He leaned close to her. Spittle flecked his lips. "I'm no traitor to my own career, my mother, the people here, my friends—real friends. But you are."

She tried to yank free of him but he wasn't budging, so she put what remained of her strength into her voice. "Is that why you follow J.G. around at night and take pictures of him? Is that for friendship's sake?"

"J.G. knows that? He told you?"

"I saw you myself. Now that's a switch, isn't it, my spying on you?"

His face a fierce mask, Hank pushed her against the car. Instinctively, she kneed him in the groin.

He groaned, let go of her and fell to his knees in the hardened mud.

Emma got in the car and left him gasping and gaping after her like a beached fish, one that finally realized there was no way he was ever going to get back in the water.

Thinking Sissy might be in her kitchen this late in the afternoon, Emma walked around to her back-porch door. She was inside all right, but not fixing supper. She was packing a small suitcase laid out on the kitchen table. Though still shaken from her exchange with Hank, Emma steeled herself not to spill what she knew about Griff until she settled with him. She had more important things to discuss with Sissy, anyway.

"Sissy," Emma called to her.

Just as her sister looked up, Emma caught a sideways glimpse of herself in the windowpane of the open door. She looked a fright, her hair like a bird's nest. She quickly tried to smooth it, then straightened her blouse, shoving it into her jeans.

"You all right?" Sissy asked as she unlocked and opened the door. "You look…"

"I know. I—let's just say I had another disagreement with Hank, our very last one."

"That jerk better not lay a hand on you," Sissy said as Emma stepped in. She noted Sissy had closed the suitcase before she'd gone to the door. Now she quickly snapped it shut, hefted it and slid it into the bottom shelf of the pantry.

"Getting ready early for a hospital run?" Emma said, trying to keep her voice steady.

"Yep. Hope it doesn't make you think I'm worried about having to go in a rush or anything."

"I think J.G. and I could agree on the fact it's good to be prepared."

Without asking, Sissy poured Emma some iced tea and plopped a big sprig of mint in it. "J.G.'s out."

"How's his back? You think he'll be able to make it through your delivery?"

"Don't rightly know. That's why," Sissy said, sinking into a chair at the table, "I'm fixin' to have my big sister right there outside the delivery room, ready to run in and save the day."

Emma's eyes filled with tears, even as she downed half the tea. She was as parched as she was exhausted.

"Sissy, I know you've got enough on your mind right

now, but I want to tell you something. This last month I've become convinced that Amrine and Ola's leaving when they were pretty far along, and then Lottie's tragedy..." She hesitated and took a big breath.

"You been cryin'?" Sissy asked. "What's frettin' you? I thought things were going better for you with Dr. Griff, Delia, and all. Hon—" she got up to hug her "—it's not your fault Lottie's baby passed any more than it was when I lost mine."

They hugged each other awkwardly, with the bulk of Sissy's pregnancy between them, as if, Emma thought, together they could protect this life that would soon be born. She held Sissy at arm's length.

"Listen to me," Emma insisted. "I just want you to know I think that someone in this area—I'm not sure exactly who yet—might be operating some sort of baby-adoption ring."

Ring. Her own choice of words snagged in Emma's mind. Perhaps there was a sort of conspiracy. That or she was sounding paranoid again, moony, as Hank had said.

"But, I'd never, never in a million years," Sissy said, wide-eyed, "give this baby up for adoption, no matter for how much money, you know that. And J.G. wouldn't neither. Pay those rumors no mind. I know you said Ola had her little one adopted, but did Amrine, too?"

"I don't know, but I can't imagine it."

"See? And Lottie didn't. She lost hers. You sure 'bout all this?"

"I know it sounds complicated. I'm looking into it further, but I just wanted to warn you to be careful."

"Oh, sure, I am. You been helping me be careful ever since you heard I finally managed to get pregnant again. But who would be behind this? You gotta have more proof than Ola, and 'sides, you said she was clear in Tennessee.''

Sissy began to look and sound so distraught Emma hated herself for attempting, and botching, her warning. After Sissy had lost the first baby and been hospitalized in Highboro, the doctor had told Mama it was partly stress that had triggered the premature birth. And here she was getting her sister all upset, when she could present no better case than this.

"I only want everything to go so well this time," Emma whispered.

"Everything will come out just fine, and that's one of J.G.'s one-liners about childbirth you can use anytime you want.''

"Thanks," Emma whispered. "That's a good one.''

20

"I hate to let you down," Emma told Jill when she got home, "but I'm going to have to take a rain check on that dinner for Griff and me tonight." Jill was reading the *Highboro Herald* at the kitchen table, but Emma didn't sit down. "Of course, if you want to call him, he might be able to meet you at Arletta's."

"You know, I sensed you weren't feeling well the second you came in," Jill commiserated. "And the way I've seen you look at Griff, why would you be setting me up to eat with him alone? Anything I can do for you or get you?"

"Just some of that dress-shop counseling," Emma admitted as she leaned against the doorway.

"Man trouble, in other words," Jill said, smacking a hand on the table, her gold bracelet hitting with a clunk. "Men. *Tell* me about it."

"What went wrong for you and your husband?" Emma asked, not wanting to explain about Griff to Jill any more than she wanted to tell Sissy.

"Ken and I found out too late that what we both wanted most in life wasn't remotely the same thing. He lied to me, but maybe he didn't know his own heart. I'll give him that much of a break. And, most of all, B—Ken didn't have the guts to stand up when others took advantage of him, of our family."

"You're stronger than he is," Emma said, awed by

Jill's sudden shift to a fierce expression and tone of voice. "You're an Appalachian woman at heart. That kind of thing happens all the time around here, and we live with it. I didn't mean that as a criticism. I'm just so tired, and I need to make some big decisions soon."

"About Griff?"

"Yes, but more than that. About whom to trust, to blame…"

"I don't mean to be crashing in on you here when you're going through hard times. But, you know," Jill added, rubbing her hands repeatedly on the knees of her designer jeans under the table, "sometimes it takes a survivor to spot another one."

"The thing is," Emma said, closing her eyes to keep the room from tilting, "I don't want to be just a survivor. That's what my mother was, what other women I've seen around here are. I want to be a—succeeder, an overcomer…

"Sorry to ramble." She smiled at Jill. "Help yourself to anything in the fridge if you want to eat here, or if you leave, take the key under the crock because I might be dead to the world when you get back."

"Oh, Emma," Jill called to her as she started away, "forgot to tell you something I learned about your friends. The Bonners used to operate a head-hunting business in New York City."

"For what sort of professionals?" Emma asked, turning back.

"Now *that* Mike wouldn't really say. 'This and that,' I think he put it, then started asking me all kinds of questions about running a West-coast dress shop. Men usually could care less about my career. I think he's really nice."

Emma nodded stiffly and said she'd see her later. Her

mind racing, she stopped on the landing and stared out through the window where the deer head had appeared. Why hadn't Trish or Mike told her they were professional headhunters? Maybe it was because their business had been to seek specific people, then "sell" them to others for a profit. For all Emma knew, the Bonners could still be head-hunting. Not just for antiques, old houses and timber, but babies from poor women they sold to rich ones.

Emma slept without moving for exactly one hour when she suddenly awoke. It was just getting dark outside. She got up, showered, pulled on fresh slacks and a yellow T-shirt that read Midwives Deliver, and hurried downstairs to her answering machine.

The red light was on, indicating she had already listened to her messages. But she couldn't recall having done so. She punched it on and listened. Griff had left three of the four messages, each time asking her to call him. For all she knew, he might be on his way here, and she didn't want that.

In the empty kitchen Emma forced herself to eat graham crackers and milk, comfort food from back when Mama used to sing songs to her, Sissy and Jake when she put them to bed. That was before folks started saying, "Nothing good ever came out of Cutshin Holler."

Jill had left a note saying she'd gone to Arletta's and Emma assumed she must have taken the other key. She locked the door and went out into the crisp, cool evening. What she wouldn't give to have Mama back, she thought sadly, Mama to trust and consult. But Mama'd made mistakes in her life—big, fatal ones. When Mama died her agony had been so bad that, given the opportunity, Emma supposed she might have provided her with enough drugs to free her from the pain, especially if the suffering had gone on for years and she'd begged for them. Emma didn't believe in euthanasia, only in life, but there must be moments of despair where you love someone so much you could give them up if that's what was best for them.

She was in the Jeep and, before she realized it, was shooting straight past the turnoff to Bonners' barn, where she'd told herself she was going to check on some things under cover of darkness. Instead, she was going to see Griff.

From down the road a ways, Jidge watched Emma's Jeep roar out of the driveway and turn toward town. Odds were, since she had looked so exhausted, she was off on some midwife emergency, but she'd follow her anyway. If Emma was the link to Shelter the Children, it was probably through her job that she got the babies. And if Jidge went back into the house and listened to Emma's phone messages again, she'd have to play catch-up by looking for her. And, anyway, Emma might have erased any messages.

There was one advantage to tailing someone out here in the sticks, Jidge mused as she sped up to keep Emma's twin taillights in view: few cars were out at night. She wondered how her private detective, Reed Gorham, would have done so far if she'd sent him to Shelter. Could he have turned up what she did in such a short time?

"Mommy just isn't completely sure," she said aloud, picturing little Mitchell, "that it's the midwife and the doctor yet, my sweet boy. I'm going to be checking on your little quilt tomorrow, but whoever lied to Mommy and sent you away from here is going to pay with much more than the fifty thousand dollars they charged for you."

When the curves on the road gentled a bit near town, Jidge fumbled in her purse. She touched Emma's big, heavy house key and then her Magnum, nestled at the bottom.

It's almost the equivalent of a small rifle, the gun expert she'd bought it from had told her. *The California Highway Patrol has used Smith & Wesson .357's like this for years because they're so reliable and have such power. Despite the size, it's got enough juice to stop a moving vehicle.*

"That will do just fine to punish the bad people," Jidge whispered, "won't it, Mommy's good boy?"

A light shone behind the curtains in Griff's apartment windows, but the front door to the clinic was locked. Emma rang the bell, telling herself she should have called first. But she knew she could not have kept the anger out of her voice and would have ended up accusing him over the phone. She wasn't sure how she'd manage to get through this. She was already shaking with frustration as she heard footsteps approaching.

She propped her hands on her hips and opened her mouth, not certain which accusation would spill out first.

Wanda Keck opened the door.

"You hurt yourself?" she asked Emma, scanning her as if looking for wounds or blood.

"I'm fine. Is Dr. Cusak here?"

"Gone to your favorite place, the Eubankses'," Wanda said with a snicker that grated on Emma's nerves. "Seems Modeen cut her thumb real bad, and Hal fetched him. You know them. Luck'ly they stay pretty much to home, so he's gone up there. I'm just finishing up lab tests with Pam. You wanta come in and wait or leave him a message?''

"It's not important," she lied, turning back to her car while Wanda shrugged and slammed the door.

A house call, Emma thought. Dr. J. Griffin Cusak making a house call and to the Eubankses.

She got in her Jeep and turned the key in the ignition, undecided about whether to go back to her original plan to search the Bonners' barn. She had her flashlight, but it would mean a big hike in and out when she was exhausted. Besides, there was a half-moon, and she should go on a night when it was pitch-dark.

"As if," she whispered, suddenly furious with herself as well as Griff, "I have the time to solve and stop all this before Sissy delivers."

She twisted around to back out of the driveway, but the health center van pulled in behind her. Griff killed his headlights and got out.

She felt panicked, frozen. She watched in her rearview mirror as he walked toward her. A torrent of emotions churned in her like spring runoff from the mountain.

He tapped on the Jeep window, and she rolled it down.

"You won't believe where I've been and all the bad things I've heard about you," he said, his voice teasing.

"Same here—about you."

"You want to come upstairs?" he asked, evidently not realizing she was serious. He reached in to touch her cheek. They were both surprised it was wet.

"Emma, what's the mat—"

"Pam and Wanda are still here," she blurted out.

"Then let's go for a drive."

"Let's just walk out back," she said, fighting for control of herself and the situation.

"Suits me." Griff reached in to unlock and open her door, but his voice had gone wary.

Emma swiped at her cheeks before she got out, welcoming the dark. She played her flashlight before her feet, leading the way around the side of the mansion. Behind was a pond, larger than the one in front, and filled only with rainwater and weeds. Beyond it, at the back of the deep yard, stood a white, wooden gazebo that glowed ghostly in the dark as they approached it. Benches curved around its gingerbread interior. Years ago, Delia had taken her and Sissy to see *The Sound of Music* in Highboro, and in the movie two love scenes had occurred in a gazebo. After that, Emma had always thought it so romantic. Now it seemed only sad, its railings and lattices strangled with ivy and honeysuckle.

She stood in the center of the gazebo and spun to face Griff, then turned off the flashlight and put it on the bench. Despite the roof and thick vines, shadows of moonlight webbed his grim face, making the angles and lines look more deeply etched.

"I know everything," she blurted.

"You found out who's behind the adoption scheme?" He came close but didn't, thank God, touch her.

"I found out you've hidden everything from me— the trial and all. Why didn't you tell me?"

He seemed to deflate and sank onto the bench, hunched over, his elbows on his splayed knees. "I wanted to," he said, his voice a near whisper. "I almost did more than once, but that night you'd been harassed, you didn't need me saying, 'Your mother's death? That's nothing, baby. Wait till you hear my story.'"

She sniffed. "And?"

"And the first time—the night we drove to Cutshin—I had other fish to fry. And I wanted you to trust me."

"I believe that, at least," Emma said, starting to pace despite the groan of the floorboards. Every time she spun around, the heavy scent of honeysuckle sank clear to her stomach. "I'm sorry you had to go through that, Griff. I know trials can be hell. Everyone thinks the worst and you're so stripped naked and scared."

"I know you understand that," he said, reaching out to snag her wrist when she walked past. Emma pulled back, and he let her keep going.

"I won't ask you if you were guilty," she said, "because you got off, but—"

"I was both guilty and innocent." With a huge sigh, he leaned back against the latticed wall. "I didn't steal those drugs, and I didn't help my father kill himself, but I knew he wanted to die and I let him. He had been bravely fighting such pain, Emma, you can't know..."

His voice trailed off. "No, like understanding the trial, I guess you can know that. Was I guilty? Not legally, because my defense team got me off on a technicality when I wanted so bad to be really cleared. I knew my father had the quaaludes, and I knew he was desperate to use them, and I didn't take them away from him. I tried to talk him out of it, I got him counseling from a family friend who's a minister, but I didn't take them away from him. I even sat through an agonizing goodbye speech before—before the night he did it. Is that what this is going to be for us tonight, Emma," Griff said, looking up at her. "A goodbye speech?"

Emma collapsed on the other side of the small circle of seats. "I have to know," she said, "if Delia put you up to watching me, to try to control me in your very special way because she knew she couldn't.''

He sat up straight. "I told you she wanted me to stay the hell away from you. I got myself in deep with her for not listening. But maybe, if you have to ask that, you don't know me. You trust me so little that it doesn't matter what I tell you.''

"You bet I don't know you, can't trust you." Her voice rose. "How can you even try to make me feel guilty for that?''

"Because whatever was in my past, you should know me now. We've been through some things together, but so what, right? Damn, I should have just listened to Delia and steered clear of you. Every time I get too close, I get burned or sliced open, and *I'm* the one who's supposed to be curing hurts, not suffering. Come on," he insisted, his voice challenging and angry now. "Let's hear the rest of it!''

"Such as?''

"Aren't you going to accuse me of stealing and selling babies? Maybe," he plunged on, "I really came to this paradise on earth to run some half-assed adoption scam, targeting your patients. That would be a great way for my mad, bad medical practice to destroy a midwife's glorious, golden one, right?''

"It is interesting that one of the drugs you were accused of stealing was pentobarbital!''

"Aha. Perfect proof," Griff shouted, jumping up and starting toward her. He gripped her upper arms and pulled her to her feet, holding her at arm's length. "You know, you'd have hit it off just fine with the compassionate doctors who took me into their partnership one month and let me go the next because they couldn't trust me even when I was found innocent.'' His eyes, his tone, his touch scalded her.

"It's been a few weeks for us, hasn't it, Emma, dancing closer to each other, my leading, you retreating and spinning away, then you leading me on again?"

He dragged her into his arms in a hard embrace. She tried to shove at him, her balled fists trapped against his chest, her feet tangling with his. He tipped her back so that their hipbones pressed together and his muscular thighs trapped her left leg.

"Stop it," Emma cried. "You're hurting me!"

"So what's new? It takes two to tango, sweetheart," Griff muttered, clamping her even harder to his body as he swayed and stepped to silent music.

"Griff," she tried to protest, but no other words came. Her breasts flattened to his chest, and she jolted when his free hand gripped her bottom to lift her closer to the thrust of him.

"Oh, that's right," he said, his voice bitterly mocking. "The steps to the dance you want to do means no touching, no trusting a man unless you want to use him. For protection, a quick kiss, a ride to Highboro, delivering a breech baby, whatever. Then we'll make this our last dance, so let's make it good."

When he turned them again, they backed up against the entry to the gazebo. Seeming surprised, he pressed her there and tilted her face to his. His mouth descended, hovering as his narrowed eyes, flint black in the dark, pierced her.

His strength, his anger fueled hers, then became a need so powerful it took her breath away. She felt awed again by the realization that she loved him, even when everything was going wrong between them.

"I used to get so scared every time I felt like this about you," she whispered. "But now…"

His mouth was poised an inch from hers. They breathed in unison.

"And now?" Griff prompted. "Haven't you learned sometimes you have to just let go, trust someone else all the way whether things look good or bad?"

Before she even knew that she would move, Emma fastened her fingers behind his neck to pull him to her. The kiss was blinding hot. His tongue plundered her mouth and she matched him. His hands raced over her, skimming and kneading bare skin everywhere he could touch, yanking up her T-shirt and diving beneath her belt to cup her bare bottom and lift her to him while her nails raked his back through his shirt. But nothing stopped the kiss.

At last, when they could hardly breathe, they broke apart. He scooped her up and plopped her in his lap on the bench inside the gazebo. The renewed frenzy of kisses and caresses toppled them sideways, half sprawled on the seat.

"Let's go upstairs," he said, gasping for breath again.

"Not in Delia's house."

"Your place…"

"Jill."

"The van, the middle of Main Street, a mountaintop, I don't care…"

They stared into each other's eyes, lit by pale, shifting moonlight through vines.

"No," he said suddenly. He pulled her up and shifted her off his lap so their hips and thighs still melded. "The first time we belong to each other, it's going to be long and so slow it will last forever. Right now, I'm good for one second, and you've been through too much. I'd like to know that what we have to build on isn't just raw emotion. The first time for us, I'm going to know you're mine because you trust me as well as want me."

She felt mesmerized, amazed at how he'd shifted moods and how she'd soared, coasted and landed right along with him. Were they really this attuned, or was she being seduced again in a whole new way? Suddenly, she didn't care. She needed him and would take the risk of trusting him, right now at least, with her eyes wide open.

"I was thinking," she said, tracing the firm contour of his lips with the tip of her index finger, "of inviting you for a consultation on the birthing bed. You seemed to be intrigued by it from the first."

"I still am. How about you suggest to Jill she should be moving on, and I'll be your nighttime housemate?" He frowned when she looked away. "What? Tell me what you're thinking."

"What you said before about my trying to use you— I know I do."

"Hey, this would be very, very mutual using, I promise."

"I mean when I ask you to help me with something. With or without you, I still have to get to the bottom of this adoption problem. I have to find Amrine and Lottie's baby."

"Which means making another try at demanding Ginger and Sam tell you who's behind Ola's and his baby—or babies—being adopted."

"Yes. I thought tomorrow morning."

Griff stood and pulled her to her feet again, this time

gently. "You've got to swear to me you won't face him alone."

"I could take Jill," Emma suggested. "Get her talking to Ginger about quilts, then talk to Sam in the next room or something. But I hesitate to use an innocent outsider for more than just questioning the Bonners. I had thought about cornering Ginger alone, but after what happened with Trish today, I want to try Sam again, to beard the lion in his own den."

"Wait a minute. What happened with Trish today?" he demanded, his voice harsh again. "It sounds like you're the one who's been keeping things back."

It was near midnight when Emma returned home, but she saw Jill had left a light on for her in the kitchen. She parked the Jeep farther up the driveway by the shed and quietly closed the car door so she wouldn't wake her. As always, though Jake was under lock and key again, she peeked at the wicker on the porch to be sure it hadn't been disturbed. Everything looked normal.

Emma heard Jill's voice as she approached the house. Puzzled, she stopped beside Jill's car and rested her hand on it. The hood was still warm. Jill must have just gotten in, so where would she be this late around Shelter? The biggest question, Emma thought as she went quietly up onto the porch and heard Jill's voice even louder, was who could be here with her this late?

Emma sank silently into the rocker, which hid her from the window light. When she heard no other voice, she realized Jill was on the phone. But at midnight? Maybe a client's call had come in for Emma, and, thinking it an emergency this late, Jill had taken it.

Another fear surfaced through her exhaustion: her guest could have been listening to her recorded messages earlier. And Jill could have gone into her bedroom to eavesdrop on her and Griff's phone call the other day when she'd heard that click on the line.

"Yeah, well, it's 12:00 a.m. here in the boondocks, so don't give me any flak for calling you at home, detective," Emma heard Jill say. "Listen, I know I let you go, but I want you to run a check for me on a couple of names. No, not *pro bono*. I'm good for your fee, you know that."

Emma wondered if Jill could be a policewoman, or a lawyer calling a legal investigator. Or could the government be on to an undercover adoption agency and Jill was FBI? That's who Emma planned to call when she got a reliable witness or lead, since she knew now Reg Merrell was against her. She sat up stiffly, straining to hear, making sure the chair didn't rock and creak.

"Like what?" Jill was saying. "Like total background, as much as you can dig up in twenty-four hours, everything down to what flavor of Kool-Aid they drank as kids, that's what. Have you got a pencil and paper?"

This, Emma thought, like too much else, didn't make sense. She and Griff had just stumbled onto Jill at random on the road. She could not have known they were coming. And she surely couldn't have faked someone shooting out her tire, could she?

"Ready?" Jill said. "Okay, one's a doctor, a G.P., primary-care type, I take it, a J. Griffin Cusak. C-U-S-A-K. I haven't got a clue what the *J.* stands for. The other is a midwife, a certified nurse midwife. Here, let me give you her state of Kentucky certification number."

Emma didn't even have that memorized, but she realized Jill was probably reading it straight off the

framed license on the wall of her office. Jill then recited
both of their license-plate numbers.

"What? Oh, yeah, her name. It's been a long day.
Emma Weston, a native of Shelter, Kentucky. You
heard me right—Shelter as in Shelter the Children
Adoption Agency."

Emma pressed her hands over her mouth and
breathed long, silent gasps. The adoption agency existed. And it had to be local.

"No way," Jill went on. "I'll call you for the information sometime after nine your time tomorrow night.
I'll have to make it a collect call again. No," she said,
her voice indignant now. "I didn't bring the baby along.
Do you think I'm completely crazy?"

Emma jerked and the chair creaked, but evidently Jill
didn't hear. Despite how her body ached, Emma felt
alert now, drenched with sweat in the crisp night air.
Completely crazy, the words revolved in her mind as
she tried to remember everything Jill had said. Things
had not made sense, but that big lead she was so certain
she'd missed, the one that was right in front of her she
hadn't seen—maybe it was Jill Lister.

She waited until the square of light that spilled from
the upstairs windows went dark on the front lawn. Giving Jill another half hour to get to sleep, Emma let herself in the house and went silently upstairs toward the
guest bedroom.

21

Emma turned on no lights upstairs, but by now her eyes were well adjusted to the moonlit dark.

Carefully, she twisted the knob of the guest room door and pushed it open a crack. At least it was not locked. And, unless she was really faking it well, Jill breathed regularly in a state of steady sleep in the old double bed.

Emma opened the door farther, slid inside and shuffled across the room to the single chair where she had seen Jill carefully deposit her purse when she'd first showed her the room. Yes, it was here now, a smear of shadow across the pale, flower-print upholstered chair. The purse would contain identification, hopefully not false. She could just wake and confront Jill but tangling with Trish had changed her. She wouldn't hesitate to act covertly anymore.

When Emma plunged her hand into the purse and grasped the billfold, her knuckles hit cold, hard metal in the same moment Jill clicked on the bedside light.

Blinking into the brightness, Emma spun to face her shocked guest with the pistol in her hand.

"I believe we still have a lot to talk about," Emma said, leveling the gun at her. It brought back memories of facing Pa with that rifle years ago, but she fought to steady her arm and hand.

"Let's start," Emma told her speechless guest, "with what you know about Shelter the Children."

I'm dead, Jidge thought. She's on to me. She—maybe Griff, too—have to be behind the agency, especially since they were arguing about drugs and babies behind the clinic tonight. But she wasn't going to let this woman know she was scared.

"Watch that thing," Jidge warned as she stared into the black hole that was the point of her own pistol. "Are you craz—"

"Don't say that!" Emma ordered, coming closer to rest her arm holding the gun on the hip-high footboard of the bed. "It's a little late in lots of ways, so I want to hear it *now,* Jill Lister, or whatever your name is."

For one second, Jidge screwed her eyes tight shut the way Mitchell did to make something he didn't like go away. Mitchell…Mommy's boy.

She opened her eyes at a strange sound. Still holding the gun on her with one hand, Emma was rummaging with the other in her purse. She pulled out her billfold and threw it on the bed.

"Get out your driver's license, credit cards, anything that's ID," Emma ordered as she walked to the door and clicked on the ceiling light. "You see, I don't have a detective to call to do this for me, since I live out here in the boondocks."

"Uh," Jidge grunted as if she'd taken a fist to her stomach. At least she realized how she'd been caught. She began to yank cards out of their tight plastic pockets and line them up on the blanket as if she were dealing a poker hand.

"I'll show it all to you, but to save you squinting at it," she told Emma, looking steadily up at her, "my name is Jidge Collister. I'm from San Francisco, and my husband's name is Ben."

She sounded, Jidge thought, as if she were at those AL-ANON meetings she'd attended for months when Ben was drinking. She could say she was here for a friend, but how many times had she heard such spineless drivel in the shop? This woman had forced her to show her hand, though Jidge was determined not to let her know she was going—come hell or high water—to see Ginger Grady tomorrow morning. Surely the woman Mike Bonner had told her about was the *G.G.* of Mitchell's little bundling quilt.

Jidge took a deep breath. "And I'm here," she continued, "because I'm trying to find who's behind an adoption agency called Shelter the Children where we got our son."

"Go on," Emma said, her voice and hand shaking. "Tell me everything you know about the agency."

"Not until you put down that gun. It's loaded."

"I'll bet it is. Were you planning to use it to shoot the woman who took you in?"

"Look, I needed protection driving alone cross-country. The gun's legally registered at home. And I don't deserve to be treated like some criminal."

Their eyes held until Emma's started to waver.

"Emma," Jidge tried again as her captor obviously struggled with something, "don't you even think about shooting me. A lot of people know where I am and with whom."

"A few here maybe, but who's to say you just didn't move on if you disappear? And at home—San Francisco is it now instead of Santa Barbara?—I doubt if many know you're here. No husband—Ken, Ben or whatever—would knowingly let a wife do this on her own. And your detective sounded real surprised when you merely mentioned this town, at least from your reaction. I'm afraid I couldn't eavesdrop quite as thoroughly as you've done with my phone calls.''

Jidge's mouth almost fell open at that. What had made her think she could spy and lie? She was starting to sweat.

"You'd be making a big mistake to use that gun," Jidge went on. "I swear to you, I'm just an outraged mother of a baby. My Mitchell was as good as sold and he shouldn't have been. Yes, I've done some wrong things, but for my boy, not just for me. Emma. Emma?'' she cried, suddenly shocked at the look of relief on Emma's face that replaced the grim glare.

To Jidge's amazement, Emma lowered the gun and clamped it under her arm, facing it away. "You'll be happy to know, Jill—Jidge Collister," she said, "that one thing a midwife has to know is when a woman's hurting, no matter how much she's flailing around or what's coming out of her mouth. There's something you haven't said about your baby, isn't there? Is he sick somehow?''

"How could you know that?''

"I think we ought to join forces," Emma interrupted in a rush. "I'm not behind the adoption ring but fixing to uncover it, too, because of babies and mothers like you. I need your information, your help and your gun."

"Okay, all right," Jidge agreed, partly because she didn't have a choice.

Emma's voice softened more. "You've obviously been forced to become a liar and a sneak, just like me lately. Determination and desperation do that," she added as she dragged the chair over beside the bed and sat in it. "Now let's really have ourselves a talk."

* * *

Emma let Jidge get her robe and slippers and go to the bathroom before returning to sit on the edge of the bed. She still held the pistol loosely in her lap. Neither of them felt exactly at ease, but expectation had replaced the tension.

"I should have known you and Griff weren't behind things," Jidge apologized, wrapping her arms around her middle and hunching slightly over her knees.

"Then you can call off your detective watchdog first thing in the morning," Emma said. "But we were a good starting point, I see that. You did just find us by accident, didn't you?"

"Yes, someone really did shoot out my tire. But I'll admit I knew your names by then and would have come looking for you. I thought it was fate you found me— well, maybe it was. You see, I'd overheard some preppie-looking guy with glasses talking to his old mother in Arletta's, something about keeping babies away from you. Like the few phrases I heard from you and Griff when I followed you last night, I just put two and two together and got five."

Emma nodded, deciding not to go into what she might have seen if she'd been anywhere near the gazebo last night. "I want you to tell me about your baby," Emma said, "but I've got one more notion to clear up first. You haven't contacted the FBI, have you? I was fixing to call them in when I got enough proof myself."

"FBI?" Jidge cried, clamping her hands around her throat. "No way! You've seen too many movies or read too many thrillers!"

"So then, you really are just an outraged mother?" Emma asked.

"Believe me, that's enough."

"I know it is. Tell me more about your son."

"I swear to God this is the truth. We got our baby boy a little over two years ago through the Shelter the Children Adoption Agency I'd found on-line, though it's not there anymore. It's black market, I knew it was. I talked my husband into it and the fees—over fifty thousand dollars."

Emma's eyes widened, but she didn't interrupt as Jidge went on. "My boy's mentally challenged, when the adoption facilitators swore he was fine." A fierceness crept into her tone again. "I knew there were some risks, but I thought they were legal ones. It's not easy or quick to get on the legit lists for Caucasian newborns these days, especially if your husband's a recovering alcoholic and you're forty-something." She shook her head ruefully, and her voice broke. "The adoption facilitator's telephone help-line disappeared too. I don't know, maybe they keep shifting names and contacts so they can't be traced."

Emma nodded, her eyes narrowed and her lips pressed tightly together.

"I only found my way here by hiring a detective and sheer dumb luck. The woman who delivered little Mitchell to us at the airport and who took the final payment spoke with a mountain accent and that's how I began to narrow down my search."

"What did she look like?" Emma prompted, leaning forward.

"I knew she was wearing a sort of disguise, but at the time I thought I understood that. *Anything* to get my hands on that baby when I saw him." Without seeming to notice what she did, Jidge picked up one of the bed pillows and hugged it to her.

"The woman?" Emma asked again.

"Oh, right. It's been over two years, but I do recall," Jidge said, her eyes glazing over as she frowned in concentration, "that she was taller than me and a little younger, late thirties to early forties. I'm not sure about her weight or shape because she wore a bright caftan, raw silk, I do remember that—bronze and gold with a Caribbean fish-and-waves abstract pattern. I think she was fair-haired, because she'd obviously darkened her eyebrows. She wore a beige turban, so I didn't see her hair. Eye color—I don't recall. Her face, honest to God, I'm not sure. As I said, I was focused on the baby, and I didn't care if Satan himself was handing him over."

Jidge's description wasn't definitive, Emma thought. Most women could look younger with a lot of makeup and a flowing caftan. It did eliminate Delia and someone like Hank's mother, but, unfortunately, Trish fit the general description, as well as lots of others around here. The "mountain talk" could even be Trish, who had such fun spoofing it.

"And Mitchell, what does he look like?" Emma asked, her eyes growing misty despite trying to analyze everything Jidge said.

"Slightly dazed, bewildered. That was how I first knew about—that he was slow. But you mean coloring. A golden boy, but with curly hair that turns slightly reddish in the sun. Sky-blue eyes. A big baby at first, but normal on all the pediatrician's charts now, except for his problem."

Emma's mind raced. The size, coloring, curly hair. It could be Ola's baby. And it could be Sam's. It all fit. Sam *had* to know who was behind Shelter the Children if he'd arranged to hand that baby over, though Emma didn't think for one minute he and Ginger could run such an intricate operation themselves. But she was right to have Griff help her corner Sam tomorrow. Once he confessed and they got him locked up, going around Reg Merrell somehow, Jidge could testify against Sam and whoever else he'd name. And little Mitchell, unlike Lottie's lost baby, could be DNA-matched to his real parents.

"Did you come here for justice, Jidge?" Emma asked in the sudden silence that stretched between them. "Or revenge?"

The woman's head jerked around, and she stared at Emma. "I'll admit, partly because they owe me, and all this has ruined my marriage. And partly so they don't do something like this again to someone else."

Emma reached out her free hand to clasp Jidge's. She kept her other on the pistol because she wasn't going to give it back. She wanted to take it with her tomorrow and not upset Griff by letting him know she had it. Besides, though she believed Jidge had leveled with her about the agency and her baby, her eyes had blazed at the word *revenge*.

"An armed avenging angel from California," Griff summed up what Emma told him the next morning as they talked in his Chrysler parked behind Quincy's Pure Oil Station. Emma had told him everything, except that she had Jidge's pistol in the fanny pack strapped around her waist, where he thought she carried just her cell phone.

"I felt guilty leaving her in the dark about the Gradys' possible part in the scheme," Emma admitted. "And, depending on what Sam says or doesn't say, we've got a few other stops to make."

"Such as?" he asked as they pulled out on the highway.

"For one thing, talking to Lottie as soon as she regains full consciousness, which Rooster says has to be soon. Also, looking around the Bonners' barn on the sly and confronting Carter and Clary Doyal about little Vinie's Walt Disney World claims."

"That is bizarre," Griff said. "You don't believe their explanation about her just getting mixed up from some TV commercial?"

"I'll bet someone from Shelter the Children tried to bribe the Doyals out of their last baby, and who knows what would have happened at that breech birth if the agency people had handled it. Maybe that dead baby Rooster buried is from some similar medical catastrophe. The so-called Shelter the Children Adoption Agency doesn't want their babies born in a hospital, one way or the other," she added with a shudder.

"Anything else? Even if I have to shuffle appointments, I'm going with you from now on."

"I still want to ask Wade to describe the person who drove him to my house the day Amrine left," Emma said. "I was so upset about Amrine—and in that downpour—I never took a peek at who it was."

"That was back when you were trusting everyone, *but* me and Delia," Griff said as he accelerated. She reached over to cover his right hand on the steering wheel. "I just hope, Emma, we're clear that things are the other way around now."

They parked away from the Gradys' property and walked up on the ridge from which they'd surveyed Knob Creek Holler weeks ago.

"Déjà vu," Griff whispered.

"I hope not. I think we're finally making progress." Emma paused, then pointed. "There he is, heading back toward his makeshift appliance showroom. And there's a new one in the collection, an oversize washer like they have in Laundromats, see?''

''Maybe for Ginger's quilts. He's not going out back, but into the shed.''

Griff was right. Sam shuffled into the ramshackle shed from which the ear-piercing sound of an electric buzz saw soon emanated. They didn't see Ginger anywhere around. At least, Emma thought, Sam had not carried a rifle in with him.

''I don't like the idea of Sam with a buzz saw in his hand,'' Griff said as if he'd read her mind about his being dangerous, ''but let's go. He's making enough racket we can sneak up on him.''

Emma held her fanny pack with the pistol and cell phone steady so they wouldn't bounce together. They hurried down the back path and darted for the cover of the shed past the tombstones that had sheltered Emma from Jake. The sound of the saw drowned the hum of the electric generator inside.

Sam's work shed had probably been an old tobacco-curing barn, since it had once been painted black. It was peeling almost to the wood and had enough knots and cracks that they could peer into it here and there. The shed had two narrow windows, but none on this side, and the chinks seemed to be safer peepholes.

They squinted in to see Sam bent over a thick board balanced between two sawhorses. Previously cut hardwood in the rough shape of a long, narrow chest was propped against the far wall.

They hurried around to the single shed door, which was ajar. When the piercing sound of sawing droned on, they stepped into the shed.

Maybe it was the man's long-honed hunter's instincts, but Sam straightened and turned. To Emma's great relief, he not only turned off the screeching saw, he put it down on the board and moved slightly away from it.

"Trespassing, ain't you?" he said, his face calm, though his voice betrayed his surprise with a little squeak.

"Just making a house call to check on that broken wrist, Mr. Grady," Griff said, taking a step farther in. "I see it's not slowing you down. Nice hardwood boards you have there."

Emma didn't like the way Griff was starting out in left field. Was he implying to her that Sam had something to do with the timber rustling she'd finally filled him in on? If so, that could be one more link to Mike Bonner, assuming Mike was paying the Gradys partly with wood as well as money for babies.

"Sam," Emma said, slowly stepping closer as Griff had done, "I came here because your hiding my brother here last time kept us from discussing Ola in more detail. And her baby."

"She done told her ma you found her and how you asked 'bout the baby," Sam said. "It was for the best, adoption."

"Maybe it was. But not if there's some irregularity in the situation. And especially not if it's become a pattern in Ola's life."

"Irregular how? Pattern?" Sam demanded, walking farther back behind his board and sawhorses as if to put a barrier between them.

"A black-market adoption, for one thing," Emma said. "And for another, Ola's physical and mental well-being. She may be young, but she can be hurt in every way by what's happened in this family."

"You got no proof of nothing 'bout no pattern."

"Let's just start with Ola's scar for this cesarean delivery," Emma accused, "which was right over the scar for her last one."

Sam's eyes widened before they narrowed to slits again. "Doc, I'd be much obliged if you'd leave and take this woman with you," he said, his voice steady but his eyes darting. His Adam's apple worked as if he were gulping air. "Don't know what in tarnation she's yammerin' about."

"She's speaking of the fact this last baby was not Ola's first, and your daughter's barely fifteen, Mr. Grady. I'm afraid that the various versions you and your wife, let alone poor Ola, gave of the father and the events surrounding this birth really cast a dubious light on—"

"Talk English, damn you!" Sam cracked out.

Before Emma could even unzip her pack, he lunged behind the cluttered workbench and grabbed a rifle.

"I'm a' tellin' you to get off my land and outta my life or else," Sam threatened, lifting the rifle but only to their knee level.

Though he handled the guard trigger with his left hand, Emma didn't trust him to miss at this range. And he was shuffling slowly around the workbench and sawhorses toward them. She stepped behind Griff as if for protection and, not looking down, dug the pistol out of the pack.

"We'll go, Mr. Grady," Griff said, holding up his hands. "We only want information about Shelter the Children because, believe me, it will come out one way or the other about who fathered Ola's babies."

"That's over now," Sam said, still aiming the rifle at them. "Swore to her ma that Ola'd move away and ain't seen her. But you mean—you know 'bout the money and all?''

Emma hid the pistol behind her hip and only partly stepped out from behind Griff. ''That's right,'' she said. ''The appliances you've been buying are only part of the proof that you've had a financial windfall. But if you'd give us some information first—''

''I said it's over, my part in it!'' Sam yelled. ''Ola knew her place, and Ginger got some things she been wanting. 'Sides, with those two middlemen and costs, we didn't get much even for Ola's baby.''

Emma fought to keep her temper so she wouldn't blow this. ''Come on, Sam,'' she coaxed. ''We know Ola had a boy this time, but had another boy before, two years ago. We've traced the first one to San Francisco. Now we need the names of the middlemen you mentioned and who's behind them.''

''Call the sheriff, see what he does,'' Sam goaded, rhythmically bouncing the rifle barrel but still not aiming higher.

''We know about Reg Merrell's being in on the take,'' Emma countered, deciding this ruse was worth the risk. ''So it's the FBI we're dealing with.''

She ignored the jerk of Griff's head at that. ''You do know,'' she pursued, ''the FBI can get involved since your grandkids, your own babies, were taken illegally across state lines.''

''It ain't illegal if we signed!'' he roared. ''She said so!''

''Who said so?'' Griff cut in. ''Who is 'she'?''

''Ola been talking to the FBI?'' he cried, his voice rising in panic. ''She tell them 'bout me?''

''Put that gun down so we can talk, Sam,'' Emma said. ''Please, for Ola and Ginger and those kids...''

Emma knew he'd crossed the line of restraint even before he leveled the rifle barrel. She elbowed Griff slightly aside and lifted the pistol, holding it straight out in both hands. Griff looked as shocked as Sam.

"Don't," she warned. "Believe me, I can be my pa's girl in using a gun if I have to. Put it *down*."

Their eyes met. She did not flinch or blink. Sam cursed low. Then, looking confused and stunned, he dropped the rifle to the floor. It hit with a thud and a puff of sawdust.

The tension in Emma's spine and arms unwound. Even with as much as Sam had said, she could call the FBI to bypass Reg Merrell. Surely they'd get Sam to tell the names of the middlemen and of the "she" behind them.

"Someone's outside," Griff whispered, startling her. "I saw something flash by the window. I'm going to check. Hold him here."

Griff darted out. The silence was deafening. Then she heard a dull thump.

"Griff?" she called quietly, then louder. "Griff?"

Still holding the gun on Sam, Emma edged slowly backward toward the door.

A blast blurred the room. Had her gun gone off? Had Sam's?

At the second shot, Sam lunged toward her, his neck spurting blood. His weight and momentum took them to the hard floor, crushing her breath and scream.

Emma must have lain there a moment, dazed and frozen in fear. Then she saw Sam sprawled on top of her, half his throat gone, his mouth open in a silent shout.

She tried to shove his weight off, a dead weight, then

managed to roll out from under him in something slippery. After the two blasts, it seemed so quiet but for the steady hum of the generator.

"Griff?"

She scrambled to her feet. Peeking outside and seeing no one, she edged around the front side of the shed closest to the house. Nothing. Back the other way, toward the tombstones, Griff was down just beyond the corner.

"Griff!"

She knelt and turned him over, feeling for his neck pulse. She was terrified when she saw blood on his throat, just like on Sam, until she realized it was from her hand. Her clothes, too—blood-splattered. She wiped her palm on the grass before she touched him again.

Thank God, he was alive. She darted a look around. Where was Ginger? Why hadn't the shots brought her running?

"Griff, wake up." Emma lightly slapped at his cheeks, then managed to sit him up and tip him over his knees as if he'd fainted. He must have stumbled and hit his head, maybe had a concussion like she got that night she almost hit the deer. Or whoever shot Sam had hit Griff first...

She propped him up against the shed and peeked around the back. The gunshots must have come from here to propel Sam into her like that. Nothing, no spent cartridges on the ground. And no chance of tracks because she stood on the concrete back stoop. Too late, she saw she was leaving faint, bloody footprints. Carefully, she peered between and behind the appliances, then darted back to Griff, who was coming to.

"Griff, wake up," Emma urged. "Someone shot Sam, killed him. Did you see someone?"

"No... Get Ginger and help."

"I'm not calling the sheriff," she insisted. "I'll get the FBI."

"It'll take hours—try state police. They can get them."

Hunkered beside him, Emma retrieved her cell phone and punched "0" for the operator. She asked for the state police, and the woman said she'd call their dispatcher, then began to question her.

"Tell them a man's been shot and killed, Emma said, giving directions and her name. She explained she was a witness to his death, but she hadn't seen who'd shot him. "And if they need to they can land a helicopter between the house and smokehouse."

The operator promised help soon. When Griff rockily got to his feet, Emma helped him stand, supporting his weight.

"I'm going to check Sam," he insisted.

"He's dead, I'm telling you. It's awful."

They stood horror-struck in the door of the shed. "Either Ginger decided it was justice time," he muttered, "or we're still being followed."

"Not by Jidge. She's back at my house, and I had her gun."

But she realized she didn't have the pistol now. It was lying partway under Sam in a pool of his blood.

A half hour later a woman shrouded in gray, drifted into the hollow through the tombstones as if she'd emerged from the grave. Emma screamed. She wore a faded poke bonnet and a long skirt, like a pioneer woman. Her hands were stained red.

"What you two doing here again?" she asked, coming to such a quick halt her skirt swayed.

Ginger. It was only Ginger in that get-up. "Your c-clothes, your hands," Emma stammered.

"I dress in my granny's old garb," Ginger said as she walked closer to the shed. "Works fine 'gainst chiggers when I pick them wild strawberries on the far ridge. See," she added and tipped a juice-stained basket of small berries toward them. Ginger gaped at Emma's clothing, also speckled with scarlet.

"Mrs. Grady," Griff said, stepping forward to take the woman's elbow firmly, despite how she tried to flinch away, "there's been an accident. We're very sorry, but someone shot your husband."

"Shot? Who did it?" she demanded, her face going slack of all emotion. "Not you? You tend him again, doc, or's he bad off?"

"Bad off," Griff said, frowning. Emma felt not only shocked but suspicious that, so far, Ginger was asking all the wrong questions and not showing one lick of emotion.

"Mrs. Grady," Griff went on, his voice calm, "someone shot at him through a knot in the shed. He's dead, and we phoned for help over half an hour ago."

"I don't believe it. Let me see him," she insisted, sounding suddenly resigned. She dropped the basket at Emma's feet, spilling strawberries that rolled away. Ginger turned and, shaking off Griff's hand, walked toward the shed, stopping at the open door. Griff and Emma stepped close behind to support her, but she stood there stolidly, unmoving.

"Reckon that coffin he was building for Hank Welling's ma gonna hafta do for hisself now," she said.

22

Emma became even more distraught when Reg Merrell's sheriff car came careening into the holler, sirens screeching and light bar flashing. Two other Highboro officers' cars followed in his wake with the Highboro rescue squad bringing up the rear. At least the medics could treat the lump on Griff's head, Emma thought.

The sheriff got out with the lights still going, slammed the door and shoved his hat on his head. "What the hell you fixin' to get the State Patrol involved in this for, Emma?" he yelled. "You're just lucky the 911 dispatcher's in our back building and told me 'fore she went calling them boys in. I got jurisdiction here."

Her control shattered. "I wanted them because I couldn't get the FBI," she goaded and felt swift satisfaction when his ruddy color blanched. "Last time you came roaring in here, you ignored who was guilty."

"I swear I won't ignore it this time," he said ominously, narrowing his eyes and shoving back his hat with two fingers, almost as if he were pointing at her.

"Officer," Sheriff Merrell called to the portly man behind him, "hold this woman for questioning as an eyewitness, according to what she told the dispatcher. Where's Ginger? The body in here? Cusak, come with me. Maybe I can get some straight answers out of you, though the ME's gonna have to pronounce him." He gestured to Griff, who glanced at Emma, then reluctantly followed him.

As they approached the shed, trailed by two officers and two paramedics, Ginger emerged from where she'd been standing just inside the door, still dry-eyed, dazed, as if she hadn't even heard the sirens or shouting.

"My condolences, Ginger," Emma heard the sheriff say, tipping his hat to the woman before he stepped inside. "Hellfire, boys," his voice rang out. "Ain't seen something this bad in my bailiwick since Jake Weston, senior, shot up Cory Eubanks!"

Sam Grady, according to the sheriff's evidence, had been shot from behind with one of his own rifles, now missing, which had been taken from his unlocked house while Ginger was out in the woods and Sam was in the shed.

"Heard you tried to borrow a rifle off a him the other day, Emma," the sheriff had told her. "Didn't come back and get it later on your own, did you? You been in their house on the sly?"

Everything he implied was skewed, yet she could just imagine him making it stick. Luckily, this time, he strode past her without waiting for an answer.

She knew darn well that Reg Merrell would have gleefully made her his prime suspect. Griff had been outside the barn and unconscious, so he couldn't testify she didn't do it. Thank God, it was obvious that Sam had fallen forward on her, and surely ballistics testing would also help. Still, more than once, the sheriff had mentioned the fact she'd come here armed.

It was Ginger the sheriff was taking into the station for further questioning—protective custody, he'd dared to call it. And it was Griff he seemed to question the most, probably because he'd been outside the shed when Sam was shot. Still, no one was read his or her rights, no one was arrested.

Meanwhile, the Highboro police, Sheriff Merrell said more than once, glowering at Emma, would be looking for leads to other possible perps. And since Ginger said that J. G. Presnell had been here delivering hardwood boards about an hour before she went for strawberries, and that he and Sam had argued over something, the sheriff was going to haul him in, too.

Soon, in a third Highboro officer's car, J.G. arrived to view the scene and give a statement. Even from where she'd been told to wait behind the house while Griff was kept closer to the shed, Emma could see and hear J.G. telling the sheriff he'd only argued briefly with Sam over the cost of the wood. She noted the sheriff did not question him about why he was delivering hardwood boards to anyone, especially with his bad back.

Then, despite the fact that gawkers were being kept out, Delia drove right in. That was all she needed, Emma thought, sitting glumly on the Gradys' picnic table as she watched the woman hurry to comfort Griff as if he were a lost child.

"Just one more thing, Emma," Sheriff Merrell said, striding back toward her. "'Bout this California woman you say you borrowed that pistol from," he added and rolled his eyes. "This Jidge Collister. Why's she here?"

"She told me she was driving cross-country to get away from marriage problems," Emma said, fighting to keep control. She had told him all this before when he'd asked her the same thing in different ways. She had, however, carefully omitted that Jidge was also looking for baby kidnappers who called themselves adoption facilitators. *That's* what she wanted to scream at him right now.

"She loves antiques," Emma recited, "and thought there'd be some good buys in this area." She gripped her hands in her lap. They had finally let her wash them in well water after they took scrapings from under her fingernails. "Someone shot out her tire outside town," Emma went on. "Griff and I picked her up and I invited her to stay a few days, use my place like a bed-and-breakfast, only free. Mountain hospitality the way it used to be, so—"

"All right, all right," Merrell said, slapping his small notebook closed. "Maybe she was after quilts."

Emma watched him head toward Delia, who now seemed to be berating Griff. Emma felt a stab of guilt. After all, she'd gotten him into this, and if he lost his job, he'd never make it as a doctor anywhere else. And the idea of his having to go through another trial, even to testify...

"Sheriff," she called after him. He swung around, about twenty feet away, glaring at her. "Why is Delia here?"

He shrugged. "Word spreads when sirens go screaming by."

"But you've got this area roped off. I recall you were at her place last time you got called here. You two go way back, and it seems you're letting her break all kinds of rules."

"Meaning?"

"Meaning nothing new but that 'Miss' Delia gets whatever she wants around here, doesn't she? Money talks..." Emma held his cold gaze.

He pointed a finger straight at her. "If that was true, girl, guess you'd be outta here. You just stay put."

Emma saw him whisper something to Delia as the woman left Griff and walked toward Emma. Despite how ragged and whipped the rest of them were, Delia looked proper, even pampered, in her matching jogging outfit and pastel makeup with not one hair out of place.

"I told Griffin he should steer clear of you and now he has another reason why," Delia began. "He doesn't need this mess you've created."

"I didn't shoot Sam. Tend to your own business for once," Emma said, sliding off the picnic table to stand facing her. "You do realize there are some things in this county, even if it is named Lowe, that are not in your control?"

"We'll see about that. As for Griffin, I've brought him good news in the midst of all this bad," Delia added smugly, drawing herself up to her full height and folding her arms over her breasts. "He's been unhappy here—and, thanks to you, in trouble, but now he's got a chance to go back to his roots and his dreams. His Lexington partners have called to say they'd like him back. They've even arranged a meeting with the state licensing board to get him off probation. Of course, I'll be sorry to lose him."

"Probation—I didn't know." What else had he still not told her? she wondered.

"You just see that you keep quiet about what you do know of his former misfortunes."

"I realize you knew all of that."

"Of course, I did. Do you think just anyone would want to come to Shelter? But I've found another doctor to replace him if he wants his old life back—someone perhaps you cannot so easily compromise and nearly destroy."

Emma glared at Delia as the woman strode back to

her car, got in and roared out of the holler. Across the way, the sheriff motioned Griff to follow him to a police car. Griff looked back over his shoulder at Emma, but the sheriff said something and he got in. She watched as J.G. was evidently told to get in the same car.

Emma wanted to run over to them but knew better. Everything seemed to stop as the paramedics finally brought Sam out in a body bag on a gurney and slid him into the back of the ambulance. The officer's car with Griff and J.G. inside pulled out right behind them. Emma lifted one hand as it went by, but Griff's face was obscured in the reflection from the cruiser window.

Shaking with anger, she marched over to Sheriff Merrell. Before she could unleash her tirade, he spun toward her slowly, one hand on his holstered pistol.

"When you gonna realize you're way out of your league, mountain midwife?" He leveled an index finger at her as if it were a gun. "Your brother-in-law and boyfriend are just damn lucky the Highboro jail's too small to lock all of you up 'til I get better answers, startin' with Ginger. I know you been up to no good or you wouldn't have parked Cusak's old car down the way and hiked in. I had it towed to the police impounding lot. And right now I'm taking you home and questioning your pistol-packing houseguest."

Jidge was gone. The only sign she had existed was the pitcher she'd bought at the Bonners', still sitting on the kitchen table.

"She leaves me a note if she's going somewhere," Emma said, more to herself than the sheriff.

She realized too late she shouldn't have mentioned a note, because he insisted she search the house for it and turn it over. And there was no telling what Jidge might have said in it, Emma thought as he drifted through the downstairs and then searched the second floor.

Emma noted Jidge's bed was so neatly made it didn't even look like it had been slept in. Her used towels in the upstairs bath were in the hamper and had been replaced with clean ones. Her toothbrush and toothpaste were gone. It was suddenly as if Emma's best living link to Shelter the Children had never existed. With Sam dead, all that he'd blurted out was no good for proof...

"You're just lucky others uptown saw her, or I'd swear you made her up and that pistol was yours," the sheriff said after she reported she'd found no note and he headed for the door.

"You checked up on her—a mere tourist?" Emma asked, surprised.

"I make it my business to know everything that's going on."

He turned back at the threshold, leaning against the screen door, his eyes narrowing ominously. "Leave it be, girl. That Cutshin streak in you's gonna do you in just like it did the rest of the Westons."

Before she realized he could be warning her off her pursuit of the adoption ring, she blurted, "Sissy's just fine, and she's a Weston, too."

He frowned. His gaze darted away, out past the porch, the drive. "Next time," he said, not looking at her again, "you so much as get one step off the path of midwifin', you'll be real sorry."

She was tempted to tell him she knew what he and his wife did on taxpayers' time—in possible crime scenes. She almost shouted that he should bring the Mrs. to the shed where Sam had been shot to give her a real thrill, since he obviously couldn't turn her on otherwise. But she feared she might need that ace up her sleeve later, because she hadn't liked the look on his face when she mentioned Sissy.

The minute Sheriff Merrell cleared the porch, Emma tore to the phone to call Sissy. The number rang and rang. Her stomach churned, and she started to sweat again. She longed to take a shower. The stench of blood clung to her. But if Sissy didn't answer, she was going to have to get in her Jeep—

Then she remembered that her Jeep was still sitting behind Quincy's gas station where she'd met Griff this morning. She was so exhausted she was no longer even thinking straight. "Damn!" she said, smacking the wall with her fist.

"That you, Emma?" She hadn't heard Sissy pick up the phone. "You cussin' 'cause our men got in trouble with the sheriff? I was just telling J.G. this beats sitting in jail when he promised he wasn't gonna do one more blessed thing to rile me right now. Then everything goes kerflooie."

"I didn't know he was home already," Emma answered. "Despite everything, how are you feeling? Physically, you know what I mean. Any cramps or spotting?"

In the background Emma could hear J.G. yelling at Sissy to hang up because Emma'd caused the whole mess today.

"She sure din't cause what's happened to us, J.G.!" Sissy shouted, making Emma's eardrums ring.

"I realize it's not a good time," Emma told Sissy, "but just remember you need to keep rested and calm. Please, for the baby. I know J.G.'s shook but I'm gonna stop by later tonight to see you, just to—"

"I gotta go."

"Sure, but you call me if you need me, or if any-thing—*anything*—seems strange or wrong."

"Don't you fret." Sissy's last words blurred as she hung up.

Locked inside her house, in the closed upstairs bath-room, under the warm water slicking her skin, for one moment, Emma almost felt she could wash her fears away.

But the turn of events—Sam's death—had deeply shaken her, though she had set herself up for the fall. Sam was dead; her Jeep wasn't here, so she felt ma-rooned; Jidge had, probably wisely, fled; Sissy had J.G. and a looming delivery to contend with, and most peo-ple she knew were more than angry with her.

Worst of all, Griff was evidently heading for Lexing-ton, probably permanently. She'd thought she and Shel-ter had begun to change him, but she still could not fault him for going after his dream.

She felt so terribly alone.

Agonizing over what to do next, she turned the show-erhead to let the water sting her skin. And then she heard some indistinguishable sound, but from where? She'd closed the downstairs windows, locked the place and taken the extra key in. But this time it was not some outside sound. It came from the house, this room, close.

With a little shriek Emma ripped the shower curtain back to reveal a bathroom as foggy as mountain mist. Thank God, the room was empty. She turned the water off and stepped out, holding the edge of the claw-footed tub so she wouldn't slip. From the old brass rack, she grabbed a towel and wrapped it around her, then peeked out into the hall, listening intently to the silence.

She was starting to worry she was getting more paranoid for herself and for Shelter's babies and mothers. And that would soon include Sissy.

She looked both ways in the upstairs hall, then stepped back into the bathroom to dry off. And there, rolled in the mouth of the pitcher Jidge had bought her, which was sitting on the closed toilet seat, was a piece of paper. She hadn't noticed the pitcher a moment ago, but the sound she'd heard could have been the bathroom door closing after someone put it there. Emma grabbed the paper, her hands still shaking as the words jumped at her.

THE WOMAN IN THE BONNET SHOT HIM. IF HER NAME IS GINGER GRADY, I'D BET MY LIFE SHE MADE THE BABY QUILT MY MITCHELL CAME WRAPPED IN, BUT SHE'S TOO OLD TO BE MITCHELL'S REAL MOTHER. WHY DIDN'T YOU TELL ME MORE? LATER.

No signature, but there didn't have to be. It was the note she'd been looking for and the one the sheriff had demanded, but no way she was sharing it with him now. Besides, since Jidge had obviously followed her again today, she could be the one who fired through that shed to kill Sam, then decided to blame Ginger. Or it could be the truth, and Jidge was, perhaps rightly, angry with her, maybe not trusting her. What did *LATER* mean? Was that a promise or a threat? Either way, Ginger was in the sheriff's hands right now, and it was impossible to ask her about the middleman and the mastermind of the adoption ring Sam had mentioned before he'd been shot.

"I didn't tell you," she whispered as if Jidge were here, "because I don't know more—yet."

In her bedroom Emma stuffed the note under her bureau, wedging it above one of the bottom drawer's wooden runners. She jolted when the phone rang. Sissy or Jidge? Hopefully Griff. She ran into her bedroom and answered, just as she wondered if her phones were bugged.

"Emma Weston."

"Emma, this's Rooster. Praise the Lord, Lottie's come to and she's talking up a storm so—"

"Don't say more right now. You're at the hospital?"

"Came home to see the girls, and they called me here so I'm gonna drive in. How 'bout I stop and get you?"

"I'll be out in front. Can we go by Quincy's so I can pick up my Jeep?"

"Sure. Won't be ten minutes."

"Listen to me," Emma said urgently. "Call the nurses' station on Lottie's floor and insist they have someone sit with her until we get there—not a police officer."

"The nurses already are, and Dr. McGill, too. I'm gonna drop the girls at Clary and Carter Doyal's and be right there."

Emma threw on her clothes and ran down to make sure her answering machine was on in case Griff called. She couldn't wait to tell him about Lottie—if he even cared now. Excited, she clasped her hands and pressed them to her lips. Finally, an open door when so many others had just slammed shut.

It took over an hour for Emma to speak with Lottie privately, and by then, her friend was winding down with exhaustion. Lottie had sobbed when Rooster told her eight days had passed, that they'd lost the baby and already had the funeral. "Can't believe it, just can't," Lottie kept saying.

"But," she whispered to Emma, while the others filed out for a conference in the hall, "I *really* can't believe that pink, crying newborn died—and Rooster says it was a girl."

"Let me talk to you a minute, and you just rest up and listen," Emma whispered, taking her hand.

"Rooster says," Lottie plunged on, "you saw my baby. I mean, saw her not long after she died."

"I did, and I don't want to upset you, but I need to know why you're still so sure the baby was a boy. It wasn't just what Dr. Cusak saw in the ultrasound, was it?"

"Laws, I thought—I *know* I seen him." Lottie frowned, concentrating. "Yeah, right when he was born, I know I seen him. Heard Trish tell someone that, too—a boy, a boy."

"Tell *you?*"

"No, tell someone helping her. I was so addlepated then, so dizzy and out of it with the coma coming on, I guess. Maybe it was the rescue squad guys."

Evidently no one had told her yet that her coma was induced. And Emma knew the rescue squad got there after the birth—and death—of the baby. Emma held Lottie's hand tighter, bending over her on the elevated bed. The voices in the hall stopped. They'd be back soon.

"Lottie, could that other person Trish talked to be Mike?"

"Not Mike. He stayed out in the other room. They called things to him real loud over the storm but he din't come in. I know folks say I'm slow in the head, but I know what I know!''

"I believe you," Emma assured the distraught woman. Lottie's expression reminded her of Jidge's when she'd told her about little Mitchell being slow. Appalachia might be a fertile field for babies, but were the adoption facilitators picking on folks here they thought were stupid? That made it even worse.

"You always treat me," Lottie interrupted her thoughts, "like I was just fine in the head. And I'm telling you there was some woman talking to Trish, and Trish yelled out to Mike that it was time for the baby—when it was already born.'' Lottie gripped her hand and sucked in sudden sobs.

"It's all right," Emma comforted. "Rooster's coming back in now. You just sleep, and we'll talk more later."

As Rooster and the doctor returned to lean over Lottie, Emma knew it wasn't all right. She stood back, picturing Mike waiting in the other room of the pool house ready to bring in a dead baby girl while the living Weston boy was whisked away by someone Lottie couldn't even recall because they'd been filling her— and her child—with drugs during the delivery. But drugs and the coma could have made her memory suspect, too.

Emma touched Rooster's arm. "You are going to stay with her, aren't you?" When he nodded, she whispered, "You so much as step out, you be sure a nurse sits with her."

"Sure," he said, matching her furtive tone. "But Dr. McGill says she's out of the woods now."

"I'll be back as soon as I can," she told Rooster.

Emma went down the hall to use a public phone to

call information. She learned from the operator that the FBI had satellite offices in several major cities in each state, and that, in Kentucky, Lexington was the closest. If she talked to Griff before he moved back there, she could ask him to stop in so the agents would have a personal contact.

Putting a handful of coins in again, she went through a series of recorded selections, then spoke to two secretaries until she finally reached an agent name Tom Marks.

"A black-market, infant-adoption ring?" he asked, interrupting her torrent of talk. "And you've got what kind of proof, ma'am?"

"Several people hold parts of the puzzle," Emma explained, "but a few will have to be coerced to talk. One's being held by the local sheriff, and there's a husband and wife here who are looking guilty. I can't trust anyone, but I'm not giving up."

"Ms. Weston, you do realize this sounds, ah, farfetched and a little tenuous, don't you? Can you tell me exactly who's behind this scheme?"

"Right now it looks like Trish and Mike Bonner, but I'll have to call you back. I do know it's a woman working with at least two middlemen who deliver babies, maybe do the deliveries after the mothers are lured, bribed, doped up out of their minds—or even kidnapped."

"Kidnapped? And taken where, Ms. Weston?"

The man was being businesslike and polite, but the subtle subtext of his questions suddenly made her realize how crazy her story must sound to him. She was getting more frustrated and angry by the minute.

"I have your name and extension," she said, "and I'll call you back as soon as I have the evidence you need. Such as another mother who disappears or another dead or stolen infant.''

''Ms. West—''

She hung up quickly when she saw Trish coming down the hall, carrying such a large bouquet of roses it hid her face. Emma darted for the emergency-exit stairs at the back of the building. Trish was obviously headed for Lottie's room.

Emma realized she was driving way over the speed limit and slowed down. She looked back again, actually wishing Jidge's car was tailing her so she wouldn't feel so alone, but she saw no one. What she was really dreading was a police car.

''You want to give the sheriff another chance to lock you up?'' she berated herself and hit the steering wheel with her fist.

She parked off the road in a pulloff local folks sometimes used to fish the stream that tumbled down from the back of the Bonners' land. It was only twilight, but she knew where Trish was, at least for a while. She just prayed Mike was out somewhere, too.

Emma summoned her courage to call Griff to fill him in about Lottie and ask if he'd have time to stop in the FBI office in Lexington. His phone rang, then his machine picked up. Surely he could not have gone already. She was damned if she was calling Delia to ask.

Taking the flashlight from the emergency midwife kit she kept in the back seat, she half hiked, half jogged in, climbing over the cattle fences at the fringe of the Bonners' land. As darkness fell, she was on the edge of their landscaped lot, assessing her next move. Maybe luck was with her for once. Both the house and barn looked dark.

Although she intended to search the barn, it was more likely to be deserted later, so she chose the house. This would be easy if the extra key was still in the magnetic box under the carriage lantern. And, as far as she knew, the Bonners still didn't have the place wired for alarms, not deep in the heart of the charming, timeless Appalachia that had attracted them here.

The front door key was there. Emma opened the door, then put the key back. "Mike," she called, just in case, "I came by to tell you Lottie's better! I'm real sorry about the misunderstanding I had with Trish." She closed the door and went into the silent house.

She decided to try Mike's office first. She was still a novice at her own desktop computer, but maybe things weren't too complicated on Mike's computer. Hopefully, he hadn't put up any more barriers in it than he had in his house.

As she tiptoed into the paneled office, the screen glowed and burbled with an animated underwater scene of fish, so restful, so calming. The room had a large window facing the driveway, so if anyone came, she'd see or hear them.

After ten minutes of trying different menus, she got into Mike's master directory and skimmed the headings. SALES was a file. She clicked into it. ANTIQUES. WOOD. OTHER. Though she was dying to know who was working with Mike and J.G. on the timber rustling, she checked OTHER.

A huge list followed including CHINA and QUILTS. There was even one file labeled FLOWERS. Out of curiosity, Emma clicked on it.

Besides orders for the perennials for their own flower beds, someone had listed entries of BOUQS./ROSES— one dated today—at a flower shop in Highboro. WES-

TON, that entry read. The second one that drew her eye
was DOYAL, dated two days ago. Trish had delivered
the one bouquet today; had she delivered one to Clary,
too?

She went back and clicked on QUILTS. BABY QS/
GGRADY spelled out the names of patterns and prices
of quilts the Bonners had evidently bought or ordered
for the future, she couldn't tell. She noted some of the
dates went back quite a ways.

"Here," Emma whispered, putting her fingernail
right on the monitor's screen to hold her place: four
quilts two years ago, ones that would match the ap-
proximate date of the delivery of Mitchell to Ben and
Jidge Collister.

Her pulse pounded, but again, she held only sand in
her hands.

She went back to WOOD, then to TIMBER. And
under it found a list of payments to RMerrell supposedly for a police-car escort of wide loads on the highway. But Emma had never seen one of those. That
would be like advertising a theft around here.

"Bingo!" she exclaimed. This was something, at
least, that couldn't be explained away. But it still didn't
link the sheriff to the baby ring. She wondered how to
print this page and if she should print others.

She was furious when she couldn't get the printer to
work, so she checked out other files, some long lists of
prices, taxes, inventories, most for the remodeling of
this place.

"Idiot!" she scolded herself. "Did you think you'd
find a listing for babies bought and sold?"

Headlights swung in the window, splashing light on
the wall before they went out. She returned the screen
to its fishbowl screen saver and hurried through the

house to the other door. When someone came in the back, she could surely risk making sounds to go out the front.

Emma jumped when her beeper went off, screeching through the house. In the dark, she fumbled to shut it off, but it sounded again just as the back door opened. She remembered she'd left her flashlight on Mike's desk, but it was too late for that. She yanked open the door and ran.

Lights came on in the house and the yard, but she was behind the barn by then. She ran farther, intending to get clear off the Bonners' land before she stopped. When her beeper sounded again, she hunkered down behind a tree and punched it to be sure Sissy wasn't calling to say she was in labor.

She wasn't sure, but she thought the number was Clary's, and she'd wanted to talk to the Doyals again, anyway. She called from the Jeep as she headed home.

"Carter, that you? Emma here."

"She with you?"

"Who?"

"Vinie!" Panic tinged his voice; he sounded as if he'd been sobbing. "She's gone again, it's pitch-dark, and we can't find her. I was just gonna come down to your place."

"I'm not home, but I'm heading there," Emma said. "I'll look around for her, then come on out, hopefully with Vinie in tow again. You keep looking there."

If she didn't know Vinie had run away before, Emma thought, she'd think that the Shelter the Children people had taken the girl to replace the Doyal baby they didn't get. And, even if the Doyals were panicked, that's exactly what she was going to ask them.

23

Emma saw the crock of red roses the minute she walked into the Doyals' living room. She'd made her way into the house past parked cars and neighbors with flashlights and lanterns who were gathering for a search party.

"You didn't find her?" Carter cried when he saw Emma.

"No, and I didn't see her on the road between there and here."

"Dear Lord, somethin's happened to her," Clary cried, bouncing little Wes in her arms as she came in from the kitchen. Though it was late, their older boy sat wide-eyed in a corner, sucking his thumb, and Rooster and Lottie's little girls were playing dolls on the floor. They smiled and waved at her as if nothing were amiss.

Emma took Clary's arms in her hands to steady her. The baby cradled between them, Emma put her forehead to Clary's and said in a low voice, "And we know Vinie wouldn't have gone to Walt Disney World on her own, don't we?"

Clary tensed but didn't draw back.

"Are the roses from the same person who offered to buy little Wes for cash or a trip for your family?" Emma pursued. "Don't you realize that Vinie's disappearance could be linked to people selling children around here?"

"No," Clary murmured, going even stiffer. "Can't be."

"Trish Bonner brought you the roses, didn't she? Did she also offer to take Wes?"

"Yes—I mean no, just the flowers. The other, it was all on the phone, and we said no, but Vinie heard us talkin' 'bout it and wouldn't let it go."

"You don't know who was on the phone?" Emma asked.

"A woman," Clary answered in a shaky voice. "From Shelter the Children. They give babies that might be poor or disadvantaged the chance to be raised up real fine by rich folks who can give them everything, and want them so bad."

So that, Emma thought, was Shelter the Children's PR spin on abduction and adoption. She held her tongue because she didn't want to stop Clary's confession, but that was all the woman said.

"Would you recognize the woman's voice if you heard it again?" Emma asked. "You sure it wasn't Trish?"

"No, a local accent."

Emma recalled Trish's practicing that on her and she shuddered.

"Hank Welling's mother? Delia?" Emma pursued.

"Delia?" Clary gasped and jerked back. "Couldn't be. But she'll be here soon with lots more help…"

Screams and shouts outside brought everyone onto the porch.

"We got her, got her…" The echoed words became a general cry as a man ran up with a dirty and scratched Vinie in his arms.

"Just down in the ravine out back, twisted her ankle in a gopher hole," someone was screaming as Emma quickly worked her way through the excited crowd and got back into her Jeep. "We'll have to run her into the doc in town, but she's gonna be fine and dandy!"

Emma didn't even stop to tell them the doctor was probably not in town and they'd have to run her clear to Highboro. Tears blurred her vision as she recalled Vinie and her parents' joy, and she grieved for the fact that folks evidently trusted Griff and now might lose him. But what about those children who, over who knew how many years, had been taken away and never given a chance for a reunion? This happy ending made her sad, and she didn't want to face Delia again right now. Besides, she had one more possible witness to see.

"That's all right. It's never too late for a good deed," Mabel Poteet told Emma. "You know, Wade's face still hurts him mightily so he ain't sleepin' well. But he'll be real pleased to have them car magazines. Beggin' his pa to let him go back to the garage even 'fore he has that skin-graft operation. I'll just go fetch him."

Wade looked bleary-eyed when he joined Emma in the Poteets' small, cluttered living room. Despite bandages hiding much of his expression, Emma saw a smile in his eyes when she handed him the stack of magazines. Cradling them, he sat beside her on the sunken sofa. She met his gaze steadily, careful not to flinch at his appearance.

"Wade, I'm sorry to bother you this late, but I need to ask you something that could really help me."

"Sure," the boy murmured, bending one leg up on the sofa to face her. "You helped me when you gave me that twenty dollars from Miz Amrine I'm gonna 'tribute to my own medical fund."

"That day Miss Amrine left," she said, picking up

on his cue, "when you hitched a ride in that truck, I never asked you who was driving and you didn't say. Or if you didn't know him, can you recall what he looked like?"

She could tell he was fighting to keep from frowning; he turned slightly away from her.

"This is so important, really," Emma urged gently.

"You been kind to me, more'n him."

"More than who?"

"Even when they took me into the clinic when I got burned, he said it was my fault."

Her insides cartwheeled. "You don't mean Dr. Cusak?"

"Naw. It's gonna get me in trouble if you tell on me though, 'cause he said he'd get me in trouble if I told."

"Sheriff Merrell?"

He nodded.

"Don't you worry one bit about breaking your word," Emma said, "because I guessed it and you didn't really tell. Was the sheriff alone or did he have his wife or anyone else with him?"

"Just him. Said he'd been doin' a bit of huntin' on the sly. Said not to tell or else. Miz Weston, where you going?" the boy cried as Emma leaped up and hurried toward the door.

"You've been a big help. Thank your mama for me."

Emma kept going out the door, across the porch. At least she had enough to really warn Sissy now.

Emma felt almost relieved when she saw lights on and J.G. still up, so she wouldn't have to wake Sissy. Even if it meant facing J.G., Sissy needed her sleep this close to her due date.

Emma tapped on the dining room window near where

he sat, head in his hands, slumped over the table. He had a liquor bottle in front of him. Was he dog drunk or just ignoring her? She tapped again.

When he raised his head, she was shocked to see he'd been crying. The overhead dining room light made the tracks of his tears glisten. He didn't let her in but lumbered to the window, wiping his face with the sleeve of his plaid shirt. He knelt and lifted the sash so they could talk through the screen.

"She ain't with you, is she?" he asked.

"Do you mean Vinie Doyal? Did they call you, too?" Emma paused at the look on J.G.'s face. "You—you don't mean Sissy?"

"Hell yes, Sissy. We had a fight—argument. She left a note, but don't say where she's gone." J.G. snorted, then coughed. The smell of alcohol on his breath nearly knocked her back, but she squatted to talk straight through the screen. Her stomach began to churn worse than it had all day.

"Well, where is she?" Emma demanded. "Maybe she went out to stay with Delia or a friend."

"I called 'round. No one seen her."

"Open the door. Let me see the note. I want to compare it with another one—Amrine's."

"Runnin' off in her condition, you believe it?" he muttered as if he hadn't heard her. "She musta called someone who picked her up. Hell, I know she's mad at me—even admitted to her 'bout the timber rustling. Far's I can tell, jus' after dark, when I thought she's upstairs, she goes stomping off with a suitcase packed she musta had hid down here."

Emma knew where she'd hidden it. But, even if Sissy was leaving J.G., why hadn't she phoned Emma for help? She should have told her sister more about the adoption ring.

"You know, I royally screwed things up," J.G. went on, "but you did, too. Hank's furious at you for something he won't say. His ma's dyin' a cancer, y'know, and I said I'd get a coffin made for him, and then that got me stuck in your mess with Sam Grady…"

He rambled on, but she wasn't listening. Regret for Mrs. Welling hardly dented her dread. Nothing mattered now, nothing but finding Sissy.

"Where are you going?" J.G. shouted as she scrambled to her feet and clattered off the porch. He came outside but nearly fell down the steps.

Emma backed the Jeep out and pulled away. She couldn't help J.G. now and figured she had only one chance to find Sissy before it was too late. She wasn't certain where to look, but, if her very pregnant sister hadn't just run off on her own, she was hazarding a guess.

If Emma followed the trail of blame, it would lead her to Trish, Mike and Reg Merrell. Trish was in Highboro, but Mike had been at their farm tonight. He could have picked Sissy up and taken her to town. Sissy was closer to her delivery date than Amrine had been when she disappeared, but exactly as far as Lottie from hers when she went into labor at the Bonners' pool house. Despite never wanting to see that swimming pool again, Emma was going where Trish had invited both Lottie and Sissy for a safe stay.

It was just after midnight when Emma drove the road to town, her thoughts as twisted as the road. Sissy might have been planning this all along, she realized. Maybe when Trish had asked Emma to pass on to Sissy the invitation to stay at their Highboro house and she didn't, Trish had arranged it herself. Had J.G.'s behavior pushed Sissy to this, or had she gotten fed up with Emma's keeping such a close watch on her? She'd rebelled about that more than once years ago.

Emma remembered to look back between curves and hills, but she didn't see any other headlights close behind her all the way to Highboro.

She parked one cul-de-sac away from the sheriff's house and two blocks from the Bonners'. Before getting out of her car, she fumbled in her traveling midwife kit. She didn't have the flashlight she'd left near Mike's computer, but she grabbed the first weapon she touched, her new pair of sharp-pointed scissors.

Emma locked the Jeep and cut across various lawns, hoping no one saw her, heading toward the two adjoining yards with the pool house between. Sissy would be all right, she tried to convince herself. Maybe this hunch was wrong. And if by some wild chance Sissy was staying with Trish and Mike, she'd have to be careful getting her away. She'd call the FBI again. She'd keep calm and—

She swore when she tripped over a tennis racket behind Sheriff Merrell's house. She sprawled to her hands and knees. At least she hadn't stabbed herself with the scissors. Then, as she got up, something Emma had missed before hit her harder than her fall. She had glimpsed a black, rusted truck in this very garage. She cursed again, at herself this time. But with so many similar dilapidated trucks around Shelter, how was she to guess it was the sheriff himself up there on the mountain that day Amrine disappeared?

Lexington looked lovely, even in the dark, Griff thought. The mere sight and smell of it helped alleviate the headache he still had from being hit on the head and the shock of seeing Sam's bloody body earlier today. Sheriff Merrell had given him permission to leave Shelter for forty-eight hours but only because Delia had insisted.

The freshly painted horse fences spread before him on both sides of the road like open arms. He kept the driver's-side window of the health center van down, both to keep him awake and to inhale the dewy scent of open meadows and freshly cut lawns. These suburban homes looked like castles compared to where he'd been, and the sculpted flower beds and manicured grass helped the brick and timbered medical building blend right in.

He parked in the familiar lot in his old spot marked Doctors Only and got out to stretch. He'd made good time, though he'd stopped in two small towns for coffee and to try to call Emma from pay phones. In his rush, he'd left his cell phone in Shelter and couldn't recall the number of hers.

So he'd gotten only her answering machine at the house and was not sure that was working as her voice sounded distorted and the thing kept beeping when he talked. He hoped she'd understand he had to settle his past and make sure his probationary license was returned to good standing. And to see if what these doctors would say after they'd deserted him in his time of need could convince him to come back.

Deserted in his time of need kept revolving in his head. If he returned to Lexington, would he be doing that to Emma? His belly hollowed out when he realized he'd never get her to move here with him, even if that's what he really wanted.

Right now, he needed to find a motel room and get a few hours' sleep before the 9:00 a.m. meeting tomorrow. Still, he couldn't get himself to leave yet. He walked up to the front glass door and looked through the plush lobby toward the long hall lined with office and examining room doors. It was a far cry from Delia's health center. Damn, how he'd love to get out from under her thumb.

"Hey, man, what you doin' there?" a voice behind him called. "It's after hours, and this ain't no walk-in clinic. You gotta have you an appointment in this fancy place."

Griff turned to see the security man walking across the lot, taking his headphones off his ears. His hips bulged with a two-way radio and a pistol he'd carried since the place had been broken into for drugs last year.

"Hi, Jermon," Griff said and held out his hand to the big man whose shaved head shone under the parking-lot lights just like the single diamond stud in his ear.

"Hey, Doc Cusak, heard about the big deal—you comin' back. After you left, I heard more than one patient asking for you, 'spite a what happened. One lady broke a lamp 'cause you weren't there to do her checkup or whatever."

Griff smiled tautly. The clients here included a good percentage of prima donnas, rich women who were used to having their own way. Only now, it seemed so selfish, so wrong. He remembered Emma accusing him of catering to patients who worked in their appointments amid horseback riding or tennis lessons at the country club. Guilt hung heavy on his heart.

"You wanta come in, see your old office?" Jermon

asked, unlocking the door. "The guy's moving on who's got it now."

"No, thanks," Griff answered. "Tomorrow's soon enough for that. I see you've been taking good care of the place."

"Sure have. But overheard talk they might be looking for a better place with that big chunk of change coming in from your patron and all."

Griff froze, staring at himself in the black mirror the glass door made as Jermon swung it open. His stunned reflection slid sideways as everything fell into place.

Delia had done it again, and he'd gone for it. She'd set this up, either to get rid of him for good because he wasn't cooperating—or worse, to get him out of town because something was coming down on Emma. Even if it cost him this chance to pull himself out of debt, even if it cost him his license forever, he had to get back to Shelter—fast.

"Hey, man, where you going?" Jermon called after him as Griff sprinted toward his car. "Wha'd I do?"

What, Griff thought, would *he* ever do if something happened to Emma before he could tell her that it had taken this journey away from her and her people to learn how much he needed them?

The Bonners' house was as dark as the sheriff's. It was late, though, Emma rationalized. Or, what if she'd miscalculated? What if Sissy wasn't here, or she was with the Bonners at Big Blue Farm? She could hear the disbelief in the voice of that FBI guy again at her claims and calculations. Exhaustion began to set in as her adrenaline rush waned. Damn, she thought, why did she always have to examine all sides of the problem, just as when she delivered a baby? And why couldn't she just force someone to confess to something for once? But she'd gone this far and she was not turning back.

Emma picked her way carefully through the hedges that separated the two properties. Branches pricked and pulled at her. It was dark, except for lights under the water that made the whole pool look like one big, blank eye staring up into the black night.

Steeling herself, she walked behind the pool house where Trish had surprised her the other day. Lottie had chosen the pool house over the big house, and Sissy might have done the same. It seemed less overwhelming, more isolated, and those women were used to that.

Keeping a hand on the smooth white siding of the pool house, Emma felt her way around to the nearest of the two windows. A dim light shone within, smothered by thick curtains. Holding her breath, she went to the door and tapped on it.

She waited, then knocked again. A brighter light came on, and Sissy opened the door. Shock showed plainly on her face framed by wild hair.

"Thank God—thank you, Lord," Emma whispered the first heartfelt prayer she'd said in years.

"Are you alone?" Emma asked.

"Of course, I'm alone." Her sister wore a terry-cloth bathrobe around her bulk. "I suppose Trish told you I'm here. She offered me a nice rest, close to my doctor and the hospital. I've got a phone in my room to call the squad—or my midwife sister—anytime I want. I'm even gonna call J.G. tomorrow, but I'm staying here 'til the baby comes. And partly because poor Trish and Mike are so broken up about what happened to Lottie."

Fear fluttered in Emma's belly again. Trish had obviously been having private talks with Sissy. She had built some sort of relationship with her little sister Emma didn't know anything about.

"Sissy, please, you've got to listen to me so—"

"We're all done doing that," a man's voice behind them said. Sissy gasped and Emma spun to see Sheriff Merrell, unshaven, in sweatshirt and jeans, pointing a pistol at them. "This time, Emma, you crossed the line."

Emma stepped in front of Sissy. "You wouldn't shoot her anyway, would you? You and the Bonners want the baby."

"Is that right?" he taunted. "Got everything all figured out like usual. Now both you get in there."

"And if you shoot me," Emma continued, trying to stall him, "someone, maybe your own wife, would hear and come running since she likes places where danger—"

The sheriff leaped at her and swung the gun. Emma ducked the blow, but he shoved her back into the room. She slammed into Sissy who went to her knees. Sissy screamed.

"Shut up!" he hissed at Sissy, closing and locking the door behind them. "We wanted to finesse this, but your midwife sister's been meddling for weeks, so we'll have to do this the hard way."

He fastened a fist in Emma's hair and banged her back against the wall once more, then pushed the pistol barrel to her temple.

"Don't hurt her," Sissy begged.

"Go on, Sissy," Emma said, blinking back tears of pain. "Get out of here through the Merrells' backyard toward the hospital. He can't risk people hearing gunshots."

The sheriff hit Emma's head into the wall again so

hard she saw stars. "She'd just set off my motion-detector alarm like you did," he said. "Sure we want that baby, but I'm not gonna be needing neither you or your sister pretty soon, unless you behave. Trish and Mike went back to Shelter, because someone got in their place tonight and was fooling with their computer and they had to check it out. Now, who could've done a thing like that?"

Emma tried not to react, not to so much as blink as he thrust his face closer to hers. At least someone had finally told the truth when he'd said they wanted the baby. Only, his confession wasn't going to do her or Sissy one bit of good, she realized as she rolled her eyes sideways to look at her sister. Sissy was grimacing and holding her big belly in a way that scared Emma to death. To death.

24

At 1:10 a.m., the sheriff let Sissy go to the bathroom—as long as she kept the door open. While she was in there, Emma heard her gasp and the telltale gush.

"It's all right, Sissy," she called out to her, staring down the man and his gun. "That's your water breaking. I'll be right in to help."

Slowly, Emma rose from the edge of the bed. "I have to help her. You do realize she's going into labor, thanks to the trauma you've caused."

"She's due, anyway," he said and ground out a cigarette. "Sooner the better."

"I had no idea you smoked, but you're just full of surprises."

"Helps keep the weight down."

"So your wife will stay interested. Fake youth and ill-gotten riches. But it doesn't seem to be helping, does it?"

"What the hell you mean?" the sheriff demanded.

Since he had the gun on her she was probably crazy to try this, but Emma needed to get Sissy to the specialist fast, at any cost.

"I'm talking," she said, daring to put her hands defiantly on her hips, "about the way you have to cater to your young wife's fascination with woman-in-jeopardy sex games. I've documented several of them, especially the one at Amrine's house just shortly after she disappeared. As a matter of fact,'' she rushed on before he blew up, ''that one's on tape and in the care of a friend of mine who's going to release it all to the *Highboro Herald,* but I can quote you chapter and verse if you don't be—''

She ducked as he lunged at her. He yanked her onto the bed and leaned over her to press the gun between her eyes.

''Well, now,'' he said low, the smoke on his breath seeming to burn her, ''you got just ten seconds to tell me who has that tape and that info. Your lover Cusak?''

She knew whoever she named was as endangered as she. In her desperation, she had underestimated his.

''Delia Lowe,'' she said.

He choked out a laugh and flecked her face with spittle. But he pulled the gun away and hauled her to her feet.

''You know, you would have made a real good deputy or detective—or a damn peeping Tom. You hiding on the stairs that day Cindy and I got our kicks at Amrine's, that it? But since you usually get your kicks out of being a midwife, I'm gonna have you deliver that baby for me. You've had your warning. Next time, I'm just gonna shoot you first. These walls muffled Lottie's cries, and I'll just bet they'd muffle a bullet.''

Even a death threat didn't panic her as much as delivering Sissy's baby. ''She needs a specialist,'' Emma said. ''You know she lost the first baby and almost bled to death.''

''Then you better do a real good job.''

''Emma, you okay out there?'' Sissy cried. ''I need you.''

Glaring at their captor, Emma hurried in to her.

* * *

The next hours were pure nightmare. Reg Merrell found and confiscated her cell phone and beeper as well as the scissors she had hidden on her. He unplugged the phone. He tied and gagged both of them with drapery cords and stuffed washcloths in their mouths, though Sissy was already getting early contractions. He went out, moved Emma's Jeep somewhere else, then returned to toss her midwife kit in her lap.

Over Sissy's grunts and groans as she tried to breathe with the gag, Emma heard the bastard make a call on her cell phone to someone he called the Baby Stork, no doubt whoever would arrive later to abduct then deliver the baby to adoptive parents. It had to be Trish or one of those middlemen Sam had mentioned before he died. At that, Emma's belly cramped, too.

When he finally untied and ungagged them, Emma went to work. Sissy and the baby were her first priority, then getting rid of him, and if she saw a way to do that first, she would.

"No more smoking in here, I don't care how long this takes," she told him. "I'll need lots of sheets and towels from the linen closet." He stood with his gun still on her while she carried in the linen.

Emma scrubbed and dried the shower curtain and laid it on Sissy's bed, telling herself that would have to do for sterile. She remade the bed on top of it. She saved a stack of towels, one for a receiving blanket. With her small bottle of Betadine, she scrubbed the bedside table and laid out her washed, meager instruments on top of it. She remembered Trish had told her she'd had the place deep-cleaned after Lottie's delivery, whatever that meant.

She checked Sissy again, gently palpating her belly. The baby was presenting in the normal position. No fear of breech here, like Clary. Unfortunately, no chance this was false labor, like Ruth Wicklow.

"Deep, slow breathing, Sissy," she reminded her, and they breathed in unison. "No panting until we want to hold back. Save your strength."

When she saw the sheriff was hovering, Emma turned on him. "At least keep over there in the corner to give her some privacy. A woman needs a calm, positive environment to deliver well, and you're hardly helping."

She heard him cock the hammer of the pistol. "You tell her what to do," he said, "but I tell you."

She nodded, forcing herself to keep calm, modulating her voice for Sissy and him. "And exactly who tells you what to do, sheriff? Trish or Mike or do they work for someone, too?"

She knew not to bait him, but she was boiling with outrage. He didn't answer, but at least that shut him up. She went back to work, sponging Sissy, rubbing her back, even helping her get up to walk around the room when they agreed it might help. At least, Emma thought, if the Shelter the Children operatives didn't oversee this baby's birth, there would be no drugs involved, like with Lottie's baby.

But Emma's stomach clenched in sync with Sissy's next contraction when she realized her small kit didn't have her drugs of pitocin or even her herbs of blue cohosh and shepherd's purse to stop hemorrhaging. She tried to recall what she did have if worse came to worst. Just raspberry tea and, of course, good old Cutshin ginseng.

"I can do this," Sissy whispered as Emma propped pillows behind her back against the headboard which, fortunately, was tight against the wall to support her when the pushing got worse. "It will be fine this time. I been praying about it."

"It'll be fine," Emma echoed, gripping both her sister's arms. "You just concentrate everything you've got on this baby coming. I swear to you I will not let Sheriff Merrell take this child or hurt you, no matter what I have to do."

"Stop that whispering over there," he ordered.

Emma released Sissy and stood to face him again. "Please let me explain something else to you, sheriff. Sissy should have her husband here for support, but all she has is me, so I'm going to keep my voice low to coach her and urge her on. We're not talking about you, believe me."

Slumped at the small table, Sheriff Merrell sat up straighter, glaring at her.

"This one's worse. A big one," Sissy cried and Emma turned back to help her.

At 2:19, when Emma examined her again, Sissy was fully dilated. She could not believe it. The first stage of labor could go as little as twenty minutes but it more often stretched from twelve to fifteen hours. Emma had partly wanted a long delivery, because that improved their chances someone would stumble on them here. But a drawn-out delivery could do in both Sissy and the baby.

Though Emma had counseled Sissy for weeks about not letting her courage crash at this point, she hadn't planned on this prison-guard scenario, so she could hardly blame her sister for panicking.

"I can't—can't do this," Sissy said suddenly, gripping Emma's hands so hard between contractions her fingers went numb. "J.G. wasn't with me last time—

and not now. It's going to happen again. I'll lose the baby. I can't do it.''

"Of course, you can," Emma said. "You're doing great, the best I've ever seen for anyone. J.G.'s going to be real proud. It's going fast, too, so it's not taking as long as last time and that will help with the other problem."

"No, no!" Sissy cried. "I've got to try to hold the baby in, hold it back. If it's still inside me, he can't take it away."

"Listen to me," Emma demanded, putting her cheek right against Sissy's slick one. "You can't fight this or you'll hurt yourself and the baby. Let me worry about the sheriff. Now, how about we pray together for this baby to be safe and sound and you too."

Sissy, despite her pain and fears, flopped back, looking determined again. "It's worth a lot if you're gonna trust the Lord now. Okay," she gritted out as another wave of pain washed through her. "With you and Him both helping me, I can do it."

This time Sissy's contraction was so strong her belly went rock hard. Emma breathed with her, massaged her in the shortening periods between the pains. She put more pillows behind her back. She whispered and encouraged her, always searching for some way, some opportunity to grab that gun.

She even considered getting Sheriff Merrell over to support Sissy's back the way J.G. would have, but she couldn't bear to have him so much as touching her sister or seeing this child born. And sometimes she and Sissy were so intent on their mutual battle to birth the baby Emma almost forgot he was here.

"Only push when you have the urge," she told Sissy.

"Your body knows when it's time. Don't wear yourself out."

But Emma knew she'd worn herself out trying to find who was behind this baby-stealing scheme. She'd worn herself out, both wanting and fighting Griff, struggling so hard against Hank, Delia, and then Trish and Mike.

"I told you I can't do this!" Sissy screamed, rearing up, her face sweat-streaked, clawing at Emma to scratch her forehead and grab a fistful of hair. "They're going to take my baby if it doesn't die. They're going to kill me if this doesn't—ah, do it first!"

The sheriff came over, waving the gun as Emma got loose from Sissy's grasp. "You keep her quiet," he ordered Emma when she stood again, holding Sissy's hands.

Emma turned around to face him. Her back was killing her, but she ached to lunge at him. "If you want a woman muzzled and managed, get her to a doctor in a hospital," she told him. "I'm a midwife, and the way she chooses to do this is the way it's going to be."

"This says diff'rent," Merrell claimed and stuck the pistol between her lips, tapping the barrel against her gritted teeth. "While Amrine's boyfriend took her away after she sent for you, I let the Poteet boy set you up, then I shot your tires out up on Mudbrook Road. And I can shoot out a lot more than that at close range. Too bad you didn't drive off the cliff that day because you been bigger trouble since."

Emma's eyes widened, and her nostrils flared. Sam hadn't shot at her that day nor maybe at Jidge's tire. Those dark brown fatigues Jidge recalled seeing on the shooter were really the uniform of the local so-called officer of the law. Emma would lay odds Jake hadn't put those dead animals on her wicker table, either, but that it was dreamed up by Trish and this bastard. Carefully, Emma stepped away from the gun and bent back over Sissy.

At 3:00 a.m., Sissy wanted to squat, so Emma put the shower curtain on the floor and helped her down onto it. For the hundredth time, Emma rechecked the baby's heart rate with her fetoscope. Down to 132, well within the safe range. Surely, the baby's heartbeat was the only normal one in the room.

"It's crowning," Emma announced triumphantly when Sissy lay back down and the baby's head finally showed. "Lots of fine, gold hair. You just pant a minute while I make sure you don't tear."

"No blood! I don't want to bleed," Sissy cried and panted until Emma told her to push again.

"I need that lamp over there set here on a table at the foot of the bed," Emma told the sheriff.

"Then you just come over here real slow and get it."

With the light in place, Emma let herself hope for a safe birth. Things looked good, she told herself, and kept telling Sissy, too.

At 3:17 a.m., the head birthed, facedown as desired. Sissy almost heaved herself off the bed with her next push. Emma watched the baby's body rotate perfectly to pop out the first shoulder, then an arm.

"You're doing just great, Sissy. The baby looks beautiful!"

But the infant's skin color was very pale. It had not started breathing yet, though that was not too unusual, and it was still getting oxygen from the umbilical cord. Emma reached up to check that the cord was still unimpeded and pulsing.

The sheriff crept closer but other than elbowing him

back once, Emma ignored him. "On this next one, you're going to push your baby out, Sissy. You can do it. Now. Push!"

At 3:23 a.m., the baby, a medium-size girl, slid free into Emma's hands. But not crying, not breathing.

"Ohhh," Sissy murmured, trying to see between her raised thighs. "Is it okay? Boy or girl?"

"A girl," Emma said, lifting the baby onto Sissy's lower belly until she could get a better hold. "I've got to clear her nose and throat. Just a sec."

At least she had her syringe with her, Emma thought with relief, though she was soon wishing she had her resuscitation oxygen bottle with the tiny baby mask.

"Why's that baby going blue?" the sheriff dared to ask.

Emma didn't so much as look at him. She pressed her stethoscope to the little girl's unmoving chest. Yes, a heartbeat, slow, but steady. But no movement, no breath.

"Blue? Isn't she breathing?" Sissy echoed, her voice shrill.

"I'm going to help her get started," Emma said and gently wiped the frowning, little face so she could get a seal there for her own mouth.

Ignoring the fact that Sissy was crying now, getting hysterical, Emma covered both the tiny nose and mouth and began to puff air into her—twenty-four puffs a minute, gently, carefully. She felt the little chest inflate against her hand. She listened again with her stethoscope and heard air movement even before she saw the chest lift, then fall. The heart rate was rising fast, so she wouldn't have to do a cardiac massage. And the baby was going from blue to white.

In minutes she had clamped out and cut the umbilical

cord, cleaned the child and put her in Sissy's arms where she wailed loudly enough to outdo her mother's relieved sobs. The baby soon cried herself into a healthy pink shade, much better than Sissy's ashen look. But when Emma bent to check on the discharge of the placenta—which had not happened yet but could take a while—Sissy had started to bleed, just the way she had at the first birth.

"Oh, she's so beautiful!" Sissy cried, cuddling her daughter.

"She sure is," Emma said, steadying her voice as she fought down this new frenzy.

She darted a glance at Reg Merrell, who had the nerve to look proud and wet-eyed, the bastard. If Sissy's bleeding increased, Emma knew she was going to have to find a way to get that gun, even if she got shot in the process. The baby might be safe, but she could still lose Sissy.

"I'm telling you—begging you," Emma whispered to the sheriff five minutes later, standing back from the bed where Sissy still waited for the placenta to deliver, "she needs the hospital. And so does the baby, who could go blind without silver nitrate drops for her eyes. Do you want to try to sell someone damaged goods?" she argued, though it made her physically ill to deal with him on his own terms. "I mean, I know Shelter the Children hasn't minded handing off retarded kids before, but—"

"What? Who was retarded?" he demanded with such surprise that Emma realized that he and his confederates didn't know about Mitchell Collister. But neither did his cronies *want* to know if they kept changing and cutting off their access to new adoptive parents.

When she saw he wouldn't budge, she bent back over Sissy. No placenta, but the cord wasn't lengthening and she dared not try to pull it. She prayed it wasn't a partially separated placenta, because they could be deadly.

At 3:48 a.m., Sissy began to hemorrhage. Emma tried to stem the blood with packing and compression. She'd give anything to have Griff here, Griff and an injection of pitocin, ergonovine or oxytocin to stimulate uterine contractions and stop this bleeding. Wishing she had her stimulating herbs, she raced for the bathroom and dumped both packets of raspberry tea into the hottest water the tap would give, then flaked some 'sang root in. Both were old midwife and Cherokee cures for female problems, including menstrual cramps and bleeding. It was all she had. Desperation was the doctor now.

As her blood soaked the sheets, Sissy looked so weak and dizzy she didn't even protest when Emma took the baby from her breast and settled her—Sarah, Sissy wanted to name her and had been whispering that name since she'd been born—between two pillows high on the bed. Then Emma got right in Sissy's face, not only to pour the herbal tincture down her throat but to talk to her.

"Listen to me now, Sissy Weston Presnell. You're gonna have to stay with me on this, stay alert here. You aren't trying to hold that afterbirth in there, are you, like holding on to the baby?"

Sissy's pupils were huge in her pale face. "Don't let him have her," she begged. "I didn't want to let her go. I should have believed you, looked out for someone who could take my baby, not trust Trish. But I was so mad at J.G."

"Keep talking," Emma said. "Keep feeling angry at J.G. for now. Sing to Sarah. Keep looking right into my eyes. I'm going to need your help, because I have to remove the placenta manually. It's going to hurt, but you've got to stay conscious. And, Sissy, you have got to put your mind to stopping the bleeding. Women have power over their body's pain and fear. You proved that today.''

The baby started to fuss, and Emma put a hand up to rock her slightly. Instantly, Sarah stilled, and Emma's love flowed out to her as if she'd borne her herself. She heard the sheriff's excited voice on the phone across the room, telling someone to come quick.

She bent over Sissy, still talking to her as she worked. Emma knew she was hurting her, but she was appalled when her sister fainted. She completed removing the clinging placenta, then tried bimanual compression to stop the bleeding, grasping Sissy's belly externally, lifting it, and pressing hard with both hands. She wasn't sure, but by the time she heard the knock on the door, she thought the bleeding was starting to ebb. Before she could react, just when she was starting to feel relieved, the sheriff darted forward and snatched little Sarah.

''Get over there on the other side of the bed, or I'll use this,'' he said, shifting the gun in a slow arc between the unconscious Sissy and Emma. He shuffled to the door.

Emma ducked, darted sideways and rushed him, hoping to seize the gun and the baby. But he swung the gun at her. Her head seemed to split apart as the door opened. Had it hit her? The gun?

She sprawled facedown on the floor between the wall and the open door, trying to make sense of two voices. Dear God, a woman's, one he was calling Baby Stork. She knew that voice, didn't she, that voice that kept weaving in and out of her ears, her head?

"You're sure you can handle everything here?" the woman asked.

"They're both out now, so I'll tie them in the back of my truck, then transfer them to the midwife's Jeep and roll it off a cliff into a river a ways from here. Just a tragic accident, and they'll think the baby got swept out somewhere by the water—not in my bailiwick for once. Then we'll have to worry about Cusak."

"I hear that may already be taken care of."

Emma became more alert at the mention of Griff's name.

"It's this little doll I want to take care of," Stork said, in baby talk now. "I'll be sure to give the little sweetie her eyedrops, a quick checkup, and get her on formula, before her plane ride far away, yes, I will."

It was when that voice shifted back from baby talk to normal that Emma realized who she was. It should be Trish, but it wasn't. She tried to move, to get up. She'd give her life for a gun, even her scissors, but they were clear across the room and her brain wasn't working with her legs.

"You know, Reg," Baby Stork said, "it's not just the midwife's place, but this whole area that's one big baby farm, like Delia always said. And she wants to see this one before I leave."

Emma sat up, scraping one shoulder along the wall, holding her pounding head in her hands. Baby Stork was Pamela Stark, and Delia was the "she" behind it all.

25

Emma fought to regain use of her limbs, but it was too late. She heard a car door close and the car drive away. Her rage at losing the baby—at Delia's ultimate betrayal—roared through her.

The sheriff started to step back into the room. Emma gathered all her strength and slammed the door into him. Still on her knees, she threw herself against his legs. As he hit the floor, she lunged for the gun. It got trapped between them. She screamed when it went off.

She was astounded that she wasn't shot, then realized Sheriff Merrell was. He grabbed his wrist in agony just long enough for her to get the gun. His arm was slick with blood. Holding the gun on him, she quickly tied and gagged him.

Emma closed the front door of the pool house. Where was her cell phone? He'd had it earlier. Or had he given it to Pam to get rid of, too? She'd drive Sissy to the hospital E.R. and then be on her way to stop Pam Stark at Delia's.

She rolled her unconscious sister onto a blanket on the floor. Ignoring the sheriff's muffled protest and bleeding wrist, she ransacked his pockets until she found his car keys. Going around him, she dragged Sissy outside.

Before she closed the door behind her, she told him, "After they treat Sissy at the hospital and I find that kidnapped baby, I'll try to remember to send some help. Help like you gave us."

Her arms ached and her back muscles screamed as she dragged Sissy on the blanket, through the bushes and across the sheriff's black yard toward his big garage. She must have set off that alarm he mentioned, because lights went on in the top floor of his house.

Praying his wife didn't see her, Emma fumbled with his keys, looking for the little one that would open the garage door. She finally found the right one. Three cars sat inside the garage, that old truck, Cindy's jade sports car and the sheriff's cruiser. The cruiser looked like the safest bet to get Sissy to the hospital.

Though it was not locked, she made sure she had a key that fit the ignition, then got Sissy onto the floor of the back seat. From the house she heard the distant shout, "Reg, that you out there? You get a call?"

As Emma backed out, she fiddled with levers and buttons, looking for the driving lights. They lit but the big bar light on the top did, too. The night pulsated with light.

She navigated the long driveway as Cindy came to the side door and screamed. "Reg, what's wrong? That you?"

Lights flashing, Emma kept on going.

Emma didn't recognize either of the doctors on duty in the E.R., but she could have hugged both of them for quickly rousing the skeleton staff and rolling Sissy in on a gurney. The best news yet, though, was that her sister was conscious again.

"Emma," Sissy whispered, "go save my baby."

"I will," Emma assured her, holding her hand as they rolled her into a curtained cubicle. "Now that you're here, I'm on my way. Don't tell them about Reg

Merrell yet," she whispered, "or they might go looking
for him and he'd send someone after me. I'll be back,
Sissy, back with the baby, I swear it..."

She didn't even bother to step into the waiting room
the nurse indicated, but bolted down the hall.

Stark the Stork had just over a half hour on her,
Emma calculated as she raced toward Shelter. Surely
she'd find her at Delia's, but what if she didn't stay a
half hour? What if Emma barely missed the baby's de-
parture for some airport?

She was tempted to keep the sheriff's emergency
lights on, but she was afraid to attract attention to herself when she got to Shelter. If someone did find the
sheriff, he'd send someone after her, and she'd be a
sitting duck in his cruiser.

She suddenly realized the only car ahead of her on
the road was a sports car. Low-slung, dark color—here
in Shelter this time of night? It looked like Cindy Merrell's and it was speeding even faster than she was.

Emma dropped back and watched as it turned into
Delia's lane.

A thousand thoughts bombarded her. Cindy had
found Reg and he'd sent her here to warn Delia. No,
he could have just called. Maybe he was in that car
himself, going to guard Delia's lane and try to pick her
off if she got near—and not just her tires this time.

Emma backed up and turned into the closest lane,
deciding to approach Delia's by foot. The only problem
was, this was Hal Eubanks's place.

If it had been any other family—even Hank's—
Emma would have run up and pounded on the door for
help. She was desperate enough to do it, anyway. Still,
what if the Eubankses refused and held her there—or
worse?

She swung in behind their barn shed and parked the cruiser. The shed door was open; their old tractor sat inside, much like the one that killed Mama. Then she remembered there was a road partway up Delia's mountain, cut through for hunters or tractors. It was accessible from just across the road, and it would get her past the sheriff. It would save her a half hour if she could drive the tractor partway up that path, however hilly it was.

She walked straight inside the shed. It was likely that the key to the big machine would be hanging here somewhere. Her hands felt the row of nails dangling right inside the half-open door. There was just one key.

She broke out in a slick sweat over her goose bumps. Forcing back those scenes of Mama dying, she grasped the key and shoved the sliding shed door open the rest of the way. It scraped and creaked but she didn't stop. Let the Eubankses scramble for their guns. Nothing mattered but getting past the sheriff and saving Sissy's baby.

The expanse of metal felt icy to the touch. She pulled herself up onto the lofty, hard-molded seat, where she towered over the ground.

Emma managed to find the keyhole and fit the key. The engine roared to life, shaking her bone deep, nightmare deep. Then it caught and settled into a rumble as she jerkily shifted gears. She was grateful Jake had once taught her to drive a stick shift on a car.

The tractor lurched forward so fast she had to duck to keep from hitting her head on the top of the door frame. She stomped the brake, bracing herself to shift again. This was madness.

She wrestled with the stiff metal steering wheel. The tractor turned sharply and nearly pitched over. She let out a little scream, then seized control of herself to turn away from the house and head down the short lane, heading for the highway. Behind her, lights came on. She heard a shout. If they chased her in the truck, they would probably catch her. She went faster.

The highway was solid blackness. Wind raked her hair and stung her eyes. She gripped the wheel so hard her hands cramped. Her whole life of saving babies lay before her, starting with saving little Sarah.

A predawn light was in the skies but not in the dark hills and hollers. She cut off on the lane and bounced over the field. And then the curving climb began.

At least it wasn't overgrown. She only hoped it was far enough from the lane the sheriff guarded—if it was him in Cindy's car, bleeding arm or not—that he would not hear her.

Emma slowed the beast to make each big turn. She'd take it only partway up, she decided. Because it made so much noise, rattling the universe, rattling her soul.

She stopped the machine on the second hairpin curve and turned it off. Pocketing the key, she started up, running.

When she'd lost Emma's trail earlier tonight, Jidge had decided to stake out the clinic because she thought either Emma could come to Griff or he'd go to her. But she'd seen neither of them. A tall, thin woman had gone in and out with a bundle in her arms. Her silhouette— her size and stance—stunned Jidge. She was certain it was the woman who had delivered Mitchell into her arms at the airport.

Pulse pounding, the new pistol she'd bought in High-boro today trembling in her tight fist, Jidge followed the woman and that baby to a big house she knew was Delia Lowe's on a hill just outside of town.

Jidge decided to leave her car down on the road and

walk up. No way she was getting trapped up there after she did what she had to. But heading up, for the first time in years she admitted that being special-sized meant she was also out of shape. Gasping, panting, with a stitch in her side, she finally stopped to stare at the house through a web of tree limbs. Lights shone from a large, elevated living area that appeared to be connected to a wraparound deck overlooking this side of the house and valley.

Keeping low, she darted for the house, first checking the side door near the closed garage. That door, like the others she tried, was closed and locked.

Furious, Jidge glared at the narrow basement windows, then bent to try them. The third one moved inward at the merest touch of her hand. Putting the safety back on her pistol so it wouldn't go off accidentally, she shoved the weapon in her back jeans pocket and forced her ample frame through the basement window.

She dropped the short distance to the floor and landed on something soft that crinkled. She was surrounded by books in sacks, maybe for that new day-care center that Emma had told her Delia Lowe was sponsoring. A place to attract mothers and babies, Jidge thought.

With only the meager light from a humming freezer and the glow of the pilot light from the large water heater to guide her, she shuffled toward the steps and felt her way up the stairs. She was reduced to lurking again, she agonized. She'd seen that old woman shoot her husband right through the chink in the shed and who knew what she'd find here.

Jidge heard voices overhead, but they faded. The basement door stood barely ajar, so at least she wasn't trapped down here. She edged up, holding her breath. She froze when she heard that baby, a newborn, she was sure. It sounded so much like Mitchell's early cries.

"Stork's got to fly this little sweetie to Chicago and then Seattle," a woman—a young woman—was saying. She must be referring to herself. Yes, that was the voice of the woman who had delivered Mitchell to her. Seattle, this time!

A torrent of emotion crashed through Jidge. How she longed to do it all again, open her arms to little Mitchell and have him be whole. But he was whole if she loved him, she reasoned, no matter what Ben said or did. She missed Mitchell and wanted to be with him—to rear him as her own, no matter who had bred and borne him.

But for now, these people had to be stopped. Jidge knew she had the element of surprise on her side. She opened the basement door and saw she was in the entry to the kitchen, directly across from the door that must go to the garage. The kitchen lay in darkness but for the hood light over the stove. She removed her trigger lock, lifted the gun and steadied herself to close the basement door so she could slip past.

Voices still came from the back of the house. "You know," the older woman—Delia—was saying, "I'd love to keep this child, to raise one of them the way Emma never let me keep her or Sissy. As a child myself, I was never wanted or loved, you know."

"You can't mean that, Miss Delia," the younger woman said. "I always pictured you having everything, being adored."

"Oh, desired by my husband, but not by—by my own people in Bitter Crick Holler. I'm so happy I can do that for beautiful babies like this—get them a loving home."

Jidge's eyes filled with tears as she listened. This woman was demented, yet she had given her such a great gift. One she knew now she could never give back.

"They will have people who value them," Delia went on, "spoil them, adore them. They won't have to face living in a wretched place like Shelter with igno-rant, dirt-poor parents who don't even have the brains or money to—"

Jidge jumped back as the door to the garage opened, slamming into her. The sheriff stood there, as shocked to see her as she was to see him. He was holding his wrist, soaked in a bloody towel. She tried to fire as his other fist flew at her. Wood splintered, someone's blood spurted. Jidge felt her nose break and her head snap back. Women screamed, and the baby wailed. Hard hands bore her to the floor and someone put a heavy foot on her chest.

"It's not Emma!" the sheriff shouted. "When I spot-ted this woman's car down there with its California plates, I thought maybe she was joining Emma here, so I just used my key to get in. I was waiting to waylay Emma, but that means she's still got my cruiser."

"Ah," Delia said, "but we've got the baby. She'll be along yet if I know Emma."

"Oh, Reg, you're hit!" the other woman cried. "Why didn't you say so?"

"Bloody but not that bad. Tie this one up. She's a suspect in Sam's death, anyway. She's been on the run from me, so I might just have her disappear for good once I get my hands on Emma again. She might've slipped past me now, so I'll guard the frontier here in-stead of going back down by the road."

The last thing Jidge saw as they hauled her off was Delia bouncing the baby so it wouldn't cry.

From her position behind a clump of azalea bushes, Emma had heard, then seen, the sheriff park his wife's car and hurry into the house. Cindy must have found and freed him. He might not have lost enough blood to slow him down, but then, she thought with satisfaction, he was getting desperate. It didn't matter if they had an arsenal, she had his gun. She was going in.

She eyed the big wooden deck that wrapped around two sides of Delia's house. One side overlooked Shelter Valley and the Eubankses' place below, but the other side, facing her, had not only a drainpipe but a fairly tall tree that nestled against it. Maybe she should risk getting up there and at least looking in—if she could just be certain Pam didn't bring the baby out and take her away.

Emma went first to Pam's car and opened it, looking for keys she could take. The car was open but there were no keys. She wished she had Wade with her. The boy would know how to disconnect the battery so the vehicle wouldn't start.

And then she thought of something better. She shifted the car into neutral, twisted the steering wheel toward the edge of the mountain on which the grounds and mansion sat and put her weight against the open door. The driveway had a slight incline. With the momentum she set up, the big, new-model car rolled steadily toward the edge of blackness and went over with a huge double crash.

Deck lights blazed on, then off. Sheriff Merrell, with his arm bandaged, Pam screaming about her car, and Delia with the baby in her arms ran out on the deck, then back in. Emma tore for the tall tree.

She started to climb. She hadn't been up a tree for years, but it was something else Jake had taught her. He'd said keep looking up, not down. To reach higher and grab for branches, even ones that didn't look strong enough.

"Thank you, Jake," she whispered and, however

much he would always hate and blame her, she forgave him in her heart.

Emma was grateful that these leaves were out in full. It was a big oak that leaned its limbs close to the house and deck. She began to inch along a good-size branch, but it soon seemed a slender limb.

Suddenly, she heard running feet under her, voices. No, not quite under her, but Pam and Reg Merrell were in the driveway in front of the attached garage. She could see, even though they didn't have the bright outside lights on, that they both had guns.

"Didn't you have the emergency brake set?" he demanded.

"No, but I've parked there before. It didn't just roll off."

"Come on, let's beat the bushes around the house."

Then they hadn't seen her, Emma realized with relief. She watched them circle the big house, moving out of earshot. Delia had to be inside with the baby. She'd rescue little Sarah before Delia's reinforcements came back.

Her legs hung free. She swung her lower body over the railing to jump inside it. Landing on the wooden deck with a soft thud and a grunt, she quickly edged forward to look inside.

"How nice we'll get a chance to chat," the voice said quite clearly from the darkness, "before we have to say goodbye for good."

With a gun in her hand, Delia lurked like a spider that had spun the web Emma had tried to tear apart. But it had now snagged Sarah. Emma stared at the infant, sleeping, held high against Delia's breast, as if waiting to be devoured.

26

Griff's entire body throbbed. Still he hunched intently over the steering wheel. He'd been riveted for the endless hours it had taken him to drive back to Shelter. Thank God, he had the van and not his old car.

He'd been trying to reason everything out and decided to try Delia's place first. And, for once, he was going to control *her,* to accuse her of lying and orchestrating his leaving Shelter and to demand if she knew anything about an underground adoption ring.

He braked hard on the highway as he neared the turn-off to the lane that twisted up toward Hill House. At night its entrance was lit by two small lanterns and a weathered wooden mailbox. Its tiny flag glowed red in his headlights.

He had just made the turn when he saw a fire down in the valley through the scrim of trees. But he kept the van climbing, forcing his eyes ahead, trying not to watch the fire below. It looked as if it had caught some trees or weeds, but there was no house there, so what was in flames? He thought of that fire at Cutshin Holler that had forced Emma and Sissy to live with Delia.

As he parked and leaped out at Delia's, he finally realized what could be blazing below. A car. Maybe a Jeep. His stomach clenched. He knew better than to call 911 in Shelter because that could bring the sheriff, so he decided to just bang on the door and demand to see Delia.

"Put the gun on the floor, Emma," Delia said quietly from her dark corner on the elevated deck. "No, instead, throw it right over the side. My pistol is so close to this tiny mite the shot would break her eardrums at the very least, so don't make me shoot."

Emma heaved her pistol into the void and heard it hit more than once, just as Pam's car had before it began to burn below.

"My, but you've created chaos, always have," Delia said. "Sit. Sit over here right on the railing so I can see you."

"How long has this gone on? And why? *Why?*" Emma demanded, but she did exactly what Delia said. She leaned lightly against the sturdy railing, ready to spring, gripping the heavy wood with both hands beside her hips. Keep her talking, Emma thought. But if this took too long, the sheriff and Pam would surely be back.

"How long?" Delia repeated. "For about six years, though it built gradually at first, this dream of mine."

"It's a nightmare! It—"

"Don't interrupt, or try to defy me anymore. And why?" Delia went on, her voice suddenly back to being pleasant. "Pam and Reg did it for the money. Sam and Ginger, too, of course. Sam and Reg have been on my payroll for years, Sam ever since he burned you out at Cutshin."

"But—Trish and Mike?" Emma asked, trying to absorb all the information.

"I've been on to their timber theft ring for a while and decided I'd give them a choice of helping me or getting exposed. And I've promised Trish a baby from somewhere in the hills. Oh, not this one, so don't look so shocked,'' she went on, bouncing the baby slightly. ''So far they've only helped me switch a dead infant we had from near Pikeville for Lottie's and make themselves scarce so we could use their little pool house again for Sissy.''

''If I'm shocked,'' Emma said, ''it's at you. Why did *you* do it?''

''So the babies would have good, loving homes, better than the Gradys' or your cousins' or the others'.''

Emma tried to control her fury. ''These people believe you are their champion, and you treat them like pet dogs, give them treats, train them, sell their litters, then—''

''That's enough!'' Delia shouted. ''I thought at first you meant why do I target your clients. First of all, I want you ruined, out of Shelter. You know I can't abide your defiance. You never were loyal. You should have adored me for all I did for you—and would have done more. Emma, you should have been my heir. And now, I was just hoping I'd get to Sissy's baby since you seem too stubborn to have a baby of your own I could take. But then, this is like taking everything from you too, isn't it?''

''All I want is Sissy's baby. Just let me have her, and I'll be gone from Shelter, from Kentucky if you want.''

''Too late, too late,'' Delia crooned as if she were singing little Sarah a lullaby.

Slowly, as Delia glanced down at the child, Emma leaned and reached forward until she heard the loud sound of Delia cocking the gun. ''Sit back, Emma,'' the older woman said, looking up again. ''All this must end tonight. Besides,'' she added with a dismissive shrug, "with Sissy gone, I would love to keep this child for myself. She'd learn to love and obey me, wouldn't you, little one?"

"Sissy's not gone," Emma insisted, fixating on that one comment. "She's at the hospital and is going to be fine. I took her there myself."

"I'm afraid not. I've seen Reg Merrell, and he called the E.R. to see if you were there. Sissy hemorrhaged to death after you left."

Emma's body jerked so hard she almost fell backward off the railing. "I don't believe you," she said, standing. "You've lied about everything. Sissy's fine."

"Quite dead," Delia said without emotion, "and I can't see that sot of a husband raising a treasure like this child. Now, I want you to just put your legs up over that railing, Emma. Go on, unless you want this motherless child to go over, too. Lean out and just let go of everything."

Emma shifted one leg over but clamped the railing between her thighs. Though she stared at the bundle in Delia's arms, she saw swirling blackness before her, a void. Sissy dead? To save her sister's child, all the lost Shelter children, Emma could gladly lean out and let go, but she could not bear that this warped woman would cuddle Sissy's child.

Emma decided then. Just as with the sheriff earlier, Delia might shoot her, but she'd fight.

"Delia, just let me touch her again."

"In your distraught state," Delia went on as if Emma hadn't spoken, "when I told you about Sissy, you jumped..."

Behind Delia, through the sliding door, Emma saw a figure, crouching low, come closer behind Delia's back. At first she thought it was the sheriff, but it was Griff.

Delia managed to get to her feet with her gun's barrel still pressed against the baby. If Griff startled her, it could go off, and he probably couldn't see the gun.

Emma was willing to jump just to get Delia to put that gun down. But with Sissy dead, that baby would need her. The babies of Shelter needed her...

Emma sobbed and shook her head to distract Delia. "I'll jump, but first please let me tell you how much I loved you. Delia, please hear me out and don't shoot that gun you have pressed up against that child."

She saw she had stopped Griff just in time, but something—a footfall, a shadow, maybe Emma's own awareness of Griff—made Delia turn to see him. Delia gave a strangled cry and pointed the gun at Griff. In that split second, Emma exploded at her, hitting her hand that held the gun, trying to seize the child.

Griff, too, lunged for the baby and the gun, but it was Emma who grabbed the child. The gun cracked loudly as both Griff and Delia went down, and he threw her off him. He and Emma bumped, sprawled together, both with their hands on the child, who now wailed between them. Someone—Griff—had Delia's gun.

"Oh, Griff, thank God," Emma cried, cuddling the infant. She and Griff knelt, leaning together, on the wooden deck.

"I drove straight back when I saw Delia's hand in setting me up again," he explained, helping Emma to her feet. "But she's behind the adoption ring, isn't she, and this is another baby she meant to sell?"

"This is Sissy's baby I helped deliver tonight. I took Sissy to the E.R., but Delia says she's—she's dead." Her own sobs mingled with the baby's as she rocked them both.

Griff looked stunned. "Then the sheriff and Pam

Stark must have been in league with her. I jumped him outside and got Pam Stark in the bargain. They're tied to trees in front, and I came in through the garage door they must have left open. But right now, we've got to call J.G. and get this baby to the hospital.''

"But where's Delia?'' Emma asked suddenly as the baby quieted and she looked around. "She must have escaped and she'll untie them outside.''

"I thought you saw,'' Griff said, steadying her with an arm around her back. He dropped the gun on the chair where Delia had sat and gripped her arm with his free hand. "Emma, she threw herself over the side.'' He shook his head. "It was as if she just flew out into the darkness.''

Cradling Sissy's child, trembling, Emma stood and, through her tears, looked out over the deck railing at the distant sky. But it wasn't really dark anymore, for dawn danced across the jagged peaks.

Griff helped Emma, still carrying Sarah, into the Highboro Hope E.R. a half hour later. The health center van, they'd figured, would be faster than calling the squad, so Griff had driven. They'd brought Jidge along; a nurse took her into a curtained cubicle. Emma felt drained, and her arms were numb from holding the child to her.

The same young, crew-cut doctor who had admitted Sissy—Dr. Kevin Witmer, Emma read on his name-plate—now held out his arms to take Sissy's daughter.

"I'll sign for any treatment she needs,'' Emma told him, her voice sounding as monotone as one of those computer recordings. She gave up the child. "Her father will be here soon, but until then I'm closest kin.''

"That's right,'' the doctor said to dash Emma's last

hope that Delia had lied about Sissy. Her heart shattered.

"I—I'd like to see my sister."

"Impossible until we finish with her," Dr. Witmer said.

Griff put his arm around Emma. She was trembling so hard she couldn't talk, couldn't move.

"We'd like an update on Mrs. Presnell," Griff said.

"You'll have to wait until she comes completely out of the anesthesia," Dr. Witmer said as he handed the baby to a nurse, "but I'd say she's stable right now."

Emma would have collapsed with relief if Griff hadn't held her up. She reached out to stroke little Sarah's satin cheek as she lay in the nurse's arms. She gurgled and yawned. Emma was sure it was her very first smile.

Epilogue

One Year Later

"I'm out of here," Emma said, putting the cell phone down. "Mary Lynn's going into labor, and it's going to be a long night." She yawned as she got up slowly from her rocking chair in front of the TV. The waiting room served double duty as their living room now.

Holding little Sary on his lap on a straight chair, J.G. said, "You kept falling asleep during this baseball game, anyway."

"After a while they all start looking alike to me," Emma said.

"You mean like newborns?" he teased.

In the birthing room, which was now half an office, Griff helped her assemble her kit, even found the fetoscope she'd mislaid on the birthing bed. She walked awkwardly, since she was still unused to carrying the weight of her pregnancy. He put his arm around her and pulled her down onto the bed. It was here they had spent their first night of their honeymoon and here, she was certain, she had later conceived.

Now she sat on his lap, though that sank them deep among the water-lily-print spread and sheets. "I'll be happy to at least drive you there, Emma."

"I'll be fine," she whispered, but she nestled closer to him, turning her face up to his. His kiss, as always, rocked her world as nothing else had. As if to second that, the fetus kicked at her and she guided Griff's hand to feel it.

"You haven't had to scuffle with anyone but me for months," he said, smiling, "but this boy's going to turn you black-and-blue."

"I really think it's a girl."

"I told you, we could easily find out."

"Nope. We're doing this the natural way with no ultrasound unless we have to, and you're going to get to play midwife—I mean midhusband—for the first time in your life. Besides, you're busy enough at the health center lately, breaking in your very own nurse and lab tech."

"And making it without Lowe dollars," he said proudly, "though the town's getting the mansion sure helped."

They were silent for a moment. Delia hadn't even been buried in town, after what she'd done came out. The Bonners had gone to a minimum-security prison. But the people of Shelter had not wanted to lose their health center, and Griff had been eager to stay on.

"Gotta get going," Emma said, wriggling off his lap. She kissed him goodbye again, and on her way out gave Sary a peck on the top of her head and punched J.G.'s shoulder.

Griff walked her outside, stowed her gear in the Jeep and waved as she drove out. When she turned out onto the road, she passed a woman walking on the narrow berm with a little girl about Sary's age in her arms. She glanced at them again in the rearview mirror. Why didn't she recognize them?

Then she did.

She hit the brakes and backed up, leaning down to look out her open window to see under the woman's baseball cap. She was dressed in shabby jeans and big flannel shirt, but the little girl looked cute in ruffled, pink denim. The woman's ambling walk, her height despite the narrow shoulders...

"Amrine!" Emma cried.

"Emma? I din't know that was you for sure when you drove out with the sun in my eyes and all. I was coming to see you. Uptown, they say you's hitched up now with that doctor of Delia's you din't like."

"I like him plenty fine now, Amrine. You've missed a few things."

"Don't I know it."

Blinded by tears, Emma jumped out and hugged Amrine along the side of the road where wildflowers bobbed against their legs.

"Your baby," Emma choked out, swiping at tears that wouldn't stop, "is beautiful, just like her mama. I was so worried about both of you. But if you wouldn't have gone missing, I would never have suspected..." She hesitated. Amrine must know nothing about all that. "Even the FBI couldn't find you when they did their big investigation of Delia's baby business."

"I din't want to be found at first, but I'm here now," her friend said. "And look at you. Near big in the belly as me when I left." She bounced her baby once and grabbed Emma's wrist with her free hand.

"Oh, Emma, Len and some nurse tried to take little Laurie away from me," Amrine said in a rush, "but I ran and lived in an abuse shelter down south and got my head on straight, like you always wanted. And then I seen on TV 'bout the trial of that nurse, even Sheriff

Merrell. I couldn't believe what Delia did and that she's dead and how you got Lottie's baby boy back for her.''

She took a ragged breath and squared her shoulders. ''I rode the bus up from Atlanta with a loan a couple of abuse shelter women gave me, but I told them I'd pay them back when I get a job here. Oh, Emma, I been so scared and down, but I'm not gonna be no more, just like you always said.''

They hugged each other hard with the bulk of their babies pressed between them.

Author's Note

Many people ask me where I get my ideas for novels. Several years ago I noticed my file of possible topics included articles on stolen babies. These items had such headlines as POLICE SAY MOTHER WAS KILLED SO ANOTHER COULD TAKE BABY, ANCESTRY ELUDES OHIO ADULTS SOLD AS BABIES, SUSPECT SAYS SHE WANTED TO BUY BABY, TOWN SECRET IS UNCOVERED IN BIRTH QUEST, and THE WOMAN WHO STOLE 5000 BABIES. ABC's "Prime Time Live" did a feature on a small-town Georgia doctor who sold hundreds of babies. Truth may indeed be stranger than fiction, but for a writer the leap is not far.

I was especially moved by a March 1995 article in *Good Housekeeping* Magazine by Claire Safran called "Stolen Babies: America's New Adoption Scandal." In this article, California, Texas, Illinois, Oregon, Tennessee and Kentucky were listed as states with "underground adoption networks." For a writer who is fascinated by Appalachia—and who lives in Columbus, Ohio, where many mountain folk come to find work, the setting was clear.

As for midwives and their ongoing disputes with doctors over philosophy and techniques, who better than a old midwife and a displaced doctor to join forces, solve the crime and save the day? I only hope that such illegal and immoral practices as baby stealing and baby selling will soon be only fiction in America.

Karen Harper, October 1998

TRUST NO ONE
CHRISTIANE HEGGAN

Julia Bradshaw had every reason to hate her ex-husband, but she didn't kill him in cold blood. Suddenly the prime suspect in Councilman Paul Bradshaw's death, Julia gets caught up in more than a case of misinterpreted circumstantial evidence.

Desperately trying to put the pieces together and clear her own name, Julia begins to trust one man...when every instinct is telling her to trust no one.

"A master at creating taut, romantic suspense."
—Literary Times

On sale mid-August 1999 wherever paperbacks are sold!

MIRA®

Let **DEBBIE MACOMBER** take you into the **HEART OF TEXAS.**

Let her take you back to...

PROMISE, TEXAS

Dear Reader,

In Promise, Texas, people know that family, home, community are the things that really count. They know that love gives meaning to every single day of their lives.

Some of the people in Promise are from old ranching families—like the Westons and the Pattersons, who first came to the hill country more than a century ago. And there are newcomers like Annie Applegate, who agrees to marry a widowed veterinarian for the sake of his children...and discovers that this marriage can lead to a great deal more.

MDM502A

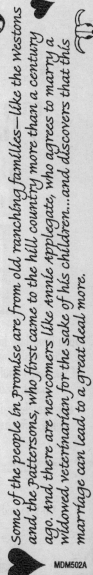

A remarkable novel of the power of friendship

MARY ALICE MONROE

THE BOOK CLUB

On the surface, it is a monthly book club. But for these five women, it is something more precious—a chance to share their hopes, fears and triumphs.

Eve, Annie, Doris, Gabriella and Midge struggle with the dilemmas life throws at them, counting on and learning from each other.

As they embrace the challenge of change, these five women will hold fast to the true magic of the book club—friendship.

On sale mid-August 1999 wherever paperbacks are sold!

MIRA

Look us up on-line at: http://www.mirabooks.com   MMAMS30

**From the middle of nowhere—
to a place of new beginnings**

CURTISS ANN MATLOCK

LOST HIGHWAYS

Meet Rainey Valentine: thirty-five, twice divorced, a woman with broken dreams but irrepressible hope. After her mother's death, Rainey packs up her inheritance—a horse trailer, an old barrel-racing mare and a lifetime's supply of Mary Kay cosmetics—and heads off, leaving Valentine, Oklahoma, in her rearview mirror.

Somewhere outside Abilene she finds him. Dazed and wandering after a car accident, Harry Furneaux is a man as lost as she is. With nowhere else to go, he joins Rainey's travels. And when their journey leads them back to Valentine, Harry and Rainey find an unexpected new direction....

On sale mid-August 1999 wherever paperbacks are sold!

MIRA

A VEILED JOURNEY

NELL BRIEN

Learning that her birth mother was a
Saudi Arabian concubine who gave up
her infant daughter to save the child's life,
Liz Ryan takes a journey that will change
her life. Accepting a job in Jeddah, she is soon
transported into the heart of a land as beautiful
as it is ruthlessly savage. And into the intimate
and hostile world of the women behind the veils.
It is a journey that will threaten all she believes…
and ultimately her life.

On sale mid-September 1999 wherever paperbacks are sold!

MIRA

Look us up on-line at: http://www.mirabooks.com   MNB528

KAREN HARPER

66433 LIBERTY'S LADY   ___ $5.50 U.S. ___ $6.50 CAN.
66278 DAWN'S EARLY LIGHT   ___ $5.50 U.S. ___ $6.50 CAN.

(limited quantities available)

TOTAL AMOUNT $_____
POSTAGE & HANDLING $_____
($1.00 for one book; 50¢ for each additional)
APPLICABLE TAXES* $_____
TOTAL PAYABLE $_____
(check or money order—please do not send cash)

To order, complete this form and send it, along with a check
or money order for the total above, payable to **MIRA Books®**,
to: **In the U.S.:** 3010 Walden Avenue, P.O. Box 9077, Buffalo,
NY 14269-9077; **In Canada:** P.O. Box 636, Fort Erie, Ontario,
L2A 5X3.

Name:_____
Address:_____ City:_____
State/Prov.:_____ Zip/Postal Code:_____
Account Number (if applicable):_____
075 CSAS

*New York residents remit applicable sales taxes.
  Canadian residents remit applicable GST and provincial taxes.

MIRA